Also by Christopher Tilghman

Roads of the Heart

The Way People Run

Mason's Retreat

In a Father's Place

THE RIGHT-HAND SHORE

THE RIGHT-HAND SHORE

CHRISTOPHER TILGHMAN

FARRAR, STRAUS AND GIROUX

NEW YORK

Farrar, Straus and Giroux
18 West 18th Street, New York 10011

Distributed in Canada by D&M Publishers, Inc.
Printed in the United States of America
First edition, 2012

Library of Congress Cataloging-in-Publication Data
Tilghman, Christopher.
The right-hand shore / Christopher Tilghman. — 1st ed.
p. cm.
ISBN 978-0-374-20348-1 (alk. paper)
1. Eastern Shore (Md. and Va.)—Fiction. 2. Domestic fiction. I. Title.

PS3570.1348 R54 2012
813'.54—dc23

2011041211

Designed by Abby Kagan

www.fsgbooks.com

1 3 5 7 9 10 8 6 4 2

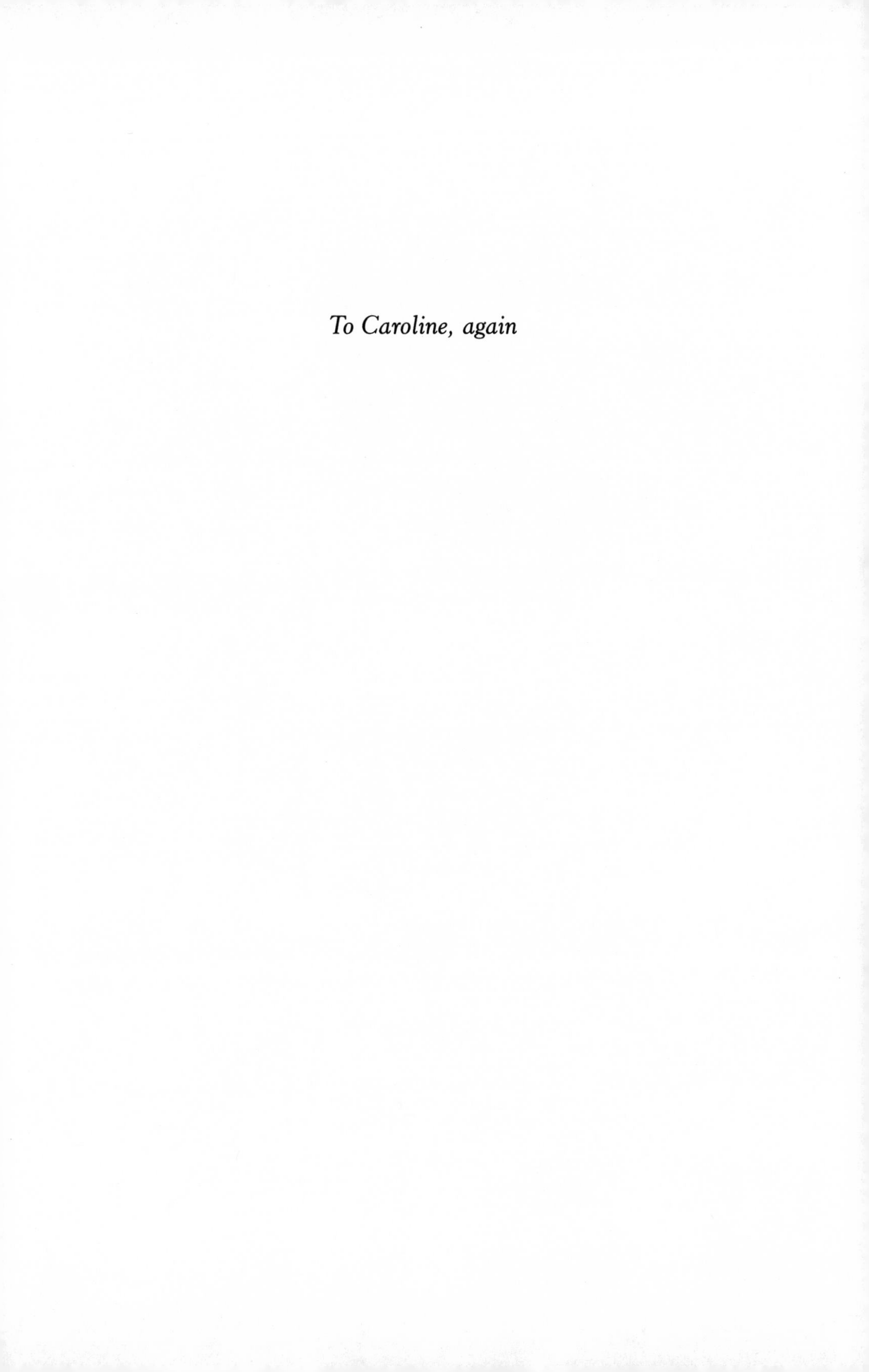

To Caroline, again

sometimes
He scours the right-hand coast, sometimes the left,
Now shaves with level wing the deep, then soars
Up to the fiery concave towering high.

—John Milton
Paradise Lost, Book II

THE RIGHT-HAND SHORE

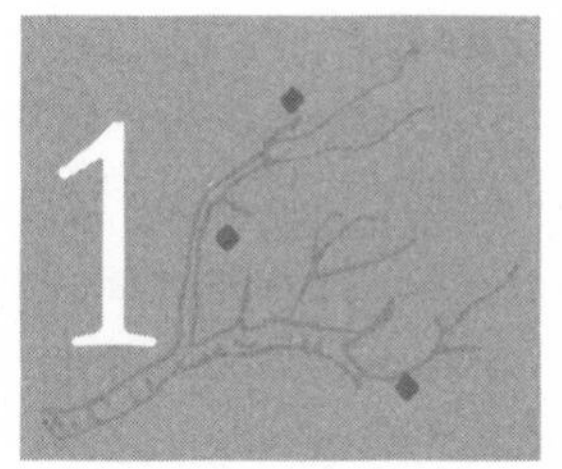

We see Miss Mary Bayly and her distant and much younger cousin Mr. Edward Mason sitting on the porch of the Mansion House on her ancestral farm, Mason's Retreat. Edward Mason has crossed his legs; one foot, Mary feels, is poised in order for her to admire his English shoes. There is a bit of mud, or worse (or better, as far as Mary would be concerned), on the left toe. The vast porch is bare except for the two wicker armchairs into which they have settled and the butler's table placed between them, on which his tea, untouched, and hers, unwanted, are getting cold. There is a slight breeze fruited with odors of the Chesapeake: sea grass pollen, clay flats, fish living and dead. It is September 8, 1920, eight o'clock in the morning, and the air above the Chester River is clear enough to reveal the rooflines of the waterman's village on Kent Island, the silhouettes of the loblollies of Hail Point, the spars and poles of the oyster dredgers. The chairs have been placed so that neither one of them can be distracted by this view.

"Certainly," says Edward Mason. "Indeed. A very sensible arrangement."

What a fool, thinks Miss Mary. She stares at Edward Mason long enough for him to show discomfort, as if those three empty and useless utterances might have contained the seeds of a bad mistake. His mustache, his flushed skin and red hair, his broad, big-eared, needy Mason face; his grand arrival on the porch where she had been waiting for him. *Madam*. He thinks he is being courtly, as if what he has learned by watching the men at whatever club he is in will get him everything they got. Well, he's not in Boston now. This place will eat him alive, she is sure of that. She's seen far better men destroyed by the place. Far better. He has no idea what he is saying, what he is agreeing to. As a

Catholic who has spent years of her life trying to emulate the love and tenderness of the Sacred Heart of Jesus—we will learn more about that later—she has a duty to slow him down.

"I'd think you'd want to reflect on it," she says. "I'm not offering you something without burden." Now she takes a sip of her tea, and though it is cold, it is still spicy, it still flowers on the tongue; this will end all too soon, in dust, eaten by insects. "Perhaps you'll want to discuss it with your wife."

"I'm certain she'll be thrilled."

"And why?" asks Mary. Why did he think she would be thrilled? Why did he claim to be "certain" about the desires of another, especially the desires of a spouse? She met Edward Mason a half hour ago, and already she believes that he thinks of no one but himself, that this wife will not be consulted. Oh, Mary could fill this girl's ears, but why bother? She married him; she deserves the life her husband provides.

Mary's questions are having, if not the desired effect, then at least an interesting one. The more she pushes back at all his frumperies, the more he takes refuge in them. It is the only hand he has to play; he'll dig deeper and deeper trying to undercut her, and he'll end up in China before he quits. What does she care? She is dying. She had taken an extra dose of morphine before he arrived, and her pain is dulled enough for her to think it amusing to inflict some on others.

"Well," he says, finally beginning to wither a little, "to take on this magnificent mantle." He waves around to indicate the surroundings—this porch on which they are sitting, its red tile floor, white columns; the structure the porch is attached to; high, square rooms and dark mahogany furnishings, the Philadelphia highboy; the lawns and box bush and flower gardens; the farm buildings and implements at the far end of the lane; the people who live there and work there by choice or by default; the pigs, chickens, sheep, and, above all, the prized Jersey cattle; the fields and pine stands and oak groves and tidal wetlands; the rats and raccoons, the fox and deer. Not to mention, hovering above in their timelessness with this landscape in their grasp, the dead souls that Mason knows nothing about.

"As in burden," states Miss Mary, insisting on her original word. She winces—a stab of pain from her abdomen. In every conceivable way she has the upper hand with this man, but still, she cannot tolerate the idea that he can observe her pain. Her suffering cannot show; her sufferings have never, ever been allowed to show. She won't let anyone but her servants observe her pain, and only them because it can't be avoided; from their wing, they can hear her howling at night. She lies in bed and bellows like a cow with a calf ripping its way down the birth canal; in her life she avoided that supremely female experience of defeat and surrender, and now this. And though Mary doesn't want her to but needs her, Valerie Hardy comes in, a lamentable angel in black and white leading her way with a candle, and gives her the morphine and strips off her soaked nightgown and dries her diseased body and slips her into something fresh and spreads out as best she can a dry sheet, and Mary can't help it: no relief, no physical pleasure in her conscripted life ever, ever felt better than this warming blossom of morphine and the crisp tang of fresh linen on her skin. "Will that do you now, Miss Mary?" asks Valerie, and Mary nods, and she hates Valerie for all of this, her own powerlessness in the face of pain, the shame of her nakedness, the ecstasy of her relief.

"I certainly wouldn't think of it that way," Edward Mason responds. "Responsibility, perhaps. A family responsibility." He coughs into the top of his fist.

"There are additional 'responsibilities,'" she says. "I gather you and your wife are Episcopalians."

"Church of England," he says proudly. "But really, we're all Catholics, aren't we?"

Mason has clearly been primed for this one and believes this old "we are all Catholics" dodge is good enough. But we are not all Catholics. "The Masons remained true to the Faith even when it cost them dearly. Your forebears did not consider the differences inconsequential." She recognizes that he knows nothing about this history, the history of the Catholics in Maryland. She lets it go, decides to leave as a codicil in her will that in order to take possession of the Retreat, the new owner must convert. It would be no impediment for Mason; he'd do it on the way home from her lawyers' offices if he could. Instead, she moves to another matter, which will, if she gauges him correctly, cause him to suck in his breath.

"The property," she says, "is to pass entire and undivided to your oldest surviving son. If you have no son, you may do with it what you like."

He had been engaged in the small matter of Catholicism and was surprised and relieved to hear that the discussion had moved on. "My wife and I hope for nothing more than a son."

"And second, you may sell or remove nothing other than farm products from the Retreat for a period of twenty-five years." She meets his eye, speaks this quarter-century delay like a prison sentence, right through his eardrums, down his throat.

Edward feels himself being unfairly attacked by this remark. He is not an idiot. He had been the awkward only child of aging parents, an uncertain and unpromising adolescent, and he had done what any animal does in order to survive, which was to make the best of what he had. He'd done all right, navigated Boston society without losing his ambitions, an accomplishment in itself. He'd completed an engineering degree at Sheffield, won a wife whom other men were mad about. He is no fool, even if he seems so to others, and he is not a crook either; at this bright and promising dawn of his life, the last thing he is thinking is that he will ever want or need to empty the house of its contents. He's assuming success in his affairs. He realizes he is being challenged, and he engages her stare. "I would expect nothing but," he says, a small tremor of indignation in his voice. "I can assure you that I would seek only to maintain the Retreat in the manner you have done."

As it turns out, this single moment is what wins him, or condemns him to, the Retreat. Miss Mary nods. She is still solidly put together, but the disease has begun to starve her face. Edward realizes that the decisions and conclusions she is drawing in these days of her life are final and irrevocable; she has a list of them to get through and no time to renegotiate. Indeed, on his way in he noticed packing crates and steamer trunks in the hall.

"I understand that you have been living in England?" she asks.

Edward has expected this. Absentee ownership, et cetera and et cetera. He protests that they have not actually taken up residence there. Not yet, he thinks, but obviously does not say. He points out that he was in Boston when her letter arrived. What a piece of luck that was! He knows that he is not the only pretender to this throne; Mary's lawyers made that clear to him, which is what got him hopping the first train down from Boston to Baltimore and then on a steamboat to the Eastern Shore to make his case. One of two Masons of the direct line from the Emigrant himself, now that Mary's line, through her mother, had daughtered out *sans* name or heir to sustain it. Edward had been only vaguely aware that his people's beginnings in America were in Maryland, and then this most intriguing letter arrived. A vast property that required only her signature for him to acquire, not that he might have much of a clue what to do with it. So what: he is in the stage of life that is all about acquisition, accumulation, increase. The answer to every offer is yes. Edward is more aware of the situation than Mary realizes. He knows Mary is dying. Everyone in the county knows that. She is not even sixty, in fact not even that close to sixty. Why, except for a mortal disease, all the rush? He believes he is fully apprised of the events in her life. He had not been on the steamer from Baltimore for more than five minutes before he casually dropped her name and the steward devoured it, told him stories about her, the downstairs version—revered as a great lady but considered two-faced by the staff. Told him one story, went away to settle other passengers, and then came back to tell him another, and even as Edward was moving down the gangplank at Love Point, this man was at his side. "She's dying, you know," he had all but shouted, and other passengers, farmers on their way back from selling their hogs and tomatoes and butter in the markets in Baltimore, ladies returning from shopping and tea, commercial travelers and drummers and farm implement salesmen, many of these people turned upon hearing this arresting phrase at high volume, and from the nods and recognition in every one of their faces, Edward deduced that they all knew he was talking about Miss Mary Bayly. Of course,

Edward also received the less welcome impression that every one of them knew exactly who he was and why he was there. That he was one of the two pretenders. So be it. Edward could rise to the competition. His rival—he had wormed this out of Mary's lawyers the day before in Baltimore—was a man whose branch had moved to Oklahoma two generations earlier, far out of the orbit, light-years farther out of the Eastern Shore and Baltimore and Philadelphia universe than Boston. Edward wasn't worried about the man from Oklahoma, if indeed he made it to the Retreat to see Mary before she died, which people now thought unlikely.

But still, to the matter of the venture in England: "I have bought a small machine tool company in Manchester and intend to live there as long as it might take to shape it up. Fine craftsmen, but badly behind the times. Now that the war in France is over, England needs to reassert herself."

The thought of England reasserting herself does not please Mary. She is no fan of the English. But it's not a fight worth picking at this moment. "How long will it take to 'shape it up'?" she asks.

Edward doesn't love the ironic tone she uses when quoting him. He will admit that she is formidable. She seems much larger than he had expected: he had imagined a tiny old spinster. Much bigger-bosomed; a muscular face, even if she was wasting away from cancer (of the female parts—yes, the county knew even that of her disease, there is no privacy to be had); even at her age much prettier than seemed possible for a person who, if the stories he'd heard were true, had spent most of her life with her brow screwed in displeasure and contempt.

"A year perhaps. Two. My wife is from Chicago. We intend to raise our children in America." This was, of course, not the truth. They had every intention of setting up shop in England, raising their children there, coming back only for triumphant visits, perhaps to this very estate. There was a chance that Miss Mary knew this; for years he had been loudly and publicly proclaiming his disdain for life in the United States, its lack of savor, of nuance, of breeding. Anyone who grew up with him or was acquainted with the family in Boston had heard him, and Miss Mary's lawyers seemed extremely well informed. Still, he had a response just in case: *Yes, in my younger days I might have thought of leaving, but now, after marrying and contemplating a family, I find—to my surprise, I will admit, a pleasant surprise I must say—that . . .*

A liar, along with everything else, thinks Mary. She could not have, and did not, expect anything better. The Masons, the men especially, bundled their own fates in with all their half-truths, secrets, and terrors. Her mother's father; her mother's brothers, both of whom had died needlessly fighting for the Confederacy in the Civil War. Mary could say this about her cancer and mean it: she was grateful to be dying of a disease that anyone, king to slave, could get, rather than to suffer one of the especial fates that seemed peculiarly Mason. She could do without the pain; it's there at this very moment, jutting its sharp elbows through the medication. The Masons; yes, the Masons. Back through the generations, the Masons, most of whom were buried just around the corner from where they now sat, one after another coming to miseries. Did anyone think all this was just family self-aggrandizement, this affectation of curses received from God, the assertion of a unique Apocalypse? Perhaps, Mary thinks. But there was a simpler answer: that the Masons just weren't very bright. Plodders—not enough imagination to add to the family coffers, not enough panache to leave them busted. Generation after generation dimly clinging to all that had gone before. Only her father, not a Mason but married to one, tried to unearth it all, gave his life trying to reverse it, to create abundance, sweetness. There is one truth, one of the deepest, most fundamental truths about her, that she would gladly admit, though no one has ever been willing to put it to her face: yes, she had loved very few men in her life. For several years she had lived in Baltimore, and young beaux had come flocking. Mary was pretty enough. *Look at those bones, that hair. That tiny waist.* But she was a little too tall, taller than half the boys who came her way. Still, she had once been engaged, but the heart was not in it. She had never met a man like her father, no one with his constancy, his capacity for love, his humor, his intellect. If only she hadn't met her own father—and Jesus—how much happier her life would have been.

Mason coughs into his handkerchief.

Yes, she has lost the thread. The pain is now staring her in the face, the pain with its witch's visage, something from Grimm's. What more to accomplish with this man? "Mr. French will show you around the property," she says, trying not to sound out of breath. "Any questions you have concerning the farm operation he can answer."

"Splendid. It's always wise to confer with the experts." He's trying to appear humble, to establish common ground, but his "experts" is as condescending as it gets.

Even with a crisis coming on, Mary cannot let this go unchallenged. "Mr. Mason, you have already been 'conferring with the experts,' as you put it. As I said, Mr. French can answer any questions. He has been the manager of the Retreat since the end of the Civil War."

There it is again, the quotes; stick around her and he'd hear this entire conversation transcribed. He stands up with the greatest relief and is overjoyed to see that she does not also rise, will not be showing him to the door.

"My lawyers will be in touch with my decision," she says in place of a goodbye.

A butler appears, his elderly black face leaning out the great doors to show him the way. How many servants? Mason wonders. Seems he has seen many, at least five gardeners; he has to admit there is much about this life that is foreign and unfamiliar in Boston and compares favorably with England. Certainly his circle of acquaintance in England has not yet risen to equivalent wealth, though he hopes it may soon. He follows the butler through the high hallway. Now that the signs point to success in this visit, he pays the contents more mind: a quite fine tea table, a nice clock or two, portraits of Masons all over the place, the usual priceless clutter. He has to admit that he is relieved that very little of it seems destined for the three large packing crates in the corner, their tops pulled to one side like hatches on a ship's holds.

"This way, sir," says the butler, and shows him to the landside door. In front of them is a parkland of mowed grass and trees of diverse species, English elm, ginkgo, copper beech; off to one side the beginning of the perennial gardens that circle three sides of the house.

Beyond this parkland are the fields, pasturage now; Edward does not know that not too long ago it was peaches, nothing but peach trees, tens of thousands of them. He does not realize that his eye is being drawn to what is not there, an echo, a pentimento. He pauses a bit while this all settles in, but the butler is hurrying him out, and Edward wonders why until, just as he reaches the bottom of the stoop, he hears a chilling, almost inhuman cry of pain from the porch. Footsteps begin running through the house. He can't help, in his own horror, gazing directly into the butler's eyes, and he sees the truth of the household. Yes, it was good that he did not delay making this trip.

Mr. French is there, waiting in the Ford in which he had retrieved Edward from the dock at Love Point. Apparently the Retreat had its own steamer landing until quite recently, when the boats still plied every river to its navigable ends. This he learned from Mr. French. Edward had found him a challenging sort, a hard but more principled man than the other people, including Mary's lawyers, who had been freely blabbing the secrets of the Retreat. No one but French, Edward observes, seems to show the most ordinary loyalties, seems to be on her side. Mr. French is clearly much older than Miss Mary, but he has remarkable posture; he reminds Edward of the gym instructor at St. Paul's School, not a pleasant association, not that Edward had spent much time under the gym teacher's supervision, not that Edward lasted very long at St. Paul's. French's voice has a boom to it, as if his broad chest has no other function than to magnify sound. An extraordinarily handsome man; if he had been born in a higher class, his looks could have taken him to the top. Whether or not Mr. French is in fact the "expert" at this farm, he looks as if he could master whatever he chose.

"Where would you like to start?" he asks.

Edward has no idea where. At the moment he is taking in the house, its squat Victorian presence, its broad overhanging eaves: the whole facade on this side seems arranged around the stoop and entrance. Not a handsome house, in his estimation. The wing to the left is of older vintage, Georgian perhaps, the remains of a fire no doubt, sometime between the landing at Jamestown and the victory at Yorktown. Somewhere in there. This part of the house is more like what he had expected to see when the idea of a farm called Mason's Retreat was first presented to him; there is smoke coming out of the chimneys at that end: the kitchen must be there, the laundry. Then there is a summer kitchen, he can tell that's what it is by the stovepipe sticking through the center of the pavilion roof, and next to it what must be a smokehouse, brick, with a vented cupola. Mr. French is now backing the car around, as Edward had said that he would like to "get a lay of the property" before "inspecting the farm operation." Involuntarily, he can hear his own phrases being quoted back to him, but this is pretty much what, last year, he said to the manager of the machine works he had just purchased, and it had seemed to go over well. He can't tell with Mr. French. At least with Miss Mary it was obvious that she hated his guts.

In a break in a thick yew hedge he sees the bone-white flash of gravestones. Those old Mason spirits; they can have no complaints. They get to have their eternal rest in a bower. This place is immaculate, the grounds set out in rigid Franco-American style, with straight lines of box bush marking off terraces as the natural terrain slopes down to the water. The whole place is abloom with late-summer flowers.

They drive out the lane, out of the shade of the beeches and pecans, and it seems to Edward that the fields stretch for miles. Mr. French is playing it very close. "This is a pasture," he says. "There's another pasture." They take a left, and they're heading toward some open water quite far ahead, but it's difficult to see much of the landscape, as they are driving through cornstalks close to ten feet high. "Corn," says Mr. French. They arrive at the end of the corn lane, and there are two magnificent mulberry trees right along the riverbank. Edward gets out, walks up to the edge, and looks down about six feet to the pebbly beach, and he is suddenly struck with the longitudinal beauty of this attenuated landscape: the river is at least two miles wide here, and then there is another spit of land, shades and degrees of green, water grasses with tufts of white blossoms, wild privet, and scraggly water elm; then, in places, a magnificent canopy of pines—he knows they are loblollies because he has just asked Mr. French, who has joined him on the bank—and beyond this array he can see or perhaps just sense the Chesapeake Bay, and the sky is a riot of waterfowl and the light strangely colorless, pure, something he pictures in Provence. Well! Without expecting it, certainly without intending it, he feels the oddest, most unearned—"unearned" is his word—burst of pride: human pride for the ability of his consciousness to appreciate what he is seeing; American pride for this landscape that seemed so immeasurable; and finally, good God, Mason pride for a family that saw this land in 1650-whatever and decided to drop anchor perhaps not a hundred feet from where he stood.

He turns to Mr. French. "It's beautiful. I hadn't imagined. It's a landscape I know nothing about. Nothing like it in New England."

"Yes, sir," says Mr. French. "We take a lot of pride."

"Just what I was thinking myself," he says.

They walk through the grasses back to the car, and Edward finally introduces to Mr. French the one doubt, the accumulation of disbelief in this unexpected turn in his life, which he had until now spoken to no one. "Miss Mary wanted to give this all to the Catholic Church, if I understand right." This fact had not been offered but had been gleaned, sifted out of the long, pompous sentences of the lawyers in Baltimore, confirmed by the steward on the ferry. He now forwards this piece of intelligence to Mr. French, uncertain of what it might yield.

"Yes, sir, I believe she did."

"So why isn't that what happened?"

"The church didn't want it. It had no use for it."

Mason might have pursued this further: When did the Catholic Church ever say no to new assets, and what, therefore, could be wrong with this one? His mind danced over the distractions of history to a more immediate truth. "So she would give it to me because I can't refuse it?"

"Yes, sir. Because you're the blood. Because you can't say no."

"Seems to me you'd have more right to it, if it were up for grabs."

Mr. French doesn't bother to answer this, and by the end of the day—a day Edward will spend in Mr. French's company even though the original plan had been to be back in Baltimore in time for lunch—he will understand that Mr. French has already had all the benefits of the place without being subject to any of its curses.

Edward shakes his head, as if asserting his free will in this matter, but it's clear to him that whatever dark forces are in play—his self-regard, his needs, the drawing power of family, the pull of the land—not only does he not have the option of saying no, he doesn't want to. How many people does he know who own vast estates on the Eastern Shore of Maryland? "Well then, let's see what you are doing with the cows."

For the next hour the previously taciturn Mr. French talks almost without pause. There is nothing about Jersey cows that he does not describe in the most minute detail: the characteristics and history of the breed, their peculiar propensity for breech births, their body weight to milk production ratios, the butterfat content of their milk, their preferred species of pasture grass, the molasses content of their silage, their choicest body parts for roasts and stews. Edward has not been raised in a milieu where mastery of large bodies of technical information wins any points, and never in his life has he heard one person spout such a quantity of it. In the farmyard Mr. French takes him first to the "hospital barn," a term Edward considers probably hyperbolic until they open the door to a gleaming tile-lined central corridor running through equally spotless and equally high-gloss stalls, where two black men in starched white coveralls—one quite aged and scarred in the face and blind, it would seem, in one eye, a father and son introduced as Robert Junior and Robert Baby—are going about their labor and ministrations to various bovine patients. Mr. French takes Edward to the "breeding office" at one end of the hospital barn, and on the wall he sees photographs of cows, paintings of cows, *portraits* of cows, and he sees ledger books of births and deaths, family trees captured at a level of detail that would make the royal family jealous.

Edward can only slump into the desk chair. He pushes back a small pile of papers to rest his arms on the desk, which makes Mr. French flinch. "Why do you do all this? Does it pay? Can it really matter all that much?" he asks.

"Does it pay?" Mr. French repeated. "No. I'd say it does not. Not anymore. Dairying has taken a different direction. But this is Miss Mary's life's work."

"Miss Mary's?"

"Yes, sir. She's made quite a study of it."

"I see that," says Edward, "but why?"

"To produce safe milk for children."

Sure, safe milk, but Edward can tell easily enough that French is being, if not coy, then evasive. Why, indeed, would the daughter of the Eastern Shore's most prominent family—at least historically speaking—devote thirty years of her life, the last thirty years of her life as it turns out, to this?

"It's what she came to," Mr. French says.

"What she came to?"

"The choices she made."

"Which choices?"

"To turn the Retreat into what it is," he answers, and with that, they are back where they started, and Edward likes and admires French more than ever because on this clever circle through his questions he has divulged nothing. God, with a manager like that at your back you would be bulletproof.

"So that's it," says Edward, meaning, The tour is over?

"No, sir. That's the husbandry."

"What's the rest?"

"The dairy."

So they are off on another round, the holding sheds, the milking barn, the milk storage, electric generators running constantly, chillers cooling the product, steam pressure sterilizers, and turbine steam bottle washers—a "sanitary dairy" it's called—and the cows come in, and six pairs of hands, some white, some black, grasp their teats and fill pails of milk, and it goes into the chilling room and then into bottles and thence to Baltimore. By now Edward is frightened—yes, that's the word—frightened by the prospect that any of the technical challenges might redound to him as owner, this "mantle" he had, he admits, so airily assumed in Miss Mary's presence, and he begins to feel the peculiar weight of the Retreat on its owners—the burden, as she said.

Everything is immaculate, like the gardens around the Mansion House—as he has learned to call it—like the white coveralls worn by the workers in the hospital barn. He thinks with dismay about his works in Manchester, the accumulations of flawed machinings tossed into a corner, decades of unfiled paperwork. Edward would like to think he'll have the place looking like, well, looking like the Retreat, but God, how exhausting to maintain it so. He gives voice to this last thought. "Miss Mary has maintained the farm in extraordinary repair," he says.

"Only way to do it," says the upright Mr. French, who adds, "but perhaps it is not quite right to say Miss Mary has 'maintained' it. She built it, sir. Everything you see, except"—he points across the farmyard—"the mule barn." He tells Edward that she tore down most everything else and started over. Three carpenters worked here nonstop for seven years. As French describes it, the whole enterprise sounds biblical. He says the carpenters built houses for themselves to live in first and then built what you see and then burned down their houses when they left.

By now Edward has learned that Mr. French is, in his own more diligent way, just as willing to divulge information as anyone he has met during this whole episode. He takes this surprising piece of evidence in silence. The whole place, every brick and batten, ear of corn and blade of grass, every genetically perfect cow and uniformed employee, is part of an obsession. Edward reflects on obsession, and on these carpenters, and his mind suddenly jumps madly to the building of the Pyramids, to the fanaticism behind them, to the thousands of slaves the pharaohs employed to ready their tombs. Somehow death is hanging over not just his visit—his visit, clearly, is about almost nothing but death—but over this place, this farm, this meticulously maintained but peculiarly joyless family estate. They're heading toward the final set of structures, the part of the operation Mr. French calls "cultivation," stables and mule barns, implement sheds, corncribs and silos, and more black people to meet Snick—yes, he heard that right—Snick

Hardy the mule driver, Raymond Gould the harness maker. Edward and Mr. French are standing in the open maw of the mule barn, and Mr. French says, as if to answer the troubling thoughts in Edward's mind, "This is where they found the boy's body."

"Aha," says Edward, because he isn't really listening. He's thinking about death in a more abstract sense, and getting the hell out of here, and this information, so apposite to his reflections, at first is processed as simply another voice in his own head. He makes sense of it in a double take. Oh yes, the boy's body . . . Of all the stories he has already heard about the place, a reference to this particular body was new to him. "I'm sorry. What did you say?"

Oral French realizes he has mentioned something Mason knows nothing about, something big, something he couldn't imagine had been left unspoken. Not that Miss Mary would have spoken of it, because she never does. But he realizes as well that even the gossips can't speak of these painful events that captured the lives of so many people: Mister Wyatt—he wonders if Miss Mary mentioned Mister Wyatt, her father, to Mason—Miss Mary; himself and his wife, Alice; Abel Terrell and his wife, Una; Uncle Pickle Hardy; Zoe and Zula and Hattie's Mary in the Mansion House; and Beal, Beal Terrell, God bless her and God bless the rest of us who have loved her, and so what if she was colored, no one—French is a powerful man, a man of principle with strong arms—no one will say a bad thing about Beal Terrell in his presence and not pay for it, and . . . and Mr. French can hardly pair the names these thirty years later, Randall and Thomas. Randall and Thomas. And Beal. Oh, French knows what he is putting Mason through, a reenactment of so many ancient emotions, grief and regret, relief and joy. He knows it is unfair because he has gone from regarding Edward as a fool to someone who was born too high to know any better. But now Mason is asking him what he means—what boy's body? But French is not going to answer. "I'm sorry, sir," he says. "I misspoke."

"I had just forgotten for a moment about the boy. Who was he again?"

"No, sir," says French. "I was supposed to show you around the farm."

He sees Mason regarding him. They are in the patch of bare earth at the center of the farmyard. French tries to imagine how Mason is seeing all this. The barns, the dairy, the dwellings for the hands and, at the far end, the grander house with three chimneys and green-and-white-striped awnings, which Mason would have to assume, correctly, is French's own domicile and which marks the east end of the farm in the same way that the Mansion House marks the western end. And in these buildings, doing their work, going about their lives at this very moment, are perhaps twenty souls—French isn't sure, for example, whether the dairyman McCready has returned from town yet—and all these people, whether they know it or not, are bound by stories, and Mr. French is trying to decide how much of any of these stories Mason should hear, because strangely he wants to tell them. But for the moment he's not going to say anything more about the boys and about Beal.

"I accept that," says Mason. "I'm here in unusual circumstances, Mr. French, but I am not here to pry into other people's business."

The tour is over, and French, out of gratitude for this last remark and out of a sudden avuncular fondness that surprises him, asks Mason if he would like to come down to his house for some lemonade. Mason accepts. They discuss the current crew of workers as they pass by their modest homes, and French corrects Mason's suggestion that good labor is hard to find. No, he says, there's been too much labor, too many good men and women on the Eastern Shore for the last hundred years, white and black, eager to work, eager to join a going concern; too much labor, a condition against all logic and the laws of economics. And too much land. There's too much of everything on the Eastern Shore. Mr. French was raised in Pennsylvania, where there was just a tiny bit less of everything than everyone needed, which yielded a fine, equitable society. French takes Mason to the back door of his four-square home, one of the few structures on the place not built by Miss Mary, and called "the French House" in his honor. He introduces him to Alice, a solid, broad-shouldered woman with a round face and chipmunk cheeks that bespeak warmth and equanimity. She's quite tall, like Mary—a race of Amazons, Edward thinks, and for a moment he tries to formulate a joke along these lines that he will share at the club when he gets back to Boston, as if he had spent weeks lost in the jungle. The three of them settle under the porch awnings to enjoy the water view, and Mr. French, buttressed by his wife's presence, the comfort of the porch, and the throat-loosening tang of lemonade, is happy to take a few minutes to tell stories of Mason's Retreat. The Retreat has been their home, a place for daughters to be born and grow, their life's work: first the peaches, then the cows. Neither orchardist nor animal husband, French is a manager, a leader of enterprises, a good judge of men. In the years to come, French will regret that he never sees Mason again, not after Miss Mary's death, when Mason became owner of the Retreat but in no way its master. In time, Mr. French will forget entirely about Edward Mason as the Retreat enters what he knows is going to be its decline, because in this century, with its already established alternating pattern of orgies of destruction and binges of consumption, there is really no obvious role for the Retreat to play. It has been remade twice in French's lifetime and denied both times. Denied a third time—denied thrice—when the Sisters of the Sacred Heart of Jesus refused it as a "retreat for prayer and contemplation." Besides those fewer and fewer workers who make their livelihood on the place, no one needs the Retreat. Mr. French will regret that he never sees Mason again, because he thinks that the man has been raised to accomplish very little in his life, but if he came to the Retreat, picked it up as it fell from Miss Mary's ravaged palm—if Mason had done that, it would have been good for him and good for the Retreat. But it didn't happen. When Mr. French died, in 1928, Mason was in England and now quite definitively a fool; the Retreat was again in decline, and no one had the slightest interest in saving it.

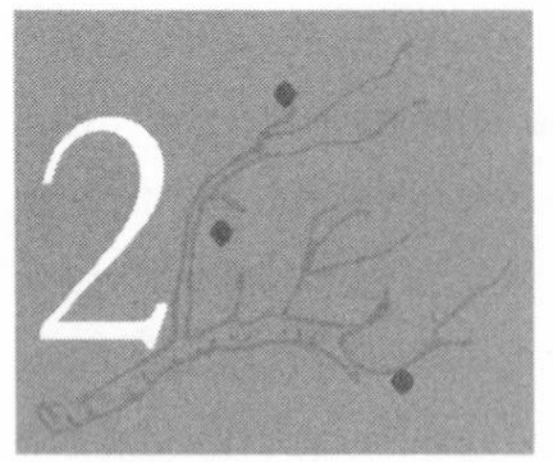

Ophelia Mason was a pretty child, with copper hair and green eyes. She had a wicker goat cart that her brother Lloyd used to hook up for her and lead around the Retreat, and she'd sit in it, a haughty lady with a parasol. One can't blame a child for her games, and some people would say to her when she went past, "Why, Miss Ophelia, don't you look right fine today." She did her lessons in what they called the Children's Office, which was right off the kitchen, in the old part of the house, where children had been doing their lessons for a hundred years and would do them again soon enough. She learned her spelling and her figures; she learned her sewing and needlepoint; she learned the customs she needed to keep living this life into eternity. At night she'd read her Bible and be put to bed in her room at the top of the stairs with its long view across the fields, and in the winter months she could hear the goose calls and the slap of frozen rain on her windows, and in the still summer months she'd hear the locust buzz and the busy traffic of raccoons and skunks, and she'd say her prayers into these sounds, asking blessings on her father and mother, on her brothers, on Hattie's Mary and Solomon and Ruth and Betty, and she believed those prayers got heard and answered and that all was well on the Retreat.

What Ophelia didn't know, back then in the 1850s, was that her father, Ogle S. Mason—everyone referred to him as the Duke; everyone, especially his wife and children, addressed him as Sir—was rich in slaves and they were eating him into the poorhouse. He had the proof in his ledgers. Months of a year the slaves lived all but idle on the Retreat. At that time the lands were in small grains, in strawberries and tomatoes, crops that grew with little need for human assistance.

The Duke hired out as many slaves as he could to Baltimore but never got the return he thought he was due; he sold a few from time to time but couldn't keep up with the population. He knew the whole thing was over anyway. The Duke was a Marylander through and through. He didn't think, he calculated; he didn't plan, he figured the odds. The western shore and northern counties were a Free State in everything but name, and Maryland would never secede just to preserve the plantations of the Eastern Shore or St. Marys County. He figured that much. Emancipation was on the way, no matter how much the Wrights and the Washbournes and the Lloyds and the Scarburghs were going to fight it, which showed how dim those old families had become, but in a way it also showed that they had some principles, even when they were dead wrong. Not him. Besides the fact that there was nothing about his farm that could afford all these souls, and besides the fact that slavery in Maryland was coming to an end, he recognized that these souls were about to pick up and leave anyway. The freedmen were whispering tales of escape and freedom in their ears. Forget the Underground Railroad: if they could just get to Baltimore, they'd be gone, which wasn't difficult, because those days half the passengers on the steamers were colored, and who knew who was free and who was slave, who were traveling on their own and who had papers saying they were doing their master's bidding? One way or another, the Duke figured, his slaves would be gone and he'd be left with nothing for his efforts. So in 1857 he made a deal with a man from Virginia, and one morning in July, a hot morning in July, that man was tying up a streaked and deck-rotted schooner at the steamer dock and off-loading a tangle of chains and leg-irons.

About a hundred people were there. Every man woman and child, black and white, slave and free. No one on the Retreat worked that day. The slaves were huddled together under the hot sun and in the yellow clay dust of the soil, maybe about forty of them, old and infirm, drooling and uncomprehending, naked babes in the arms of their whimpering mothers, young husbands and fathers who had done exactly what they had been told to do all their lives, teenage boys already burnished by hard labor, and—the most prized by the man from Virginia—the teenage girls, healthy girls. For an hour or so they just stood there in the breathless heat while the Duke and the man from Virginia did their business deal on the dock. Some of the slaves had brought bundles of clothes and who knew what possessions, and some just stood there with nothing but the clothes on their backs, because what difference would make one more or one less ratty pair of trousers, didn't make any difference at all, because they were all being sold south. Every single one of them. That was the deal the Duke made with the man from Virginia. Every one but the house slaves, no matter how old or how young, how well and fit or sick and crippled. *All or nothing; take it or leave it.* He sold them for what might have seemed thirty cents on the dollar, and the weasel-faced man from Virginia just couldn't stop himself from panting with pleasure, cackling as he counted out the money, his eyes wide with astonishment at this windfall and not a little fear that even at this late moment the deal might not go through, this rich harvest of slaves that he would start reselling the next day, and by week's end he'd be rich, richer than he ever dreamed. It didn't set the Duke back one bit to see his customer's glee; it didn't bother him to think that the man from Virginia would get rich, or get ruined, by this deal. *He* wasn't that man, so who cared what happened to him. He was selling about $15,000 worth of slaves for $4,000, $6,000—no one knew for sure, and he had no reason to tell anyone. The way things were going, he'd have nothing to show for them at all, so as he figured it, thirty cents on the dollar was a windfall to him, pure profit, and the man from Virginia was a fool.

There were about twenty whites on the other side of the landing, under the shade of the mulberries and locusts. Some were there to gawk at a scene of pure human misery. The Swems, farming a miserable bog at the northern tip of Mason's Neck, lived in a shack, and their children died one by one of the fever; Bill Swem figured there might be something to gain when others are suffering, some crumb of misfortune he could pocket and sell later. Mr. Francis Lloyd had driven over in his phaeton from Blaketon House to see with his own eyes—his own damn God-fearing eyes—if Mason would go through with it. He never stirred from his carriage, just spat out brown strings of tobacco juice into a pool on Retreat land, as if to show his contempt for the land itself. But for the rest of them, their hearts were breaking. They were there to say goodbye. Alice Yeardley, who became Mrs. French, was there with her father, who was the blacksmith on the Retreat and was losing the best apprentice he ever had, a boy with a bad leg named Clarence, a boy he cared about.

Ophelia was fifteen years old; she was wearing a white dress and a broad-brimmed straw hat, and she was crying. She knew these people. She looked into the line, and there was Little May Flower, just Ophelia's age, not a friend but could have been. Little was crying too; these two girls, one looking in, one looking out through tears.

"Hush," said her mother. "They knew this could happen. They know they're another man's property."

Next to Little was Sweet Cecilia, the girl who came in from the fields sometimes when they needed an extra hand at the Mansion House. Little and Sweet were a pair, friends, and they were holding on to each other; they knew what was wanted of them, even if Ophelia didn't. But next to them were red-haired Jacob Beets and Levi, and when Ophelia's eyes met theirs, she jumped because she was afraid of them—those two especially because they always seemed to take notice of her when she went by and said things to her or about her that she couldn't understand. She'd once seen Jacob Beets chained naked to a fence post in the heat of the day, and her mother in horror had brought her fan down over Ophelia's face before she could see all of his body, but not before she saw the cleaved musculature on his arms and chest. Levi and Jacob Beets could snap her in two, and she had a vision of them bolting out of the line and coming for her, and as if prophesying his own demise, Jacob Beets fixed on her eyes and gave her the smile of an unrepentant murderer being led to the gallows, the look of one who would someday enjoy revenge. She grabbed for her mother's hand. She stopped crying; she was glad they were going. And the old woman Milkie: everyone said she was the witch; she'd caused the two-headed calf, the heat wave in '53, when all the chickens died. Ophelia was glad she was going too.

A couple of men had come out from town, one of them the publisher of the *Queen Anne's Voice*. "What's he doing this for?" he asked

Ophelia's brother Richard. He nodded upriver to the fields of wheat. "How're you going to bring that in?"

Richard was his father's son, a hard man, an Esau to his brother Lloyd's Jacob, and he pointed over to a third cluster of people who were there that day, behind an imaginary barricade they themselves had demarcated, the freedmen and freed women and the house slaves, about eight of them, who were staying behind even as their mothers and fathers and children and spouses were being sent south.

"There's all the labor we need," said Richard. "They got nowhere else to go anyway."

Ophelia had not noticed this third group and had not realized that the house slaves, Hattie's Mary and Solomon and Betty and Ruth and the two boys, were being spared, and that the free families in Tuckertown, the Hardys and Hollydays and Terrells, weren't going anywhere. Abel Terrell was just a boy then. The next morning Pickle Hardy, uncle to about twenty of the slaves in the line, would be harnessing the mules back at the Retreat, and the free blacks would be there doing for wages what the slaves had been doing yesterday for nothing. *Homo economicus*, doing what made sense all around. Ophelia had overheard her father arguing this with his fellow slave owners: *Don't this make sense?* he asked. *Pay them for just the exact amount of labor you need?* And the free blacks were the best of the lot anyway, proven and self-selected, people of strength and courage, people who could take charge. For harvest, if it came to it, the Retreat would supplement them with the dregs of the whites. They'd keep an eye on the whites down the sights of a rifle barrel; if you needed a whip, it was for them; if you worried about your wives and daughters, those were the men you watched every step of the day.

Suddenly Ophelia felt better. The mean slaves, the scary ones, were getting on the boat, and the nice people, those who always greeted her and made a fuss about her red hair, they were staying. She breathed out, and this relaxing breath felt good, like a nice stretch in the morning while still in bed. That was how she became conscripted into the very heart of this day, and this moment of relief and joy and even gratitude to her father was a shame she bore for the rest of her life, but that's the way it was in Maryland in those days. In the North, there was one principle, one war, one story; in the South, one cause, one defense, one history; but in the borders, in the middle ground, there were as many principles and wars and histories as there were human beings to hold them, to survive them, to preserve them.

The negotiations on the dock continued in a low rumble during these static and windless minutes; the two men were squatted down in the attitude of defecation. The slaves waited with only a faint murmur of grief, the fussing of babes and whimpering of the young children. A mother was sitting on the ground nursing; an old man turned his back on the whites and urinated. And then, as if this were the sign everyone had been waiting for through the hot center of the day, a breeze rose up. It came down the river in a pebbled line across the water, and it came over the croplands in a disturbance of dust, swirling pillars "such as that which took Isaiah to Heaven," said Hattie's Mary after they had left, certain in her faith that there was some sort of salvation yet to come. The wind caught the skirts and tatters of the slaves' clothes and the hems and hat ribbons and neckties of the whites, and it caught the slack gray sails of the schooner and they began to flap and strain the sheets and halyards, and everyone knew that this was a wind the man from Virginia could catch that would speed him and his cargo in a dead run out into the Bay and south, past the wide mouth of the Potomac to Hampton Roads, then to the James and in a broad reach west and close-hauled head north up the river, and in two days, maybe three, they'd be in the slave market in Richmond.

With this wind came the end, and with it came the cries and wails, the unanswered prayers to God and to Abraham and Isaac, the appeals to that hard and calculating man for mercy. The crew of the schooner watched, clutching their handguns and rifles. The whites were still; Ophelia was holding on to her brother Lloyd, who was murmuring to her, and to himself, that this was *all for the good, the good of the Retreat*, that this was the way they had to look at it: *what was good for the Retreat*. The freedmen watched. And then, finally, whoever it was at the head of the line of slaves—whoever and whyever—turned and took the first step onto the dock, and then the next one, and the next one, and soon they were just loading themselves into the holds, and why? What force on earth compelled them to do that when they could have rebelled? Why not die resisting? Well, to live. To live long enough to see Richmond turned into a pile of rubble; to see the man from Virginia hunted down by a troop of Massachusetts boys and then turned over to the freed slaves who would promptly castrate him and hang him from a tree; to see, one morning, coming on foot out of the North Carolina mist, your husband, Robert Turner, who never for one day forgot you, coming to take you home. To see all that, which was prophesied, every cannonball and flame and severed vein of it, by none other than the Duke himself. He had the gift of prophecy; he just didn't know how to use it for the good of mankind.

How's that lemonade doing? Need an extra squeeze?

Can anyone imagine what this place felt like in the following days? The line of slave quarters was a pitiful and inhuman repository, but it was also a home, and the babes and children played there, and there was a life there, love and anger, tears and music. Now the quarters were empty, as if a plague had swept through, in one corner a half-carved doll, along one windowsill a collection of red stones, a pot with greens wilting in the sun. Silence in the barns and sheds. In the Mansion House, Ophelia tiptoed around in her nightgown as if the quiet that had descended on the Retreat was the whole point, as if all human activity should now be stilled. The stove was cold in the kitchen, and she found Betty, her maid, huddled on the floor in a dark corner of the laundry, crying for her father and for her friends Little and Sweet.

"What's he need money for, Miss Ophelia? Wan't there enough food here for all of us? Did we take so much more than what we earned? Did we eat more than the mules and give less service? Who on the Retreat was ever in need? Isn't you cared for in the Mansion House? Your daddy. What fault did he find? What was all this miserableness for?"

No one, especially not Ophelia, could answer those questions. And her father wasn't really done yet. Her father didn't think for a minute that by selling all the field slaves and manumitting all the house slaves—manumitting all the house slaves but not telling them he'd done so, though it might not have made that much difference to them—that he was off the hook for what was coming. That wasn't the point anyway, not guilt or innocence, amends or retribution. Money wasn't the point either, though that's how the whole thing got measured. It was just this figuring in the man's head, it was opinions hardened into some kind of crazy science, which could prove to some that science is best left in its own place and let God take care of the rest. Even when there were Federal troops camped on the lawn of the Mansion House, Ophelia's father never pretended that he was anything but what he was: a Maryland planter, a landowner with four thousand acres to do something with and not a whole lot of options, a former slave owner who saw nothing wrong with slavery even if, as it turned out, the natural limit of the institution had moved south during his lifetime. The war, when it came, wasn't about owning slaves for him, but about the right to have disposed of slaves however he wished, and for that right he'd resist to the end.

In the months and years between selling the slaves and the outbreak of the war, the rumors about a Great Insurrection flew on the Eastern Shore. One could take her pick which rumor to fear most—a runaway slave army from Accomack Plantation at the southern tip of the shore, working its path of murder and destruction up through Salisbury and Easton; freedmen pouring over from New Jersey and moving south through Elkton and Chestertown and Denton, coming down the rivers in oyster skiffs, picking up recruits along the way. Whatever the rumor, it seemed that just about everyone was zeroing in on the Retreat. At this point there was no one who liked the Duke—not the other planters, not much the working whites, even less the freed blacks, but each time one of those rumors started to fly, everyone would end up on the Retreat in the Mansion House and in the manager's house, or in the barns with the mules or in the dairy with the cows, in the implement sheds and in the old slave quarters, now empty and crumbling. They ended up at the Retreat because there weren't any slaves there anymore and because, to the degree that any of those people knew a thing about military tactics, the Retreat was well situated for "defense," this neck of land mostly surrounded by water, and broad open fields in every direction with plenty of tree stands to lodge in and snipe.

Landscape to stage an orderly *retreat*, one might say, though when the place was named by the Emigrant in 1657, it was not the withdrawal of an army he was thinking of, but of a single man, himself, a defeated English Catholic, his family's schemes exposed by the failure of the Gunpowder Plot, personally betrayed by Cromwell, living out his life in exile in the New World.

The rumors came in with riders at nightfall, and on those nights Ophelia sat with the ladies in the waterside parlor under the portraits of the Richards and Elizabeths and Edwards who would have hardly foreseen such a gathering as this, such cowering from these docile and domesticated beings, with the shutters drawn on the French doors and only a single lantern burning so as not to attract attention, and when Betty brought them tea, they asked her what was going on.

"No word, Miss Susannah," she'd say to Miss Ophelia's mother.

"I heard they're at the outskirts of Easton," Mrs. Lloyd would announce, or, "They're stealing boats so they can float down the Choptank." Or, "They're cutting us off neck by neck, that's the plan."

"I ain't heard word of that," Betty would answer, whatever the rumor of the night. "No word of such things, Miss Mercy."

And when Betty or Ruth would leave, Mercy Lloyd would say, "Do you think those nigger girls would tell us anything? They know what's happening. They'll slink into the night when the men get here, slave or freed, it hardly matters. They'll all be gone into the night."

That woman always got Ophelia's mother going, and even as her mother tried to calm her, fear seeped through Ophelia's body like black, cold blood. She could hear the low and tense reports delivered in her father's office by one of her brothers or the husbands of one of the ladies. She'd listen to Mrs. Lloyd's wild hallucinations and she imagined the slave armies all too well, could see them boarding punts and skipjacks with their corn knives sharpened to a shine, like pirates, blackened faces with the glint of bloodshot eyes; or like the mobs of the French peasants and their pitchforks, sweeping onto the estate from their starving huts, and she wondered if her father's head would end up on a pike; or like Nat Turner and his band, risen and rotting from their executions to continue a ghostly revenge. She could imagine these things because all this had happened in history and seemed to be happening now, but what really scared her, the nightmare from which she could not waken, was Jacob Beets and that Levi breaking through the door, escaped somehow from Virginia and come back to take their revenge. She'd think, In the next second the shutters will splinter and the glass will shatter, and Jacob Beets will come through with a bloody ax in his hand and hack me to bits. Then she'd feel a gray hand on her arm, and it would be Mrs. Neale, the widow from Carleton Farm, and she'd be saying, "Don't you listen to this, child. Nothing's going to happen. Change is coming, but not like this. This is all rumor." Mrs. Neale was a lonely person, and she was there those evenings for company as much as anything.

This went on for two years or so, and finally, when the most likely of all these scenarios of insurrection actually happened, the rumor they should have worried about all along but had never in fact imagined—which was a bunch of fanatical white abolitionists coming down from the North and picking a fight all on their own—when that happened in Harpers Ferry, it did look as if the bugle had finally sounded in earnest. The war began for Ophelia the night the news of John Brown's raid reached the Eastern Shore. She was seventeen. She spent that next night sleepless in her bedroom, with its long landview, and this time she did hear men out there, shouts and some gunfire, even if she could discern that these were sporadic, almost accidental firings and not anything sustained. This time she did see flames out there beyond the fields, a high conflagration that created a dome of orange in the moonless sky, and she could see the showers of cinders alighting in the rows of young corn. What was burning was not a home or a barn, but the steamer dock, as good an object for destruction as any, but in the morning it seemed less likely that it had been chosen as a target of Negro retribution than the mistake of a tense and careless man with a lantern. This time Mrs. Lloyd had to be slapped out of hallucinatory panic by her husband. Ophelia understood that the woman was mad anyway, a hysterical, pathetic sow of a woman, but even if all those events on that night could be explained, even as she sat on her bed and stared out the window until dawn finally arrived, she decided then and there that she no longer wanted to live on the Retreat, she no longer wanted to live on the Eastern Shore. She wanted to go to Baltimore, which was having its own share of conflicts and riots and would soon become an occupied city under martial law, but at least it was on the other side of the Bay. None of this was unlikely for her; none of it could have been called wishful. Her oldest brother, Richard, would inherit every bucket and buckle on the Retreat in due time—and that time did seem closer now, with her father consumed by his woes and worries—and she would be free of it.

In three years' time, both Mason brothers were dead, three companies of the Massachusetts Eighth Regiment were camped in the fields that could be seen from Ophelia's bedroom window, and her father was in detention in a cell at Fort McHenry. They kept him there for a month, but the rumors—spread liberally by his neighbors—that he was a captain of a secessionist militia proved to be untrue; he never cared about anyone else enough to join, much less lead, an army. As soon as he returned, he recommenced his scheming, driven now to preserve Mason's Retreat for himself through the agency of his daughter's marriage. He foresaw the next few years with slightly less precision than the events leading up to this moment, but he knew what he feared more than anything else, more than his own death: that with the inevitable victory of the North and the destruction of the South, the lands of the middle ground would become neither spoils for the victors nor charity for the defeated, but a sort of peace offering to all who had suffered. To be precise, what that meant to this man was that the Retreat and all the other slave-owning plantations of the Eastern Shore would be confiscated and given to the newly emancipated slaves or to anyone the federal government now judged more worthy to own it than himself: German abolitionist shopkeepers, Pennsylvanian second sons looking for a new plot of land, families from Maine, Irish immigrants. It would be broken up and given out, like crumbles from a Christmas fruitcake. But there was a solution. The death of his sons had in fact opened the way for his daughter, and if Ophelia's father could marry her to someone unspoiled by slavery, unbesmirched by suspect loyalties, whatever the policies concerning the plantation lands of the Eastern Shore, the Retreat might be safe.

About a month after Lloyd was killed, Ophelia's fondest wishes were granted and she was sent to Baltimore, accompanied by her maid, Betty, into the protection of her mother's cousins the Mapps, who would find her a husband. What she packed was no shimmering display of fashion and wealth, but threadbare remnants of earlier times, grayed muslin and percale in place of taffeta and crepe de chine. Her mother did her best, but since the war started, such fabrics were unavailable, and anyway, it had been some years since the Masons could afford such things. On the morning she left, her mother gave her a Bible, her great-aunt's pearls, and a talk on the facts of life, in which she told Ophelia that there was "a certain feeling" she might experience from time to time and must resist. Ophelia understood that her mother was not referring to feelings of love, which she had been led to believe she shouldn't resist, but some other sensation.

It had been perhaps four years since Ophelia had been any farther off the Retreat than Sunday services and her brothers' funerals at Holy Redeemer in Queenstown. She had forgotten almost everything about life except fear and grief. She had forgotten that there were other views than the long, mournful one from her landside window, the fields, the river, the sun that always came up to her right and set to her left, the storms that always overtook her from behind; that the air away from the Retreat could be fragrant with honeysuckle and fruit blossoms; that there was something other than silence, something to break it—laughter, chatter, children playing—other than the summer rattling of the insects and the winter howl of the wind; that as the road made its way to town, the land could unfold with dips and hollows and snug places to rest and secure places to tarry. As they began to approach the first buildings of town, she realized she had forgotten that men were engaged in labor and commerce that had nothing to do with the Retreat; that women could be seen not just in church clothes, but in easy work dresses, a plait of their hair falling without causing distress; that they could laugh and have friends and sit on a porch eating fruit; that one could live without shame for things you had absolutely nothing to do with. Ophelia had not realized that for most of the Eastern Shore the war existed only as distant catastrophe and not intimate tragedy; there was no reason for any Union army to drive down the peninsula, and no way for any Confederate army to march up it. Above all, Ophelia had forgotten that she was female, and pretty, that her copper hair was a kind of gold and her eyes emeralds that people stopped and gaped at. Solomon guided them through the center of town, past the courthouse, the smithy, the apothecary, and the Family Grocery, with its extravagant signs and the promise of delights in its dark recesses: sweets, ribbons and combs, paper tablets, soap smelling of lavender and sage. She craned her neck to watch these places recede. On the steamer landing a crowd was gathered, soldiers and gentlemen, ladies and daughters, young lovers preparing to part, and farmers with enormous pigs in crates, chickens sticking their fearful, soon-to-be-removed heads through the slats of their boxes, and baskets of tomatoes and strawberries. When they pulled up, Ophelia grabbed Betty's hand and Betty took hers, and they squeezed tight because they both knew they were on an adventure that could change their lives.

When they reached the wharf in Baltimore, Mrs. Mapp was there in her carriage, and her coachman drove them out into the narrow wharfside street and into a tangle of wagons and drays and carts. The cobblestones were slick with garbage and dung. Ophelia had been to Baltimore a few times with her mother long before, but she wasn't sure she had ever seen so many people and so much activity in one place. She glanced at the fortifications on the hill across the harbor and she could barely make out the black-spouted barrels of cannons trained down on them, and the dark shapes of artillerymen lounging on the ramparts, but at this distance she couldn't tell whether these soldiers were in gray or blue, and she didn't care; she was just relieved that they were there keeping order and that for now, the guns were silent.

Mrs. Mapp saw which way her glance went. "We are not untouched by this war," she said, "but you will be safe in my house, and you will see that civilization has survived here."

Ophelia moved into a room on the third floor of the Mapps' mansion on Mount Vernon Place, and Betty moved onto the fourth floor with the other girls. In the mornings, Ophelia pulled back the curtains and opened the window shutter and gazed out at the stolid looming monument to George Washington and the tree-lined square in front of the house. She often saw three boys under the care of two nursemaids playing tag on the grass and, less often, one or two girls of their approximate age watching them intently from the edge of the lawn. If she was awake early, she'd see the carriages pulling up at the stoops to take the great men of industry to their places of work, and if it was later she'd see the first of the women in high fashion strolling off to make calls in the neighborhood. It seemed that Ophelia had landed in a little Eden, a Parnassus high above the world's strife, where the children were allowed to laugh and play games, where women were safe and free and men were gazing into the future as if each day was a new beginning. Often she'd get back into bed, pull her bedclothes over her head, and stifle a small squeal of joy in her pillow.

When finally persuaded to leave her bedroom each morning during the months she lived with the Mapps, Ophelia would have breakfast with Mrs. Mapp and her daughter, who lived next door and was the mother of some of the children Ophelia watched in the park, and they would plan a day more exciting than the one before. An hour of reading and needlepoint, then get dressed, a lunch of maybe terrapin soup, tongue, and almond pie at the town house of one of Mrs. Mapp's friends, where there might be a long discussion of summer plans or of the typhoid season or of war news; or a light meal set in the back parlor at the house of her new friends, Becky and Molly Helm, with the good chance that their brother Frederick, who was between the two girls in age, would pop in and tease them. Or maybe just a walk in the morning and lunch at the Mapps', nothing but broth on account of Mrs. Mapp's weight. Then a nap, with letters written home and entries in her diary, and perhaps another walk with Betty, and when the late spring afternoon began to turn a slight rose color, back to dress for the main event, the dinner with the Mapps, their daughter Eveline, and her husband, Ralph Delaney—whom Ophelia found tedious—but then a concert, a lecture, a night at the theater.

This was all busy, busy work, and Ophelia knew what it was about for Mrs. Mapp, and for her parents, which was to find her a husband, a husband who lived in Baltimore. Fine, more than fine, with her. It thrilled her that in the course of the typical day she encountered dozens of men, men tipping their hats on the street to Mrs. Mapp and then to her with what seemed and must have been far more warmth. But though it thrilled her, most of them baffled her. A sly and slightly ironic look from that one with the pearl overcoat and sparse mustache: What was that about? What had amused him, and why did he feel it necessary or proper to let her see it? At lunch, arriving at Mrs. Garrett's, did it not seem that the two young men about her age, the homely one from Princeton and the Federal lieutenant, had found themselves there at that moment because they had been promised something, and was it right for them to inspect her like that? At the lecture hall during intermission, Mrs. Mapp placed them both with their backs to the large mirror, to the right of the potted palms, to the left of the staircase, and a parade of mothers with sons came to introduce themselves, sons too old and smelling of brandy or too young and trying too hard to be intelligent, and one who had lost an arm at the First Battle of Bull Run, and one who had lost an eye at the Second Battle of Bull Run. "Don't even consider him," whispered Mrs. Mapp about the one missing an eye, which meant he had fought on the side of the secessionists, forgetting that Ophelia's two brothers had fought, and died, with the Confederacy. There was the terribly sad one with a gray face and sunken eyes, who was dead three days later. And more, and each time Ophelia asked herself if she was feeling anything that her mother might have considered "a certain feeling," she decided that she was not.

One night she was at the theater for what she understood was a famous production of *The Rivals* by someone named Sheridan, and she and Mrs. Mapp were passing the first intermission in their places directly opposite the center of the three entrances. The lobby was hot and swooning with silk and pomade, and the truth was that after almost two months of this, with the hot summer now approaching, when everyone would flee the typhoid epidemics, it seemed that they must be coming to the end of the ranks of possibilities, with no results. "You're pretty enough," Mrs. Mapp had said, "but your parents made no effort to teach you how to converse." That, of course, and the fact that she was Catholic. Ophelia watched Mary Garrett, her fair and bare back against a mirror, effortlessly attracting men in a way that seemed both coquettish and calculating, and Ophelia knew that however determined she was never to go back to the Retreat, she was ill equipped to flourish here in Baltimore.

"I believe the scene change is taking quite a bit longer than usual," Mrs. Mapp said, comparable to a comment about the weather. Ophelia almost felt sorry for her, and in fact she was right. This intermission was a failure anyway.

Across the room, in the direction of the orchestra doors, there was a small commotion, and at the same time, out of the crowd came Mr. Mapp, looking extremely pleased with himself. "Have you heard?" he said to his wife and Ophelia. "Our Lucius has dropped dead in his dressing room."

Mrs. Mapp grabbed her husband by the sleeve. "Dead? Christopher Gilson? Here?" she asked, but by now the word "dead" was traveling from twosome to threesome, and both Mapps went off into the crowd.

Ophelia remained where she was. She had no idea who or what they were talking about; she was tired of being in a place she did not understand; she wished she were in her bedroom on the third floor of the Mapp town house or at the Retreat in the kitchen, talking to Hattie's Mary and Betty, or anywhere, and just then she was joined by a very tall but pleasant-looking man—a little gaunt, hollow-cheeked, a vague resemblance to President Lincoln, which would not have helped him much even in the Unionist enclaves of the city. He was over thirty, she supposed, old but not too old, a man who seemed in every way—a hesitant manner, dinner clothes slightly out-of-date and perhaps heedlessly put on—different from the others she had met in the past month.

This man took up a place at her side, two spectators on the unfolding scene in front of them, and said that this was quite "an excitement."

Men weren't supposed to talk to young women they hadn't been introduced to, and women, especially young women, weren't supposed to respond, but at this point Ophelia hardly cared. "What has happened?" she asked.

"The lead has dropped dead."

"In what way?" she asked, and what she meant was whether this was part of the play somehow, since she'd already heard two names for the dead man. In the past two months she'd sat in on long conversations about people she didn't know, only to discover that they were characters from novels—Dickens, Jane Austen, writers she hadn't read.

"The old-fashioned way, I think," he said. He said this after a pause, as if, she thought later, her question had bewildered him, but it was just the way he conversed, composing his sentences before speaking.

By now the crowd had moved forward, and over the tops of their heads Ophelia could see one of the tall orchestra doors opening. She turned again to this man and said, "Yes. But what does it mean?"

"It means that he won't be able to perform the dueling scene in Act Five."

Ophelia heard this and then realized what stupid things she had been saying, and how kind and silly he was being to her, and how good being stupid and kind and silly felt after trying so hard for these weeks to be brilliant and catty and droll. She brought her hand up to her face and started to laugh just as the crowd was stilling for the announcement. Heads turned with disapproval, and it was as if everyone in Baltimore who had found disfavor with her for one reason or another was there: the women who had disapproved of her gawky stride and her country table manners, the men and boys who had inspected her and found her too skinny, too flat-chested, too red-haired. She gloved her giggles and turned to the tall man, and he still seemed willing to remain at her side. The stage manager, the famous Joseph Jefferson, began to address the audience. His voice was very high, and he often squeaked when making announcements, but these words flowed from the heart. "The Holliday Theatre," he said, "regrets to inform you that our dear friend Christopher Gilson, whose Macbeth we will always remember, whose Tony Lumpkin celebrated with such charm the rebirth of the stage in Baltimore, whose—"

"What's he saying?" whispered Ophelia to this stranger at her side, with whom she now felt more comfortable than she had with anyone in weeks.

"He's talking about the roles Mr. Gilson played."

"—collapsed in his dressing room and has been pronounced dead by Dr. Richard Whitlaw. His understudy is in the theater, but in honor of his passing"—and here he did squeak a little—"we are canceling the performance."

He left his remarks to that and would not have been able to be heard had he continued. The crowd erupted, moans of dismay and shock, tears. Mrs. Mapp had found her way back to Ophelia, and she glanced at the man at her side. Ophelia could see her considering the strengths and weaknesses of him as a candidate and deciding that actually he would do quite nicely. Considerable wealth. A fine house on Charles Street. Unitarians, but therefore inoffensive. She ought to have considered him earlier. She introduced this man to Ophelia as Mr. Wyatt Bayly.

They were married the next summer, in 1864, at the Retreat, and Mary was born a year later. Everyone knew that the Duke would not live much longer, and no doubt he was taking with him to his grave the satisfaction that he had figured it all just about right, that Mr. Wyatt was from a Unionist family and rich, that he had been willing, eager in fact, to convert to the Faith, and that if land was taken—which it was, here and there, but mostly down in St. Marys—it wouldn't be his land. Mary had been born by the time he died, and with the first child popping out so expeditiously, a son, and a future, couldn't be far behind.

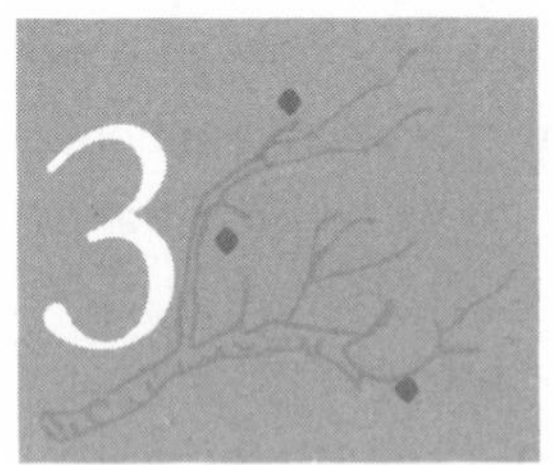

One chilly morning in April 1872, not much after sunrise, Wyatt Bayly stood with his back to the river, glancing inland. Behind him, out on the oyster flats, tongers were at work, their twenty-foot-long tong handles rising and falling, closing and spreading, as if machines were in control and not men. In front of him, in a field that stretched along a mile of rivershore broken only by the occasional slice of drainage into the river, a field that had produced nothing of market value in a hundred and fifty years, there were now approximately eleven thousand young peach trees, a bright froth of blossoms lined up in rows following the barely discernible swell and dip of this sandy patch of land. For all his self-satisfaction, Wyatt could gaze at this display and feel humbled by the urgency of the plants, eleven thousand living creatures expressing a dogged drive to make good and quick use of the time allotted to them. The blossoms expressed the essence of all this. The trees' daintiness belied the raw energy driving up from the roots, across the graft unions, into the hardwood, and out the stems, detonating the buds into blossoms; and this force became fragrance and continued up into the sky. Wyatt believed that if he could throw a canvas over the entire orchard, he could catch this energy and rise all the way to the moon.

"Well," he said to Abel Terrell, standing at his side, "I think we have done it."

"Yes, sir, Mister Wyatt," said Abel. "I believe so." Abel Terrell, child of a free man and a free woman, had been about ten years old when the slaves were sold at the landing, about a half mile upriver from where they stood now. Abel had performed or supervised the grafting of almost every one of those eleven thousand trees. Between the cambium layers of rootstock and scion of virtually every one of them, there was a drop of his saliva, his sweat, or his blood. He did not engage in imagery about the life force of plants. To get through this life, he was placing his bets on three things: his own labor, his wife's love, and his children's future. He took off his straw hat and ran his hand over his round, quickly balding pate. "The Campbells and Yorks look right fine."

"The best soil in this section," said Wyatt.

"Like you said, Mister Wyatt."

Yes, as I have been saying, thought Wyatt. He had made a study of this, the sandy, well-drained soil along the watercourses; everyone agreed that it was what you wanted for peaches. This is where you could plant with confidence. Most of the big orchards were higher on the river, closer to Delaware. A mistake, he thought. Here, there was a good amount of clay to keep the moisture up during dry years. Perfect. Along the wider watercourses you got a good winterlong blow, but by the time the fruit had set, the breezes were gentle, sometimes perfectly still, which, in the opinion of the scholars Wyatt consulted, you wanted in order to avoid spreading blight. Blights were always a problem, but the answers to them were in science, derived from the logic of the earth. Wyatt had made a study of this, this planet. It was in his blood to do so. His grandfather had founded the family fortune on a granite quarry in Cecil County that at one time seemed to be providing every cornerstone and every lintel for every brick building from Philadelphia to Richmond. His father had followed his nose west to the seeping black pits of western Pennsylvania and knew that this product of the earth, this rock oil, was going to become useful, and Wyatt's older brother had moved to Pittsburgh and was building a petroleum company on the land holdings his father had amassed. To some minds, to his father's and brother's minds, the earth held its real secrets and its true riches deep inside. What was outcropped on the surface, the coal lumps, the granite, the oil seeps, the gold in California's mountain creeks, the salt on the flats, was just advertising, just a taste. Men had to be used—and to die—to get the real stuff; technology, steam-driven augers and drills and pumps, was needed. If the earth wasn't going to give up its wealth willingly, it would be taken by brute force.

Wyatt really didn't disagree with too much of that. The necessity for manpower, the benefits of technology. Still, he had no idea why, but even as a small child he was fascinated by plants, not flowers or vines or box bushes in a line, but the homeliest of volunteers, a gnarled spruce growing out of solid rock, dandelions year after year making the push between the cobblestones of Baltimore. He thought the dandelions were pretty and brave, and it saddened him when they were trampled. They never gave up. When he was perhaps five, a large mock orange tree had been cut down on his grandparents' farm in Towson, and over time he watched as that stump put out a hundred shoots. They cut them back, thinking the stump would dissolve, but then someone on the farm decided that the original tree had been handsome where it was and they should let the tree do what it wanted to do, which was to survive and propagate in that very spot, so they kept cutting the shoots back, but let one live. In time, that great subterranean being understood it was being given this reprieve, and it stopped putting out new shoots and poured everything it had into the sapling growing out of its rotting stump. Wyatt had been caught from time to time talking to the sapling. This was a drama of life, of will, which he watched for about ten years. His mother thought his focus on it a little odd, and his father found it completely unsatisfactory, hardly a manly way to act. Later, when Wyatt refused to volunteer for the militias, his father dismissed him with a question: What else could be expected from a boy who played with flowers? He should be attending to the livestock, if anything. But in the other beings on the farm Wyatt had little interest; when they died or, more accurately, when they were killed, they stayed dead. It was the nature of these beings to give up, to give up their lives, as humans did. Wyatt placed no store in the afterlife. What he believed in was that mock orange stump—not a promise of eternity, but a will to occupy it. As a young boy, and later as a businessman, a grower, and an orchardist, Wyatt placed his full faith and protection in the unstoppable determination of plants to live.

"And what do you think, Mr. French?"

"Surely," said Wyatt, when Mr. French didn't answer, "even you can regard this with some pleasure. Wouldn't you think," he said to Abel, "Mr. French would regard this with pleasure?"

Abel did not want to be forced to make a comment about his boss, though he liked Mr. French, trusted him for the most part, and didn't have much choice for the rest. "Mr. French, he'll find some rub to this."

Oral French, manager of Mason's Retreat, was a worrier. He was a Pennsylvanian whose studies at State College had been interrupted by two years of mercifully bloodless service as a quartermaster in the Union army, and he had been recommended to Wyatt as a young man of superior intellect and character by Wyatt's uncle, who had been French's commander. He had been studying law, but he took the job as manager of the Retreat despite the fact that he knew nothing about farming. Wyatt didn't need a farmer; he needed someone who knew something about money and men, which Mr. French did. He knew that nothing in this world was more unreliable than money and men.

"The Heaths are looking poorly." Mr. French could hardly tell one variety from another, but he could not bear to leave optimism unchallenged. Bad business, bad luck.

"They're lates," said Abel. "The earlies are the key."

Yes, Wyatt reflected, the earlies were indeed the key to his plans. This whole enterprise was about being early, about earliness in all its forms. To every complaint from his wife about how hard he was working, about how he was working like a common field hand alongside the Negroes—and what had he hired Mr. French for, anyway?—earliness was the answer. Maybe this was so because as a man, he had gotten such a late start in a career, a marriage. Early Campbells and early Yorks in the markets of Baltimore, or of Philadelphia, New York, or Boston—a week before the earlies from New Jersey. Even a few days ahead of Delaware. There it was in a single sentence, the whole logic behind his business plan. The first peaches of the summer, and then for the rest of the summer the Smocks and Crocketts and finally the late Yellows and the Heaths, each time a week ahead of the growers in New Jersey. For a week Wyatt and his fellow peach growers on the Eastern Shore could be the foxes in the henhouse; they could sit down to a banquet. That was the key, which Mr. French could well appreciate from a business perspective, even if he couldn't tell a Smock if it bit him.

"If we can get the crews," said Mr. French, and here there was no denying the challenges on his mind. Wyatt turned to face the water because the river too was a key to his plans. Everything about Chesapeake country was about the rivers. The low skiffs of the tongers were almost at their waterlines from the weight of the mounds of oysters in their centers, a good day for the Negro oystermen, a good season. Shipping oysters to New York might be a good business, but not for Wyatt, who didn't understand oysters. Hard to imagine what it would be like to be an oyster. Why spend all that life force to create such a gnarled, imperfectly shaped shell?

Yes, Mr. French knew what he was saying now: those early Campbells and early Yorks were not good shippers; they had to leave the Retreat not a minute too soon and not a minute too late, and every part of that could be well arranged, except for the crews to pick them and the boats to haul them, and that was Mr. French's job. His nearly impossible job. Nothing about labor made sense anymore. The war and Reconstruction had raised hell when it came to labor, which should be the simplest matter of all. The freed slaves, the ones who hadn't taken off in search of family or in search of confiscated slave-owner land that they could claim in St. Marys County or in the Confederacy, their forty acres and a mule, or in search of children taken away by the Orphans' Court and returned to a bondage called apprenticeship—well, they had no idea what labor was all about. They knew work, they knew travail more than well enough, and they'd do it sunup to sundown without complaint, with hardly a cup of water to nourish them. They just didn't understand jobs, and how could they? They'd come for a day, and at nightfall you'd say, *You gonna be here tomorrow bright and early?* and they'd say, *Sure thing, Boss, bright and early,* and sometimes they'd come and sometimes they wouldn't. Mr. French was from an abolitionist family, and he knew that when the former slave owners called these men "unreliable," they were angling for some way to put them back into bondage. They'd already tried a couple of ploys and would try a few more tricks before Reconstruction was done. So Mr. French wasn't going to call these emancipated souls unreliable, but he couldn't depend on them either, and he spent his days and weeks before peak labor times trying to get commitments from free blacks or Irishmen right off the boats at the immigrant pier in Baltimore. Three times a summer he needed a crew of about thirty men, and as many wives and children as came with them, and they'd move them into the former slave cabins, a gesture Mr. French didn't love, no one did, but that was the shelter they had to offer. Mr. French had heard that Poles and Germans were starting to come over, and he was ready to sign them up.

Sign them up, said Wyatt. *Sign them all up.* Why delay? No delay in any of this. As soon as Wyatt and Ophelia were married and the Union troops had cleared out, he and Abel and whoever they could get, sometimes just two or three, sometimes twenty or thirty, were out in the old pastures and strawberry beds and cornfields planting pits for rootstock; they planted pits for rootstock by the tens of thousands, from April to June. Wyatt would go to bed hallucinating, as if from each pit they planted would spring a soldier, whole armies marching across the fields in rigid array. If the rains or the freeze or the soil was bad, they'd get nothing at all, but if the sequence was right, they'd get a healthy plant sticking up about two feet above the grass in about four months, the first half of what they needed for a peach tree. They'd get roots that were born in this soil, that had this soil woven into their fibers, roots that knew their own home ground.

"We worked hard for this," said Wyatt. He meant all kinds of work, but mostly the physical kind. The kind that left your hands rough but your head clear. His angular and awkward-looking frame would never fill out, but no one would mistake him for a schoolteacher even after, in a sense, he became a schoolteacher. "I want to thank you for your hard work," he said. He continued a bit, telling them, in the ardor of the moment, of his respect for and gratitude to them. Mr. French looked at his shoes, kicked the dirt. Abel said nothing to this, did nothing about this.

When they had all the rootstock they needed and it was time to make the grafts and plant them, they set up tents at the heads of the rows and brought in the budsticks, and Abel's grafters would set to those young saplings, with Abel doing ten in the time it took anyone else to do two, and most of his grafts would take, and most of anyone else's would not. He was a sight to see, leaning over those plants like a dentist: his knife blazing and a mouthful of scions staying moist and vigorous in his saliva, wounding the seedling's firmest branchling, joining the root and the budstock in a savage blending of fluids, binding the joint with twine and clay. Like magic: a man-made tree. Sometimes he'd cut himself, and the next five or ten would be wrapped in his blood. There wasn't a single knife on the farm that had to be sharper than a grafting knife, honed on only one side. Abel was left-handed, so Wyatt had one made especially for him, and all day as he worked; he'd go back and forth from the stock and the scions to the leather strop, and all day his knife remained sharp enough to cut a silk scarf falling through the air.

During those days Ophelia, and Mary in Betty's arms, often rode out in a carriage to see them work. Mary was two or three when they were grafting the first growth, and she was tall and healthy, with her father's black hair and not, to Wyatt's disappointment, her mother's red. Betty would take her over to watch the workers, and Wyatt would get into the seat beside Ophelia under the shade of the carriage roof. She'd take off her glove and take his hand, and the pressure of her flesh could, for a moment, displace peach trees from his mind, and he could lose it altogether anytime he thought back to the first time, some weeks into their marriage, when he finally was allowed to look frankly at her naked body, and of all the unexpected beauties, nothing quite so delighted him as her red body hair, her copper pubic patch. He hadn't dreamed that this would be so, and therefore assumed that no other man would suspect it, that no other husband would imagine that Wyatt's wife's body offered a secret treasure that their wives' did not. It seemed almost indecent, yet pure, adolescent, untouched. Right there in the carriage, all this could come to mind, and he knew she felt it too, this "certain feeling" her mother had warned her about. It was all easy, back then.

"Is it going well?" Ophelia asked the first time she was there to watch Abel grafting. "Whatever those boys are doing."

Even Wyatt had to admit that what Abel and the grafters were making looked unlikely: just sticks attached to roots, as Ophelia might say. "They look like sticks, but they're beginning to marry. Next spring we'll prune off every leaf and bud of the parent, and the graft will sprout."

"It sounds mean," she teased. "You're being mean to your trees, letting their bodies be taken over by an invader."

"Well," he said. "It doesn't hurt. At least I don't think so." He wanted to go on, tell her more, tell her that the year after that they would replant the new tree in the orchard lands along the river, but he wasn't going to press his luck.

She considered what he had said. "Does it work?" she asked finally.

"I hope so," Wyatt answered. "A lot of wasted effort if it doesn't."

She took back her hand so she could swivel about in the seat, contemplate the vast rivershore land that he had told her he intended to turn entirely into orchard. She could not help letting a sigh escape: Would it take a year, five years?

Wyatt knew exactly what she was thinking, what that sigh meant. "Don't worry," he said.

"When will you know?"

"That's the thing about peaches. They grow quickly." He failed to add that individual trees didn't live very long; what perhaps looked like planting oaks for the ages was actually more like nursing a flower that bloomed a few hours and then was gone. The process never ended: new seedlings, new grafts, new trees to take over the ones that had lived their useful life, some only five years. What was certain, timeless, and ageless for Wyatt was the collective tree, the immortal fruit. "We'll know when they blossom. Then we'll get peaches."

"But these are just saplings."

"They look like saplings, but the budsticks are from mature trees. They know they are mature. The stem will flower and fruit despite the fact that it's now part of this young plant."

She had heard enough about peaches. "You and your trees," she said. " 'They know they are mature.' "

"Well. They do."

On that certainty they sat for a moment; he was beginning to think he should get back to the work. "I don't think I will ever be able to come out here and feel anything but horror," she said. They were in the north corner that day, just beginning the slow cultivation of this entire stretch of rivershore. She pointed at the other end, a mile away, where the charred remains of the pier still stood, the blackened ends of the piles being lapped lightly by the soft, brackish water of the river. She couldn't see them from where they were, but she could feel them. "Nowhere out here."

"I would hope that what we're doing could make that go away for you. This is not cursed land. It is vital, rich, fertile, blameless land. The trees are pure, the product of black labor and white labor side by side." He nodded toward Abel, with his blazing hands and his mouthful of scions.

She turned to him straight on, her green eyes fixed on him from the recesses of her sunbonnet, her lips so tensed they almost disappeared. "The land knows what happened on it just as much as your peach branches know they are mature. What happens on the land is never past. Never."

Another time, Mary was four and, as she did often, asked her mother to take her out to the fields. Ophelia was pregnant. She had believed almost from her first missed period that this pregnancy would not go well, knowledge that had come to her with the immediacy of a vision. She asked Betty—who had two of her own by then—what it meant, her certainties, and Betty had heard that the pregnancies a woman lost were babies that were too good for this world, that it was a case of God being selfish, realizing He had almost carelessly given away an angel, and Ophelia's vision was like Mary being visited by the angel Gabriel, but for the opposite reason. She was being told she'd have to give him back. God made mistakes from time to time but put them to rights directly. She said women mourned a lost pregnancy more than their husbands because they had felt the touch of an angel. A theology of loss, Wyatt called it when Ophelia told him, faith in disaster: Wyatt, man of the Enlightenment, trying to free his wife from the superstitions of the home ground.

"Look at this place," he said to her that afternoon, waving at the undulations of peach blossoms. He coughed to cover up the quivering in his voice. "Smell the fruit of this land," he said, forgetting whom he was talking to.

By now the planting effort had gotten them into the center of the rivershore fields, and the charred posts of the dock house were plainly visible from where they sat. Ophelia could smell this fetid land all right, the acrid sweat of human beings in misery, the rotten air of the holds of a derelict schooner, the choke of clay dust in the nostrils. That day would never leave her. Not long ago, driving off to pay a call, she had gone by three or four black workers and her blood was chilled when she recognized one of them, the man who had scared her as a child, Jacob Beets. That night she begged Wyatt to let him go, and Wyatt didn't know who he was, said he would talk to Mr. French, but why, he wondered, after all this time, after this rebirth, this redemption, would she worry about him? He'd come back to the place of his birth, like most people. Rather than frighten her, that should reassure her.

"I think I want to go to Baltimore for this birth," she said.

"If you wish," he answered, enthusiasm gone. They sat in the carriage without speaking for a minute or two and watched Betty and Mary emerge from the trees. "But I don't think there's any reason for alarm. Besides, what do they have over there that we don't have?"

She let it go; in fact, they had nothing over there in the way of attendance upon a birth that they did not have on the Retreat. The point was Baltimore, not the birth. Mary came over to the carriage and tried to pull Wyatt out. She was already tall, a physical child, boyish in manner, something her mother was trying to repress. "Show me my trees," Mary said. He had told her a few days earlier that they had planted a whole section of trees and named it after her. Marysland in Maryland, he had said, and then she asked why the states were named after girls and not boys. They were all queens, just like you, he answered, but she persisted: "Who was Queen Georgia?" she asked. Wyatt said that Georgia was a name for a state before it was a name for a girl. Carolina, he said, was for Princess Caroline.

"I want to see my trees."

He appealed to Betty, who took her off, wailing.

"You seem troubled," he said to his wife.

"I'll be glad when all this is done. It's taking much longer than I imagined."

There was no mystery about what she was saying: *When these trees are finally planted, then we can move back to Charles Street.* He had not promised this, but he had allowed her to believe he had promised it. The truth was, when this land was done, he intended to continue south onto the lands they called the Waverly lands, and then almost to Queenstown Harbor. Fifty thousand trees, that's what he had in mind. No impulse to please his wife was going to change that. And by the time they got the Queenstown Heights planted, the original trees on the Retreat would be exhausted, time to dig them up and replant. He didn't know exactly how he was going to finesse this with her, what arrangement would satisfy her if she persisted. Already between them was this vague understanding that their marriage would not be typical, and the agreement that this was no one's fault, or that the fault was so evenly shared that no one could be blamed.

"I'll be much less encumbered soon. We will have a wonderful winter in town with our two"—he gripped her hand, still gloved, for luck and confidence—"children. Perhaps this year the new Holliday Theatre will be open. Our special spot," he added.

"Yes," she said. "Our special spot."

And then Mary was six, and complaining that it was too hot to visit the trees. The planting had made it to the southern end of the rivershore lands; the Mansion House was only five hundred yards away, its red clay tile roof a backdrop through the pines and beeches of the parklands. Ophelia pulled the reins to a stop almost on the spot where the slaves had stood; on Wyatt's orders, the remains of the old pier and pier house had now been completely removed, eradicated, planted over with shore grasses and day lilies, but after all these years, even he felt the lingering malevolence of this place. For five years they had been working with this as the goal, the end point. Who knew what Abel Terrell thought of it. Who among the whites could possibly imagine what sort of legend that day had now become in Tuckertown—a cautionary tale to misbehaving children? A myth of the darkest moment promising redemption and victory in the light? Or was there too much misery to speak of it at all? Perhaps Ophelia was right about the land, but not because evil was *in* the land—he could not go that far, would not—but *on* it. The fact that she was willing to come out here, to this very spot, to talk to him gave him warning that this was a conversation she would not put off.

Wyatt came over to the carriage and, as usual, climbed in. Mary would not get out, though Betty was pulling her across the seat. "C'mon now, Miss Mary," said Betty. "Let your mama and papa visit."

"Oh, for heaven's sake," snapped Ophelia. "Just take her back to the Mansion House."

"I'm pregnant again," she announced when Mary and Betty had left. She wasn't looking at him when she said this; in profile, her jaw was set, as if she did not want her lips to tremble.

"Lovely," he said, reaching for her hand, which she did not offer up. "When will you be delivering?"

"I shall be in Baltimore," she said. "I won't let you talk me out of it this time."

"I hope you do not still think the death of our child was something that could have been prevented."

"I don't know," she said. "But I can't bear the thought of giving birth in the same room where Edward died." The priest had baptized the dying child, and they buried his body under his own name beside the remains of an earlier failed Mason pregnancy marked only as "Promised Child." Wyatt had never referred to this son as anything but "the one we lost."

Wyatt heard this with some relief, as if this were all there was to it. Because this time he could understand her fear, her superstition, and if that's all there was to it, it didn't have so very much to do with him, or with their marriage, or with the Retreat. But he didn't think that was all there was to this.

"With your permission, I will be leaving this afternoon."

"Surely you won't be spending July and August in the city. It's much too dangerous. I couldn't allow that."

She had been planning this for some time, with or without his permission. Of course she wouldn't risk the epidemics. "We will be with your family at Chestnut House."

It was Wyatt's turn to be silent and hers to dissemble. Because by now the sides were drawn: to the east, the Retreat and the peaches; to the west, Charles Street, the farm in Towson, Wyatt's parents and his sister, Cecile. In between, as always, the Bay, a border, a barrier, a moat. Oh, thought Ophelia, what changes with a two-hour steamship ride! "I could want nothing more than to have you accompany me."

"You know I can't do that. Not now, certainly. I'm especially sorry that I cannot, given your condition."

"My condition is fine, Wyatt. There's nothing wrong with this pregnancy. I would want us together for any reason, but I don't expect it. You have your trees. There will always be trees. If God sent a plague of locusts upon us, everything would be bare except your peach trees. If God desired to inflict on you the one loss you could not endure, he would send a plague to destroy your trees." She realized that she was getting a little hysterical, but she did not want to stop. "Trees and trees and more trees," she said. "Ten thousand, twenty thousand. If you had fifty thousand, you'd want a hundred. I realize now that I had incorrect expectations."

Wyatt didn't think they were incorrect, whatever they were. He felt that the situation had changed, success had changed it, and as a result, she was unfair to call their original plans "expectations." Could she not see, he wondered, that they could have both lives? The Retreat was going to shine, emerge out of the smudge of tobacco, the dishonor of its slaveholding past, the vicious conniving of her father's last days. But to Wyatt's astonishment, Ophelia now so hated this place that she had even speculated, one evening not so long ago, whether it had been right to take it from the Indians. She was now arguing that the whole American adventure was about forced labor from the beginning—indentures, African slaves. Who cared, thought Wyatt, for all this history? Wyatt hated history now that he thought about it; it was history that he hated about Baltimore. Blow it up. Had he lived long enough to see the fire of 1904, he would have been pleased. Yet here he was, having to argue history with his wife. But for all of Ophelia's umbrage, she gave honor and respect to the Mapps, and to his own family on Charles Street, growing rich on other people's labor. Wyatt did not want to lose his beloved copper-haired Ophelia over any disagreement, any conflict about mere abstractions, or lose her to anyone. But most of all, he did not want to lose her to the Mapps.

"Whatever your expectations are," he said, "I will try to meet them."

Ophelia thought of him that summer she spent with her in-laws in the gentle rolling hills of Towson. A blameless farm, a tidy house in the elbow of two grassy knolls that had been much added to over the years, it still felt at its heart like the modest Quaker cabin it had once been, with its small parlors, deep-set windows, and low ceilings. The barns and the springhouse were in the same hollow, close and handy for those who did the work, and the chestnut and maple trees that shaded the yards and lanes were northern species, firm, unyielding, with none of the untidy indolence of the sycamores and magnolias across the Bay.

That summer in Towson, Mary played with her two cousins, Cynthia and Dolly. She was six that year, tall and dark and, to Ophelia's eye, rather willful; not well-mannered, she played mean. Cynthia was the oldest of the three, an awkward girl with poor vision, and her sister, Dolly, at five, worshipped Mary and would do anything thoughtless or spiteful to her older sister if she thought it could win her the tiniest bit of favor. They played hide-and-seek, but when it was Cynthia's turn to hide, Mary suggested that they go inside and play cards instead of looking for her, which Dolly thought was a fine idea. They painted eyeglasses on Cynthia's doll, which could be washed off the porcelain of her face, but not out of her hair.

In that summer of Ophelia's pregnancy, as the baby grew and gave her a gentle, reassuring kick each time it seemed that he, Thomas, was too still, she realized how completely her hopes had gone awry since her marriage. How had it happened that while she was escaping to the west, to Baltimore to find a husband, she had met the man who had similar thoughts of escaping, but in the opposite direction, to the east, to land where he could plant peach trees? Their marriage had become like a meeting of steamboats in the middle of the Bay. Perhaps if they could have stayed there, tied alongside, they would have been happy. She could not blame Wyatt for her feelings about the Retreat, about her father, and she understood how passionately he believed he could plant all of that away—away from her and away from the land, as if the trees selectively drew in the poisons from the soil and, in their magic, transformed them into sweetness. How could he not be right about this, how could anything as innocent as a peach tree not lend a kind of grace to the soil around its roots? Ophelia understood this spiritual side of her husband's work far better than he imagined, but what she also had figured out—maybe it was that summer in Towson of Thomas's coming into the world that she figured this out, or maybe it was some time before—about her diffident husband, with his halting manner of speech and his eagerness to avoid the scrutiny of society, was that Wyatt was a deeply *ambitious* man. That he was one of those people who felt called upon to prove and re-prove himself. This would not, did not, come as a surprise to Mr. French or to Abel, or to the men who worked under him or the other landowners, former slave owners—Lloyds, Wrights, Scarburghs—similarly land-impoverished gentry who, as the summers wore on, were busily buying Wyatt's rootstock and sending their employees to spend a day or a week with Abel just to learn a thing or two. Wyatt was a businessman, of a sort that was unfamiliar to Ophelia, who held in contempt connivers like her father, Marylanders merely holding on to what they had and not actually trying to put something new into the world. Wyatt wanted peach trees to line the Chester River from Kent Island to Millington, and he was going to make it happen. She knew she should admire it, but instead she felt as if she were being engulfed.

Ophelia sat on her shore and grew silently fat and wondered about the past, and Wyatt stood on his shore and planned for the future. When Thomas was born in October, she was back in the Bayly mansion on Charles Street. He'd kicked a couple of times before she went into labor to let her know he was all right, and Wyatt was there, holding her hand until things began in earnest and he was shown the door. It was a very short labor; both of Ophelia's previous deliveries had been short. Wyatt played cards with Mary in the parlor until they heard not the cry of the newborn, because Thomas didn't cry, but the purposeful yet unpanicked bustle and excited chatter of the maids and nurses that signaled all had gone well. At length his mother came in to tell him the good news. An hour later the bloodied sheets and full basins had all been removed and Thomas had been taken away, and Wyatt came in to sit with her while she dozed. The heavy tapestry curtains of the room had been replaced for the birth by white muslin, and it was a very warm day for October, and as the breezes flowed in, the curtains moved to their own music. Wyatt now had a son, if the boy survived—the doctor had branded him "sturdy," although he would have preferred more vigor in his inaugural moments—and Wyatt was now thinking exactly what Ophelia would have hoped he wasn't thinking, which was that he had an heir, not for these Bayly properties in Baltimore and Towson, whose future disposition did not much concern him, but for the Retreat, his adopted domain. He sat in that white room giving the stirring Ophelia a caress on the cheek, and she smiled wanly but happily to feel her husband's hand and to know the baby had been born living and she had survived the birth.

The day before Wyatt and Mr. French and Abel Terrell stood, that early morning in April, on this spot surveying their field of trees, Ophelia had returned with Mary and the infant Thomas, the first time she had set foot on the Retreat for many months. Everyone on the farm knew that there had been more to Miss Ophelia's departure last summer than simply a visit to her in-laws or, indeed, simply anxieties about the new pregnancy. No one knew what to expect upon her return. Everyone knew that something was going a little haywire in the Mansion House, and the first whispers against Ophelia had become a shake of the head, words and eye-rolling exchanged in the kitchen and laundry at full volume, a cruel joke ended with a gob of spit at the ground. Wyatt had the gift to be admired, to be liked, and Ophelia did not. Ophelia's pain? No one cared all that much for it; no one really believed in it.

"We'll start preparing the Waverly lands in the fall," said Wyatt. If that's what Ophelia expected, then she would get it.

Mr. French groaned. Who in this county, or in Kent or Talbot, was going in so deep: ten thousand trees, fifty thousand, a hundred thousand? A hundred and ten to the acre, so how many acres is that? Did it make sense?

"I'll try to get ten thousand pits this fall. We'll plant on the creek-lands," Wyatt said, and turned for the wagon. He could see it all. A million peach trees between the Retreat and Chestertown, perhaps three miles of winding river, one long peach orchard. Peaches on both sides of the river, high up on the bluffs, or so low it would look as if they had marched up onto dry land from the shallows, lines and lines of trees, the power of them all together, the promise of them, the queen fruit, Chesapeake gold, the first good news for the Eastern Shore since tobacco had played out a hundred and fifty years earlier. No one but Wyatt knew how good it was going to be. A boom, and people would get rich and build big, square houses, "peach houses," as they had already been called in Delaware and in the other parts of the peninsula that had bought into this fabulous rejuvenation of the shore. It was a time of destiny, 1872. Maryland had finessed its way, just barely, through the Civil War; the border states were poised, fleet and unfettered, while the Confederacy had barely begun digging out of the ruins.

Mr. French brought the wagon over, Abel jumped in back and Wyatt took the seat, and they headed away from the river and back to the farm. The modest celebration was over. Work to be done. As they progressed, the rows of trees came forward in disarray, snapped rigidly in line for a single mule step, and then receded at their ease. There would be fruit this year, not much of it, and before things moved along too much, Wyatt would send Abel and a crew of pruners out to relieve the trees that were getting too ambitious for their size. These grafted trees had barely missed a season as they recovered from their wounds and were now doing what God intended them to do.

When Wyatt returned from this outing, he slipped into his office through the kitchen and sat at his desk, listening to the unfamiliar sounds of life going on around him. He could not deny that his family was the imperiled part of the dream, his dream of children growing up self-reliant and clearheaded, scholars of the country with none of the pretensions of Baltimore. He and Ophelia had lunch at a small table in the main parlor. Every piece of furniture in the house, the tables and chairs, the bedclothes, radiated the damp chill of the Chesapeake spring. Above the mantel was a portrait of Cousin Albert in his colonel's uniform, pointing toward the battlefield in Yorktown, toward—so said the painter—the very spot where he had been killed a day before Cornwallis's surrender. The house smelled as if it had died. The winds off the water rattled the French doors and made the gaslights and candles flicker.

Still, to Wyatt's eye, Ophelia did not seem especially dissatisfied with all this. She had grown up here; this was home. "So," he said. "How do you find it all?"

She glanced up from her soup with a slight smile, of the sort she might use at dinner parties. "How do I find what, Wyatt?"

With just the two of them in the room, he did not quite see that using his name was necessary. "Well, being back home after all these months?"

"I have been thinking of a day much like this, with that cold wind, when I was Mary's age and Richard and Lloyd had been fighting. It was one of those awful days when everyone just tries to avoid everyone else. My mother had taken to her room. I was sitting in the Children's Office, and Hattie's Mary came in with a tea tray and set it down in front of me. I'd never been allowed to have tea, and I didn't understand that it was for me. Hattie's Mary poured a cup as if there were nothing unusual and held it out to me. I'll never forget it. It makes me cry to think of the joy that gave me."

Wyatt could think of nothing to say for a few moments. "Well then," he said at last, "not a happy thought."

"I'm not sure," she answered. "It depends what part of it you concentrate upon."

"I suppose it does."

Betty came in to remove the lunch plates and to bring tea in no doubt the very pot from Ophelia's story, and again she gave him that brave, almost coquettish smile as she acknowledged this coincidence, or this continuity, whatever it could be called.

"I have been thinking about the children," she said.

"Yes?" he said. Being able to say "children" must have given her—after the stillbirth—as much joy as it gave Wyatt, but her tone was grim.

"I want to understand what your expectations are for them, for their upbringing and education."

There was that word again. He had no expectations, merely assumed that Mary and Thomas would, one way or the other, become grounded in the arts and sciences, that they might soon sit on the porch of the Retreat and debate the meaning of Platonic dialogues, that in the evening he and Ophelia would sit in this room in front of a rosy fire and listen to them recite Longfellow.

"Perhaps you should tell me what is on your mind," he said.

"I think we should give Mary the sort of experiences and education that will suit her for a life well beyond the Retreat."

"I agree. I agree that both children should be equipped to choose their own ways in the world."

Wyatt had told the truth. He meant it without qualification, and although it would seem, at least regarding Mary, to align perfectly with Ophelia, this was not going to end the discussion. "Then, for example," he said, "what sorts of things would you have in mind?"

"As long as you ask, I think we must send Mary to France."

At first Wyatt could make no sense of this remark. Of all the things he might have imagined she had been thinking about. "To France? What are you talking about?"

"For a year. To the Convent of the Sacred Heart for schooling. My cousin is eager to arrange it."

Wyatt had heard plenty about the Society of the Sacred Heart, and about Mary Aloysia Hardey, a cousin of Ophelia's who had been raised on the western shore and, once having entered the order, founded convents and schools for girls from Quebec to Havana. She was already a saint as far as Ophelia was concerned. "But there's been a war going on in Paris. Have you forgotten about that?"

"Not now. Not for a few years. Besides, they have signed a treaty."

A treaty? When had a treaty between the French and Prussians ever amounted to more than a few years' respite? "There could be another revolution in Paris any day."

"I am not going to debate world affairs with you. I'm not talking about France. I'm talking about Mary. Going to France is just one of the ideas I have in mind. I mention it now so you will understand that I will return to the Retreat only under certain conditions."

"And what are those conditions?"

"That I be allowed to save Mary from all this." She waved her hand around the room; the air displaced by her hand was damp and cutting. "That I be allowed to raise her properly. That she be under my guidance."

"Sending her off alone to France? Is that being under your guidance?"

"Of course not. I would accompany her for the year. Cecile and I have been planning."

"Cecile!" barked Wyatt. He always said his sister's name with an exasperated emphasis on the second syllable. "What does Ce*cile* have to do with this?"

"She's going to come. Cynthia and Dolly would also be going to the school."

"But they're not Catholic."

Ophelia answered that Protestant girls had been attending the Sacred Heart schools for years, that there was no problem. In any event, Mother Aloysia had offered to clear the way.

"It figures that Cecile would worm her way into this somehow."

"I know you don't like her, but she has been a godsend to me."

Wyatt was well aware, if not that his sister had been sent by God to comfort his wife, that Ophelia thought of her this way, that more and more she took Cecile's lead, almost as if brother and sister were in competition for her favor. If so, he was losing. "Where, exactly, would you be living?"

"The Countess de Millay has apartments in Paris that she has offered to us."

"Countess!" He knew this woman, a friend of Cecile's when they were growing up, only then her name was Becky Talbot.

"Wyatt," said Ophelia, turning to him, "anticipating all this has been giving me great joy. You may have your peach trees, and you will have Thomas as the heir to all you have created, and I will raise Mary to understand that the world is vast and full of beauty and art."

"Does she have to go to France to learn that? If she must go to a convent school, why not here in her own country? Why in France?"

Ophelia had won. France was the Mother House of the Society, she explained. They had girls from all over the world there. The very best Catholic families. Mary would perfect her French. She would receive instruction in the sciences as well as the humanities. "The Society is very firm on this, that girls must learn the sciences. I would think that would win your approval."

Wyatt shrugged.

"Mary will acquire the knowledge she needs to succeed in this world."

"And what of your other child, a son we have named Thomas?"

"His place is here with you. He will live a boy's life and become a fine young man."

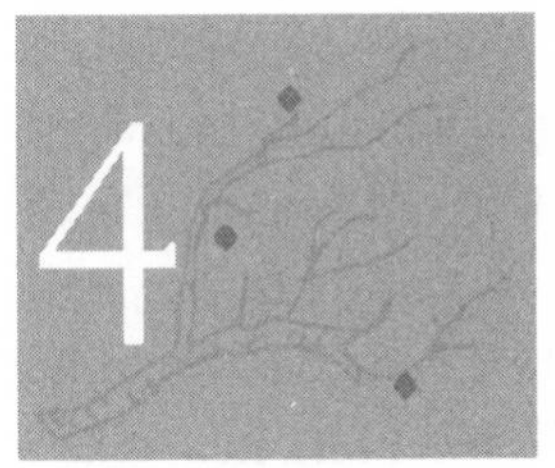

Thomas woke up early. He was seven, and he still slept in what the household called the "baby bed," a half-size sleigh bed at the foot of the four-poster that he would soon be forced to move into by his own growth or by Hattie's Mary's edicts that it "wan't right for a big boy to keep sleeping in no crib." Thomas liked the baby bed, and when he woke up in the darkness, with the four posts rising in the room like tree trunks, the heavy dark chest and armoire lurking in the corners like beasts, and the fireplace with its charred mouth open wide as if it were trying to draw him in, he felt safe in his little sleigh. With his hair brushing the headboard, he could stretch out his toes and reach out his arms and feel the four sides protecting him from the wild.

As Thomas lay there in the dullest of dawn lights, he could hear the household preparing for the new day. He heard everything from his sleigh bed. From the kitchen far off in the help quarters came the clatter of Solomon filling the kitchen coal can, the scrape and clang of iron as Zoe fired and fed the cookstove, and the seesawing complaints of the hand pump as Tabitha Hollyday drew the water for the day—for cooking, for washing, for laundry, for cleaning out the chamber pots. From the study directly below him he could hear his father's chronic morning throat clearing; he liked that sound because it meant his father was near, though both Mary and his mother complained about it. There was a thumping that sounded like a carpet being whacked on a line, though it was too early for that. Someone moving stovewood? A grouse beating its wings? He pondered this for a few minutes as the details of his room began to emerge from the dark mists. He could hear cowbells outside, and the bright ping of harness buckles and chains, and then a cat or a raccoon or some other feral beast in the woods just beyond the graveyard spitting out the last venomous snarl of a night's worth of fighting.

The day before had been full of one of his mother's and Mary's departures. They departed and returned so many times that he could never keep straight whether it was to Baltimore and the house on Charles Street, in order for Mary to go to Miss Davis's Academy—ugh, thought Thomas, an academy that was all girls!—or to Towson and the cousins. More girls! There had been the usual stack of traveling cases and hatboxes and glove boxes in the hall, and his mother's escritoire, on which she would write him countless boring letters, and steamer trunks, and his mother would keep telling him she would be back again in a month or at Christmas or some distant point in a future that Thomas had no possible desire or ability to imagine. On those mornings his mother's gaiety seemed, even to a seven-year-old, sort of frantic, her green eyes unfocused and feverish, her words wet and eager. As usual, Thomas kept being told to get out of the way, and as usual, Mary was sweet to him one moment and mean the next. Hattie's Mary once said that dogs that were treated the way Mary treated Thomas got so confused they went crazy and had to be shot. A sister like that builds character, said Hattie's Mary, that it surely does, and Thomas believed her, taking it not as a slur against Mary, but as a suggestion that he ought to feel gratitude. Yesterday Mary squabbled and complained about everything. She kept saying she did not want to go, that she would *in no circumstances cooperate*, that Cynthia and Dolly smelled like *pigs*, but when the carriage finally arrived to take them to the steamer dock, she was the first person in. Their luggage, loaded into two hay wagons, had been taken ahead. They all went to the dock to see the party off in the steamer to Baltimore, and the Retreat returned to its centuries-old calm, and to Thomas.

Thomas understood that the house found the whole thing a bit peculiar; there was whispering about it in the kitchen—a mother leaving her husband and child. Mrs. French, of all people, had paid a call to offer whatever assistance might be needed during his mother's absence, and though Thomas heard nothing of their conversation, it was clear that his mother was offended. Thomas was glad he was not being taken with them. There was nothing or nobody anywhere outside the Retreat that he needed or wanted. He had Hattie's Mary and Tabitha Hollyday to care for him, to wake him and dress him and feed him and to answer almost any question that ever came to his mind to ask. Hattie's Mary had a soft lap and huge breasts, and once in that warm burrow, he asked her why her name was Hattie's Mary and not just Mary like his sister, and she said she had been given it as a slave name but had chosen to keep it as a way of always having her mother with her. This need to keep her mother close struck Thomas as a bit peculiar. Then he asked her what happened to her mother, and she answered that there are some questions you should never ask. You should never ask a prisoner what he did to get put in jail, never ask a widow whether she gets lonely in bed, and never ask a freed slave what happened to her family. Thomas was perhaps four when she gave him these answers, and he retained them until he could make sense of them, one by one.

Tabitha Hollyday—daughter of free blacks Reggie Hollyday, cabinetmaker and preacher, and Zemirah Hardy, cook at Blaketon next door and sister of Zoe Gale—had come to work at the Mansion House when she was fourteen, which was about the time Mary was born. She was a Hardy *and* a Hollyday; she was beholden to no one. Hattie's Mary told Thomas that Tabitha was the most "eli-gible" girl in Tuckertown, most eli-gible colored girl in the county, and men came to call from time to time and, as Thomas heard it from Tabitha, she sent them *packing* with *loooong faces.* Thomas liked to think of all those men with loooong faces slinking back into the woods around Tuckertown. Tabitha was always talking. She worked in the Mansion House, helped her aunt Zoe and cousin Zula in the kitchen, did laundry, and cared for Thomas; it was a good job with decent pay. She was the first colored person Thomas knew who seemed to do things because she wanted to, was willing to, and not because she had to. Hattie's Mary sheltered Thomas when he needed refuge, but Tabitha Hollyday had other plans for him, it seemed; she wanted him to test the limits, to misbehave, which was fine with Thomas.

So it didn't matter to him which one woke him that morning or any morning, and now that the sky outside had advanced from purple haze to white and cloudy and all the night shadows were gone from his room, leaving only the dark corners that no amount of blazing sunlight outside would ever illuminate, he heard Tabitha's firm footfall on the stairs, and when she opened the door, as she had been doing for years, she called out, "Thomas, you in there or did Monkey come in the night and eat you up?"

Thomas giggled, though he had had more than a few nightmares about Monkey over the years. Tabitha came over and stood above him. "When are you going to move into your grown-up bed, Thomas? You look like a little white china baby doll in there. And you know there's nothing Monkey likes more for breakfast than little white baby dolls."

Thomas made a fist and held it above his chest. "I'd bash him in the mouth and break all his teeth, and he'd go into the corner and cry."

Tabitha went to the chest, pulled out his clothes for the day, and turned and looked out the window while he slid off his nightshirt and pulled on his underdrawers. "Your friend Randall's out there, waiting for you," she said.

Thomas didn't need to go to the window. He knew that Randall would be there, half hidden between the kerosene shed and a box bush. That summer, they all knew that every morning Randall would be out there next to the shed or behind a pile of brush where the back lawn of the Mansion House met the first line of peach trees, his face patient and impassive. From the kitchen they could see him out there, just the dot of his little black head peeking over the box bush, motionless, gazing up at Thomas's window, waiting for him to come down, knowing he would, as if they were connected by invisible twine: one pulled, the other jumped, wherever he was. Randall would stand there beside the brush pile, thinking, *C'mon now, Thomas. Time to go,* and Thomas would snap up in bed saying, *Directly, directly.* Mister Wyatt, Abel Terrell, Miss Ophelia, Una Terrell, Zoe and Hattie's Mary and Tabitha—everyone who was supposed to keep an eye on the boys knew that Randall was there, felt the exclusions of this private language, this fierce allegiance. Anyone could see it. One day that summer, when Willis Freemantle, the county commissioner, came to call, he made a minute's conversation on the way to Wyatt's office by asking Thomas how old he was, and Thomas, said, "We're seven." Freemantle looked confused, as well he might have been, and glanced around for this *we.* Randall wasn't there; at that time he'd never set foot in the Mansion House, just a few paces into the summer kitchen in hot weather and a half step across the threshold of the kitchen in the winter. Wyatt could see Freemantle deciding that everyone out here on Mason's Retreat was crazy, not just the nigger cook, not just this moody Wyatt Bayly and probably his Mason wife, now off God knew where, but the kids too, this pasty boy that probably would get sick and die any day. And who knew about that girl, the tall one, Mary. *We're seven.* Freemantle might have told this to his wife later: *Can you imagine? Like he was talking about the ghosts.*

"So what you and Randall got cooked up for today?" asked Tabitha. She was buttoning his shirt.

"Nothing," said Thomas, unbuttoning the top button. The shirt was getting a little small on him. Thomas had been a scrawny newborn, but he'd quickly put on a covering of baby fat and hadn't shed it yet.

"Now, don't be impolite. Don't say 'nothing' to nobody. You say, 'Well, Miss Tabitha, I don't surely know yet, but when I decide, I will be happy to tell you.' "

Thomas laughed again. Tabitha putting on these airs, mimicking his mother. *Miss* Tabitha; it was a funny idea to call her that, a reckless idea. He finished dressing and ran down the servants' stairway into the kitchen. Zoe squinted at him, dropped his plate of herring and corn bread on the table, dipped his cup into the milk pail. "Thank you, Aunt Zoe," he said. She waved at him gruffly, but as he ate his breakfast, he could feel the ease in the house like a holiday morning, with his mother gone. It was always like this. Solomon came in, paused to pop a piece of corn bread into his mouth and ask his wife if she wanted a magnolia blossom for their room. "That would be right nice," said Hattie's Mary. Yesterday, with Ophelia in the house, she would have said, "Solomon, I swear you're getting lazier every year. Pretty soon Miss Ophelia going to be waiting on you." But now there were just the men to serve—Mister Wyatt, whom everyone thought a fine and fair and decent man, and Thomas.

Thomas finished eating and headed for the door. "Where you going?" snapped Aunt Zoe. "I don't know of no little boys going out to play that leaves a nice piece of fish like this on his plate."

He looked at his plate, saw a small piece of herring. "You put it there after I was done," he said.

"You left your plate on the table."

When Thomas was finally released, he ran to the kerosene shed. Randall was sitting against one wall, weaving a salamander trap out of long grasses. He looked up from his project as Thomas approached through the thick grass, but they did not speak; their planning, as always, was wordless. They didn't even need to be looking at each other to make a plan—they were like ants, or they'd change direction in midair like a flock of geese. They just knew, no words even then, at best a shrug and a nod one direction or another, out to the river toward the glimmering of water light or to the farm, the darkness of the lofts.

The clouds were burning off; it was going to be a fine day, with a nice southwestern breeze, the kind of day they usually liked to spend at the water. No question, then; the rivershore it was. Randall jumped up at Thomas's side. Randall was a head taller but ten pounds lighter; a stick, his father called him, a stalk. They set out through the orchards on pathways that wound like shuttles through the groves. In the orchards there wasn't much time or place, just slight undulations of the land and the grid of trees and cart roads. The boys knew that if they turned for the river when they got to the 312th row of trees, they'd end up at their fort, and sometimes Thomas counted them all the way, but most times he would get to ten or so before he lost interest—not that losing time and place was hard for him and Randall. They made up ghost stories about people lost in the orchards, and they weren't entirely exaggerating: from time to time when they were playing on the shore they'd see one of the workers break out into the clean air in relief, and he'd stand there panting, as if he had almost drowned. In spring, the scent of the blossoms, the sticky, sweet air, could become frightening, as if, deep in these miles and miles of trees, there was no air other than what the blossoms breathed in and breathed out, and if a man stayed there too long, he'd simply be absorbed by the trees. In the harvests, which would be starting very soon and would run all through the summer, when the trees stood stooped under the load and seemingly exhausted by the effort, the orchards came alive to the rumble of the peach carts, the braying of the mules, and the footsteps and chatter of fifty men and women and children too. Randall would be there when the crew was light because he had to be; Thomas too, because he went everywhere Randall went. As the lines of pickers worked across the woof and warp of the trees, the skunks and raccoons would scuttle on ahead, the bees and wasps would make a high fuzz as they feasted on the rotting drops, and finally there would be a whistle or bell from the schooner or freight steamer heading upriver into the peach dock, and the noises would turn from grim and earnest to almost celebratory as the pickers rushed to fill up the last of their baskets and get them out to the river on time. Every peach sent back downriver on the boat was one more peach you'd never see again. That was the joke. As the steamer cast off, *There goes one peach I'm right glad I'll never see again. Oh yeah, which one was that? I can't describe it, but I'd know it when I saw it.*

Today Randall and Thomas had the orchards to themselves, and on the Heaths and Crawfords the fruit was still green and cherry-size, and they had a fine fight with them, Randall circling around Thomas with a pocketful for a surprise attack, only to discover that Thomas was lying in wait up a tree, concealed like a sniper. Later, when the fruit got bigger, and when, in the unlikely event that they hit each other, it would hurt, the boys would turn peach throwing into contests of marksmanship, and even later, with the earliest ripening fruits, you could smack a tree trunk dead center and send a splattering of peach guts in a ten-foot arc.

They tired of their fight and headed up to the peach dock and the rivershore. The clay banks were low there, on some stretches just a foot above the sand that was dotted with clumps of grass dislodged by the latest northeast wind. They kept crab nets in the dock shack, and sometimes they'd strip down, Thomas to his underdrawers and Randall to his bare bottom because he didn't have underwear, and they'd wade through the seaweed, come upon a nice fat crab resting over a perch nest or hiding, feeling safe in a forest of water celery, and it was a quick motion that did it, a stab just in front where you thought the crab would go, and then you draw the net from the water, fiery with trapped animal. Randall, or Thomas, would hoot, and unless the crab was especially big or a breeding double or a peeler or a papershell—or what-all made this crab worth saving—it would then be let go.

When they came to the bank, they jumped across the crumbled clay onto the sand and stones and headed down toward Piney Point, where they had a fort they'd hollowed into the clay banks under the root-ball of a pine just about to fall over into the waves. They hadn't been there in a while, and they agreed with a nod that it was Thomas's turn to poke his head in first to make sure bees or raccoons hadn't taken up residence in their absence. From the cave they spent the rest of the morning collecting stones—red ones, black, or white—luminescent shards of oyster shells, scissor clams, and horseshoe crab peels. Over the years, and the years to come, they would spend thousands of hours on the beach like this, way at opposite ends, consumed in the hunt, pawing through the piles for the perfect stone out of a million, and sometimes an arrowhead would be sitting there, first time in the light for three hundred years, still sharp, and after an hour or two of solitary hunting, the boys would turn and draw back together and open their palms to show off the prizes, and they would agree without discussion which was the best, a pale ochre-red one banded with an unbroken white strip, or a piece of quartz with a shape visible in the center like a ship in a bottle or a fly in amber, or a perfect cube, a number 7, or a disk as flat as a wafer. They'd fling the rest in a shower over the water. Then they'd fling the best into the water. They took nothing away; there was no reason to. They'd walk along in the shallows, and when the jellyfish were there in numbers, they'd scoop them up and throw them at each other, a satisfying sort of ammunition; a jellyfish couldn't sting through the callus on the palm of your hand, but did a fine job on someone's naked back, except that Randall and Thomas didn't try to do that; they didn't want to hurt each other. Randall said that his black skin couldn't be stung the way Thomas's pearly back would be, and they both reckoned this was true. Still. They hated it when one of them got hurt, fell hard, stubbed his toe, took a tree branch across the face. While the one cried, the other would curl down beside him and wait it out.

Sometimes they'd wade off Piney Point out into the river, a half mile, three-quarters, out on the shifting sandbars to wait for a steamer to come by, the *Emma A. Ford* on her way up to Chestertown, or the *Gratitude* back down from the Corsica landings, top speed in the Chester channel, company pennants and ensigns flying, the walking beams seesawing explosively overhead, paddles in response slapping the water into an ecstatic froth below, smoke so black and heavy it left behind a sheen in the wake. The boys would wave, and that was the joke—them out there in the middle of the river, as if they had walked on the water or as if their legs were thirty feet long—but they got few takers from the passengers on the rails. Not decks full of sightseers on these lines, just business: on the freight decks, cattle and sheep and butter and strawberries and tomatoes to Baltimore; in the saloons, county administrators and salesmen clutching their sample cases; in the staterooms, rich women and their daughters heading to the western shore to shop and have tea. The steamships were like the trains coming through the mountains, carrying not only cargo and passengers but also a whole manner of living in a corridor across the wilderness, and Thomas and Randall were just there, waving them through the pass.

The boys, Randall and Thomas: everyone called them "the boys," and there wasn't much chance of confusion. Six child-rearing families on or near the Retreat and more than a dozen daughters, but just the two boys, born within a week of each other, Randall at his parents' house in Tuckertown, Thomas in Baltimore. The girls: Mary; the Frenches' three daughters; Randall's twin older sisters and one younger; the Hardys' two; the Gale girls, Zula, Zayne, and Darby; Robert Senior Turner's one with his wife, Emily, until she went back to her ex-slave husband in North Carolina. Robert Senior also had a son, Robert Junior, with a woman in Cookestown, and though he came to live with his father after a few years, no one thought of him as a child of the Retreat. Besides, there was something about Robert Junior, even as a small child, that people didn't trust.

Compared with the girls, either one of the boys seemed like the runts of their litters, the piglets you'd find the next day ice-cold in the straw. But they survived. Randall had an older sister between him and the twins who had died of yellow fever when he was two; the pestilence swirled about and within his house, yet he never had a tremor or sniffle.

The boys. Someday their lives would be put to other responsibilities: Thomas was an heir, his name was in the will before he was a week old; and Randall, no inheritance for him, but if he survived his frail infancy, he could work for the next forty years, and his father and mother and sisters could stay in their house, and with luck, the next generation would even out the disproportionate cluster of girls with a brace of boys. Until then, the boys could do what-all and no one minded.

So it was only logical that they would play together these years. If during harvests—the peaches, corn, wheat, and straw—Randall was put to work, Thomas was out there with him, sharing some of the responsibilities if not Mr. French's boot. At harvest, most of the girls worked too. And for the rest of the time they didn't need Randall anyway. Labor was a problem in those days: too many men when you didn't want them, too few when you did. Before the war, on the Eastern Shore, too many colored men, slaves and free, and half the slaves were hired out to Baltimore to work in the markets, the shipyards, to work as servants. After the war, with the peaches, Mr. French needed families to come move into the old slave quarters for most of the summer; with the families there, the workers would stay put. Mr. French didn't need those dusty men, white and black, crabbing up to him in the morning—the white men tugging their forelocks and the colored men sucking their lips—who'd work for nothing but food and fresh hay to sleep in. Mr. French would tell the white ones to head north, keep going until it got so cold only a fool would think of living there, and he told the colored ones to head west, until the mountains got too high to cross, until they'd get where they were the only Negro within a hundred miles. Mr. French usually said "Negro," rarely "colored," never worse. He gave this advice to the dusty men because to his way of thinking, it was the smart thing for them to do. But he also said it because he was afraid of them—the whites, anyway. Sometimes it was one older man and a couple of teenagers eager to impress; that was the mix he most distrusted. Sooner or later this older guy says to the kids, *As long as we can't get food for wages, why don't we just go and take it for nothing?*

Some mornings Randall and Thomas hooked up with the hands after milking, when they were all standing around waiting for the day's word from Mr. French and when Uncle Pickle Hardy led the mules out of the barn in their traces, saying "good mule" or "bad mule," and that was about it, and they seemed to want to be good, for Pickle, anyway, and went where they were told. Sixty mules, maybe more, and Pickle knew every one of them by name and temperament, and which of the other mules they didn't like and which ones they were sweet on. So no matter what, there was always a wagon or a dray of some sort to ride in, and the boys jumped up and settled into the residue of the most recent load, cow manure or corn husks or oyster shells, and when they were settled, Mr. French's rat terrier, Spud, jumped up too. Sometimes the wagon would be full on the return trip, and they'd end up walking home for lunch across the flat landscape, so they'd stay closer to home in the afternoon, and when they thought no one was looking, they'd hunt down the turkeys and ducks and pelt them with corncobs; and if they got away with that, they'd drop into the pigpen and harass the piglets until the sows came after them and they'd run for their lives. They'd catch pigeons in crab nets and clip their wings, as if that would turn them into pets and not just simply food for blacksnakes; or they'd erect parapets at either end of the half-full corncribs and lob rounds at each other. Sometimes one of them would get hurt doing that, a nasty, burning scrape as the ear of corn rubbed by. They'd take Spud out to the manure pile and set him to work doing what his breed was bred to do, which was to catch rats by the hundreds, catch them and kill them with the most economical snap of his head, except when he caught one that was not much smaller than he was, and the boys would hunt it down and brain it with ax handles; and if it was too hot to do any of these things, they'd go into the cool shade of the mule barn and sit in the breeze that always flowed through it and practice knife throwing, and finally, if it was too hot to do even that, they'd sit side by side and whittle. Then they'd get to feeling ready for lunch or a snack, and they'd go to whatever back door on the place they judged most likely to give them a nice piece of bread with butter and lard, a little touch of ham, a glass of milk, except it was never Randall's house, because his family lived in Tuckertown, which was too far to go just for lunch, and Thomas never went there anyway and didn't think to find that strange or inequitable. It was sometimes to Mrs. French they'd go, but most often over to the Mansion House, across the gulley and past the icehouse and the house gardens and the chicken coop and the sheds and the smokehouse, until they were standing at the back door of the summer kitchen, as wordless and obvious as a dog begging for a bone.

So after they had spent the morning on the rivershore collecting rocks, they headed back to the Mansion House, and Randall stood back while Thomas bartered for their lunch. Randall was afraid of Aunt Zoe Gale; everybody was, and it amazed him that Thomas thought she was funny, that he laughed when she played tricks on him or called him "a dirty worm." That worked fine for Zoe; she could almost say what she felt and the Masons would think she didn't mean it. *They's whiteness on the outside but dirt in their souls.* The boys realized even then that what they each could or did find funny was one thing that separated them. Thomas had known never to tell Randall that Tabitha threatened him with Monkey; Monkey was not a joke in Tuckertown. In Tuckertown, Monkey was sometimes on your side but usually getting ready to betray you. Thomas knew for sure that Randall never told him a lot of what went on in Tuckertown, the jokes they made about his family, his father, his mother. But Thomas did not really understand that Zoe Gale was not a joke in Tuckertown. Zoe was "*touchéd,*" they said, as was her youngest daughter, Darby, as, in time, would Darby's daughter Valerie be touched with strange ideas and weak eyes. That's why Zoe became a cook, because she didn't need to see very well to get around a kitchen. Darby was born when her mother was the impossibly old age of forty-four, and if Zoe hadn't been known and feared for the visions that often compelled her, everyone on the Retreat and in Tuckertown would have blamed Darby's similar behavior on the fact that a child born to a mother forty-four years old was certain not to be normal. That and the fact that no one knew for certain who her father was—couldn't be Zoe's husband, Mobby, with Darby's light skin and him so coal black.

Zoe had a habit of talking to the food as she prepared it. Solomon and Hattie's Mary and Tabitha—they all made fun of Zoe when she and Zula left at night, but they didn't tangle with her. She'd talk to the goose as she snagged it with a strong hand around the ankles, talk to it as she led it to the elm block and then say, *Lay your head down, goose.* And when it did, she would take its head off with a bloodstained hatchet, and she'd talk to it as she gutted and plucked it; talk to it as she stuffed it, salted and larded it, and put it in a roasting pan; and bid it farewell when she slid it into the oven.

There were plenty of people afraid of Zoe, and she could get the tongues or see something in the shadows in church of a Sunday, the kind of vision that sent you home feeling as if the Devil himself had you in his sights. Thomas paid none of this any mind, just stood there silently at the door to the summer kitchen. From the cool shade under the pavilion, knife in hand over the cook table, in conversation with Zula, she noticed them immediately but made no sign. Randall stepped forward to nudge Thomas, then quickly stepped back. They didn't know what time it was, but they were hungry.

"What you want, boy?" Zoe said finally, looking over Thomas's shoulder and, as much as her eyes could look as if they fixed on something, fixed directly on Randall.

"We're hungry, Aunt Zoe," Randall said, almost whimpering.

"You got your own mama to feed you, ain't that so?"

"Yes, Aunt Zoe."

"Well, you wait out here, and I'll bring you some ham and bread. Thomas, you come in and wash."

That was the way it always was: "Randall wait here and I'll fetch you sumpin'," and "Thomas you wash and sit down for a sandwich." The boys never talked about this, just the same way they ignored the fact that Thomas had never been to Randall's house in Tuckertown. There would be no need to remark on such things, the most usual sort of arrangements anyone could imagine. Zoe was the only person in the world who brought it to Thomas's mind that he was white and Randall was black, that he was the owner's son and Randall's father worked in the orchards. Zoe never let either boy forget it for an instant, and how could she: she had watched her boyfriend, the man she planned to marry, get on the schooner bound for Richmond, and he was one of about twenty of them that no one had ever heard a word of or from again. And there was more to it than that, something that had to do especially with Randall, which was that Abel Terrell had risen too high in Zoe's estimation, mistook a whiteman's favor—that's how she said it, "whiteman"—for his respect, had allowed himself and his family to consort with whitemen who were foolish enough to open the way for them. In the end, as far as Zoe was concerned, what happened to them was their own fault.

She let Thomas go past her on the way to the washbasin, but she kept poor Randall on the spot and said, "Randall, why you playing with this whiteman's boy? No good comes when the lions and lambs lie down together." She often said that, but other times it was that no good comes when Jacob plays with Esau, or when Cain plays with Abel, and when she got on one of those tirades, Hattie's Mary would glance at Solomon, and Solomon would give a nudge to Zoe's older daughter Zula, and Zula would say, "Now, Mama, let the boys have their fun. No harm in that."

That afternoon the boys helped Mrs. French pick peas. Randall's little sister, Beal, was already there, and Randall tried to make her go home until Mrs. French scolded him and then invited Beal in for lemonade just to punish the boys for being mean. Beal was five. A baby. The Frenches' youngest daughter, Doris, was four, but she was not encouraged to play with Beal. They finished the afternoon with their feet draped in the marshy backwaters of Mason's Creek.

In the fall of that year Thomas started going to Miss Comstock's school in Cookestown. Miss Comstock was a lady of some age with bad breath and rotting teeth, and even Thomas recognized that she didn't know all that much about the subjects, and he didn't like the six or seven town kids who were in the school with him; they teased him because he was just a farm boy and called him Peach Blossom; as far as Thomas was concerned, they were frightened of every living thing, it seemed, and weren't half as smart as Randall. Though there was a school from time to time in Tuckertown, there wasn't in these years, and Una Terrell was doing her best with Randall and the girls at home. After a week, Thomas told his father at bedtime that he hated Miss Comstock's because it took close to an hour to get there and the kids were stupid. "Why can't Randall come to Miss Comstock's?" His father was sitting on the bed beside him, the four-poster; the baby bed was now in the attic. Thomas expected Papa to say it was because Randall was colored, and Thomas was ready to say that didn't mean anything to him, that Abel Terrell was colored, and, in fact, his father seemed to start saying that very thing, until he stopped himself in midsentence, took in a breath, and sat quite motionless for a minute or two.

"Papa?"

"Yes, Thomas?" he answered unconvincingly.

"Is something wrong? Did I say something wrong?"

Papa cleared his throat, a peculiar sort of rhythmic grating that Thomas realized, at that moment, was what his father did when he was lost in thought. But it was almost two years later, the summer of 1881, when Mary and his mother had departed for France, wherever that was, that Thomas understood what his father had been thinking at that moment. The departure for France had been quite like the earlier ones, except this would be for a full year, and even Tabitha, much less Zoe and Hattie's Mary, thought it was indecent.

"Is Mary gone for good?" asked Randall.

"No. Why do you say that?"

"When people say they going for a year, they go for good, even if the grown-ups say they'll be back directly."

"I don't know," said Thomas. Maybe she was gone for good. Maybe that would be better—himself and his father and Randall on the Retreat alone. Maybe Randall could move into her bedroom and they would just be a family. He couldn't imagine ever needing more, wanting anyone else in his life besides Randall and Papa and Hattie's Mary and Tabitha and Solomon, and yes, Uncle Pickle and a few others.

As soon as the women had departed, Solomon and Robert Senior opened up the old room called the Children's Office—where lessons had been taught for a hundred years—and they smoked out the bees, whitewashed the walls, repaired the windows, removed the child-size desks, and brought in a broad maple table and three sturdy Windsor chairs. From Philadelphia came textbooks and supplies, inkpots and tablets, pencils, lead and colored, a globe, a small marble bust of Julius Caesar, and three wall maps—the United States, Europe, and the Ancient World. Even Thomas knew what this was: the best-equipped schoolroom in Queen Anne's County. He told Randall all about it.

"So what's it for?" asked Randall.

"Well, there's three chairs," he said.

"So?"

"There's one for the teacher, and one for me, and one for you." This was something Thomas had been thinking, guessing, hoping for the past few weeks.

"Nawww," said Randall. "Nawww," he repeated, shaking his head.

One early evening in August, Thomas spied his father walking down the lane to the stable, and an impulse told him to scout it out. The evening was fresh, a drying breeze from the northwest, the first hint that the season was about to change. Thomas came forward, and they walked a few paces together. "Where are you going, Papa? Can I come? Can we take the saddle horses? Can I ride Dixie?"

"Hush," his father said. They reached the stable, and Wyatt rang the bell for the coachman, who appeared from his rooms behind the stalls, still chewing his supper. Thomas followed him as he harnessed Big Bob to Wyatt's runabout, but when he was almost done, his father told the coachman he'd changed his mind, that he would take Rickie and the depot wagon—which was a little odd, some sort of evening call, but in the depot wagon?

They set off down the lane; Thomas had not been invited, but he was not told to get down when he jumped in back. It had been a dry summer, and as each footfall kicked up a small puff of fine yellow clay, the wheels left two curtains of dust. They were headed away from the river and the orchards, and at either side of them were the fields of corn and alfalfa and sorghum, and in front of them were the darkening woods, with their high canopy of pecan and mulberry, and the pungent bramble of the floor, a nest of holly and thorn and chiggers and snakes. Almost every time Thomas went down the lane, which wasn't often—for Mass in Queenstown and that was about it—he held his breath as they passed from the flat expanse of the croplands into this border of woods, as if he were entering a tunnel that he might never exit.

Tuckertown was a strip hacked out of this frightening growth, a line of eight dwellings—three two-story houses and five shacks—built by the Masons and the Lloyds in the early 1850s. Randall's family lived halfway down, in one of the houses, and as the wagon entered the top of the Tuckertown lane, Thomas could hear the fuss. The murmur went down the line, beginning with the first alarm from the front porch of Zoe Gale's house, where she and Mobby and Robert Senior Turner were taking their ease. The word went through Zoe's kitchen, out her back door, low across the swept earth yard to Reggie Hollyday's, carried upstairs by his youngest granddaughter, Minnow, as she was called then, and then flung out the bedroom window by his wife, Mill, almost vengefully onto the roof of the next shack, which was lived in by two bachelor Everetts—moved in one day from God knew where—who worked for the Lloyds at Blaketon and who had a feud with the Hardy/Hollydays over a mess of firewood years before. But still, they passed the message through the trunks of two enormous tulip poplars to the one structure painted recently enough to be called blue, where more Hardys lived, the young couple with a spastic child, and then handed like an unwelcome gift to Randall's sister Beal, who was playing a game with twigs and a length of harness leather, and she looked up in time to see Mister Wyatt heading her way and she screamed in terror and ran for Randall.

Thomas watched her run and saw Randall put her in front of him, his hands on her shoulders, and walk them both around the side of their front porch. Randall's parents were already standing outside, and their two older twin daughters, Ruth and Ruthie—not Ruthie's given name, but a family joke that became a name—with their faces just visible out of the darkness of the front entrance. From the scarlet fever that killed the sister between them and Randall, Ruthie's hearing had been impaired, and she never went anywhere without Ruth to relay what people said.

Thomas remained in the back of the depot wagon. His father walked forward, said good evening. Abel said good evening, shoved his hands deep into his pockets, kicked a pebble in the dirt, and for a moment they shared a little business—the last of the Crawfords gone in maybe a week's time, the Gooby boy seemed like a right fine worker. Thomas guessed they'd had this conversation about five times already today. He wondered if the Terrells would invite his father in, but they did not.

"Evening, Una," he said to Randall's mother after the business chat was over.

She said "Evening," and was trying to be friendly, but it didn't sound that way to Thomas. "A rough ride for you, Mister Wyatt?" she added, and Thomas knew she was saying, *Why come here and why in a wagon? What does this mean, you coming to my house in a depot wagon, neither day business nor an evening call?* All of Tuckertown was looking at them now and asking what he was up to, here in a wagon with his boy in the back—the Hollydays, the Hardys, the Everett brothers who worked for the Lloyds, Uncle Pickle Hardy, Robert Senior and Aunt Zoe, all asking the same thing.

Wyatt said it was an especially fine and cool August evening, then waited for Abel to respond. Thomas had heard his father and Abel Terrell and Mr. French talk for hours; he'd heard Abel say to his father, "Now, that's the poorest idea you've had since the Queenstown blufflands," and he had heard Abel say to Mr. French, "Mr. French, your frettin' ain't going to get a single damn peach picked, and you know I'm right about that." Thomas and Randall had heard their parents debate as equals in the orchards, and no one there called Abel "Boy" or threatened him because he showed disrespect. But neither of the boys had ever seen Abel speak to Mister Wyatt in front of his own house, and Abel was a different man there. In an instant he was uncertain and stuttering, and his eyelids were fluttering and he was squinting, and he asked finally if Mister Wyatt wanted to come sit on the porch, and Wyatt said, "No, I wouldn't think of troubling you like that." Thomas glanced at Una, and her steelier and sharper eyes said, *Then why are you troubling us at all?*

"I've just got an idea that I'd like to talk to you about," he said.

Abel answered, "And what was that, if you don't mind my asking?"

"Well, it's about Randall," Wyatt said. Thomas shot his glance over at Randall. *See? I told you.* Beal no longer seemed as frightened as she had been; she had wriggled from Randall's arms and was squatting in the dirt in front of him. They could all hear Ruthie whisper loudly to Ruth, "What did he say, something about an *anvil*?"

"About Randall's schooling," said Wyatt.

Well then. Thomas watched as Abel's shoulders relaxed, as he kicked the dirt, showed a deep breath of relief: this would have nothing to do with him. Schooling was for the women to talk about—except, thought Thomas, except in my family.

"Schooling?" said Una. "What schooling for Randall?"

So Wyatt explained what he was up to. He told them the history of Randall and Thomas's strange and deep bond—which of course was no news to anyone but had perhaps not been pondered, considered, *studied* by anyone as much as Wyatt. Then he told them that he had his doubts about Thomas at Miss Comstock's or in the county school. Thomas glanced over at Randall, who had sat down beside Beal, and she now had her head in his lap; Thomas was motionless, one skinny white arm draped over the side of the wagon. Wyatt told Randall's mother about a tutor he had hired and the supplies he'd bought, and Thomas noticed then that the nervous one at this point in the conversation was his father, trying to explain himself to Una, and when it was time for him to make his pitch, he was the one fumbling for a word or two. He told them that it was abundantly clear to him that Randall was an extremely bright boy, and that often, he had observed, Randall was a beat or two ahead of Thomas. Thomas didn't love hearing this, but okay. Maybe not *often,* but sometimes. At length Wyatt said what was on his mind. He was wondering—no, the word he used was "determined"—he had determined that Randall should attend these lessons in the Mansion House with Thomas.

Once he stopped, no one said anything. In the background, a murmur as the gist of this speech was being relayed to either end of Tuckertown, and in the woods, the sound of a high and fair breeze. Beal had by this time crabbed away from Randall and was sitting in the dirt peering at something: ants at work carrying off a dead grasshopper? A locust husk? A scab on her shin? But then Thomas saw what he thought was a tear beginning in Una's eyes, and maybe it was just gratitude, and maybe that tear confirmed to Thomas that Randall's parents would allow this, but it came to Thomas borne on some sort of extra sense—he did not know why, but he often felt that he witnessed people on the inside more than was usual, adults especially, with all their attempts to conceal, with their manners and customs. Una's tears meant something else: *Why not the girls too?* She wouldn't give voice to this, so Mister Wyatt wouldn't have to explain the obvious, which was that Randall and Thomas made a nice, manageable unit, and if he invited a single girl to join them, he'd get eleven, or was it twelve of the other daughters, white and colored, and that just wasn't what he was up to.

"Randall has his chores," said Abel.

Wyatt said this wouldn't interfere with Randall's chores, and it wouldn't interfere with his labor during the harvests and the wages he got for it.

"Where?" said Una. "Where's this schooling going to be?"

Again, she was speaking Thomas's train of thought, her questions and her fears attending each new turn in the conversation. If in the Mansion House, then *where* in the Mansion House, and if not just in the kitchen, then in what kind of room—she'd never been in any room but the kitchen, as far as Thomas knew—and then, finally, where all this was headed, into the most practical of it, if Randall is going to spend all this time in some room of the Mansion House, she asked, "What is Randall supposed to wear?"

These negotiations continued, but by now Thomas understood that it would go forward, and he was less interested in the discussion. He could feel this mother's protectiveness and her ambitions for her children and her determination to hammer out every detail, yet at the same time she was going over this material with Mister Wyatt, she was figuring what she would have to do to even out somewhat the opportunities for Ruth and Esther—never "Ruthie" from her—and for Beal, and Thomas had a sudden and completely unexpected realization, something that would alter his relationship with Randall from now on, which was that Thomas's mother did not feel the same way about her son as Randall's mama did about him; that of all the people he understood in such a precocious way, he read very little in his mother's moods and desires because there probably wasn't that much to them; that his own mother, if in Una's place, would be thinking at this moment of nothing but what it meant for her, whether it might mean that she was relieved of even more duties on the Retreat and could therefore make the afternoon steamer to Baltimore. And from that moment on, he lived and breathed with the knowledge that he had been lucky in his father, lucky, as it turned out, in his fierce sister, but had grown up a motherless child.

Wyatt finished his business with the agreement with Una that the lessons would start in a week, and he bid good night to Abel, called in a greeting to Ruth and Ruthie, said, "Night, child," to Beal, but didn't meet Randall's eyes or speak with him. Thomas finally waved as they set forth back to the Retreat, all eyes on him, everyone just waiting until they passed Zoe's before the entire village could descend on the Terrells and ask for chapter and verse; and every single man, woman, and child could only wonder if this was a good idea. As usual, Wyatt had everything worked out, an answer for every question, a reply to every doubt, an assurance for every fear except the big one, the one that could be answered by neither himself nor the Terrells as they stood on the hard earth in front of their tidy home—a home that Wyatt supposed he owned half of, if anyone cared. The big fear was the lambs and the lions, as Zoe had tagged it. Because where would it lead? Not for Randall. If there was one thing the Eastern Shore needed, it was more educated colored men. No one could foresee, in that evening in 1881, that the last decade of the nineteenth century and the first half of the twentieth century would be almost as bad as the centuries before Emancipation, maybe worse, given that there was no North and no South this time, no place to escape to, no abolitionists making a case for dignity and equality, just a general agreement about the Negro's role in the new century. But still, Wyatt persisted: the only solution for a clearly gifted boy like Randall was education. The only place for Randall to go was into the white world as far as it would permit him, and if thus far that was only a mildewed and unused back office in the old wing of the Mansion House on Mason's Retreat, then it was a start. The problem, as always, was Thomas. Because if there was one place on earth Thomas could not go, where no one wanted him and no one would permit him, it was into the colored world. But that was the danger here, was it not? Thomas seemed to have no sense of himself apart from Randall. It was all fine that the souls and intellects of these two unusual boys had joined at some previously unsuspected space between white and colored. Far too late to do anything about *that*, but what then?

That first morning of school, Hattie's Mary brought Thomas back to the Children's Office, and Tabitha grasped Randall by the hand at the back door and dragged him through the kitchen, his eyes wide with the fear that some great ill would befall him in the Mansion House. This fear had come out of nowhere for Randall, was not something he anticipated at all, and because it was unexpected, it quickly turned into panic, and he tried to run. Tabitha was stronger than she looked, and she shoved him through the door, kept a foot on his thigh as she closed it, just as you would with a dog or any other livestock you wanted to close into a pen, and Randall started to cry, running his hands over the front of his shirt, grasping the pencil his mother had given him that morning and slid into the pencil pocket, the first pencil he'd ever owned. Thomas did what the boys always did for each other, which was to come over and sit with him while he snuffled and finally pulled himself together. Miss Henderson was a nice person, a handsome if not pretty girl from a progressive farm family in Prince George's County, and she stayed for two years, and it was mostly because she was so good that the whole project went forward, even though so many people wished it didn't. Because there were no other white servants living in the Mansion House, she boarded on the farm with Mr. and Mrs. French, without any question a most proper arrangement, and at length she married their nephew, who was studying medicine at Johns Hopkins.

On that first morning, Miss Henderson had a boy sniffling in the back corner of her classroom and another seated equally uncomfortably, so she went over to the boy at the door, put a hand on his shoulder, and led him to a chair. She walked over to her side of the table and sat down. She let them take in the room. There were windows on two sides behind them, and behind her was a fireplace with a broad gumwood mantel on which she had placed her specimens: rocks, bones, rusted iron, feathers, nuts, seedpods, shells, knotted rope, robins' eggs, dried bear scat, a raccoon skull, the sorts of things they had spent most of their nine years together collecting. Some of her stuff wasn't all that bad: the skull, a pickled pig fetus, a blacksnake skin that she ran along the back of her collection on the mantel and allowed to drape almost to the floor. Thomas glanced at Randall: *Are you okay?* On either side of the fireplace she had mounted two of the maps—the United States, all thirty-eight of them plus territories, and the Ancient World, with engravings of its many wonders ringing the shape of the Mediterranean: the Colossus, the Hanging Gardens, the Acropolis, aqueducts, roads, forums, the Pyramids. *All of this,* she seemed to be saying to the boys, *is yours if you just let me give it to you.* Finally she spoke, asking, "Which one of you is Thomas and which one of you is Randall?" They couldn't help it; they laughed. *Silliest thing you ever heard. Imagine not knowing which one is Thomas and which is Randall? Like not knowing which one is white and which is colored.* She let them laugh, but she wasn't going to let them off the hook without an answer.

"You don't know which one of you is Thomas and which one of you is Randall?" she asked again. Now they were stumped: What possible way to answer this question?

"You know which is which," said Thomas finally. He nodded toward Randall as if saying, *Just take a look.*

"Of course I do," she answered. "But do you?"

It was that way with Miss Henderson the whole time: these riddles, these questions. She sat them down and put a reader in front of them and then said nothing. They shrugged; they knew how to read, pretty much. Randall had a mother who was going to make sure he knew how; Thomas had a father who would do the same. At length Thomas said, "That's baby words. 'The farm milks the cow.' "

"No," said Randall. " 'The *farmer* milks the cow.' "

"That's what I said," said Thomas.

"No it ain't," said Randall. "You said the *farm* milks the cow. How's that going to work?"

Miss Henderson may not have known it, but she had probably just been privileged to overhear the longest conversation between the boys ever recorded by adult ears. She took away the reader and gave them a slate tablet with addition and subtraction problems chalked in. Randall shook his head, and Thomas spent the next few minutes solving some of them. Okay, she marked to herself, *Randall a better reader; Thomas better at figures.*

For lunch Thomas went off to the butler's landing, where Hattie's Mary gave him his sandwich and milk and sat with him while he ate, as she had for almost every lunch in his life, and Randall went back to the kitchen, where Zula gave him his sandwich and sat with him while he ate. After a few days Thomas moved himself and his plate to the kitchen, and they ate together, as they would for so many lunches over the years to come. When they had finished, the boys were put out the door. Neither of them understood that this was something called recess, and no one had told them that, so Randall headed straight home to tell his mother and sisters all about school, except that Mr. French caught up with him in his wagon before he got there and brought him back for the afternoon's session.

Wyatt watched as the boys grew through that first winter, listened with satisfaction and pride to Miss Henderson's reports, and it was not troubling to him that she agreed that Randall was the more natural student, such an unusual Negro boy, as long as she made it equally understood that when Thomas applied himself, their results were comparable. Their subjects the first winter were reading, spelling, penmanship, arithmetic, Latin, and what Miss Henderson called "story time," which they loved, which was simply her sitting in front of them and telling them the stories civilization is built on: ancient and American history, Greek myth, European fairy tales, narratives from the Old Testament, magic from the Prophets, parables from the Gospels, American folktales, Jack tales, Monkey tales: this young woman could do them all, with voices that made the boys squeal. Miss Henderson—until he died, she remained dear to Wyatt's heart, a person who could do anything. More times than not, Tabitha and sometimes even Zoe could be found lurking on the other side of the door during Miss Henderson's story time, the door, it appears, having been conveniently left ajar. *Now I'm going to tell you about a man who went down to Hell to find his dead wife,* she'd say, and it seemed not to matter to her, and certainly didn't matter to the boys, whether they kept all these genres, regions, eras, and cultures straight, whether they knew that there were no chariot races in Iowa, for example, or whether it was in the Chesapeake in a classic Bay line squall that the Spanish Armada had met its match. It was like the mélange on the mantelpiece; she collected things, she didn't catalog them. Part of this was because geography was not Betty Henderson's strength. The girl never got it straight that the Eastern Shore was called that because it was its own region *east* of the Bay, on a map to the *right* of Baltimore and of her family home in Prince George's County. Part of this was because that is how she herself had learned, if not how she had been taught. She might have been fired from any teaching job in America but this one. And part of it was because it didn't matter when, where. Just who and what. Wyatt knew that. What mattered was the story, and later, when they were stronger readers, when they were approaching adulthood, they could go back and unravel this cultural braid of recorded experience and understanding and be the better for both, the hearing and the unbraiding. Wyatt wondered how she knew all these stories and concluded that she must have been a lonely and studious child and that her farm family must have gone to remarkable lengths to provide her with the books she needed. He'd go by the door and hear the milky drone of story time, and he'd stop, lean toward the panel, and hear her description of Aeneas escaping the destruction of Troy—in many of her stories she would make up what she didn't know or what wasn't known, but in this case, what would remain with both boys was some faint connection between the Iliad and the Aeneid—to Wyatt what she was doing suddenly seemed so physical: filling them up, those two willing vessels, packing them full, coloring in their brains, and it occurred to him that they could take what she taught them anywhere in the world—anywhere he could imagine—and speak the language of the ages. He was trained as a scientist, an engineer; never would he have thought that all these stories mattered. About this time, as well, Wyatt figured out that he was falling in love with her, the children's tutor, an employee in his home, so it was a miserable relief, a fortunate devastation, that at the end of the second year, she announced that she was marrying Dr. William French, Mr. French's nephew, and would therefore no longer be available to teach the children. Which was probably good for the boys as well, because now they were ready for a sterner, more demanding teacher, and harder, less soluble lessons.

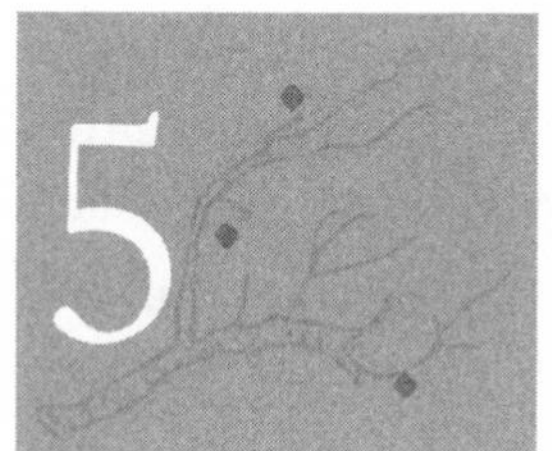

Off in the convent, there was stirring. The building awoke every morning like a beast from hibernation, with a twitching, a stretch. In the first misty light of dawn Mary could hear the dairy boy outside, delivering milk. It was the time of Greater Silence, but the lay sisters always greeted the tradespeople with blessings and treats—the same for the baker's two daughters and for the coachmen dropping off the day students in time for chapel—a blessing and coffee. Off in the wings of the Hôtel—when Mary learned she would be going to the Pensionnat du Sacré-Cœur at the Hôtel Biron in Paris, she thought it odd that a religious order would run a school in a hotel, but it wasn't that sort of hotel—the ladies were rising, the "mesdames," the professed nuns. So much for Mary to learn, the difference between the ladies and the sisters; whom you called *Madame,* whom you called *Soeur*; who wore white veils, who wore black veils. Only yesterday Mary had figured out that only the ladies wore silver crosses, but not all ladies wore them. It was almost six in the morning. My time, thought Mary, my private time. She had rarely in her young life been alone; here, in the most communal environment yet, in a hall where twenty other girls slept alongside her, she could conjure up absolute, blessed solitude. Alone with the Virgin Mary, she thought. The dim light was coming in from the small windows high above the partitions between cubicles; Mary could arch her head back into her pillow and see the airy fabric of dust rising in the light. When the Hôtel was an aristocrat's palace, back in the ancien régime, this vast space had been a ballroom—that's what the other girls said, *une salle de bal*—and even though all the murals, all the *luxe,* had been whitewashed out, traces of vermillion and crimson, of *l'or,* still showed through here and there.

Down at the end of the dormitory, Madame Bernault and Soeur Lisette were stirring in their cubicles, stretching the last moments between sleep and work. In the cubicle next to Mary, her cousin Cynthia, and in the next cubicle beyond, Cynthia's sister, Dolly—nothing but snores from them. When the bell tinkled, they'd keep snoring, and they'd roll over when Soeur Lisette came into their cubicles to shake them, and they'd keep snoring until a Ribbon—a head girl with a sash around her waist and shoulders—was permitted to cup a handful of water and splash it in one or the other of their faces; and all the girls—now dressed, almost ready to go down to chapel—would get to gather around and squeal with mirth at the lazy Americans, and it was known that Cynthia and Dolly were Protestants, and so the girls thought Mary was also lazy and a Protestant, and she was neither.

She'd been at the Hôtel for a month, she and her cousins. They had what Mary thought was a thrilling start of it, setting sail from New York in a June northeaster, winds and driving rain, though it became less fun when the storm confined them belowdecks in their cramped stateroom or the fetid ladies' lounge for days. Mary had pictured glittering crystal and vast elegant spaces, but even this, the *Pereire*, the flagship of the French Line, could not conceal the fact that most of its space belowdecks was given over to the boilers and the coal bins and the men who manned them, and above decks was a maze of masts and lines and sails and the men who manned them, and in between, more people had been crammed than could possibly be imagined. The odors in the air of these interior spaces came in waves, now the greasy spice of lamp oil, now the char of coal dust; in the dining salon the congealed residue of roast meats; in the passageways and on the stairs not the perfume of French style, but the sweaty bodies and human wastes from the steerage decks below. Moving from one space to another meant only the risk of being thrown against the sides of the passageway or smashing a head into a thwartships beam, and when one reached the saloon, the men would all jump to their feet and sway in unison as if dancing, and the full blast of dinner aromas would drive Mary and her mother back to their stateroom, where first one, then the other would heave without much effect into chamber pots. The nights were full of what her mother called "horrors," the lurching of the ship and the grinding rumble of the screw shaft and every sleepless half hour the clang of the accumulating bells and the tramping of the changing watch overhead, and in their cabin the swaying and rolling and rattling of every fixture and convenience—a lamp on its gimbals throwing distorted, nauseating shadows across the spaces, the thump and crash of what sounded like a loose door in some adjoining space that no one, no porter, no steward, not even the ship's bursar or captain was ever able, in the entire voyage, to locate and secure. From time to time the captain, a red-faced Frenchman with little English but a desire to spread cheer, would come by with apples and oranges to give the sick women, and at least four times a day a sturdy and solicitous Vermonter—whom Mary had nicknamed Thresher Man because selling threshers and other farm implements was his business in Europe—would come to inquire if the missus and the young miss were feeling better, and would they like to join him for a spot of air on the quarterdeck. In the middle of the second or third night Ophelia announced that she was giving up. She simply could tolerate no more of this. "I can carry on no longer. I have fought hard, and now I am giving up."

Mary pulled herself close to the edge of her bunk and peered down. In the swaying light she could see that her mother had risen, grasping the edge of the washstand as if she were preparing to pick up her coat and return to New York. "I'm not sure," Mary said, "that giving up will have much effect."

Oh, it had been grand, thought Mary for the rest of her life, that wild voyage into the unknown.

The first ray of yellow sun pierced the window above; soon Madame Bernault would be coming down the center aisle, and with her, the tiny silver bell that didn't so much wake the girls as whisper to them. Mary rolled onto her side, felt the rough weave of the pillowcase on her cheek, and gazed at the minimal contents of her cubicle—a white iron washstand, a small wooden side chair with a wicker seat, her dressing box in which, last night, she had carefully placed her clothes for the day. She pictured the other bedrooms in her life: the vast cavern at the

Retreat, with its dark, brooding armoire, a fireplace like a white marble gate, and portraits of her forebears, who seemed to exercise a stronger claim to the space than she did; her room on the third floor on Charles Street; the attic room at Chestnut House, which was simple and cozy, but whose angled eaves and low ceiling made her feel like a giant in a dollhouse, not a feeling she liked, now that everyone—everyone—commented on her height. Yes, she was happy here in her cubicle. Even if it was to be hers for only this year, it had been assigned to her by God, which made it a work of grace. No? Wasn't it a work of grace, this room, this place, the love and attention of women who had chosen to serve Jesus by teaching girls?

Oh, the joy. Her mother had counseled her that she would feel homesick and frightened, that all would be strange and she would feel awkward and out of place, that she should pray for comfort, and, after all, Cynthia and Dolly would be there, so she wouldn't be all alone, would she? No, I'm sorry to say, Mama, I am not all alone. Cynthia is a whiner and dull at her studies just the way she always was, and Dolly is a spoiled brat, and at this rate neither of them will last until Christmas. Oops. I mustn't think unkind thoughts. *Grâce, o mon Dieu! Voyez le démon qui s'élance de l'abîme, courant à d'horribles conquêtes.* But no, thinks Mary, I am not homesick and lonely. I do miss Papa. *Grâce, grâce pour mon père Wyatt, o mon Dieu.* And Thomas, and . . . *Grâce pour mon frère Thomas, et pour vos servants* Hattie's Mary and—I mean *et—et Solomon et Betty et Zoe. Ainsi soit-il.*

Thus it is. A sense of forgiveness, not just for others, but for herself. Not that, at her age, she could conjure that many awful sins: she once asked her father why Robert Senior sucked in his lips when he talked to white people, and her father told her she was wrong to notice such things; she had touched herself between her legs one night and it tingled; she had heard bad stories about her mother's father from Zoe and had believed they were true without asking anyone else; she told her friends that the priest in Queenstown smelled bad in the confession booth, and then, the next week at confession, had to admit to him that this is what she had said. Mary was a blameless baptized beast; she felt that was so about her, except that others sometimes seemed to blame her anyway. It had been this way at Miss Davis's, with her cousins, and at the Retreat. She wanted so much to be loved and felt it so little. Why? A mystery. Still—a fault spoken aloud to herself as rebuke and reminder—I am eager for praise, to be acknowledged. Was this the sin of pride that priests and servants and even her mother had warned her against? Warned her *especially?* She still could not see it: she couldn't see why trying to do one's very best was a sin; she couldn't see why she was supposed to pretend that other girls had recited well when they had not. Lying was a sin, was it not? The ladies were so kind here, so encouraging to even the most hopeless cases. *Très bien, Christine.* Wasn't that lying, when Christine's recitation had been *affreuse*?

Finally she heard the somewhat heavy clomp of Madame Bernault's feet on the floor, a definitive close for her reflections. She stuffed her pillow over her head and hummed in order not to hear Madame Bernault using her chamber pot, but then she held her breath so she could hear the rest of the sounds: a mumbled prayer, a splashing from the washstand, and a slight, horsey snort as Madame Bernault cleared the water from her nostrils, a stretching and a rustling as she, and now Soeur Lisette, disrobed and withdrew from their own dressing boxes their undergarments, their habits, the clink of the chain of Madame Bernault's cross as she pulled it over her head, the stiff pinning of fluted caps, the swish of their veils. Finally, the clatter of wooden rings as both women pulled aside their cubicle curtains almost in unison, and the first bright ping of her call to service.

Cynthia groaned, a good sign; Dolly was her problem, not Mary's. Mary got up, dressed in her uniform, a lavender skirt with white bodice, and at the second tinkling of the bell she pulled aside her alcove curtain and took her position for inspection, her dressing box in hand. Madame Bernault was a Canadian who had spent much of her vocation in Louisiana and only just last year, 1880, had been called home to the Mother House. She was used to things being slightly out of order, so when the girls lined up, her criticisms were typically mild, her manner indulgent. Messy hair, a dragging shoelace, a smudged shirt; there were others, not just Mary's cousins, who were sloppy in their dress, and Madame Bernault would take an extra minute to nudge them into respectability. Mary believed that Madame Bernault was lax, too forgiving, that it wasn't so hard to dress and groom properly, that these girls should be scolded. But this morning it was Celeste, already her best friend, who had not pared her nails.

"All right then, girls. Double time," Madame Bernault said. Mary didn't understand this idiom in French, but she knew this was one of those mornings when her *cours*, the *troisième cours*, was late. They took their usual places in twos, matched by height, which meant that Mary was at the absolute end of the line with a homesick Chilean girl named Anna, and then raced to the *vestiaire* to leave their dressing boxes and thence to their classrooms—where their teacher, Madame Rolando, had been waiting impatiently—for hasty prayers, a rushed assumption of veils, a grappling for prayer books, and finally back out to the corridor to pass in front of *la maîtresse générale*, Mother de Lapeyrouse, who had spent no time in Louisiana and was there to spot the slightest infraction of order—no tall girl slipped away from her partner to walk with a beloved shorter friend, no eccentrically tied veil, no whispering, no hands held, no smirks. If any of the girls in Mary's *cours* were out of breath from their usual morning sprint, she tried to swallow her breath on the way past.

And so it was every morning—from Mass to a cold breakfast; thence to the classrooms, where the desks, arranged against the walls on all four sides, served as altars for prayers, carrels for study, box seats—with chairs turned—for recitations and readings in the center, confinement for punishment; on to the refectory for dinner; and after that a chance to take walks on the vast grounds of the Hôtel, the steep gray rooftops of Paris visible through some of the trees. When the girls were certain they were out of sight of the ladies for a few seconds, they would walk arm in arm or clasp each other at the waist, because here at the Hôtel Biron, where so many of the rules seemed, to Mary, simply an opportunity for leniency on the part of the ladies, the one rule that was enforced was that their bodies were given to Christ, that even the youngest of girls, five and six years old, who might try to crawl into the lap of a lady or a sister or an older girl would be put gently but firmly back on her feet. Not without, Mary noticed, the smallest second's hug, a moment of delight in those firm, warm little bodies, but rebuffed just the same. This was one rule Mary did find difficult to follow; one rule she broke whenever she had the chance. So in those few moments in the park, the girls would touch each other, and for the rest of her life, there was no physical intimacy that gave Mary as much pleasure as Celeste's fingertips on her cheeks, no pleasure accepted that she returned as greedily as her hands brushing Celeste's hair or rubbing the nape of Celeste's neck and feeling her goose bumps rise.

They sewed in the afternoons, mending their own clothes or making fancywork, during which time they were allowed to talk for a half hour; then they had to work in silence as Madame D'Orsey, the one lady, the one person at the Hôtel whom Mary did not like, came around, inspected their work, and most of the time forced the girls to rip out what they had done and start over. A snack, *goûter,* at four, then classrooms, supper, recreation, and finally, before returning to the dormitories, the daily *examen* in the classroom, the part of the day most girls dreaded, but not Mary. Madame Rolando would stand in the center of the room and her eyes would dart to one kneeling girl and she would ask, "Did you give your heart to God today when you awoke?" "Yes, Madame Rolando, I promised God that I would give myself to the Heart of Jesus." To another, "Have you been jealous of the success of others?" "Yes, Madame Rolando, but I have prayed to be released from the sin of covetousness." "Have you spoken falsely to conceal your faults?" "Were you paying attention during the history lesson?" "Have you tried to follow the example of our blessed founding mother, Madeleine Sophie?" The girls were not allowed to divert their eyes in order to avoid being called upon, but Mary wanted nothing more than to be examined; her eyes shone with eagerness; she allowed them to cloud with disdain for stupid responses. She was going to be a Ribbon, the first American Ribbon in quite some time, and she didn't much care what it took. And when she noticed that Madame Rolando called on her less and less, she squirmed on her bony knees and let a small pout form on her mouth.

"You are very eager, Mary," said Madame Rolando one evening when Mary had just come from a few moments' prayer in chapel.

"Yes," said Mary. "I always try to do my best."

"The whole spirit of this house is a spirit of love and tenderness for our Lord, and for his august Mother. All is done here for love, and it leads to love. Do you understand that, Mary?"

"Yes," said Mary again. She added that she had tried to open her heart.

"But you are unkind to your cousins, who have not been raised in the Faith and have less successfully learned their French and face far greater challenges than you do."

There it was again, Cynthia and Dolly. As hard as she tried to rid herself of their grasp holding her back from success, the more she was saddled with them. She mumbled that she would be better.

"You must learn to give yourself to God. When you do, you will not have to try to be better, you will be better. Do you understand?"

With her head down in shame, Mary nodded.

"Have a little confidence in God, Mary. I wish you trusted yourself less and trusted Him more. He will help you. He is asking something more of you than what you are giving each day, as good as you are at your lessons, as eager to serve. The troubles He sends you are proof of this."

And so Mary spent the next few days and weeks trying to think *quels troubles* were being sent her way, because she couldn't imagine what they might be. As far as she could tell, she had been experiencing no woes, no grief. From then on, whenever she saw Madame Rolando outside of the class—in evening recreation when the girls were playing *cache-cache* or mounting a drama or gathered around Madame Dusaussoy at the piano to sing folk songs—whenever she passed Madame Rolando, she made sure to be smiling and laughing and gay, and the more she did this, the more she felt a hollowness inside, as if her whole body were rebelling against the falsity of her forced gestures. Then she decided on a different tack—that she didn't want to be happy, and silly, that she would be serious and pious, and there could be no *troubles* in that—but Madame Rolando seemed to have anticipated that, telling her she could not find grace turning inward, so she began to spend more and more of the evening recreation hours in the chapel. Many girls did this, stopped in their classrooms for their veils and slipped into an empty pew. The gas lamps only heightened the mystery—the perfumes of the altar flowers and the incense from Mass on feast days, the figures of ladies in their stalls or sisters in the gallery, pupils kneeling here and there, and almost silent comings and goings—and at these times Mary did feel that she had a dim glimpse of what Madame Rolando was talking about, a sense that if her troubles had become no more than trying to figure out what they were, that here, all this circumspection fell away for a moment. But then she would leave the chapel and have to walk past the very spot in the corridor where Madame Rolando had taken her aside these weeks ago, and she would again be filled with doubt.

Every Sunday her mother would come to Mass, sitting in the enclosure railed off by the side of the high altar, sometimes joined by Aunt Cecile and sometimes by other great ladies of the faubourg, and before lunch, parents and daughters could visit, sitting in benches in the park grounds when the weather was fair, or in the elegant parlors at the main entrance of the Hôtel that were reserved for commerce and intercourse with *le monde*. The other students were fascinated by Ophelia, this fashionably dressed American woman with such extraordinary red hair; and Mary was usually happy to see her, to hear her stories of the week, the calls made to houses that sounded so grand, the theater and the opera. Mary could tell that her mother was thriving here, so much so that it was becoming unimaginable that her mother would ever set foot on the Retreat again. But after "Madame Rolando," as she had begun to think of the conversation, everything sooner or later fell under the gaze of her examinations and doubts. Was her own mother the cause or the source of her troubles? Mary began to try to probe into her mother's stories and ask whether she, a good Catholic woman, the daughter of a Maryland family that had remained true to the Faith despite persecution, test oaths, and disenfranchisement, whether her mother was really giving her heart to Christ, whether these pastimes could in any way be thought of as virtuous and apostolic. Was not the Sacred Heart in the world? Wasn't this the point? It seemed to Mary that each day now she was becoming more confused and that these visits were giving her less and less joy. And then there was the fact that every Sunday *sans exception* the conversation, sooner or later, turned to Cynthia and Dolly.

"I wish you would try harder to help them," Ophelia said one day.

Mary answered that she was trying, and in fact, since "Madame Rolando," she had taken Cynthia and Dolly on as her proper burden. She made sure they were awake, risking being caught by Madame Bernault as she left her cubicle before the second bell, whispering corrections to their French, making sure they weren't off alone, the two of them, during recreation, and she was sick of it, sick of caring about them.

"They don't take Protestant girls anymore," said her mother, as if that explained their difficulties, which it did not. Since the first few weeks, when the novelty of arrival had made all the new girls subject to chatter, this fact had not once come up. It magnified their difficulties, but was not the cause. "It was only because of my cousin Mary Aloysia that they made this exception."

Mary knew this, knew that there was almost no woman in the Society of the Sacred Heart more revered than Mother Hardey, knew that the reason the school didn't accept Protestant girls anymore was because so many of them converted to Catholicism, which began to arouse suspicions of what exactly the school was all about. As far as Cynthia and Dolly were concerned, there was little danger of that.

"It will be a terrible inconvenience to me if Cecile goes home," Ophelia said, meaning, if the girls withdrew from school. "And so dangerous to make the crossing in winter."

So Mary went back and redoubled her efforts with her cousins because now, in addition to the remonstrations of Madame Rolando and, in truth, Madame Bernault, she had her mother's inconvenience to think about and, finally, the very lives of her aunt and cousins should their ship get caught in a squall in the North Atlantic and go down with all souls aboard. Sometimes Mary thought she would burst; one night she decided that if all three of them withdrew and all five of them boarded a ship in January and they all drowned, that would be the best solution all around. On her weekly visits, her mother had in fact stopped voicing her concern about the cousins and started asking Mary if she was getting enough sleep, telling her that there were dark circles under her eyes, that she seemed wan and of pale coloring, and asking was she getting enough to eat. As Christmas approached, Madame Rolando seemed to be taking pains to be nice to her, to ask her questions at *examen* that would allow her to show what she knew, to compliment her on her French, but even that seemed false, and Mary wondered how a person of such faith as Madame Rolando could commit such sins of false witness, of flattery, of worldly relations in this place where all love passed not from person to person, as she herself had said, but from person to God to person.

In the middle of all this, in the middle of Christmas preparations, Madame Bernault sought Mary out after dinner and told her to get her cloak, they were going outside. Mary did as she was told, but this was so unusual, so out of order that there could only be some terrible cause at the end of it, and she panicked when, seated in the carriage, Madame Bernault told her they were going to the Mother House, 33 Boulevard des Invalides, at the far end of the park. "There's nothing wrong. Don't be nervous, Mary," said Madame Bernault, but it didn't help that she was nearly trembling herself, and that furthermore, it was obvious to Mary that she had no clue why this one child, the American Mary Bayly, would be called to *le trente-trois*, when Madame Bernault herself had been a professed religious in the order for thirty-five years—all but one of them in Canada and Louisiana, it was true—and had never set foot inside the Mother House door.

They arrived and were shown into a parlor to wait, and after a few minutes a religious of at least seventy came to them. Madame Bernault almost swooned as they exchanged blessings, and as much as Mary admired and respected her dorm mother, suddenly the *madame*'s whole demeanor had changed, and she was acting not so much as a servant of the Lord, but of man—in this case of woman. Mary was trying to figure out what this transformation meant, but then the old nun beckoned her to follow and showed the way to a small anteroom, a small library where she was asked to sit down in a brocaded chair of the very highest style.

"So how are you, dear?" said the nun, not only in English, not only with the unheard-of affectionate "dear," but with an unmistakable Maryland twang magnified by her years in Louisiana—the sound of Baltimore society and of the fields and pastures of the western shore—and Mary realized that this was her mother's cousin, in fact, her own cousin removed, Mary Aloysia Hardey, the legend, described as an "angel" by President Lincoln, blessed by Gregory XVI, confidante of the founding mother herself, Madeleine Sophie Barat.

Mary could only nod. She mumbled something about "Mother Hardey."

"They all say you're a smart girl, and I see that it's so. I hear nothing but the best reports about your lessons. But you should call me Mother Aloysia."

"Thank you, Mother Aloysia."

"I've just come back from America. I saw your father not a month ago, and he sends his warmest wishes and wants you to know he's very proud of you."

This was all entirely too much for Mary: this legendary woman, the Maryland accent, a greeting brought from Papa personally, a sudden desperate wish that she were home at the Retreat, where she could forget about Cynthia and Dolly, about Madame Rolando, and she would not have to figure out all these puzzles about whom to trust and where to put one's faith and what to pray for. Mary burst into tears, and when Mother Aloysia gave her a handkerchief, she cried even harder, and it felt as good as anything she had done in a long time.

When she reached the last few sniffles and heaves, Mother Aloysia said, "Tell me what is making you so sad."

So Mary did, starting from the day she arrived, when she had felt such warmth and kindness from everyone and wanted so much to be a part of it that she had tried so hard to do well, and then Madame Rolando had told her that she was committing sins of pride—and she was right, said Mary, Madame Rolando was right—and that she was being mean to her cousins, and she was, and that she was trying, but obviously hadn't tried hard enough, because now she was here in the Mother House to be told that she had failed and was being sent home.

"Who said you were being sent home?"

"No one. But it's true, isn't it?"

"Not at all. Nothing could be less the case. It's Cynthia and Dolly who are going home. They are more than welcome to stay, but we have all decided that it is best for everyone, and the reason I'm telling you this is that no one is more to blame for it not working out than myself. We put your cousins in an awful situation, and I understand that we have put you in an uncomfortable spot. So let's rejoice that we have seen the way forward."

Mary didn't know whether to rejoice or start crying again, but yes, best for everyone, except her mother, who would now be inconvenienced by not having her companion in Paris.

Mother Aloysia went on to say that her cousins were already packed and, in fact, had already departed with Cecile and with her mother for England, where they would be staying with family until the season seemed safe for a crossing, and that her mother would then return to Paris and was very happy with the way it had all turned out. "What that means," said Aloysia, "is that you will be staying here for the Christmas holidays, and I'll tell you right now, there will be no lack of joy in these weeks. You will see a side of our school, and of our order, that most students never even suspect.

"And finally, I'll share what any religious knows, what Mother de Lapeyrouse knows, what Madame Rolando knows—that many of the teachings of our faith are contrary to reason, that there is paradox at the heart of it, beginning with the irreconcilability of the Passion, that the questions you're asking are the right questions and the doubts and fears you are feeling are evidence of grace as much as evidence of trouble. You still have much thinking to do; you must learn to feel love; but I'm sure you will succeed."

Throughout the years after this conversation, Mary tried to succeed, tried to become a spiritual person, but of all Mother Aloysia's words that day, what was truest was that the Christmas holidays would be some of the happiest days of her life. For weeks they had all been preparing the crèche, with wax figures, a baby Jesus, horned cattle; and the midnight Mass, with the robes and gold service brought from

Notre Dame, and the flowers, the incense, the candles, the singing of "Adeste Fideles," all bewildered Mary in their majesty. On a blue and biting Christmas morning, the carriages lined up past the porter's lodge and into the courtyard of the Hôtel, and coachmen in livery and fathers in great fur coats and dowdy old governesses in threadbare wool all came in to collect the girls who were going home. And for two weeks, the thirty or so who stayed behind had the run of the Hôtel, making pastries in the kitchen, which no girl normally would be allowed to enter, singing carols and songs with the ladies, who played *cache-cache* with as much enthusiasm as the girls, their caps askew, veils flying, bosoms heaving, cross chains clanking. At night, staying up sometimes as much as a half hour late, the girls sneaked up to the highest attic windows in the turrets, flung open the glass, and stood openmouthed as they gazed across the river and over the rooftops at Paris, the Louvre, the Palais-Royal, the lights up the Champs-Élysées toward the Arc de Triomphe, and the twinkle of the carriage lamps on their way to the most unimaginable, most forbidden pleasures; and for these breathless convent girls staring out into the black December night, the worldliness of this view and of society in some way became one with the sacredness of the spot from which they were observing, and it seemed to Mary that she could have it all, that difficulties would vanish wherever she wished to go, that her troubles were over.

At the end of the school year, when Mary and Ophelia returned to the United States—after Mary had won her precious Ribbon and once again been warned by Madame Rolando that it would be taken away if Mary expressed the barest hint of vaingloriousness, and after a calm and swift passage on the *Pereire*—they did not go to Towson, as was her mother's preference during the summer, but straight to the Retreat. One thing that had changed during the year was her mother and Aunt Cecile's relationship: a complete rupture, it seemed to Mary, had occurred. Her father was at the station in Baltimore to greet them, and when Mary saw him on the platform, taller than she remembered, and thinner, and tanned like a farmer, she was surprised to realize that in Paris he would be taken for a servant or, at best, a tradesman. It shocked her to recall that her father worked for a living, worked with his hands alongside the peasantry, the Negroes. She accepted his great, exuberant, almost unseemly hug and returned it with all her love for him intact, but she noticed that he smelled not of the cold stone and cedar paneling of the Hôtel Biron, but of the soil, of mules, of fermenting peaches.

Thomas was there too, ten years old now, standing back from all these greetings as if they meant very little to him. He accepted with some protest his mother's embrace, was embarrassed by her tears and wary of Mary's approach. Months ago, Mary had concluded that she was being called to be nicer to her brother, Thomas, but now, face-to-face with the boy, she could think of nothing to say. Her eleven months in the society and community of women had left her with no idea what boys liked to talk about; men, she could understand, fathers and porters and coachmen, but boys had become deeply mysterious. She greeted Thomas, placed a hand on his cheek, and patted it lightly the way a grown woman might. He asked her if she had had fun in Paris and was she looking forward to getting back to the Retreat.

Yes, she thought, she was eager to be home at the Retreat, but as she climbed into the coach for the trip to the steamship depot, she began to recognize how hard this was going to be. Solomon was waiting on the Retreat steamer dock, and all around them the orchards were buzzing with the sounds of harvest, mules braying, men cursing, babies crying, and Mary thought all this was wrong, all this labor should be given to Christ, not to the profane business of commerce in fruit, even if Christ himself spoke so often of the olive tree and fig branch and of sowing and reaping. She tried to be rational about this, to remind herself that someone had to grow food in order for humanity to survive, but she didn't know what she thought of the fact that this someone happened to be her father.

"A fine crop this year," Wyatt said. They were riding in the carriage. "A perfect season."

"That's splendid," said Ophelia.

"We have completed the planting on the Waverly lands," he said, and Mary saw that he suddenly regretted saying this, and she saw the flicker of dismay on her mother's face, and it made her feel a little better, realizing that reunions after so many months are awkward, a collision between two worlds no matter how near or far the worlds might be.

"It is good to be home, Papa," she said, trying it out.

He turned to look at her and said, "Thomas and I have been counting the days, haven't we, Thomas?"

Thomas made a grunt that sounded as if he agreed.

"Oh?" said Mary to Thomas. "So how many days have I been gone?"

"I forget."

"Three hundred and twenty-nine."

"Mary," said her mother. "Enough of that. Thomas isn't supposed to know exactly."

Hattie's Mary was at the door to give Mary a great hug, and Mary followed her into the hallway, almost as ancient and unchanging as the Hôtel Biron, every bit as musty, with Mason portraits and hunting prints on the walls where there would have been saints and devotional scenes at the Hôtel. Through the hall and out past the porch she could see the water, not the Seine, but Mason Creek. Mary didn't know exactly what she felt about all this, so she narrated each step to herself: Now I am walking into the hall. I am seeing the portrait of the second Richard. I am seeing the spot on the matting where the dog had diarrhea. I am looking out the door to the creek, and to the river, and I am wondering if I am happy to be home.

"My, my, my," said Hattie's Mary. "You're most as tall as your pap now."

Mary tried to be nice, and to say that she had grown only an inch, that she had been weighed and measured upon arrival at the school and on departure, so she knew it was so.

"Well now, you go on in and say your hellos to Zoe. She'll be right cross if you don't."

So Mary did, through the butler's pantry door and into the kitchen, passing through these spaces as if she'd never left, and Zoe and Tabitha Hollyday were there waiting for her. Zoe was already out of sorts about something, standing back from her worktable with arms folded, and she reminded Mary of the cook at the Hôtel, Madame Laynez, who, like the sewing teacher, Madame D'Orsey, was unusually disagreeable and was consequently *sacristine* and rarely in contact with the pupils. "Good day to you, Zoe," she said.

"Ain't we proper now," Zoe snapped. "Good day to you, Miss Mary."

The plain fact is that she doesn't like us, thought Mary.

Mary took dinner in the dining room with her mother and father, the first time she had been seated there with her parents on any day other than a holiday or feast. She took her place and sat, silent and hands crossed, waiting for the *benedicte,* which, though he had converted to Catholicism to please Ophelia, was something her father rarely bothered with, and it was left to her mother to nudge him. He mumbled some words about mercies and safe returns, and Mary said "amen," but she continued to sit with a sort of practiced and orthodox stiffness that was curious enough for her father to ask if she had forgotten how to converse in English.

"We always begin the meal in silence. We're not allowed to talk until the bell sounds."

Wyatt rolled his eyes at Ophelia. "Mary, you're home now. I want to hear all about what happened and what you did, but I'm not going to ring a bell to get you started."

Over the next few days Mary resumed the life of a daughter of the Eastern Shore. She preserved, in some sort of imagined simulacrum, the office of hours and the devotions connected with them. It was hot and muggy, and she was dressed in her lightest white muslins, which she spent the first week lengthening and altering because, in truth, she had grown more than the inch in height and in bust that she admitted to. She and Tabitha sewed together back in the cedar-paneled linen room, which reminded Mary of the *vestiaire* at the Hôtel, with its built-in cabinets and drawers. She had not gotten to know Tabitha at all before she left, a young woman not that many years older than she, and they had fun together; Mary liked being the better seamstress, thanks to Madame D'Orsey, but Tabitha was a handy and competent person and learned Mary's fancy stitches without much difficulty. For the first few sessions Mary thought she might contribute to Tabitha's religious education, for she was not Catholic, but Tabitha responded only with "You don't say!" and "Well, I'll be," and Mary dropped it. Instead, they talked of the farm, and the feeling that all through the county and beyond, the great prosperity was upon them, that in no small measure due to her father, people were making money as never before, even the colored who worked for wages and could sell their services to a higher bidder next door for a penny or two more a day, and even for the pickers, who knew they had the farmers over a barrel.

"And how is Thomas? What kind of boy is he?"

"Now, Thomas. He's a funny one," said Tabitha.

"He likes you a lot. He told me about Monkey."

"Him and Randall. Quite a pair. They're as tight as ticks. You just watch them."

Mary tried to fulfill her vows to be a better older sister, tried to take Thomas aside to play cards or to draw together, but he had no interest in these pastimes, no interest, it seemed, in her or anyone else but Randall. So Mary was denied that project, and as the summer descended upon them with its indolence, she realized that unless she took positive steps, she could easily pass the months doing nothing but what ladies do: paying calls with her mother around town, reading in the parlor, or writing letters in French to her friends, and before she knew it, the summer would be over.

None of that had much appeal, and though she wrote hundreds of pages of letters to her friends in France, in Chile, in Singapore, that summer, as in several summers to come, Mary spent as much of each day as she possibly could at her father's side. She spent many hours in the orchards and came to understand that there was a rivalry cleaving her thinking—between her mother's faith and her father's science. She'd always been more than aware of her mother's faith in holy mystery; and she had only recently come to understand that for Catholics—perhaps for Protestant denominations as well, though she couldn't be certain—things were holy precisely because they were only *hoped for*; they were *not seen*. She realized that the gulf between her mother and her father was more fundamental than merely faith and science; it was about the nature of knowledge, about *épistémologie*, as she had learned to call it. Her father believed that scientific inquiry could lay bare any uncertainty, that there was nothing that could not be seen sooner or later. Her father lived in the assurance that all would one day be revealed, and he was even confident enough to believe that this final day was not so far off, perhaps even in his lifetime. She had thought of her father's vocation simply as "the Retreat," but there was much more to it. The trees were the manifestation of all that he believed: he worshipped this natural world, this growing of things, this standing alongside the processes of trees and fruit, and he believed that whatever the calamities of early frost—and he had already lost one entire crop to it—he could trust in the abundance of this Retreat land, so perfectly situated, with such ideal soil. The earth made sense to him; God had done a superb job in creation and was now elsewhere, engaged in creating new worlds.

Not that her father didn't fret. He and Mary would set off in a soaking July rainstorm, both in their moleskins and watermen's hats, and all the while he would be saying that the rain would turn the orchard roads into soup and picking would be impossible. Or that in a week without a breath of wind the bugeyes wouldn't make it to the dock, and if they did, they'd be becalmed with a full load and the peaches would rot in the sun. Along the way they might see Abel Terrell out doing the same thing her father was doing: fretting. He would tip his hat to Mary and tell her she looked right fine in her farm gear, and then he'd lean against the buckboard side at Wyatt's feet, and Mary could hardly follow what they were saying, things about blight here and there, leaf curl, or the pattern of shootlets that had forced their way out since pruning. The trees, said her father, were never silent. They were always trying to be heard.

Mary loved this time, but as the letters from her friends came back, each one of them sooner or later asked when she would be returning to the Hôtel Biron. In June, when she left, Mary had not so much lied as extemporized, saying that her return was up in the air, all very complicated, aspects of her father's business, but that yes, she would certainly be returning in the fall. Leaving Paris without this little invention to sustain her would have been unbearable to her. But as the summer began to wane and the crystal hazy white of early summer light began to shade into a creamy yellow, she'd begun to wonder what was next. In answer, one day, her mother and father called her into the study.

"We have been discussing your plans for the fall," said her father. He was at his desk, and her mother sat in one of the severe ladder-backs reserved for people who came to do business with Wyatt. From the expressions on her parents' faces, it appeared that these discussions were not going well. Mary sat on a stool. "It seemed best," her father continued, "to ask you what you wanted."

Mary knew perfectly well what she wanted, wanted with all her heart, which was to go back to the Hôtel Biron. She answered that she would do whatever they wanted her to do.

"Tell her what we have been discussing," said Ophelia.

"The course would seem as obvious to her as it does to us," he snapped. He turned to Mary and laid out what was, as he supposed, obvious to Mary: in a month she would return to Baltimore with Ophelia and enroll for one final year in Miss Davis's Academy. Her mother was in the process of buying a new house on Mount Vernon Place, which meant she would no longer have to share space with Cynthia and Dolly. After that, they would see.

Mary said nothing in response. What they were proposing to her, she knew, had little to do with schooling or with houses and everything to do with her parents' marriage. She had hardly left her father's side all summer, but in September her mother would take possession of her, her future and her life.

"What about Thomas?" she asked.

Both her parents showed surprise at this turn. "What about him?" asked her father.

"Where's he going to live? Is he just going to do this school with Randall?"

"Thomas is the son, and his place is here," said her mother.

The three of them sat in silence, and it seemed to Mary that if she sat there much longer, her parents' miserableness would flood the room and she would drown. Last Christmas, one of the girls in the *première* was not going to return, because she was preparing to be married.

Mary had been standing at the icy window overlooking the courtyard when the glittering four-in-hand of the mother of the girl's fiancé arrived, and she watched with horror as a gloved hand pulled the girl inside behind the brocaded curtains. Mary felt that the girl had been drawn into a darkened prison, and when the coach arrived at whatever palace it came from, she would be swept inside and never seen again by anybody. Mary shouldn't have known or been able to discern these stresses in a marriage, but she felt them to her core. Forget the marital act, which in any event couldn't be all that different from what she had been observing among farm animals her whole life, and none of them seemed the worse for wear; forget the pain and danger of childbirth, which she would survive or not survive, depending on God's will. Of all the potential hardships of marriage, this slow, dispiriting tug-of-war between two people simply trying to *be,* yet being thwarted, seemed the least supportable. That gloved hand pulling the young woman into the carriage: the tugging would never stop.

When she was dismissed, she walked out into the broad central hall, which ran through the heart of the house from the landing at the lane to the porch and the lawns sloping into the creek. In the hottest, stillest, muggiest days of summer, if there was air moving anywhere in the county, it would be moving through this space. She stood under the pendant lamp in the center of the hall and looked first over her shoulder to the landside and then ahead of her to the water. Two sides: the land, the water. Her father was a person of the land, the soil, the firmness of place. Her mother was of the water, the escape, the freedom, the clean wash of the tides. Mary understood that if she resisted her parents' accommodations, she would be ripped in two, and so in that moment she gave herself to both. She called this private understanding "the covenant," and in the years to come, she grew to value its utility, even if she recognized that the time would soon come when she would have to make a choice for herself.

But for the moment she was free to make her own accommodations, to find joy in the activities of the Retreat, in the hum and tremors of the orchards during peach picking. Thomas often drove one of the carts, and sometimes Mary rode with him, balancing in the footwell, her hand on his shoulder. Thomas was mad at her the first time she jumped up—he was always mad at her, as a defensive tactic—but when he figured out that she was just along for the ride and not trying to take his job, he found he liked her company. They made a sight: Mary on the cart, as straight and tall as a flagpole, Thomas hunched over the reins, passing down the lanes between the trees as if it were a feast-day procession.

"I never imagined it like this," said Mary one day when the air was clear and the water was choppy and, in this light, quite green. They were drawing toward the dock with the last load while the brilliant white steamer waited impatiently for them. "It was just something the men did."

Thomas was only ten, but Mary had figured out that he was a pensive little sort, had been since he was a baby; she wished she didn't get the feeling that there was much he would not reveal. "Papa says we are all equal before the land," he said.

"Before God. He means that we are all equal before God."

"No. He said 'the land.' That's what he thinks."

Mary looked down at him, but all she could see was the top of his straw hat. "What do you think?" she asked.

"I like driving the mules," he said. "This is Ruby."

They had reached the dock, and Mary jumped down from her perch while the men unloaded the baskets. The work rose in intensity each day before the arrival of the steamer, and when it was full and had pulled up its gangplanks, clanged down the freight hatches, and given out a long, piercing blast of its whistle, a lull, an exhale, and a relaxation settled over the orchards for a few minutes. Thomas pulled the cart to the shade of the mulberries, and Mary walked over with him.

"Thomas, do you miss Mama when she's gone?"

"I used to," he answered. It was very matter-of-fact. "Papa says it's not about me or about him, but about the Retreat. She likes to be in the city."

"Yes. He's right. The city."

Thomas continued. "But I don't understand what she doesn't like here. We have everything anyone could ever want. It's perfect. Papa says when I'm old enough, he wants to send me to college, but I don't want to go. What would happen if I had to go to Paris or somewhere?"

Mary laughed. "You'd like Paris," she said, but when Thomas replied that he didn't think he would, she realized that he was right. "He probably means Philadelphia," she said.

"I guess," he said glumly.

In that instant, this little boy seemed very alone. Mary could not presume to know anything about him that others did not, but it seemed she was talking to someone who had been bruised a bit behind the legend and camaraderie of Thomas-and-Randall; he was a twin caught out in the open alone. It seemed to Mary in that moment that a part of him had been left behind in this plan of their father's, all this coddling—a part of him had been supplanted. It was a fleeting impression, but a strong one. The noise of work was beginning to rise again from the orchards; the mule perked her ears. Thomas's cheer seemed to have returned, but Mary grabbed his hands on the reins to hold him back for a second longer. "You know you can always count on me," she said. "You know I will always be here for you."

Thomas made a face. It was a funny face, a look of horror at the thought that she would always be with him.

"Oh, I know I've been a mean older sister, and I'm sure you've been just as happy to have me gone. But really, I want you to know that whatever happens between Mama and Papa, I will always be here. This isn't a joke I'm making."

"Okay."

"I will do whatever I have to do to give you a happy life."

"Gee," said Thomas, a little unnerved that the stakes had suddenly gotten so huge. He looked around and saw a happy life, the orchards, his friends Randall and Beal, Uncle Pickle and the mules. *A happy life?* he seemed to be saying. *What are you talking about?* Mary didn't know, couldn't answer, except what suddenly seemed logical to her was that at some time in the future, perhaps even very soon, she would be called to be Thomas's protector. That it was given to her to be a sister, if not a *soeur.* That within her father and mother's negotiations, division of the spoils, Mary here, Thomas there, no one—especially not, until this moment, Mary herself—had ever reckoned on Mary and Thomas as brother and sister, as a pair, as two young people whose lives would forever be intertwined.

From out of the trees they heard what was unmistakably Randall's voice, a tiny little pip-squeak of a soprano, probably one of those voices the choirs in Europe would have fought over. No, she said to herself. She would not fall into this exceptionalism about Randall, a nice enough farm boy, but a voice that might tour Europe? Really.

"Thomas, we ain't making jam here!" he shouted. There was laughter around him; the words "making jam" worked back into the orchards. Thomas laughed too, seemed to be trying to come up with a response, but then seemed to decide on silence as a tactic. Make Randall come looking for him.

"Thomas, who's that girl that keeps following us?" Mary asked.

"Oh, that's nobody. That's just Beal."

Beal. Yes, Randall's sister. She seemed always to be there, a few rows over, darting through the trees, a nymph on delicate hooves, always keeping Thomas in the view of her pale eyes. Mary had heard of her, Randall's sister, the pretty girl. No one seemed to mind that she wasn't picking; there were children much younger than she who were put to hard labor, spanked and cuffed when their attention wandered, yelled at in a number of languages, but everyone liked Beal, this dryad of the orchards, even the mothers who had just finished beating their children brightened and softened when she came into view. It struck Mary that people treated her as if she were a little off, as if she'd had a fever in the head as a baby, but it wasn't a mental deficiency that kept her apart, it was her beauty. Mary began noticing her, and soon watching her had turned into an odd preoccupation. She was eight that summer, still a child, a girl for whom skirts and hats seemed an afterthought and strangely unnecessary, as if she hardly knew or cared that she was dressed, that no one else would mind or notice if she appeared naked, brown and boyish and smooth-limbed. Mary tried to talk to her a couple of times but didn't get very far, which only made her want to claim more of the child, as if she wanted to *own* her. As if Beal might always accompany her, like a child who might never age but would always be this little sliver of beauty. Mary was appalled at these thoughts; in slaveholding times, beautiful children could become favorites of the main house and then of the owner. Were her daydreams about Beal indistinguishable from such evil customs? But Mary was drawn to this child physically. Eros was present; Beal was Eros, and Mary was Psyche, or some garbled version of this myth. When Mary was fifteen and in her bed at the Hôtel, she had been touching herself idly, then more avidly, and finally had inserted a fingertip between her legs and been jolted immediately by unexplained pleasures. She understood in that moment, even as she caught her breath, that this was the "certain feeling" her mother had once talked about, but her mother had never suggested that she could feel this alone. Her shame was immense, and she confessed it to the Father, who reacted with an embarrassed stammer from the other side of the curtain. Later in life it occurred to Mary that this priest must have heard the same confession from dozens of pious little adolescents, and he might have been prepared for it with something a little more useful than throat clearing. Mary did the thing again from time to time, when she couldn't resist, but she never confessed it again, just took it as a shamefulness that she shared only with God. But here, in her bed at the Retreat, tired and loose from a day's hard work, she found herself wanting to do it more than ever, and her confusion about it rose as she recognized that Beal seemed to be inspiring some of this. But it was not really this beautiful child, and not at all that this beautiful child was a girl, a female like herself, that aroused such ardors; it was more her elusiveness, the motion of her body through the trees, the tangibility of something so untouchable, the freedom of the surrender to the vision of this girl as a night visitor.

The last weeks of summer were drawing to a close; the covenant would soon be enforced and she would return to Baltimore. One evening she found her father alone on the porch awaiting the call to dinner; her mother would come down to join them at the last possible moment. The same was in some ways true of her father; he spent his days holed up in his office if he wasn't in the orchards, but in the evening, as the sun began to redden, he usually took a seat here on the porch, gazing down the terraces and through the massive trunks of the pecan trees and out at the water. Mary loved this time of the workday and had figured out that everyone did, this quiet, rhythmic interlude between toil and family, when conversation was easy and almost any random thought or observation would get its due. Without forethought, without any particular slant, she asked her father why her mother was so unhappy here, why she hated the Retreat.

"Well," he said, "her father, your grandfather, was not a kind man. He was not a good man, if you want to know the truth. The Retreat reminds her of him. A place like this holds history. It drives you back into the past just living here. That's it, I think."

"Is that why she doesn't want me to be here?"

In the pale light she could see him setting his jaw and nodding to himself, as if she had asked a very good question, which she had. "She thinks the Retreat is unlucky. She worries about you here."

"But not Thomas."

"I suppose she thinks Thomas doesn't have any choice. The Retreat will be his someday, and he'll have to make his peace with it. Because he is a boy, a man, he'll have the power to change it, to undo the deeds of her father." He paused. "I think it's all silly superstition. I don't agree with her about any of it, as I guess you've figured out."

She certainly did have that much figured out. She heard her mother emerge from upstairs, and it suddenly felt urgent that she share one thought with him alone. "I've had fun with Thomas."

"I'm delighted to hear that. Isn't he remarkable? And Randall."

Well, Mary wished he hadn't said it quite like that, as if this school of his was an experiment and not just an education. It seemed Papa was more interested in the process than the boy. Her stomach registered a sudden hollow moment of nameless fear: Was anyone really looking out for Thomas? Anyone other than Randall—and what could the future really hold for this unlikely and increasingly inappropriate bond? Something would break the bond, and then where would Thomas be?

"Sometimes I worry about him."

"Why in the world?" said Wyatt.

Why in the world indeed. Because he seemed touched by an odd loneliness. She had known a couple of girls like that at the Hôtel Biron—the one from Hong Kong who never said a word in any language, the sickly girl whose family lived in Algeria—girls who seemed to have too much on their young minds. If you asked them, they'd say they were content, but they seemed sad to Mary.

"Don't worry about him," said Wyatt when she didn't answer. "Besides, your mother and I have agreed."

Mary tried to picture them agreeing, what sort of words, what sort of gestures; she tried to imagine the scene, but it was almost difficult to conceive of them even speaking, these days.

"You'll have a lot to figure out, but you're a smart girl. There's nothing you can't do with your life. I want you to know that."

On her last day at the Hôtel, Mary had been summoned one final time for an audience with Mother de Lapeyrouse. "I would like to wish you well on your departure," she said in that classically indirect French manner. *Je voudrais* . . . "I have these talks with girls who I feel are exceptional." She paused, as if Mary might thank her for the compliment, which she did not; she did not get the sense that this audience was designed to make her feel proud. "You are an unusual child, to my eyes. You are like so many American girls we have had here. Precocious."

Mary had heard that before. *Précoce.* Not a compliment. Worldly, an adult in miniature; this was the universal complaint in Europe, from London to Vienna, about American children. The conversation was going in the direction she might have expected.

"But you are much more. You are a brilliant scholar, as I have just written to your father." She added, "I hope the translation of my letter performed by Madame Menendez is adequate. I do not have your gift for languages."

Here Mary did thank her, and regretted immediately that she had, as if she were finally speaking only to underscore the Mother's admission of weakness.

"Under more typical circumstances I would have considered asking an exceptional student like you to consider staying with us in juniorate as training for the novitiate. As Mother Barat used to say, we need *saintes savantes,* and we have plenty of *saintes* and not enough *savantes.*

But you, Mary, are not really a saint. When faith and reason cannot be reconciled, a saint chooses faith, and you chose reason. Do you understand what I am saying?"

"Yes, Mother," said Mary.

"I'm speaking to you like this because I have to give you what wisdom God has sent to me about you, and it is harsh wisdom. You don't have a vocation, but I don't see in you either a woman who wishes to marry anytime soon. I have been teaching girls, the brightest girls, for many years, and I am not a scholar like you, but I understand girls. I think your mind is exceptional, but here in Europe and, as I understand, in your home country as well, a woman like you will need great fortitude to find even the smallest place for her talents."

Ainsi soit-il. Thus it is. So be it. A harsh truth, perhaps. A cruel goodbye. The next day, the carriage drew up with her mother inside to retrace their steps back to America, and despite her harmless fibs, she had known she would never see this beloved place again. Until her last days Mary would remember the joy and excitement and pride she had felt at the Hôtel Biron in the morning, any morning, filing into the chapel. Years later, when she couldn't sleep, and especially during those white nights of her illness, she would comfort herself by picturing that grand Gothic sanctuary, golden light streaming in from high windows, the white caps of the sisters dotted about in the dark galleries, the kneeling figures of the ladies in the high stalls down each side of the chapel, and the two lines of girls, the littlest first, the babies, marching down the broad center aisle in complete silence through the bars of light and shadow to the sanctuary railing. All these girls, all these women, and just the celebrant, who was a priest and therefore not really male. Mary had never imagined that women could be so strong, that one woman, their founder, had created this vast communion, an order that went around the world. In the year Mary spent at the Hôtel Biron, she filed into the chapel perhaps five hundred times, and it was often on God that she reflected, but it was always women she marveled at. When she finally returned to the Retreat to take up the burden that God, it seemed, had reserved for her, after she had gone back to join a community that in every meaningful respect was peopled only by men, she'd be comforted in those first few years by thinking back to her community of women. She'd hear the grandfather clock in the hall chime midnight, and she'd think, In Paris the girls are being wakened by the ladies' bells; and at half past midnight in Maryland, she'd think, The girls are marching to the classrooms, the girls are passing in review in front of the Mother, the girls are entering the chapel, and sometimes, when memory and matter seemed to join just right, she'd bring this simultaneity into her bedroom, and her heart would pound just as it did when she was a student. And then this transport through time and space became impossible. The Second Republic decided that women, if they were nuns, were no longer qualified to teach girls, and in 1905 the Society was expelled from France; the sisters and ladies dispersed to other vicarages in other, more hospitable countries; and the Hôtel Biron was seized, the altar and stalls dismantled and sent to Australia, and the chapel abandoned, awaiting the wrecker's ball. After that, Mary lost one of the most precious sinews of her soul, and she had nothing soft and gentle and contemplative to put in its place. Wrote the Superior General about the expulsion in the pages of *The Dove from the Ark*, the Society's newsletter, "Israel under its olive and fig trees forgot the wonders of the desert, the manna and the divine law. With war and persecution come special graces." Yes, Mother, thought Mary, picturing herself at sixteen, her ribbon around her waist, but I don't want the kind of special grace that war and persecution bring.

Wyatt pondered things as the years passed and the boys grew: his marriage, his daughter Mary's prospects for marriage, the peach crop, and the never-ending fight against the natural forces and blights that devastated orchards. He was as confident of success against the blights as he was about the boys, though he stayed up late at night worrying about both. Randall was truly gifted; Thomas, a little dreamy. They all said this: *a hard worker, but easily distracted.* There was something about Thomas that most of the tutors didn't like. They found him unlovable; he tried to please, but he read it wrong, got forced smiles in return, got *Very good, Thomas,* or *That's fine.* Randall basked in proprietary, teacherly pride, but he wanted Thomas to share as much of it as he could. *I thought Thomas was correct,* he'd say, or *Thomas is better at equations than I am.*

"It's all right," Thomas said after a particularly vigorous defense, Randall arguing that Thomas's essay should get higher marks than his. They were twelve; they'd finished for the day and were walking over to the farm to see the new litter of piglets. They didn't chase the pigs anymore, not since Mr. French figured out that this was why the sows were eating their farrow and the piglets that survived weren't putting on enough weight. They'd never seen him so mad. Randall got spanked; Thomas got banished to his room. "She was just saying what she thought," Thomas added.

"I think you're the smartest person I know," Randall said, and he meant it, Thomas could tell that, because he returned the compliment. No one else in the world was smart enough to understand the things on each other's minds. They were both so smart they didn't even need the other to explain himself, to finish a sentence; everyone else was a little slow on the uptake.

"You remember things better," said Thomas. They reached the barn and leaned over the low rail into the farrowing pen; even in the gloom the piglets were shiny and pink; they looked like little elephants that hadn't yet grown their trunks.

"Aw," said Randall. "I don't neither. I just study harder." And that was true. In Tuckertown they hardly knew what to make of it, light from the Terrells' house deep into the evening, Randall leaning over his books, nine, ten o'clock at night. *Who's paying for all that kerosene, is what I wonder* or, *Randall's using up his eyes. Keeps this up and he'll end up as blind as Zoe.*

The boys were reading Catullus, Virgil, and Plautus. Gearing up for Hume and Locke, and Pope and Milton, and Newton and Darwin. Thomas Jefferson and Ralph Waldo Emerson would have approved. Money was no impediment. They were studying chemistry by then in a lab set up in an old, recently superseded laundry house, with well water pumped through, and they would do their chemistry experiments and then discard the chemicals into the drain, and the experiment would pass underground for a hundred yards and blossom into the creek and kill all the fish and vegetation within a number of feet of the outlet. The teachers were now young men from Hopkins, from College Park. One of them, a boy named Brian McCloskey, was an aspiring astronomer, and Wyatt had a telescope shipped in from Philadelphia and installed on a platform along the shoreline of the river.

Night after night that fall, Mr. McCloskey, who lived alone at the edge of the farmyard in a snug little shack that had always been called the Huntsman's Cottage, hitched up a mule to a wagon, swung by the Mansion House first to pick up Thomas, and waited at the clearing on the lane for Randall to appear from Tuckertown. Neither Thomas nor Randall had ever been allowed to make this kind of nighttime prowl—they were thirteen that year—and often at the end of an evening's work they would both be asleep side by side in the back of the wagon. Mr. McCloskey would drive to the Terrells', shake Randall and wait for him to stagger into his house, and then drive to the Mansion House and wait for Tabitha to come fetch Thomas.

Between the picking up and dropping off, Thomas and Randall learned about the heavens. They began with the constellations, and Mr. McCloskey was often bemused by their fractured versions of the myths behind them: Orion and Diana as lovers who liked to hunt together (Diana gave him his belt the last time she saw him); the Gemini: Castor was white, Pollux was black. That fall the boys learned as much classical mythology, the kind Miss Henderson didn't bother with, as astronomy. They observed the planets as they made their way around their orbits: the red rocks of Mars, Saturn's rings, Jupiter's moons. They moved on to the stars—the early ones at dusk, the infinite plenitude in the darkest hours of moonless nights. Mr. McCloskey had a story about each one, as if they were companions for him, which they were; he was a solitary person. Mrs. French fretted about him.

"I'm giving you Time," said Mr. McCloskey one night, taking a few more minutes at the telescope to himself, speaking the mysteries captured through the eyepiece. "You're not looking at space," he said. "You're looking at Time." The boys found this a little puzzling, and as they sat huddled together in the wagon bed, they discussed what he meant. It was early November by then; the fields were black and cold; the orchards were sleeping; the water was a void stretching out before them, and Thomas felt Randall's warm body beside him, and he believed he knew what Time meant, that the real experience of time was timelessness, that he and Randall were making their own kind of time, their own kind of space, and nothing was ever going to change that. One thing Thomas knew about himself: when he gave his heart, it was for life; if he couldn't trust the hearts of the people around him—his mother, his sister, even his father—he could trust his own.

Around that time, Wyatt decided that the boys were ready for fitness and manly exercise, even if such arts weren't among the strengths of the studious lads Wyatt hired, and on the first afternoon of this new regime the boys and the tutor assembled on the threshing floor of the old granary. The building was now chiefly the home of blacksnakes and raccoons, but the floor was smoothed by a hundred years of labor, and an old rug had been placed in the center as a wrestling mat.

As soon as the boys entered, they had their shirts and shoes off, and they lined up opposite each other with delight in their eyes. They could hardly believe that they would get to roughhouse during school hours.

"Too late to run," said Thomas. "I've got you now." He reached up his hands, ready to grab Randall by the forearms.

"I am Achilles. You're Hector," said Randall, and he also dropped into a crouch, and both of them waited, ready to join, an embrace of flesh. Miss Henderson had told them that when the gods became bored on Parnassus, they used to wrestle, wrestle naked, but because they were gods, they didn't have privates, so they weren't embarrassed. But the tutor—this was the next one after McCloskey—seemed suddenly unable or unwilling to give the word for them to commence, and at length the boys straightened up and looked at him questioningly.

"Are you sure this is what you're supposed to do?" said the tutor.

"Isn't that what my papa said? Fitness and wrestling?" said Thomas.

"Yes, but—" And seemingly without meaning to, he held his hands apart and gestured, first at Thomas's pasty, almost translucent torso and then at Randall's deep hue, and both boys instantly guessed the meaning of this hesitation: he could not imagine that Thomas would want to touch Randall's skin, that Thomas would be willing to mingle with Randall's sweat, that as they wrestled, he would submit without distaste to the hot warmth of Randall's breath on his neck. Would any of this be *proper*? As to what this black boy might think about this kind of intimacy with a white, the tutor had no clue. However much of all this, in that split second, the boys understood in detail, the meaning was clear. They looked at each other, suddenly abashed; they had a signal, an expression they had used for years whenever anyone in their hearing commented on their differences, a disdainful widening of the eyes and a slight, dismissive upturn of their heads, and they did that now, except they both knew that this was a little different, not just about the color of their skin, but about their flesh, their bodies, and they were being told that black skin and white flesh should be kept separate.

"Gee," said Thomas. "Randall and I always wrestle. Don't we?" he said, pushing it back to Randall, but he got no support. Instead, Thomas realized that Randall was hurt and he was angry, and he had retrieved his shirt.

"Perhaps we should do some stretching exercises," said the tutor.

Later, Thomas tried to discuss this incident with Randall, but he got nowhere, and besides, there was change happening in their bodies, and they both knew they had to leave their boyhood games behind. Randall reached puberty first and even began to gain some weight, to fill out, a handsome man, a black man with the features white people would regard as handsome, light skin, sharp jaw, smaller lips. Then Thomas began to mature, and the fine features one appreciated in Randall—the delicacy of them, the sculpted core of his face—were exactly the features one might have improved upon in Thomas: a blunter, more manly chin and brow for Thomas, a stronger, fuller mouth, a little more gold in his pale skin. There was no way people on the Retreat could avoid making these odd accountings: they had for so long contemplated these two boys side by side that their features had become almost one, as if their two faces were actually the same, just seen in different light, in different shadow. But now, out of this twinned childhood, two very different young men were emerging.

The boys had their first fight when they were fourteen, a shoving match that no one saw begin but that ended outside when Randall pushed Thomas down into the snow. Tabitha and Zula heard the commotion and came running. "What's alla this about?" said Zula, holding on to Randall while Tabitha picked Thomas up, brushed the snow off his pants and his back. The boys glared at each other, but they didn't say what it was about.

"Somebody laugh at somebody?" asked Zula. "Somebody hurt somebody's feelings?"

Thomas shrugged; Randall shook his head, then nodded: *Yeh, sure. That's it.*

"You apologize," said Zula. "Go ahead. You tell Thomas you're sorry."

Randall did, and they were forced to shake on it and were left to themselves with a fair amount of boys-will-be-boys chatter, and that was all there was to it, except that the house talked of almost nothing but this fight for the next few days. Thomas heard them off in the kitchen when he was doing his homework: *had him down on the snow; what in glory's name was he thinking?* Thomas read the fear in Hattie's Mary's eyes. Because a fight between Thomas and Randall wasn't just boys being boys, wasn't just boys raised as close as brothers and inevitably going to have to separate; it was a fight between employer's son and employee's son, between a white man and a black man. *The lions and the lambs,* said Zoe. *Two nations are in thy womb,* said Zoe. They all knew what she meant; they had all heard her say this before. *Two manner of people shall be separated from thy bowels. The one people will be stronger than the other people.*

That summer Randall worked alongside his father, learning the ways of the orchards, and Thomas stayed mostly in the Mansion House. Mary was home that summer and she tried to teach him French, which he resisted. "Don't you care about *anything?*" said Mary, slamming the grammar book closed at the end of the final attempt.

Thomas was brought up short by this, hadn't imagined that such a thing could be said to him, someone who had so many ideas in his head, was always finding little wrinkles of time and behavior to dissect, at times so full of impulses and shards of thought that his eyes hurt. "Well, yes," he protested.

"What, then? What are your interests?" said Mary, as if he should be able to list his top five, like book titles.

Thomas didn't know what his interests were; he'd never asked himself that question. But actually Randall had been saying somewhat the same thing, now that Thomas thought about it: *Don't any of this matter to you?* Randall had said once, and Thomas couldn't remember what they were talking about, but no, whatever it was, it didn't much matter. He wanted to do well, please his father, keep up with Randall, but beyond that, no: Latin and chemistry did not much matter. *Thomas, the difference between you and me is that I like to work and you don't,* said Randall. That time he'd meant it as commiseration, cheering up his best friend after he had failed a test miserably. *Don't worry about it,* Randall was saying; *it don't matter as much for you as it does for me.* That stung; all these comments did. It was fine for Randall if he could just sit down and memorize his tables, do his problems, read his chapters. It didn't work that way for Thomas. He wished it did; he'd look over and see Randall absorbed in his reading or working his pencil through a problem, his lips moving, lost in an equation, transported to ancient Rome. Almost anything Randall encountered interested him. Thomas saw this; he wasn't stupid, but because he had all these *things* in his head, so much crowded into the middle, he couldn't do what Randall did. When he sat down to read, he had to prepare the way, rearrange the mental furniture in order to get a place to work; he had to go through a catalog of thoughts in his head and one by one put them to rest, to the side, and if that process took most of the hour allotted to reading, then obviously he wasn't going to get as many pages turned as he should.

That summer, if Thomas hung around with anyone, it was Beal, and people shook their heads about that—Thomas, almost fully grown, playing games. Thomas didn't care; she was good company for an hour or two. She worshipped him and was willing to do anything he wanted; she was as tired of hearing about Randall as Thomas was, an alliance of sorts. Thomas could see the admiring wonder in her eyes, and he knew that no one else on the Retreat thought of him as so special, so talented, so wise. One evening he ran into Randall in the barnyard, and he asked how things were going with Abel in the orchards.

"Good," said Randall. "The earlies are all done."

Earlies. Orchard talk. Business. Thomas didn't want to hear it. "Randall the orchardist," he said. "The big man."

"At least I don't spend my days playing with a *girl,*" he answered.

Thomas was so surprised and hurt that he almost found himself begging Randall to be nicer to him. "What's wrong with that?" he said finally.

Randall put down the tools he was carrying and put a hand on Thomas's shoulder. They were standing at the entrance to the machine shop, and the other men were coming and going, dropping off their tools at the end of the day. "Look," he said. "We just ain't children anymore. We ain't going down to the rivershore to collect stones anymore. She ain't just some baby following us around anymore. That's over."

In the end, it was Tabitha he went to, the adult he could talk to, the person he trusted. She was about thirty-five now, and though people had said for years that she'd be leaving for Baltimore or Philadelphia or New York any day, she had married the new harness maker Raymond Gould and had two children of her own; Raymond was a wizard with leather but a fool with drink, and he disappeared for days or weeks at a time. Tabitha still worked at the Mansion House, and—beyond trying to keep a lid on her aunt Zoe and taking care of Thomas and, increasingly, Hattie's Mary and Solomon—not everybody could figure out exactly why. She just seemed to be one of those people who made things work, who fixed problems, had a way of seeing through the complexities of tradition and change, coming up with a simple but pretty clever solution. People gave her that much. And besides, Tabitha knew things, crazy things about the world, things about the Retreat, about Mister Wyatt's thinking. Thomas had realized from the beginning that people in Tuckertown didn't like her, but she didn't seem to mind, probably didn't even notice. She helped Solomon down the stairs in the morning and set him up in his chair in the maid's room off the laundry, and even though he'd always agreed when his wife called Tabitha a "hussy," he didn't seem to mind her attention, called her Chile and Darling and lately Leah, which was the name of his sister who had died decades ago.

She didn't need to supervise Thomas's lunch anymore, but from time to time she stopped to sit with him at the family table on the butler's landing. She had a particular way of dropping herself free-fall into a seat, as if nothing was going to remove her until she was ready. Tabitha was big, powerful, but never fat. One day she took a seat loudly. "Phew," she said. "Hot. I'll say it's hot." She pulled a chair over to her side, propped up her feet, and made a show of fanning air up her skirt.

Thomas kept eating his sandwich, feeling miserable and unloved, and there was Tabitha, his protector, and he asked her why people didn't like him. What had he done?

"What are you saying? Why you asking this?"

"Because it's true," he said. Because Randall was mean to him at school and didn't have any time for him even when he wasn't working. Because Mary said he was a dope. "Because the only person who is nice to me is a *girl*."

"What's wrong with that?"

"She's a baby."

"Maybe you haven't noticed, but Beal is no baby. She's twelve years old and the most beautiful young girl I ever seen."

Thomas, in fact, had noticed this. Who could not—those eyes? "Ever since Randall and me had a fight about her reading with us, he just gets mad if I mention her name."

"Hmmm," said Tabitha. "So that's what the fight was about."

"Well, yes. No."

They heard Solomon calling for her, and she held up one finger to still Thomas and called out, "I'll be right there, darlin'." She held her ear cocked toward him, but that seemed to satisfy. "Probably needs a hand to the outhouse," she said to Thomas.

Thomas wished she hadn't added that, but it was the sort of thing she would say. She leaned forward and grabbed Thomas's two hands across the table. "Look. You're doing fine, Thomas. I'm proud of you. You've got a lonely life here, and let me tell you, I wouldn't trade all your privileges for one night in Tuckertown. A day doesn't go by that I don't think that."

Thomas wondered why this made him feel better, but it did.

"If Beal Terrell is nice to you and talks to you, that's fine. That Beal . . ." she said, and then wandered off into her own mind—a thought about Beal, some moment, a recollection she did not share. She snapped back. "If Randall has a problem with that and tries to get in the way, he'll have me to contend with."

"Well," said Thomas. He tried to pull his hands free. Getting Randall in trouble wasn't actually what he was after here.

"You just keep your mind on your work, Thomas. You always were a dreamy child. Maybe that's why I like you."

"Would you say if you didn't like me?" said Thomas, already feeling a bit better, beginning to see a way forward in Tabitha's peculiarly free world.

"Oh, yes. I wouldn't say, but you'd know. That you would."

That fall, Thomas tried to grow up, to concentrate, to not be dreamy, to be *interested*, and for a while the new tutor, Mr. Richards, seemed fooled into thinking Thomas and Randall were on the same plane, but soon enough the truth began to dawn on him, and Thomas began to read the nastiness and sarcasm creeping in. Mr. Richards, it turned out, was a sick sort of individual; one time, late in the day, he asked the boys if they wanted to come to his room and play "a floating game." They had no idea what he meant, but they didn't like the sound of it one bit—and then in November, Thomas got ill. For a week there was no school and everyone tiptoed around his bedroom, and he was confined to darkness for weeks. He didn't know what was happening with Randall, so when their studies started again in January, he was surprised to discover that Mr. Richards had been fired—dumped, literally, by the side of the road just outside the Retreat's boundary line—and that Thomas's own father had taken up the task with Randall. For six weeks his father and Randall had worked together, read Latin, studied botany; and Thomas could see the pleasure and the delight his father felt as Randall surprised him once again with some acute observation. He could see his father drop his pencil and nod, the way he did when someone did something all but miraculous. Yes, Randall was a miracle. When classes started again—Mr. Townley had been hired after the New Year—Randall tried hard never to make any reference to that period, but it would come out; *Mister Wyatt and I went over that when you were sick*, he'd have to say from time to time. Thomas would hear this, and his stomach would clench; his stomach was always cramped, his limbs hurt. Randall was in the orchards side by side with his own father, and where was Abel when he was in the orchards? Side by side with Wyatt. When Thomas fell sick, his mother had come back from Baltimore, and for a time he took joy in her being there, as if he would give his father away, repudiate the Retreat, the peaches, and join his mother, return with her to Baltimore, where Mary was now in college, let Randall move into his room in the Mansion House, since that's what his father wanted, but though Thomas dropped hints to his mother that this was what he was thinking, she seemed either not to hear them or, when his comments became more overt, to respond simply that she *knew* Thomas loved the Retreat and his father and that he would *never* be happy on Mount Vernon. "Too much high society for a boy," she said gaily. When she returned to Baltimore in January, he didn't even bother to say goodbye; what difference did it make where she was? Where Mary was. He was once again left alone in the Mansion House to prowl at night, and often enough he ended up just outside his father's office, with its line of light showing under the door, as if in that room all was brilliant and bright, unlike the dark, creaking gloom of the building around it.

"It's not that Thomas is untalented," he overheard Mr. Townley saying to Wyatt one night in his office. "I believe that in any school he would be among the stronger students."

Wyatt said something Thomas could not hear, but the tone was enough to reveal that this conversation was in the manner of consoling Wyatt, that Mr. Townley was bucking him up.

"It's just that Randall is so exceptional," the tutor said. "He is a Negro like no other I have ever heard of. We cannot hold him back."

"My son is not holding anyone back," Wyatt snapped. This Thomas heard loud and clear.

"Forgive me. I didn't mean to imply that."

There was silence for a while, Wyatt clearing his throat, shuffling papers, the creak of the springs on his desk chair, the floor creaking as Mr. Townley shifted his weight. "The problem is Randall's future, not Thomas's," said Wyatt finally.

"Yes. That was my point," said Mr. Townley.

Thomas thought about this for a few days, but he knew what his father and his tutor were saying: under more normal circumstances, maybe one would be thinking that this arrangement should be ended, that these teenage boys should now go off to school, where they could find friends more like them, that the tensions between them now, so much a part of the house, meant nothing more than that they had outgrown the Children's Office. But what was to become of Randall? In a year or two they would be ready—young, but ready—for college, but for now, there was no other place in the wide world for Randall. He fit nowhere. Thomas knew that. And he understood and ultimately accepted the notion that his own schooling was held captive by the circumstances his father had created.

"I need to talk about the school," said Wyatt to Thomas one Sunday afternoon in the spring. They'd called it "the school" for years.

A few months earlier Thomas might have let everything out to his father, might have allowed himself to say, *Even you like Randall more than me,* and then his father might have put his arm on his shoulder, even though he was now sixteen, and might have said every word Thomas had so wanted to hear: *I love you. You're my son. You're every bit as smart as Randall. You are a fine young man. I'm proud of you.* But the time for that was past, and in any event Tabitha had already said much of it, and he knew his father would do and say none of those things. "What about it?" answered Thomas. "The school is fine."

"Mr. Townley believes you aren't applying yourself as well as you might."

"I'm sorry, Papa. I will try harder."

"Good," said his father, as if that was all that needed to be said. But he added, "You and Randall don't seem to get along very well these days."

Randall! Could there not be a single moment with his father when Randall did not stand between them? "We get along fine."

"Why do I get the feeling something isn't right between you?"

"I don't know," said Thomas. He'd been saying all year: *There's nothing going on between me and Randall. I don't know what you're talking about. There's no* something *between us.*

"Would you rather go to school in Cookestown? That could happen."

"I don't want to go to school in Cookestown," said Thomas, and that much of the conversation, at least, was the truth. He didn't want to go to Cookestown, and that's where it all was left.

Thomas went back to his solitary prowls, and his father went back to his peaches although by now, in 1888 and 1889, it was becoming more and more clear to everyone that all was not well in the orchards. No one was talking about it, at least not to Thomas or, as seemed quite clear, to Randall either. "There's some disease or something," said Randall one day. "I think the Heaths are all dying."

"What does your father say about it?" asked Thomas.

"He doesn't say anything about it. What about Mister Wyatt?"

"He just sits in his office and worries." The boys laughed. What else could they do? Thomas and Randall were well raised, and they tried not to quarrel. They were brothers in their hearts and could never escape it. And if they were brothers, then in some way they shared a sister, even if the subject was taboo between them. Beal was now working at Blaketon and did no more hanging around the farmyard, but from time to time she'd come up to the Mansion House to visit with Tabitha. Thomas would hear her voice coming from the kitchen and he'd listen for the squeak of the door that meant she was going home, and he'd dart out to the side and walk her most of the way home. He did not feel he had to apologize for this; when it got dark, you were supposed to walk women home. Sometimes Tabitha would say, *I think Beal is droppin' by this evening. You want to 'company the lady home?* The summer evening air was creamy, with just enough breeze to clear the air of the smells of manure and kerosene, and on those evenings the Retreat felt easy and safe, all those families in their houses, children bathed and in bed, the men on their porches watching the water lap in the creek, and none of them noticing Thomas and Beal on a path that skirted the back of all this, a new path that they were wearing through the vines, the raspberries and blackberries, between the barns and the pastures; no one would see them unless they were looking, and even then, at night, they could become almost invisible.

Wyatt's grand experiment came, at last, to a close. By most standards the boys were both already a year or two into college studies, but college was the next thing. One evening Wyatt retraced his steps of many years before, back to Tuckertown, where he heard the murmur pass from house to house—though the two bachelor brothers who worked for the Lloyds had long ago moved to Pittsburgh and had been replaced by a man with seven children—and he ended up in front of

Abel Terrell and Una, saying, "The boy's got gifts. He's ready for college, and I'm sending him. I'm clothing him and buying his books." There was no real protest. They worried about him going to the city, to Washington, D.C., and not down to Hampton, where Ruthie had gone for a year, which had done just fine by her, taught her how to lip-read a little better, prepared her for work as a teacher. But Wyatt had selected Howard, and Howard it was. If he hadn't done this, Una Terrell would have gotten into her best clothes, reversed Wyatt's route to the Mansion House, waited in the kitchen with Zoe and Zula until he came out to see her, and said, *You've ruined him for the country life and you've made him more one of yours than one of mine, and now you owe him, you owe him for what he's done for you, given you hope, so I'll be thanking you for finding a college for him and paying for it and clothing him and buying his books, and I'll be thanking you the rest of my life and for whatever of eternity I get to experience.* She would have said that and meant every word, but she never had to.

As for Thomas, he'd go up the road to Benjamin Franklin's university, as had been customary on the Eastern Shore, and Wyatt could not help thinking that academically, Randall might be reaching below himself at Howard and Thomas would be reaching above himself at the University of Pennsylvania, but either way, they were ready. The project that had in the past decade consumed untold hours of his time and a great deal of his money—no one could guess how much—was now done, and he was proud of the boys, standing side by side on the last day in the Children's Office, which, as it turned out—at first simply because there was no reason and later because it was too painful—he would never enter again. He was proud of them for being fine young men, for their hard work, and he was proud of all they had come through, even if one of them was a lion and one of them was a lamb.

A few days before he was to leave, Thomas was in his room when Tabitha came in and told him that Randall was wanting to see him. In the Children's Office, naturally; there was no other place in the house for this meeting, and when he got there, Thomas found Randall in front of the map of the Ancient World. They had both sat across from that map for eight years; they had both memorized every line of it, every engraving of ruins, every speck of the routes supposedly taken by Ulysses and Alexander, every thread of canvas unraveling on the edges. "Hey," said Thomas.

Randall turned. "Hey," he said. They eyed each other. Thomas couldn't help realizing that he had not really looked at Randall in a long time; he didn't seem so imposing to him now. Thomas was taller now, if still skinnier. The image of little Randall crying at the door, his pencil clenched in his fist, came to Thomas.

"When are you leaving?" asked Thomas. The big table was between them.

"Tomorrow. You?"

"Next week."

Neither of them said anything for a few moments.

"Well," said Randall, "I came to say goodbye."

"Yes. Me too," answered Thomas, wishing him well.

"I came to thank you."

"You should thank my father. Not me. Besides, if you hadn't been here, I probably would have had to go to the county school."

"Well. I know what your family has done for me."

Again an awkward pause, and Thomas had by now concluded that this was all there was to it, a thanks and a goodbye.

"But I got to say one more thing, Thomas." The tone had changed. Randall was pointing his finger.

"Oh, yeh? What was that?"

"You keep away from my sister."

"I'm not messing around with your sister," said Thomas. "She's got a right to do what she wants."

"I'm telling you to stay away from her," said Randall again, and this time he had moved so the table was no longer in the way. "If I have to fight you over this, I will. I'll never get out of the way, do you hear me? You let her be, Thomas. You touch her, and I swear, I'll kill you."

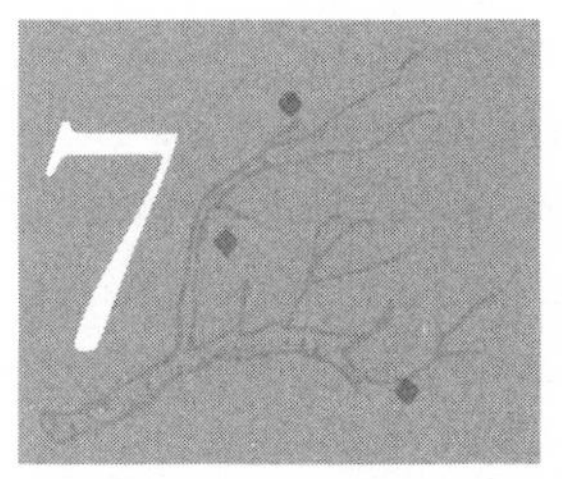

Beal was five when she started following Randall and Thomas. They held a power over her, like a mother over its calf. She couldn't break it. She didn't try. Her parents were always awake and stirring at dawn, even before the night sounds gave way to the finches and mourning doves. Her older twin sisters Ruth and Ruthie slept in as long as they possibly could; but Randall, Randall was up just when the sun began to feather between the sparse branches of the white pines behind Tuckertown, he was up when the crows took over from the finches, and if he had no work and no chores, he was through the kitchen like a runner snake and out the door on the shortcut to the Retreat, and Beal had to be quick and make sure she wasn't snagged by her mother. "Beal, where you off to so sudden this morning?"

"Just down the lane to see those baby jackrabbits."

"Well, I don't want you going into the woods, you hear?"

And it was "Yes, ma'am," then down the woods path at Randall's heels, or just behind them. What could happen on this path, the path her father and Pickle Hardy and Reggie Hollyday trod every day, and Zoe and Zula, and lately Tabitha Hollyday—they all walked down this path, and nothing had ever happened to them. And Randall had been walking down this path to the Retreat since he was Beal's age. The first hundred yards in the pines, the footing was firm but cushioned by moss and a layer of needles, and there was a sweet pitch fragrance—Beal thought of it as perfume, because her mother had perfume, a tiny bottle she never opened that her father had bought her, and Beal assumed it smelled of pine trees. On this part of the path a corner of Zoe's house remained visible, a straight shot back to Tuckertown in case one had to run as fast as one could back to safety. *In case't one got chased by a skunk, or sumpin'.* Then the long, windy, mushy part, working along the rancid flats and fingers at the end of Mason Creek, with the yellow-gray smell of swamp gas and maybe a little more chance of snakes—Beal didn't like this part of the path—and when the season was wet, she'd see the footsteps of the grown-ups sinking deep and hope they didn't sink all the way to over their heads, but that was silly: quicksand didn't exist, just another of Tabitha's stories. If she started to sink, she'd call out and Randall would hear her, and he'd come back and toss her a rope or a vine, *or sumpin'.* He could make a rope out of his pants and shirt, though then he'd be bare naked. Beal's mother would get mad at her when she asked if one of Tabitha's stories was true, and though she was always reassured to hear it wasn't, she stopped telling her mother the things Tabitha said. Her parents didn't like Tabitha. After the marshy part, the creek widened and the water became sweeter, and she'd see flashing through the trees the chimneys of Mr. French's house and then the scrubby woods ended. There was this one big white rock right where the path reached the fields, a rock that marked the path; it was as big as Beal, the only rock like that she'd ever seen in a country of pebbles, but no one else seemed to pay it any mind at all. She asked Tabitha where it came from and Tabitha said it was a piece of the mountain where Noah and the Ark ran aground after the Flood. She never said how it got here, to Maryland, to the Retreat. Beal could crawl up on this rock, and there it all was, the Retreat buildings clustered along the creek banks, the barns and the dairy, the help shacks and the foremen's houses, the line of old, rotting slave quarters slowly being consumed by ivy, home of raccoons, woodchucks, a beehive in every gable. All around this, hundreds of acres of fields: crops on these inland lands, but out there toward the broad river, the orchards.

Beal could stand there on that piece of the mountain where Noah and the Ark ran aground after the Flood and see all this, but then she'd remember that she was following Randall, that she was trying not to be caught. If it was corn they'd planted at this far end, if it was late in the season, Beal could still keep hidden, but if the corn was low or it was wheat, she'd have to keep back in the water oaks and cordgrass and watch as Randall's little black head bobbed forward, always bobbing toward the Mansion House, always bobbing toward Thomas. But still, from here she could follow him clear across the farmyard, just squint and wait for movement, and maybe it would be Uncle Pickle Hardy and the mules, or her father and Mr. French and Mister Wyatt, but sooner or later she'd spot Randall on his beeline to the Mansion House and to Thomas. And she'd sneak over past Mr. French's house and past the barns, and if her father spotted her, he'd give her a whupping and send her home, and her mother would whup her when she got there, but how could she not follow the boys?

If she got past the farmyard safe and sound, she could run along the thick lines of box bush that bordered the park behind the Mansion House, and from there she could spy on Randall as he waited for Thomas, and when Thomas came out, if the boys set off for the rivershore, she was set. If they suddenly turned and headed for the farmyard, she'd have to scurry, run along the line of boxwood with her chest pounding, not even stopping if she got a bramble or a twig stuck in the soles of her feet. She had a few places she liked to hide on the shore at the edge of the orchards, and it didn't much matter what the boys were doing, she just felt good watching them, wanting to be part of their games, but this was good enough. At home, Beal was a lurker; she went through their little house silently, and if her parents were in the kitchen talking about something interesting, she could steal to the doorway and maybe they were talking about Ruth and Ruthie or about the peaches or about Zoe; Beal could make herself invisible, at least until her mother called out, "Beal, I see you there, and little girls who eavesdrop get their ears boxed."

"I wasn't hearing nothing," she'd call out.

"Anything. Wasn't hearing anything. Now git."

Sometimes that would happen when she was watching the boys. Randall would call out, "Beal, you're a big fat pig, and I see you there spying on us." She'd come down from a peach tree or crawl out from under a wagon, and to show that she could do what she wanted, she'd walk over to them and say, "I ain't spying on you."

"Liar."

Here she'd run out of things to say, so maybe she'd say, "Hey, Thomas."

Thomas would say, "Hey, Beal," and sometimes it might seem that he was going to invite her to play with them, and sometimes he did, but most of the time Randall would shoo her away, or as they were preparing to head off, he'd hold up one finger and tell her that if she followed them, she'd fall into one of the traps they had prepared and he'd sell her to some whiteman in Mississippi or send her to the Orphans' Court. She'd protest that there weren't no slavery no more, but the Orphans' Court scared her, scared her even more than that man Jacob Beets, who hung around sometimes, looked at her with wounded, hollow eyes. Jacob Beets scared her, but the Orphans' Court scared her more: they could come onto the Retreat and take her anytime they wanted, make her apprentice to some white family until she was eighteen or twenty-one, that's what she had heard—and the first day Randall threatened her with it, she sat down in the hay in front of the mule barn and started to cry.

From the loft window above she heard Mr. French's voice saying, "Who's that making all that fuss?"

She wanted to run, but in a second he was standing above her in the doorframe. His laced-up boots looked huge. "That you, Beal? What's got you going like that?"

She liked Mr. French, even though her father was always complaining about him; on Sundays she liked to spy on him playing with his daughters. So she told him what Randall had said about the Orphans' Court, and he told her that those bastards knew better than to take on Mister Wyatt, and besides, if one of them set a foot on the Retreat, he'd shoot him dead and that would be that. "Okay now?"

"Yes, sir," she said. She rubbed a greasy forearm across her nose.

"Come here," he said. He reached out for her hand. "I'm going to town, and I'll give you a ride home." Around the corner of the shed he had a team hitched to a wagon, and he picked her up and placed her on the seat and her heart was beating fast because she almost never got to ride, and when she did, it was never, ever in the seat, up there on top of the world. Mr. French pulled himself up beside her, took the reins, snicked the team to attention, and then said to her, "Where to, Miss Beal?"

She giggled, and off they went down the lane, and it didn't matter so much to her that she was going to be punished by her mother and that she was probably going to get a lesson about staying out of Mr. French's hair; he was the manager of the farm, and besides, she shouldn't take favors from a whiteman—any whiteman, you never knew what they were going to expect in return. Beal knew all of that was coming, but she didn't care. When Mr. French got home that evening, Mrs. French said, "What child was that up with you on the wagon this afternoon? Was that the little Terrell girl?"

"Beal. Her name is Beal." He didn't say that he found her a haunting child, with huge amber eyes and strangely luminous skin, a lovely little girl who chattered away to him all the way down the lane about the goings-on in Tuckertown and the stories Tabitha told her. Mr. French didn't say any of this, because it would have seemed disloyal to his own daughters, two older than Beal and one just turned three. As much as he loved them, it seemed that none of them were destined to become beauties; they didn't have whatever it was, those eyes, this strange promise, this assurance of beauty and grace, that this little Negro girl had.

When Randall and Thomas started doing their lessons at the Retreat, Beal's mother and the other women of Tuckertown and Cookestown got the Negro school going again. It was held in an old tobacco barn that Mister Wyatt had fixed up, and it wasn't ideal—dark, and impossible to heat—but it was just across the road from Tuckertown on Retreat land and safer as a result. The teacher was Beal's sister Ruthie, though during school she was to be called Esther. By now Ruth had gone to work for the Lloyds. Though Esther was a little deaf and the boys could whisper to each other behind their books and not get caught, she had a gift and a calling for teaching. She became famous for her work, and that's what she did her whole life, even though she had two schools burned from under her and a husband who stole and drank up every penny she ever made.

At school, it seemed to Beal that her sister, the Hollydays, and the children from Cookestown were always shushing her. Other girls made the talk-talk-talk sign with their hands at her, even that stupid Myrtle Venn, who never voluntarily said a single word the whole time she was in school, never raised her hand to answer a question, mumbled through her recitations, when Beal would have gladly done them for her. She didn't know why, if no one else was going to say anything, she couldn't say what was on her mind. The boys made fun of her. Mason Cooke and Ulysses Gould pulled up her skirt, put glue in her hair; when they began to be able to write, they chalked notes on her bench, like *you smel.* At home she asked Ruthie—only their mother called her Esther at home—what it all meant, although it seemed to Ruthie that Beal knew perfectly well what it meant, all this attention from the boys, this resistance from the girls.

In 1884, when the boys were thirteen and Beal eleven, Mister Wyatt sent Ruthie to Hampton Normal for a year, and the teacher at Tuckertown was a frail older woman from Cookestown who meant well but had little learning to impart. Before the war her father had been sold by the Lloyds for teaching her to read; when they bought him, they didn't know he was literate. Things at the school became lax. That year Beal took to following Randall again, only now, on those occasions when he'd come home from the Retreat for lunch, Beal tagged along when he went back, and Randall didn't mind so much; she kept the walk interesting. They'd end up at the summer kitchen door at the Retreat, and Zula or Tabitha often welcomed her in for a sit. They liked Beal, everyone did; even Zoe liked her, was sweet on her. What was to become of her nobody knew.

One day in the fall, the boys' teacher—Miss DeCourcey it was then—asked her if she wanted to come into the Children's Office and read with the boys. "A bright-looking girl like you," said Miss DeCourcey, as if one glance from Beal had bewitched her. Beal could see the horror on Zoe's face, then rage, and, finally, a silent slash of her arm telling Beal that no way, no way was she to do this—*This fool white girl has no idea what she's doing, but we know, don't we, we know that this is all wrong. Don't we agree on that, child?* Beal knew she should agree, but Randall had been doing his schooling up here now for three years, and no ill had come of it, and she'd never been farther than this into the Mansion House and had been hearing about the classroom for so long, and all the wonders in it, so she figured she'd take up this invitation just once. She followed Miss DeCourcey down the low brick passageway between the kitchen and maids' rooms and laundry, and into the office. Randall and Thomas both had their noses in their history books, Thomas slouched so far in his seat that he could rest the heavy volume on the table and peer directly into it, nothing but his curly brown thatch visible. Thomas had not started to grow yet, to become tall like his sister, Mary, and he was always slumping and drooping, and everyone was always telling him to straighten up.

"What's *she* doing here?" said Randall.

"She's just going to come in and read a bit. I don't see any harm in that," said Miss DeCourcey. "And what are you reading in school now, dear?"

They weren't reading much of anything in her school that year, and the truth was, Beal was probably as bright as Randall but wasn't all that interested in books. So she said she was reading the *Freedman's Reader*, because that was the one book in school they had enough copies of not to have to share.

"Well, then try this," said Miss DeCourcey, and Randall snickered because it was a simple book, but Beal didn't care. She tried to focus on it, but she was too excited; the letters danced in front of her eyes. Thomas had straightened up a little, so that every once in a while his eyes popped over the pages and he could glance at her. After a few minutes it seemed that he was staring at her. Mason Cooke and Ulysses Gould never stared at her, they just punched her. Thomas kept looking and it made her nervous, but she didn't really want him to stop.

That winter she stopped in often. Randall never warmed to this. "It's not fair," he said when the family was having supper. "It's my school."

Beal knew her parents had mixed ideas about this, but fair—that was something her mother cared about. "It's your school by the grace of Mister Wyatt, and if Miss Whatever invites Beal in, then that's fair."

"Thomas doesn't mind," said Beal.

Randall slammed down his fork. "You keep Thomas out of this. He's my friend, not yours. What he wants doesn't matter anyway."

Their father sat quietly and ate his supper; his silence was enough to let the present situation stand: Beal could go in from time to time, if invited.

"Just don't let that Tabitha fill your head with nonsense," said her mother.

When she came into the office, Thomas always said, "Hey, Beal," the way they had done since they were young children, and she noticed that he sat up straighter as the winter went along. One day she came in and Miss DeCourcey wasn't there, was home with her ailing mother. Randall looked up and told her to get out.

"I just readin' a bit," she said, grabbing hold of a book, *Julius Caesar,* in Latin, as it turned out.

"You readin' nothing. You don't belong here," said Randall.

"Let her stay," said Thomas. "What is she bothering?"

"You keep out of it. This is between me and Beal."

"Is not. I've got a right to say. This is my house," and at that, the two boys were out of their chairs, pushing and shoving. Beal began to think this was all a bad idea. She got frightened and sneaked out a side door no one ever used and ran home through the snow without her coat. Randall came back an hour or so later with her coat, and he threw it at her and told her for the hundredth time to keep away, keep away from the Mansion House, keep away from Thomas. But she didn't.

All this stayed between the children. No one seemed to be paying all that much attention to what was going on in the back rooms at the Retreat that year. Miss Ophelia was in Baltimore, Beal guessed. Beal wouldn't recognize her if she saw her. Miss Mary was in Baltimore, she guessed, maybe going to college, which seemed more peculiar for a woman than going to a convent in Paris, France. Mister Wyatt and Beal's father seemed more caught up in the orchards than ever before, and it seemed to Beal that the harder they worked, the darker her father's moods, as if the branches had reached out at them and wouldn't let them go, as if what was supposed to be sweet and luscious contained some sort of horror, a sight you didn't want to see, ever. Mr. French was the only man on the place, white or black, who ever said a word to her as she crossed the farmyard on these afternoons. "So now we're studying with the boys, Miss Beal?"

She giggled—the old joke between them. "I'm just reading with them by and by."

"You be careful," he said, and she didn't know exactly what he meant, careful of *what*? but he was a gloomy man in the best of circumstances, so her father had said for years. He was always prophesying ruin, trouble with the hired men, trouble with shipping, trouble with late frost, early hurricanes, summer-long drought.

Beal had decided that year that it was time for her to bring herself up from Tuckertown. Tuckertown—it had embraced her, rocked her as a baby, sheltered her and the other children from the wild goings-on in those years after Emancipation. Tuckertown wasn't a bunch of sharecroppers or people waiting forever to be given forty acres and a mule, but people like her father, from freed families for the most part, people with jobs. Sure, every man, woman, and child above ten years old had to work the peach harvest to make ends meet, but ends did meet, and they all ate well. And Tuckertown wasn't a bunch of huts and lean-tos, but a regular street with houses and swept front yards, a watering trough at one end and a church at the other. In Tuckertown, Beal had been carefully schooled in the intricacies of life: whom she was allowed to talk to, whom she wasn't; how to walk so as not to be noticed; how to look down at her feet when a whiteman was talking to her and how, almost always, to pretend she didn't understand what he was saying; how to put her faith in the Retreat and Mister Wyatt but, at the same time, not to trust them, a pretty feat that: untrusting faith. Most of these lessons she got from her mother, but Zoe—from her house at the top of the street, the place you had to pass if you were going anywhere, the porch with all-seeing eyes—Zoe was the high priestess of these accommodations, and you didn't cross her, because she was the tiniest bit crazy. You didn't cross Zoe. Now, Tabitha, she had her own mind. Who knew where Tabitha got the stories and wild ideas she spouted—from the men who came calling, everyone supposed, but where did *they* get those ideas: stories of Africa and telephones and a trade union of ship caulkers in Baltimore even the yard owners couldn't bust up—but Tabitha didn't cross Zoe. Zoe, who was maybe sixty, was freed by Ophelia's father in 1857 and had worked her whole life in the Mansion House kitchen. In her near blindness she saw everything from there, she knew; but lately people had been whispering that she was getting too old to understand the new world they lived in. Tabitha—she was a different voice in Tuckertown, the voice of 1885, for glory's sake, a new day for the colored. No other way to put it. And Mister Wyatt's peaches were making them rich.

It was Tabitha's voice Beal was listening to when she stopped in at the Mansion House, walked through the kitchen with no other sound in her ears, Zoe frozen in her work, the pot held an inch or two off the stove top, the mixing spoon in mid-spin, staring at her. Miss DeCourcey was not one of the strongest of tutors in the Retreat school, a girl not much given to hard work, not much of a favorite of Mrs. French's, with whom she and all the other female teachers boarded, and she was happy enough to let Thomas do things like teaching Beal how to say "You are a big fat pig" in Latin, which he said was *"Voss es a magnus pinguis sus."* Zoe would hear those bursts of laughter come from the children in that room, and she'd fume and tremble.

At the end of the year, when Mister Wyatt quizzed the boys on this and that and saw how little they seemed to have learned, he fired Miss DeCourcey—the first teacher he'd ever fired—and for the next year hired the first of the men. Ruthie came back from Hampton, and though she had not found a husband there, which was what even Una had hoped, the lip-reading helped and the Tuckertown school was back on track.

That summer Beal was twelve, and she was working in the orchards, as Randall had done, whenever her father said they needed her, but often she'd go over to the farmyard with the men at first light, and there would be families and children she didn't know, speaking languages she'd never heard, and the parents of these strange white families were always pushing their children—much younger than Beal—ahead into the wagons for a place on the crew, and Beal was only too happy to be pushed aside and end up at the end of the line, and by then there was nobody left who could tell her what to do. She would hang around the farmyard, and sure enough, often enough, she'd see Thomas working his way through the box bush and across the gulley from the Mansion House. In the beginning he always had some chore, and though Beal didn't believe any of it was real, she'd follow him to find a spade in the toolhouse or go searching for Uncle Pickle, who he knew would be out in the orchards tending to the mules and drays. Then sometimes he'd come over, and he'd say, *Hey, Beal. What are you doing?* and she'd have to say something like *I'm s'posed to take Spud over to the granary and see if he can catch that big rat,* and Thomas would not say *Which big rat,* because once they'd gotten past these little subterfuges, they could just visit for a while. She was the one with the ideas, stuff Tabitha had said to her, things she'd heard, and Thomas would listen to her and then say, *Now, that's just crazy,* or more often, he'd listen and then try to explain, *See, what she meant was.* Beal didn't know Thomas was floundering up there in the Mansion House, but she sensed that he needed her friendship, and now he and Randall had fought—fought over her—and in those first days she felt sorry for him.

"Why are you spending time with him?" Randall would say.

"Because he doesn't have anyone to talk to. You're being mean to him, and his mama don't care that he was ever born, and Mister Wyatt only cares about peaches. So what's he supposed to do up there in the Mansion House?"

Randall nodded; he still loved Thomas, as far as Beal could tell, and they were just going through a fight.

"And I'm not spending time with him. When I see him, we talk. Tha's only proper." She liked saying that it was only "proper." But the truth was, she didn't have anyone much to talk to either. Robert Junior Turner used to visit with her from time to time, but he had long gone to man's work in the orchards, and the spastic Hardy girl was closer to her age, but she could hardly speak and in no way could she run and play.

People had been telling Beal she was beautiful since she was old enough to understand it, but even as she entered puberty, she had no real idea what they were talking about. From time to time she'd look in her parents' mirror, bring her hands to her cheeks, pull and tug her nose, peel her lips back, then let her face snap back into normal, and she'd ask herself, *What's so beautiful 'bout that?* She'd overheard a man caller saying to Tabitha once that she was "a *fine* woman," and Beal recognized that there was something about Tabitha's big frame and big breasts and smooth skin in that, but also something about the way she acted, the way she behaved. *Fine.* Beal wouldn't have wanted her own mother referred to in that way. People said Una was "han'some"; that meant skinny, Beal supposed, and also direct, plainspoken. Ruth and Ruthie were just "Ruth and Ruthie," as if no one ever looked at either one individually for long enough to appraise their looks. Darby Gale was "precious" until it became clear that even if she had none of her mother Zoe's looks, which was good, she had all too much of her madness, her spells. Other women in Tuckertown were "good-lookin' " and "easy on the eye" and "right fair," but only Beal was "beautiful." Sometimes even white women she'd see on the Retreat, town women come to call at the Mansion House, would tell her that she was a beautiful child. *Those eyes,* the white women would say to each other, as if they were talking about an animal, or a painting; *such an unusual color.* Sometimes the immigrant families who worked as pickers in the summer would say things to her or about her in their own foreign tongues, but Beal knew, from the tone of voice that was now familiar to her, that they were saying she was beautiful. *Bootiful,* said Uncle Pickle. *Come here, Bootiful, and let an old man feel the sap rise.*

But Thomas never said anything about her looks, and now that she was twelve, she wanted him to notice her. She'd put a sprig of lavender in her hair, make a belt out of a red scarf that was too torn for her mother to wear, iron her skirt, and starch her shirt, but Thomas never seemed to notice. She didn't know what she was doing with all this, just thinking that if everyone called her beautiful, there was no reason that Thomas shouldn't too. On the way home she'd have to jettison her flowers, muss up her clothes so Randall wouldn't tease her, or worse—accuse her of things she had no idea about and neither did he—and it was all a waste of time, except that she couldn't stop trying.

And then, about the middle of that long summer, before the peaches started to die in earnest and before it had become clear that Emancipation maybe wasn't everything it was supposed to be, a summer that was hot, when the air shimmered with bees and locusts, she was watching Thomas walk across the farmyard, and it came to her that for all the time she spent trying to make him notice her, she had never really looked at him, and that he was beautiful. It wasn't in his features, which were so finely drawn, so dainty that he seemed breakable. He had, she supposed, the face of an angel, or one of those English choirboys Tabitha told her about, except Beal couldn't imagine an angel having such a troubled brow, lines worn into the skin at too young an age. So often pretending that he was happy, that he didn't care about Randall or about a family that didn't seem to pay him any mind, but she knew the truth. The truth was what made his face beautiful. That trouble ran as deep as a well, and seeing it in those eyes, you could fall in, right to the bottom. That's what beautiful meant, Beal supposed, this depth—not a flower behind an ear or a fancy way of walking, but this mystery of seeing so much of a person's soul yet knowing you hadn't seen any of it. Beal didn't think this was love—what a stupid idea, and besides, Thomas was white and she was colored, so love was impossible—she thought it was beauty, and for a while it made her nervous to think that every time someone said that to her, they were looking partway into her deepest secrets, just as she was now doing with Thomas.

The word had passed that Ruthie could get some letters and figures into the densest of heads, so there were now twelve kids in the Tuckertown school, even if neither Mason Cooke nor Ulysses Gould came back. People still played mean jokes on Ruthie—Miss Terrell—but there was no fun in it, and often when people thought she hadn't heard something, she was just playing possum anyway; you might get whipped on the way out, and you knew why. Beal was proud of Ruthie; she had good reason to be. Ruth had gotten married and had moved with her husband to Kent County, and that had freed Ruthie; people no longer thought of her as disabled, as half a person.

Most people expected Beal to be a genius like Randall, but she wasn't, didn't care to be. Ruthie complained about her to their mother, and it began to seem a bad piece of luck to have your older sister be your teacher. "She's just as smart as Randall," Ruthie would say. "She thinks she's fooling me, but during reading she's just daydreaming." She sounded disgusted. "Dr. Washington says that the Negro can take his place alongside the white only through education. What's going to happen to her?"

"Oh," said her mother. "I suspect Beal will end up comfortable enough."

"Because she's so pretty?"

Beal heard this coming from the kitchen, over the clank of dishes, her father's snores. She was supposed to be doing arithmetic homework.

"No," said Una. "Because she's got her own ideas. She's got a different kind of future. I can't explain to you why I feel that."

"Well, if she keeps hanging around Tabitha, you know what that future is going to be. She'll end up in Baltimore at Fells Point."

Beal heard this with a gasp of breath, heard her own shock at the same time that she heard her mother slap Ruthie's cheek. "Esther. Don't you ever say that about your sister. Never."

There was a silence. Then, "I'm sorry, Mama."

"I declare." Her mother was still panting. "You bring her as far in her studies as you can, and then we'll let her take that job over at Blaketon Zemirah was talking about. She'll take an honorable job in a respectable house, and we'll see what the future holds."

Beal tried to take Ruthie's stark prediction as a warning. For a time she avoided Tabitha, but there was no reason in the end, and Tabitha wouldn't let her be anyway. Beal went back to school for another year with all sorts of ambitions, all sorts of resolutions, but by the following May, it was clear that she had reached the point her mother delineated, and she took the job at Blaketon. Nobody liked the Lloyds much, and at first it felt to Beal that she'd switched sides, a Retreat family working at Blaketon, but soon she began to like it. Zemirah was a less interesting person than her sister, Zoe, but life was a whole lot more restful around her, and the girls from Cookestown who worked there became friends, and there were even some boys she liked, a nice, shy boy named Lester who reminded her of Thomas.

But that was the problem—the only problem in her life. She missed Thomas, so was there any wonder that in the evening from time to time Beal would change out of her maid clothes and into her light work skirt and best shirt and find herself on the path toward the Retreat to visit with Hattie's Mary, who was fading fast, and that Thomas, after spending the day at his lessons or, in summer, working alongside his father in the orchards, would slip away from the dark, empty Mansion House to walk her home? Or that they would make a plan and meet at a bench Thomas had made out of two elm butts and an oak plank in a private and sheltered spot between the granary and the water, a small high spot that caught whatever breeze might be blowing, a sort of dune that was so sandy that the grasses never got long enough to harbor chiggers? This was a place where slaves used to court, but no one thought that's what was going on with these two young people, least of all the young people themselves.

So it was "Hey, Beal," and "Hey, Thomas," and they'd sit down at either end of the bench, Beal with her ankles drawn beneath her, her hands folded in her lap, or maybe fiddling with something she picked up in the barnyard, a shard of leather, a rusty nail.

"Did your daddy get a letter back from Miss Mary?" she'd ask, because Thomas had told her that they all thought Mary was going to get engaged, and Wyatt had written her to ask if it was true. Or, "Tabitha says the governor was up to the Mansion House t'other day," which was true, but who cared about the governor of Maryland? She'd ask this sort of thing, but it was just a way to start talking, and she didn't care what the answer was anyway.

He'd say, "This is a nice breeze, don't you think?"

"First breeze in a week, I'd say. Up at Blaketon, there isn't a breath."

"They cutting hay yet?"

"Not yet," she'd say. Or, "Just started this morning with that new mowing machine, and the rabbits and skunks and voles were all running for their lives." Or, "Still seems pretty strange to me to be selling hay. Who would have ever thought anyone would pay money just for grass." Or, "I declare, no flower grows back in as fast as black-eyes do," and she'd hold up a blossom, maybe sniff at it, at the light, sweet smell of it, as if it had just come from some white person's linen closet.

"I was thinking about you today," he'd say.

"That so. What about?"

"Oh, nothing." And it would go on like that, except that somewhere they'd find themselves talking about whatever was on their minds, and sometimes these were happy things and sometimes not, but Beal, walking home briskly so she wouldn't get caught, always felt that he had taken on her need, the need to speak her mind, and she felt relieved of extra weight, and lifted.

No matter what either one of them did, every time she'd meet Thomas, Randall would know about it the next day. Zoe told him, or Zula. Or someone on the farm spotted them and made sure to tell him because they knew it would make him angry. But Beal wasn't going to back down. "Thomas is my friend," she'd say. "He used to be your friend, but he's not a genius like you are, so you don't have time for him. So what you getting so exercised about, Randall? What business is this of yours? You want to know 'what went on,' well, you come with me someday. I'm sick of you spying on me." They both knew she was simply quoting him from so many years ago. "I'm sick of you asking questions 'round about me and what I do with my time. You just g'wan back to your books, Randall. That's all you care about. Let everyone else just be."

The next day, Beal would replay her visits with Thomas. In the upstairs spaces at Blaketon, as she went about her chores in the bedrooms and private spaces, she would picture Thomas at the Retreat. Even though it was Philomen Lloyd's bed she was making, she'd imagine Thomas, his head asleep on the pillow. Ruthie was right; she was always daydreaming. "What did you do to yourself?" Thomas asked after she had burned the flesh on the bottom of her hand with an iron, left a long red sear between the coral of her palm and the golden brown of her knuckles. He took her hand in his and flattened it so he could see. "Does it hurt?" "Of course it hurts," she answered. Thomas could ask stupid questions, but so could she. She winced, remembering that she had asked whether Mr. French had been born in France; she didn't really think he had been; she couldn't really remember exactly what she was trying to say. She asked Thomas about Mary's life in Baltimore, the love affair everyone was talking about, and he didn't play coy, he just didn't know anything. "Whatever it was, she's always going to be the boss" was what Thomas said after it became known that Mary had broken off with her beau. In Beal's whole world, the Retreat, Blaketon, Tuckertown, and Cookestown, there was maybe no one about whom people knew less than Mary, no one who seemed to have more blank spots in her history. Thomas didn't talk to Mary very much. "Not like I can talk to you," he said. Beal didn't know exactly how that made her feel, to have him say that their whole friendship had been built on their saying to each other what they couldn't say to anyone else. That was one of the reasons Randall got jealous of them, but it was his own fault: Randall didn't ever understand how special she was, didn't understand how special *he* was. Well. It didn't really matter that much anymore what he thought; it was now the spring of 1889, and in the fall Randall would go off to college, which was good—good for him and for her. But Thomas would be going too. He didn't want to go. "I'm not going," he stated. They were sitting on the bench, even though it was chilly and getting dark.

"You always makes things so hard on yourself, Thomas. You always fight things. Philadelphia," she said in a tone of wonder. "Imagine!"

He crossed his hands and stared out at the creek for a few moments. Beal wished she could take it back—Philadelphia. "I'm sorry, Thomas," she said. "I didn't mean to say anything about all that."

He waved his hand at her: *You're forgiven; forget it.*

"I mean . . ." she said.

"It's nothing. Papa got a letter from one of my professors. They're all ready for me."

"Is that bad?" She hated to see Thomas this way. Defiant. Fearful. Fearfully defiant, really, which was something else again: all balled up, rigid like a possum.

"It doesn't mean anything. I don't know why I'm going there, anyway. I don't want to be there. I just want to be here."

In a few minutes it would be dark. Beal could be a hundred years old and she'd still be reluctant to walk that woods path to Tuckertown much after dusk. "I'd like to see it. Philadelphia, Baltimore. That's the truth."

Her pleasure, her wonder lightened the mood. He turned to her. "Maybe I could take you someday."

Beal stood up and swept the tree buds from her shirt. "Oh, Thomas, how you going to do that? Dress me up as your maid or something? How are you and me supposed to go to Baltimore?"

Maybe he didn't want to go to Philadelphia or Baltimore, but she loved to hear about these places, so he told her about electric lights in the houses, about water closets and indoor plumbing. Well, that wasn't so special: both the Retreat and Blaketon had water closets, and thank the good Lord for that, since there was no way Beal would have taken that job if it involved emptying chamber pots. He told her about the telephone, which his mother had just gotten in Baltimore, but mostly just to call the fire department. These were the stories Beal really wanted to hear, the city, out yonder. All summer, just passing the time until he left, and not always just sitting on that bench, though it was a good spot. They'd take a walk out through the orchards the way Tabitha and her men callers used to, sit on the dock, because who else was she supposed to take a walk with? Out there on the dock, she'd think about waiting for the steamer and, when it came by, getting aboard, going to Baltimore or Annapolis. She used to imagine doing this alone, being a lady who had done all this before a number of times and knew the ropes. But now, ever since Thomas had said he'd like to take her to Baltimore, she imagined a different scenario. Maybe the steamer would be one of those that went down overnight to Norfolk, or maybe it was even one that went out into the Atlantic and up the coast to New York City. When she stepped aboard, she'd be alone, as she had always imagined, but waiting for her on the deck would be Thomas. Maybe he'd gotten aboard from the dock at Piney Point; she wasn't sure about that part. But he'd be waiting for her, and—because from the moment she stepped aboard a steamer for New York, she'd *be* in New York—she'd take his arm, and they would go below to the same stateroom and lie down in the same bed.

Randall left for Howard on the first day of September. Beal hugged him long and hard before he got into the carriage for the steamer; she loved him, was proud of him; there had never been a Randall in the county before. All of Tuckertown and most of Cookestown was there to send him off—their pride, their champion—as well as some of Cookestown, white and black, who were sick of hearing about this boy, this college boy, and who went home that day licking their wounds. Beal hoped Zoe would let him go without some wild outburst, and she did, even if her tears seemed not those of joy or of sorrow, but of dread. Randall was wearing the suit Mister Wyatt had ordered from his own tailor, and he carried his clothes in a carpetbag his mother had saved for all summer. He was a regular gentleman, a man of the world.

That evening, when Beal got home from work, her mother was waiting for her on the porch. It seemed to Beal that her *han'some* mother was in a mood, now that Randall was gone, to take care of other issues in the house. As soon as she saw her mother with her fearsome scowl, Beal knew what this was about.

"Evening, Mama," she called out.

Mama pointed to the step and told her to sit down. The door to the house was closed; Ruthie and her daddy, if he was home, had been told to stay out of the way. "How you doing, Baby?"

"I doing okay. I be right fine." Beal knew what she was saying: *I doing; I be.* Taking refuge. No one could accuse her of reaching up. The low western sun was coming through the pines, a filtered gentle light, and for all the scowling, there was no way for Mama's skin not to look golden. Beal got her skin from her mother, cinnamon. Coffee, they said. *Cuffee, now where do you suppose your skin come from?*

"You know what we need to talk about?"

"No, Mama. I don't think I do."

Her mother didn't pay any attention at all to this disclaimer, didn't even pretend she believed it for a moment. "Thomas has been brother to my son and daughter for many years, and he's a good boy. A good boy, but not wise to the world. He won't mean to hurt anyone, but he will. Do you know what I'm saying? I should have put a stop to this long ago. Years ago. I just didn't know how. How to be true to all three of you children at the same time. I have prayed and prayed for guidance, but none has come. But now Randall is gone. He's gone, and if you want to know how it looks to me, I'd say he's never coming back, and God be with him in that white world. You're my last, and it's time we looked at what the future holds for you."

"How am I supposed to know my future? Am I supposed to ask Zoe to read it for me?"

"Don't you be snappy to me. I'm telling you that Thomas Bayly is not your future. Do you understand that? Don't make that mistake."

"Mistake?"

"The mistake of feeling we can plan our own lives. We believed that. We believed it on Emancipation Day, November the first, 1864, and it hasn't come to pass."

"Mama," Beal said. "I don't know about this history, and about all this future. Thomas is my friend, that's all. He's my brother, just like you say. We don't care about black and white. We don't care about all this history."

" 'We don't care' this; 'we don't care' that. Listen to yourself. Who's this 'we'? How far has this gone?"

"Ain't gone anywhere."

"And it never can. Oh, Baby, Baby Girl. You are the prettiest thing I ever saw, but this can't go anywhere. It's got to stop."

This? It? Let Mama listen to herself. "Randall's been telling you a bunch of lies."

"He's just trying to do what's best for you. You'll figure out someday that he'd do about anything to protect you. You put all that stuff about Randall aside."

Beal knew that Randall was trying to protect her, but she also knew that Randall knew nothing about love. There. She'd said the word, said it out loud to herself because Mama was trying to take it away from her. "So what do you want me to do?"

"Well. Thomas is leaving next week, as I expect you know."

"On Tuesday."

Her mother winced slightly. "Okay. On Tuesday. And when he goes, that'll be the end of this. You're grown up now, fifteen. It wouldn't be any more proper for you to spend time with *any* boy, the way you have with Thomas over the years."

So her mother had given her one more week of "this"—one more week of Thomas, and she took it by living her life the way she had been, they had been. And on the Monday before Thomas was to leave, Beal could think of nothing but him. She got yelled at by Zemirah; Mrs. Lloyd threatened to fire her. She could not help herself. She could not imagine life without the boys. *Life without the boys,* she repeated to herself, but she knew it wasn't Randall who was on her mind. Tabitha had brought her a message the day before: *Meet me at the peach dock.* She and Tabitha both knew what that meant, even though Tabitha probably wasn't aware of how many times she and some man had been spied on in off-hours on the peach dock. Tabitha wanted this to happen; all summer she had been how they communicated. *What if Randall finds out,* Beal asked Tabitha, and Tabitha said, *You let me take care of Randall.* Beal got home at five, ate her supper without a word; no one spoke. She went up to her room and changed, and when she came back down, heading for the door, her mother made a grab for her arm, a lunge, but she missed. "Where you going, Beal? Abel—" she called. "You stop this child."

Beal was crying. "I'm just going to say goodbye to him. That's what you want, right? Say goodbye to him once and for all."

"You will not." Again, her mother called for her father, but Beal was off now, into the woods and down the path, through the pine groves, across the marshy stretch, past the rock, and into the cornfields. She couldn't cry and run at the same time, so she had stopped crying. She was following the path behind the farmyard that she and Thomas had made when he used to walk her home, but when she drew up to the Frenches' house, she ducked into the corn a few rows and made her way down an alley, the sharp, drooping leaves slicing her arms and legs with spidery traces, banging painfully into dense cobs hanging in her way, once or twice setting off an explosion of pollen from the tassels of late plants. She came to the lane, hesitated—to check whether her father had hitched up the mule and come to head her off, but he had not—and she crossed, walking now, breathless, into the poor, sick orchards.

I love him, she said to herself, maybe for the first time. *I love Thomas. Mama's right. Nothing will come of this, but I love him.* The light was yellow, the kind of evening that blossoms after a thundershower. Far ahead, down the row of trees, she saw Thomas standing there.

She reached the dock, lightly stepped her way over the splinters of the decking. He'd been sitting on a bollard, but he stood up when she approached. When she stood to face him, he gathered her into his arms. "I love you, Beal. I want to marry you."

"I love you, Thomas, but don't talk crazy."

He had her body gripped. His heart was breaking, he said, and so was hers. There was a wind blowing down the river, the same north wind that filled the sails of the schooner long before either one of them was born. She would do anything to make Thomas feel better, to make herself feel better. She let him lay her down on the dock. She didn't know if what they had done was what her mother had once called "married folks' doings," whether such doings were even possible if you weren't married, but when it was over, she left him there and ran through the orchards, as if now, at long last, they were free, and through the yellow light and green leaves, he followed the luminescence of her gray skirt and the white ribbon bobbing in her hair.

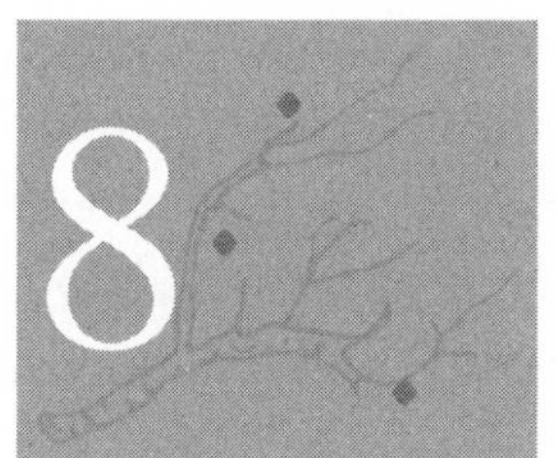

There is a knocking from what Edward Mason judges to be the back door of the Frenches' house.

"Oh, Lord," says Mrs. French, "we've been talking for hours." She gets up from her chair with some difficulty; she's been back and forth all morning with the same uncertain launch. Once on her feet, she's not nimble, but she is solid. She's a stout woman, and she must be well past seventy. Mr. French must be a few years older; some of the colored, who would appear to be still alive, older still. Edward has already begun to form the unwelcome notion that people over in the "Mansion House," as they call it, don't live very long, while the plainer folk on the "farm side of the gulley" persist to fantastically advanced age.

Once up, Mrs. French steadies herself, runs her hands down her dress to give time for her head to clear. An impressive woman, thinks Edward. From a perch in her kitchen in this house, she seems to have missed very little of the furtive traffic on the Retreat. She goes back into the house, and Edward and Mr. French sit in the anticipatory silence of this interruption, a few muffled voices, and then Mrs. French is back, leading a young black woman, maybe twenty years old, birdlike, a curious darting sense about her eyes, as if she is always startled.

"Valerie, this here is Mr. Mason," she says. Edward is surprised to be introduced to a servant, but happy to offer a warm nod, which excites her eyes to furious activity. She's in kitchen whites, a slight smear of egg on her left sleeve.

She has a message for Mr. Mason: Miss Mary finds she will be available to receive a call from him later this afternoon. The way she delivers this gives Edward the clear impression that the purpose of the meeting is for Mary to deliver an answer. He is not happy about getting this message in front of the Frenches. All three of them, maybe even including this girl, all four of them, wondering the same thing: *Well, is he going to get the Retreat or not? An answer so soon?* It seemed that the other pretender from Oklahoma was not scheduled to visit until the end of the month. So "soon" means that (a) Edward has succeeded brilliantly, has so impressed Miss Mary that no further searching for an heir is necessary; or (b) that he has so bombed with her that no matter how much of a cretin the man from Oklahoma is, the place is his for the asking; or (c) something else. Edward cannot imagine what "c" would be. The lawyers offering to sell him a cow? Accusing him of stealing a teaspoon? The girl with the vaguely reptilian eyes is still standing in front of him; the Frenches are looking at him.

"Then do tell Miss Bayly that I will be delighted to return, and in the meantime I am pleased to be her humble servant." He likes that last bit and hopes she will report it exactly so. A little archaic—"I am, sir, most aff'ly, your ob. Serv."—but in the context of all this history, it sounds about right. He begins to reach for a coin to give her when he notices the stiffening of Mr. French. Ah, tipping would be bad form. He covers by making a show of straightening his waistcoat and checking his watch.

"It's dinnertime, then," says Mrs. French after Valerie leaves. Edward is still holding his watch. "You'll be hungry after we have been boring you with all these old stories."

"Not at all," says Edward. He hadn't imagined that he would still be here at lunchtime, had looked forward to a late luncheon back in his hotel's fine dining room. He certainly hadn't imagined being served by the Frenches, but breakfast had been quite a while ago; the Belvedere had to open the kitchen early to boil him an egg. A solid farm repast sounds perfect: a roasted portion of one of those beasts he had seen earlier, boiled potatoes, if he smelled right, a mess o' peas. Wasn't that what they said, "mess o' "? An entertaining notion: lunch with farmers. And boring? He doesn't think he has been bored. He doesn't know what to make of all these stories. Mauled perhaps, mauled by the pull of the past, still so fresh for these people. Expressing interest in the place had struck him as a wise move at the beginning; it wouldn't have seemed political for Mr. French to report that he was indifferent to the privations of Miss Mary's family—of his family. But—well. "Bored" wouldn't be the word.

Mrs. French shows him to the washroom, hands him a towel. A remarkable person, really. Both of them, but at this moment he's most taken with her: the daughter of a blacksmith, born before the Civil War, lived on this place all her life, almost surely never set foot out of the state of Maryland, yet not provincial, he wouldn't say. She makes no apology; even when she interrupts her husband, she seems to be providing precisely the tidbit Edward wanted to hear. Despite dramatic differences in circumstances, she has the same blunt but equitable manner one can still find among the Yankee dames of Beacon Hill, the same alertness, the same presence. He closes the door, evacuates about a gallon of lemonade, and plunges his hands into the washbasin he has filled. The water has a distinct odor of sulfur or iron oxides, or worse, something organic; it is so hard it takes a full minute to rinse off the yellow laundry soap that has been provided. He pauses to look out the tiny window over the stubble of some crop recently harvested, and suddenly he sees again whatever it was about this landscape—he tries to define it better but can't—that had so caught him at the river's edge. Flat—flat and broad, as if the land were offering itself for a higher and better use. A *self-effacing* landscape, Edward decides; an empty canvas. Not *welcoming,* he wouldn't say, but *amenable.* Wyatt Bayly must have felt that with his peach trees—that this land would be amenable to growing peaches. As Edward has grasped the layout, he's looking now toward the acreage that so recently was planted with tens of thousands of peach trees. Hard to imagine anything in such numbers, and today there's not even the slightest residue of them, no stumps that he can discern; perhaps some Schliemann could unearth the foundations of the docks, the bad one and the good one, the one where the slaves were sold, and the one where—if the Frenches were to be believed, although how, indeed, could they know such a thing?—that boy and the colored girl met for assignations. Whatever was ailing the peach trees, it did the trick. Wiped them out. It seems, well, indecent; perhaps not unfair, but *indecent.* Wyatt Bayly sounds like a self-absorbed but decent man.

Edward emerges from the washroom and follows the voices around the corner to the dining room. Mrs. French has placed them in the formal space; through the kitchen door Edward can see the corner of a table where, he assumes, most meals are served. Their dining-room table is round, firm on a heavy, carved pedestal, and big enough for six or eight upholstered side chairs. Edward can imagine this room filled with French family friends and relations, but for the two of them plus their guest, the size of the table is awkward. The whole house is still furnished in Victorian style, but less cluttered than the type practiced in Boston, less of those heavy draperies over everything, less darkness. His wife, Edith, grew up in Chicago, and she finds everything about Edward's family's home "funereal"; the new midwestern look is spare and clean, "geometrical." "Arts and Crafts," she says it's called. "Mission." Okay, but Edward likes "comfortable." This, the Frenches' house, is comfortable; he admires the ample light coming through the broad windows, a rich, refracted glow.

They sit, Mr. French with the rigid posture of the patriarch, a window at his back; he is surrounded by a penumbra of sunlight. In New England they might call his manner flinty; except for the frayed collar and well-worn tie, he could be the president of Harvard. Edward does not know whether there will be grace or other remarks, but Mrs. French immediately passes him the platter of beef. The meal is exactly what he had pictured, although he had not imagined he would be served a tall glass of milk. He dives in, and they all eat in silence for a few minutes, an almost communal silence. For a flicker, perhaps the tiniest glimpse of the truth in Edward's life, he can see that this would be good, that he could live quite a different sort of life here, that he might be less aware of his weaknesses here, that he could be content. He doubts the same would be true of Edith, who has ambitions for a more gilded life. "This is very kind of you," he says. The Frenches seem surprised by this, as if kindness had nothing to do with it, and Edward realizes that it really didn't: in rural life, when mealtime comes, what is one to do, throw the guests out the door? "Treating me with such elegance," he adds, holding a single hand up to make it clear that he is referring to the room. The Frenches are immediately put at ease now that he has acknowledged that they have put on an infrequent show for this visitor from the North.

"Bit of a reach," says Mr. French, half standing to pass Edward the potatoes for a second helping.

The beef is fine; Edward would love a little horseradish but does not ask for it.

"Tell us about Mrs. Mason," says Mrs. French. "Is she with you in Baltimore?"

Edward tells them that she is not; she is in Newport, Rhode Island, visiting a distant aunt.

"Then her family is from Rhode Island?" asks Mrs. French.

No, he explains to them. She grew up in Winnetka, Illinois. Her father owns a moving and storage business in Chicago. He tells them that they met in Paris just before the war broke out. They were married at her home in Illinois this past June.

"Ah," says Mrs. French. "Are you planning to settle in Chicago?"

Edward is once again on his guard and tells them about the business he has purchased in England, that the first stop in their marriage will be Manchester. He tells them that it will just be for a few years, et cetera, but he needn't have dissembled: both Frenches have been dizzied by all this geography, all this transience. They have been following his recitation like spectators at a tennis match. Edward doesn't blame them; from the perspective of this place, the life he has been leading and plans to continue leading is rootless and exhausting. The conversation halts.

"Miss Mary sure did love Paris," says Mr. French.

"She has never been back?"

"No. By the time"—he pauses just long enough for Edward to recognize that in this phrase "by the time" is elided considerable event—"well, by the time she'd come back to help Mr. Wyatt, she was putting her energies into the Retreat."

"And this love affair in Baltimore?" he asks.

The Frenches share a look. By now Edward is convinced that they know more about Mary than she does. He means this literally—more about the life and family she grew up in than she does, more about what people say about her, more about her legacy. "Oh," says Mrs. French. "We wouldn't want to make you listen to another whole story. We've been talking your ear off as it is."

Edward takes this opportunity to reprise the line that had won him such favor earlier in the morning—wouldn't want to pry; no, certainly—though he does wonder: this well-educated, upright, rich, perhaps beautiful young woman who never married. How did she become a farmer? Why a spinster? And what became of Thomas, presumably the titular heir?

As Edward has been reflecting, Mr. French seems also to have been forming a thought. At last it bursts forth with a little more vehemence than this careful manager has displayed previously. "One thing you should understand about all this. Miss Mary is a fine woman. She's known throughout the county for her charitable giving. She may not quite add up, but there will be a full church at her funeral. She got few mercies, but she followed the teachings of her religion as best she could."

Edward nods; it's all he can do. As far as he can recall, he is acquainted with no Catholics other than the Irish help. At this time he does not know that he will become a Catholic himself if Miss Mary bestows the Retreat upon him. Mrs. French is clambering up to clear the table. He wonders if there will be a sweet.

"She was a gracious lady," Mr. French continues. Edward thinks that perhaps he's going to get the whole story whether he wants it or not. "It's too bad you had to meet her now, when she's so ill. She's in great pain. Life has hardened her. She can't have been at her best this morning. Tea on the porch of the Mansion House was once a great affair, all the best ladies in the county coming to call." Mr. French pauses to grasp these moments, these images from not so long ago. "Twice a year she gave tea on the porch for everyone on the Retreat, everyone in Tuckertown who worked for us. You can imagine the talk about that, the colored coming right to the front door. Not that on any other day they'd try it; not that on any other day I myself would try to do it. But on those days it was what we were supposed to do. The mothers would spend weeks worrying about what the children were going to wear, telling them to behave. I remember Betty Gale talking with her boys on the way up the lane. *I got two words for you. Behave.*" Mr. French laughs.

Mrs. French returns from the kitchen with slices of pie. "First sweet potatoes of the season," she announces proudly.

Edward has never really thought of potatoes as having a season, of being either better or worse at any point during the year, and would never have imagined that a potato pie would be served for dessert. He takes a bite and finds it perhaps indistinguishable from pumpkin, perhaps more tart, and creamier. Quite delicious. She offers him another piece, and he takes it and admits he's never heard of sweet potato pie.

"Imagine that," says Mrs. French.

Once again there is a knocking on the kitchen door. Once again Mrs. French rights herself, limping a little now, Edward perceives, and from the kitchen comes a different sort of tone than earlier—friendship, pleasure. "Oral," she yells, "look who's come to call," and she returns to the room leading a remarkable-looking man, at once ancient and physically imposing, as if age has given him the appearance of wisdom without robbing him of his mature strength. His head is like an orb of black marble, face a perfect oval, mustache nearly completely gray. His glance is firm, perhaps avoiding Edward's eyes, but untroubled by the moment. His trunk and arms are quite a bit more massive than Edward has been imagining—heavy around the middle, broad red suspenders, a clean work shirt. Edward does not need to be told who this is. He had been imagining a more wiry physique; it didn't seem one would need such brute force to cultivate something as delicate as a peach, but that was many years ago. Mrs. French brings him fully into the room, looks at him sideways as he receives the first greetings, and gives him a warm and easy pat on his upper arm.

Mr. French has risen, gone over to shake his hand, and he introduces him to Edward. Edward returns the handshake, summons up a few words of respect, but he finds himself stripped of words. He can't imagine saying that they had been speaking of him, that he was pleased to meet him in person. Things like that. Polite things. To Edward's surprise, he can't imagine what to say to this man whose children's lives seem at this very moment to hang in the balance. Yes, twenty, thirty years ago, all of this, but in Edward's life only an hour or two, and he has been listening to these stories with interest, yes, with interest, but it was as if these people being spoken of were in a novel. One believes in fictional characters only as much as one needs to. But here in front of him is Abel Terrell, one of the main players in this . . . well, at this point "drama" would be the right word, but there seemed tragedy lurking ahead. Edward has the realization—the realization of a lifetime—that these stories were for keeps.

"What brings you up here?" asks Mr. French. He's pleased. Edward now knows the end of one of the strains of this narrative: Abel and the Frenches would seem to have survived their lives together as a good deal more than manager and employee, more indeed than merely friends. He wonders: Is Abel's wife—an odd name, what was it?—also still alive?

"Little Val dropped by," Abel answers, and Edward can't tell if he's trying to be subtle or trying to be completely forthright, because obviously he is saying that the Negro girl tipped him off about the Frenches' guest, and he wanted to come up and have a look.

"Well then," says Mrs. French, "let's go have a seat. Mr. Mason dropped by for lemonade and we got to telling old stories and, well, poor man, he hasn't gotten any peace since then."

"That a fact," says Abel, and he looks at Edward, yet Edward is still without words. He doesn't really understand why this man has so silenced him. Edward knows too much about him; he's been fodder for gossip. That's part of it. But maybe it's because the stories he's heard up to now, as bad as they are, still seem to have a good bit of worse ground to get through, that Abel in particular has more tragic events he must endure, and seeing the man now, it's as if Edward can foresee his agony, his death. The plot of the stories is prophecy for Abel. How could Edward speak from that unwelcome prospect? If Edward didn't already feel circumspect around the man, this last thought made him tremble.

Edward follows them back to the porch and takes the same seat he'd sat in all morning, facing the house. Through the doorway he can see half of a historical print about the signing of something, lots of men in wigs, lots of white men, now that he thinks about it; he'd meant to examine what it was, but he forgot to look on the way to lunch.

"So, Abel, how you getting on?" says Mrs. French.

"Good. Right good. Ruthie and me are right good."

Mrs. French turns to Edward to tell him what he has just figured out. "Abel's wife died, well, two months ago. Abel?"

"June the thirtieth."

"I'm very sorry to hear that," says Edward at last, and it is true: he *is* very sorry to hear it. He has only just met her, this strong woman who wouldn't take a gift without bargaining, who wouldn't see a hard fate without seeking to change it. Wait, thinks Edward. Una can't be dead. She's got more to do. She's got to mind Beal, solve the problem as mothers do, something.

"His daughter Esther lives with him, and Ruth and her family come by just as often as they can," she continues.

"A comfort, I'm sure." He is wondering about the girl, the pretty one.

There's a silence, and then Mr. French says, as if following Edward's lead, "Heard from Beal, Abel?"

"Oh, yeah. Beal's right good. She sends word from time to time."

Mr. French nods, but Edward understands that Beal is now far away, and not just in space. The word that comes "from time to time" does not come as often as any of them might wish.

The day has gotten hot, much hotter it seems than before they went in for lunch. The air is still. Edward feels he can hear individual droplets of water lapping the shoreline, the ripple of a single fish in the center of the creek. He wonders what is happening up at the Mansion House under this silencing dome of captured air. A beautiful place, but perhaps not a happy one. What will Edith make of it, if she ever sees it? He feels a long way away from her; he feels the distance between them and can wonder in an instant like this one whether their marriage will be as successful as all predicted, whether this whole foray to England will be good for them, whether this pregnancy will bear them a child. It all feels a little pointless, actually. In the thrall of all this history, no one seems to have a shred of free will. In the alternate recourse to science, as Miss Bayly is practicing it with her herd, as perhaps her father had practiced it with his trees, all enterprise is slave to natural forces that are only dimly and partially adumbrated. All slaves to something. Edward has been here for a few hours, and already his future seems as writ as Abel's, as if his life is a story being told by someone else, as if he is being dreamed, but dreamed willfully, with an ending in mind. He doesn't want to hear his story, would be terrified that someone might inadvertently say, *Oh yes, he died in England a few years later,* or, *After Edith left him, he married his first cousin Thelma and they had nine children,* or perhaps the worst, *Nobody knows what became of him. He got on the ship that day, and it was the last anyone heard of him.*

"Hot day for this late in the season," says Mr. French.

"Not a bit of air."

"You been keeping out of the sun, Abel? I saw you t'other day out in your garden. Not even a hat on your silly bald head."

"Sun never bothered me, Mrs. French."

The quiet is companionable; Edward feels that within these stray comments a very intimate kind of visiting is going on, built on bonds that grow out of sharing hard labor and deep history, neither of which Edward Mason knows anything about.

"Those days . . ." Mr. French begins, and then, because he realizes this might not be clear to the guest, he turns to Edward. "Days like this in the orchards, you can't imagine how closed in you'd feel. You'd look over your head and see the air just a few feet out of your reach. Sometimes you just wanted to chop every one of them down. Which was—" He stops. Which was evidently precisely what happened.

"We put in long hours," says Abel, "but no longer than Mister Wyatt."

"He did what he could," says Mrs. French. "The poor man. To work so hard and then have it all end so suddenly."

"Oh," says Abel. "We always knew what we were up against."

And Edward asks what it was, what they were up against.

The yellows. We always knew we were up against the yellows. Maybe at first I didn't know, but what did I know about peaches anyway? Mister Wyatt knew. He knew we were always up against the yellows.

In Pennsylvania, New Jersey, the Hudson River valley, growers had been fighting the peach yellows, fighting and losing the battles for years. This is an American disease. It started in the North, one tree I guess, then a few more. Like that. I don't know where that tree was, maybe just on a farm, a few peach trees, six or eight, and one day the missus goes out to see how they coming on, and there, on one tree the fruit seems to be damn near ripe and it's only July. At first she thinks it's a blessing, a miracle, fresh peaches here in New York not much past the Fourth. She's already thinking about dinnertime, fresh peaches and cream. She's thinking, *Well, maybe it has been unusually hot and dry these past few weeks, maybe that's it,* but truth is, the spring was wet and late and damned if they didn't think the last frost was going to wipe out the peaches for the year. But here's this fruit, big, tree-ripe. She stands back to look better at the tree and sees that in fact it isn't the whole tree ripening like that, but just one header—ten, fifteen fruit-bearing branches—so there goes the hot-summer theory. She's back to the miracle idea, and she's right, you might say, if all change in nature is a miracle. She doesn't know it, but her tree is the first peach tree in creation with the yellows, that God chose her hillside and her tree to announce part of His plan, sent Gabriel to breathe on her tree, and she's the first farmer, the first Eve in the garden who's sat and scratched her head and said, *Now, ain't that right peculiar.* Well, she thinks, enough of this staring good fortune in the face. She pulls out her apron and picks five or six; they're soft, easily bruised, ripe no matter how you say it. She carries them back to her house, lays them out on her worktable, and by now this whole thing is starting to spook her, this sight of ripe peaches on her worktable in July. She cuts into the first one. She's the first person ever to do this. She notices right away that the flesh has a lot of red in it, not just flecks of scarlet around the pit where we love to see it, but red coloring throughout the flesh, masses of flesh out to the skin soaked in a deep red, like the peach had been bleeding on the tree. She drops her knife, backs off a step, then steps forward again and picks up one of the halves, notices what she hadn't seen earlier, that the skin is spotted with red, the spots arranged in bands, you might say, a sort of warning. Hmmm, she thinks. She picks up a knife and cuts off a wedge, a small wedge, because now she's a little nervous about putting the thing in her mouth—imagine that, nervous about taking a bite from the peaches from her own trees, the best in the valley, the trees the neighbors envy and come to help pick because everyone knows she gets way more peaches than she knows what to do with. She bites off the tip of her wedge, isn't sure she got enough of a sample, and bites off half of it. Well, there's no taste to it. Wet, but not juicy, not sweet, just kind of tepid, salty if anything. There ain't much to the flesh, just this mass that dissolves into stringy paste on the tongue. She spits it out, hacks into two or three more, and sees the same thing, some even redder, some that look pretty normal, but when she tastes them, the same sickly result. When her husband and sons come in for the day she says, *Here now, Henry, look at this peach.* And he says, *Woman, why do I have to look at this peach?* but she's holding it right in front of him, and his mind goes through everything his wife's mind went through that afternoon, and he tastes it, and Henry's a man with a lot else on his mind in high summer, but this peach ain't right, and this tree ain't right, so let's say Henry's a man that don't wait for a weak calf to get her strength, or don't wait for a used-up horse to wander off in the pasture to die. He's a firm Bible-reading man who believes you must cast out the wicked and diseased, so the next morning he goes out and chops down that tree, even though the wife thinks that sawing off the header would be enough. He burns the tree on its own stump, and a few days later, when the coals are cool, he hooks up his team and pulls out the stump and burns it and its roots. And let's say that's the last of this nonsense this family sees in their lifetime, and even if they have a chance once in years to come to recall that strange early peach, they think it was over and done with when Henry burned the tree. But it wasn't. It was in the land, in the air. No one knew what-all, but the yellows had come.

Mister Wyatt knew that the yellows had wiped out the peach trees along the Hudson and in Connecticut and a good part of New Jersey, and by the time we were getting started, there was something up in Delaware and the peach business was moving our way, the stretches inland in Kent and Queen Anne's and Talbot counties. His plan was simple: Why just up there in Millington, where the river was little more than a trickle and the winds over Delaware picked up the dust and the pollen and disease? Why not here, where the Chester was three miles wide and the Bay was right around the point and the breezes came off the water clean and rich? That was, to listen to him, where peaches belonged in the first place. Peaches in Queen Anne's County were peaches catching up with their own virgin soil. Peaches lining the Bay, the rivers, thousands of miles of watercourses, good air and good drainage. Some protection from the frosts, that's what people thought, that peaches along considerable sheets of water suffered less damage from frost. Mister Wyatt had done a study of it; he was always studying over there in his office, late into the night, and no one to bother him, with Miss Ophelia away so much of the time. He'd done studies of apples and peaches in New England and cotton in Mississippi and even wine grapes in France, and he believed that crops being grown in the wrong place, the wrong soil, the wrong climate, the wrong time, these were the crops that were going to get something like the yellows. He thought that anything as sweet and fragile as a peach tree would be choosy about where it wanted to grow. He'd say, *Abel, why do you think wine grapes on one side of a river in France make wine and the grapes on the other bank make vinegar?* Well, I didn't know nothing about wine grapes in France, so I said, *Can't tell you, sir,* or *Wouldn't know, sir.* Mister Wyatt figured that sooner or later the peach tree would be led like Moses into the Promised Land. You may think that's funny, trees walking down the road on their roots toward a good place to live, but that was the way Mister Wyatt talked. Peach trees headed for the Retreat, a place so perfect to his way of thinking that anyone had to wonder whether he married Miss Ophelia for love or for the land. Mister Wyatt had all the money in the world to buy whatever he might have wanted, but the Retreat wasn't for sale.

If you think going to work for the Masons was an easy decision, then no one's told you about the Duke. But the war was over, the Duke was dead, and Mister Wyatt offered himself as a friend of the Negro. "You," he said to me—this was over in the farmyard, right about where the hospital barn is now, and he'd put the word out that all free men should have a job and good wages, but not many showed up, since the last time any colored showed up in numbers at the Retreat, they either got herded into a schooner or watched their friends and families get herded into a schooner. "You there," he said to me. "You look like a man that wants a good job for good wages."

Sure, I said, but who had a choice anyway? If I didn't want Ruth and Ruthie taken from us by the Orphans' Court, I had to work for a man powerful enough to stand up to them, and the Masons filled the bill. What devil do you want to make your deal with? We were living in Cookestown then, with my wife's family, and there were houses in Tuckertown empty. I didn't have any idea what he was fixing to plant; planting anything at all was a step in the right direction. No one was making money growing wheat, that was certain. There was a lot of land in those days that the forests were taking back. "Sure," I said. "I'm a man looking for a good job at good wages."

"Can you read, do figures?"

"Yessir, I can read. I can do figures."

"Ever eaten a peach?" he asked.

It wasn't a question I expected, but so what, back then you answered whatever it was and hoped for the best. "Sure, I've eaten a peach."

"A Maryland peach?"

"Well, sir, I'd say since it grew in my daddy's front yard, it was a Queen Anne's County peach."

"The best peach of all," he said, and that was how it started. He sent me back to Cookestown in a wagon with Pickle Hardy, and I packed up my wife and babies and we moved into the house in Tuckertown I live in today. The next day I was out clearing the first ground for rootstock. That was 1865, fifty-five years ago. The year Miss Mary was born.

We knew we were up against the yellows, but Mister Wyatt figured with the Retreat land and location we had the first part of the problem taken care of. From the beginning, we took care of that land, we nursed it, we gave it everything it ever wanted, as if it was a growing baby. In the early years we spent almost as much time cultivating the rivershore lands in preparation for replanting as we did on growing and grafting the trees. Cow manure, potash and phosphoric acid, superphosphate of lime and ashes, we spread it all on those acres, and you should have seen the wildflowers that sprang up there in the spring; this soil was so fertile you could spit on it and the next day you'd have an oak tree. You'd be afraid to walk on it for fear your boots would begin to take root. Mister Wyatt inspected every inch of that land, took test tube samples back to his office to analyze, which people made fun of: dirt in a test tube! *You know what this dirt is? No, Professor, what is it? This dirt is dirt.* All at the same time we were growing our own rootstock right on the Retreat, on virgin land fifty, a hundred miles from the yellows, and he was buying pits from canners in the Carolinas and budstock from growers in New Jersey whose trees had survived the yellows, *demonstrated their resistance.* That's what he said, and it got sad, at the end. *These trees had demonstrated their resistance,* he was still saying when the sky was black with the smoke of burning peachwood.

It wasn't as if Wyatt Bayly was ever going to trust these precautions; only that he would do whatever could be done at every stage, and if the yellows came, we'd be ready for them. We'd beat them back with our labor, our science, our good practices. Every year Mister Wyatt would make it known to the pickers that he'd give a quarter to the man, woman, or child who brought him fruit that gave evidence of having ripened early, a quarter if it turned out they be the yellows. People tried all sorts of tricks, but they never worked; Mister Wyatt was too smart, he knew too much to be fooled. An expert can't be fooled, that's what I thought. We kept our eyes open, cruised the orchards day by day when other work was slack. Those were the days when I learned about peaches, because Mister Wyatt was always talking, a quiet man normally, but a teacher in the orchards. I learned how to tell a variety just by looking at a square inch of the bark; there wasn't a blight or disease I couldn't spot from a hundred yards, brown rot, leaf curl, catfacing. I could look at a tree and just know it looked poorly, know it was sick, know it was infected with something and needed to be put out of its misery. Misery! Mister Wyatt had my mind twisted to his way of thinking, and I didn't mind at all, never did, never will, no matter what was to come. It was like I could feel my brain take it all in like food; I'd walk back home at the end of the day, and I was tired, but my mind was sharp; it was as if anytime my eyes alighted on something, a machine in my head started breaking it down into little bits of fact; I felt I could look at anything and understand it; I felt there was no mystery I couldn't solve if I put the machine onto it. Imagine what that felt like for a man from my circumstances. Even after yellow fever took our daughter Michal, I just thought I had to work harder so the next time around we'd be safe.

By '83 the Delaware peach industry was just about dead, so Mister Wyatt figured we had to get over there and learn what we could. I didn't expect that he meant I'd go along, but one morning in September at dawn, he was out in front in his runabout yelling for me, and my wife thought it was on account of trouble that he was there, but what he was saying is that we had to get going or we'd miss the train. Just like that. Do you think I had ever been on a train? Una was running around trying to iron my Sunday suit and shirt, mad at me I hadn't planned this better, but how was I supposed to know? And I was glad of that suit when I got on that passenger car, because I got taken notice of, you can be sure of that, but Mister Wyatt sat us down and we rode over to New Castle and didn't pay any mind to stares and grumbles.

A grower met us at the station, some acquaintance of Mister Wyatt, loaded me and my suit in the back of a market wagon, and we headed out to his farm. The fields all around the town seemed uncultivated, except that here or there were these tangled, blackened mounds, and it wasn't until we passed one close to the road that I realized they were the root clumps of peach trees, thousands of them left to rot. I thought it was the sorriest sight I'd ever see, until I saw the same mounds on the Retreat just a few years later. Across the way we saw the first stand of orchard, Mr. Thatcher's land, as it turned out. He was a right proper man, a man that looked as if he had done some labor, answered all of Mister Wyatt's questions on the way from town and didn't treat me with particular disrespect, but you could tell that he was about as played out as his trees.

Everyone knew that premature ripening was the first sign, but no one understood—no one except for one who had watched his life's work get hollowed out from the inside, like this man Thatcher—that from the first too-early ripening, from the first time you saw red spots on the skin, you might as well just mow the orchard down like corn. We headed off into the trees, didn't even stop for a cup of water. I was already sweating in my suit, worried about ripping the trousers; my wife made me wear it and would kill me if I ruined it. The man seemed to be in a hurry, a hurry to wrap this up. We'd come in the middle of something, as if he was packing and leaving for California. I almost expected to see furniture in the carts leaving his house, this square brick palace on the Delaware plain.

We stopped. "There," he said. "That's as good an example as any." In front of us was one sad tree. It pained me to gaze on something so unhealthy, as if I could feel the hurt of a man all stove in from life's work and arthritis. The tree seemed to be under attack not just from one disease, but from the plagues of Egypt, plague of locusts, plague of boils, plague of darkness. The leaves were pale, curled, and stiff; they were yellowing at the top of the tree, still green at the base, but they crumbled in the hand. It was covered in spiky little branchlets, like hog's bristle; the trunk, the headers, every branch of any size was being swarmed by these pests, this unnatural growth. Mister Wyatt reached forward and cut one of them off with his knife.

"Will they produce leaves?" he asked Mr. Thatcher.

"Yes. But the tree usually dies before that," he said.

"Did it bear this season?" I asked.

"I couldn't tell you about this one." A lot of trees to remember, but the fact was, if you asked Mister Wyatt that same question on the Retreat, he'd know the answer. "They can be fine one year and barren the next. Or set plenty of fruit, and it ripens in July and falls off the tree."

"And what treatment?" asked Mister Wyatt.

The man laughed, not at Mister Wyatt, not at the question, but at some of his private toils and troubles. That man, he took a lot out of us, myself and Mister Wyatt that day; he aged us ten years, and it wasn't his fault; he showed us what we came to see. "I cannot recommend anything," he said. "I have no success stories. I don't know why we ever got into this. I don't know what was so wrong with growing corn and wheat. One season out of three the peach crop is ruined by the frost. One season there's so much fruit you can't find baskets, and all you get is fifty cents for your trouble; the next season the earlies are fine and you figure you'll be all right, and the lates . . ." He didn't finish. He spat. "And this. Insects? Parasites? Fungus? Bacteria? Can't be insects, so it has to be fungus. Can't be bacteria, so it's got to be some other parasite. Seems to me there has got to be something else on the list, but I don't care anymore. I'll leave you to it."

He waved his hand down the line. "Over yonder you'll see some Smocks that look just fine, but don't draw conclusions from that. My neighbor's Smocks were the first to go. This isn't about varieties. When you're ready, my boy will give you a lift back to town." He began to walk away, but then turned. "Bayly, everyone says you're a real smart grower. Hell, I've even heard this boy here is a fine orchardist," he said, pointing at me. "I wish you well, but I don't think things are going to be well. I think you're next, is all. Good day."

Mister Wyatt had a black case with him, seemed a sort of a doctor's case, and in fact, that's what it was, a case with test tubes, boxes, wax envelopes, microscope slides. So we spent the next several hours gathering specimens—from the soil at the base of the diseased trees to the sickly leaves at the top, cuttings of buds and branchlets, smears of sap and fruit juice, bark, heartwood he extracted with a boring machine, root wood. He wasn't going to be next if he could help it; he was going to solve this; he was going to figure out just what it was that we were fighting. It's hard to fight an enemy if you can't get him in your sights, and that was the problem we had with the yellows: no one knew what they were. Thatcher was right: everyone knew what it wasn't, but no one knew what it was. We didn't talk much that day, a grim sort of mission over there in Delaware, to jump ahead into our future, to see what plagues the Lord had in mind for us. We didn't have anything to eat for lunch, but that never bothered me much, or him. My suit came through just fine. We worked until midafternoon, hitched a ride back to the train stop, and rode back home. Mister Wyatt looked into the yellows that day, and for the first time, he was scared. Who could not be troubled by the sights we saw, a whole way of life, it seemed, falling prey to disease. On the train coming back, every once in a while he'd say something like, *It's the good air of the watercourses, Abel. That's what's going to be the difference.* Or, *I saw no evidence of potash. I don't know why they didn't use potash.* I didn't say anything back, but we both knew that Mr. Thatcher meant it when he said they'd tried everything—potash, spraying with Paris green, pouring boiling water around the roots, sulphates and alkalies on the bark. He must have tried them all, and soon so would we, but by the time we were doing some of that, the heart had gone out of Mister Wyatt's fight. That was all in the future, but on that train ride home, we both could see it coming.

It hurts to recall those days, before the yellows, before we lost the children, before Mister Wyatt died. Hard to imagine that innocence could have survived the war, the strife; hard to believe that an innocence that could survive those times would be anything other than false hope, but it did, it was. In Tuckertown we made the mistakes of the innocent, the mistakes of the good-hearted. We had our disagreements. The Everett brothers were always making trouble for people, starting with themselves. Those brothers could fight; more than once they had to be pulled apart before one killed the other, and you wondered what drove them to feel such fury. But when one of them got fired by the Lloyds, the other quit, and they went to Pittsburgh, and they married sisters, so we heard. The Everetts were smart; they weren't going to live out their lives as field hands, which was the work they had at Blaketon, and even though they created quarrels all around them, everyone liked them. Sundays we'd be starting the dinner in the back and they'd smell the chicken or butt in the pit and come wandering over, one walking on ahead, the other waiting for the high sign. *Want some fine tomatoes to go wid' that? Want some nice yaller squash?* which was a joke because as soon as anyone had tomatoes or summer squash, everyone had more than they knew what to do with. They were handsome men, the Everetts, small but well made, clever with machinery, and the younger one, Daniel, had an eye on Tabitha Hollyday for years, but she lived with her parents not ten feet away. It was tight quarters; if you sneezed in Tuckertown, you'd get a *Lord bless you* from one side, and *Close that window, someone at Terrell's is sick again* from the other side. Not that Tabitha was a saint. There was always a little misbehaving going on. In those years there was a woman named Delilah Samson—that was her name, though I can't be sure it was the one her parents gave her—who lived in the last shack before the swamp, probably just squatting there, and maybe she had a husband and maybe she didn't, but there were always men around, and I think both Everetts paid calls down at that end from time to time. Delilah, a big woman, the kind of woman some men go crazy over. Aunt Zoe at the top of the lane, Delilah Samson at the bottom, quite a fair distance between them; one woman coiled like a spring, the other as loose as a dog.

But those Sundays in summer I'd start cooking a shoulder in the pit, and the Everetts would come over with their tomatoes and squash, and the Hollydays would bring down a chicken and throw it on, and Zoe and Mobby Gale and Zula and Robert Senior came down the road with buckwheat cakes and greens and lemonade, and we had peaches and syrup and peach pie and peach wine. I'd built a table on a pair of stumps behind our house, and people would bring over their chairs. Everyone still in church clothes, the girls with white ribbons in their hair. We were proud people. Most of us owned those houses, bought them over time at a fair price from Mister Wyatt, not given to us like we were sharecroppers. Some of us swept our yards and some of us let the grass grow, but we were all house-proud. We had furniture; the women made curtains and cut out pictures to put on the walls. We knew how to use our hands, not just our backs. Our children were getting schooling. We could sit together on those days and you could look around the yard and you'd say, *That Reggie Hollyday can make anything out of leather. There isn't a better mule driver in the state of Maryland than Uncle Pickle.* Zemirah Hardy and Zoe—Miss Fat and Miss Thin, the children called them—would sit and tell stories; they were sisters, and they were always arguing about who was the best cook, but being with Zemirah settled Zoe's mind a bit, took the demons out. The babies would crawl around the yard and the bigger children would play their games, and the men, Raymond Gould and Robert Senior Turner and Reggie Hollyday and Pickle Hardy and even the Everetts, could look at it all and know we were being given only what we'd worked for. We'd look at the troubles going on at the Retreat between Mister Wyatt and Miss Ophelia, and the plotting and conniving going on at Blaketon between those three Lloyd sons, and we'd feel we were the right people in the right place and would have switched places with no other people on earth. In the evening, after everyone had wandered back to their houses and after we'd done the dishes, my wife and I could sit on our front porch for a few minutes and feel that nothing was being denied us, nothing that really mattered.

What I see now is how it was all built on sand. Get in a balloon a hundred feet into the air and look down, and you'd see the line of our houses with the swamp at the end and the scrub forests threatening to engulf us; get five hundred feet in the air and you'd see the Retreat on one side and Blaketon on the other and the paths through the woods, and you'd recognize that the only reason we existed at all was to provide our labor; get a thousand feet in the air and you'd see all of Mason's Neck, and you'd begin to see how indifferent the land is to our hopes. Get ten thousand feet in the air and you have the whole county, and the Bay, and in the middle of it now is this little dot, what we called home. What we thought then was so firm and steadfast was just a little mote in the eye; you could blink it away and never think about it again. Well, I won't find fault with our innocence, even if it offended others. Even if others thought it was vainglory. Even if God thought we deserved to be knocked back a few pegs. But I've thought about those days a good bit. What were we doing wrong? That's the feeling I get about those days, that we were making mistakes we knew nothing about. I'm not talking about the peaches. Those peaches were dead from the moment we put the first pit in the ground—no mistakes in that, just science. I'm meaning we were trying to build a whole new country out of free men and women, free black and free white, and in Tuckertown we thought we'd done it. We lived better than half the whites we came in contact with, and that was how we measured equality. There was no lack of evil around us, but we thought change had come, freedom had come. We had come out of bondage. The Israelites enslaved in Babylon and Egypt had their Promised Land; we had our Maryland, neither North nor South but in the center, where the good things happen to people who mind their own business. Where the mercies happen. Back then, when all this started, more than any other time in the history of our country, we had the chance to do it right.

Ain't a disease a human gets, but in some ways I think we caught the yellows. When things began to turn sour, the first people who felt it was us.

Mister Wyatt had done his studies; by then he was saying that what was causing it, whatever it was, was just too small for his microscope to see. In October of 1888 he brought in an expert from Michigan, Professor Quigley, who had been writing about the yellows since early in the decade. I never saw such a sort of man as that, his stiff collar, his weak, soft hands; he smelled of powder and mustache wax, and he had two or three different monocles around his neck and a jeweler's loupe. Not the sort of person Mister Wyatt would favor, but he brought him in, and that afternoon we went out to the orchards, the professor and Mister Wyatt, Mr. French and me.

We got halfway out to the river, and he stopped to gather a small handful of soil in his palm and inspect it through one of the monocles. When he was done, he took out a large white handkerchief to wipe off his hands, and then he handed it to me to hold during the rest of the afternoon. "The orchard seems to be kept in a proper state of cultivation," he said, as if he was surprised. "The general health of an orchard begins in the soil. It is a well-known fact that if the digestive, circulatory, and respiratory organs in man are in their proper state, there is not near as much danger of the body contracting a disease."

We didn't need to bring someone in from Michigan to tell us that, and I expected Mister Wyatt to defend us, but he said nothing.

We started walking again, heading toward the lower river orchards, the place where we had lost the most trees. Lower land, only a few feet above the river level, but more than sandy enough to keep the roots from getting overwatered. There was no reason we could figure that this part of the orchards would be so much worse.

"Ah," he said, reaching out to rub his hands along the tips of the branchlets infecting a limb hanging over our path. He waved Mr. French and me over. "Observe these. A sure and infallible guide to the detection of the yellows."

I don't know why, but it fell to me to respond; maybe it always falls to the least among us to respond to the stupidest remark. "You don't say."

The professor wouldn't have dreamed he'd get sarcasm from a colored person, and he continued to list the clues and symptoms that had by then grown right familiar. Mister Wyatt didn't bother to cut him off; in fact, he seemed to be barely listening, so it was Mr. French and myself that had to listen to this stuff, about peculiarities of the bark. "Leaves are the lungs of the trees," he said. "Even a fool can detect fungoid growth." This last got a reaction from Mister Wyatt, but not much. I would have expected more from him; it was as if he was happy enough to bring this man all the way from Michigan just to have him call us fools.

"Here now," he said, pulling apart a slightly rotted section. We'd gotten to the corner where all the trees were dead; none of us liked to go there. There were marshes beyond the trees, and they smelled of decay. "Fungus mycelium." He held his hand out for his handkerchief, but he was directing his comments to Mister Wyatt. Even the professor had figured out by now that one of his students didn't seem to be paying much attention.

Mister Wyatt glanced at the sample, almost shrugged. "You're convinced that the yellows are a fungus?" he said finally.

"The disease—how can I put this more plainly?—is due to a fungoid growth in the aerial portions of the tree."

Mister Wyatt answered, but he didn't seem to be talking to this fool professor. As he had been doing these past few years, he was talking to himself. "I'm not saying there isn't a fungus in this tree. I am uncertain that it is related to the yellows."

The professor handed me his handkerchief; he was getting more from his student now than he bargained for. "It is caused either by a fungus or by a bacterium. As you would have little way of determining for yourself, microscopic analysis has revealed no bacterium in any constituent of the diseased tree or its fruit."

The professor had not seen Mister Wyatt's office, that was sure; he had more microscopes and scientific equipment than Johns Hopkins. He was hearing nothing new, but he didn't bother to correct the professor. "And how is it transmitted?" he asked.

The professor didn't like this. "Through the passage of spores or living mycelia. Through the winds distributing them hither and thither."

Mister Wyatt asked if insects played a role in this transmission. Here the professor went off on a long argument about why honeybees could not possibly be the cause. "Why is it that orchards close to affected orchards do not become diseased? Why is it possible in some cases that the disease is limited to only a few trees in a healthy orchard? Do we assume the honeybee only visits certain trees?" He added this last remark with a satisfied chuckle, as if this point always carried the day for him.

"I wasn't talking about bees," said Mister Wyatt. "I was talking about leaf-cutters."

And here they were off again; here is why Mister Wyatt seemed to have brought this man all the way from Michigan, not to learn how to fight the disease, but to debate its cause, to discuss a matter of botany as if it had nothing to do with our lives, our living. That's why he had hardly been paying attention most of the morning, not that we had heard anything new anyway. It was then that I realized Mister Wyatt had already given up. He hadn't brought this man from Michigan to consult on treatment, on how to save the Retreat's peach crop. He knew it was lost; he'd let us keep up the fight, but it was the trees themselves that were letting him down; he'd only go so far with a patient that had lost its will to live. "Why does this fungus, unlike any other, only grow on peach trees?" he asked.

This caused a bit of stammering from the professor. There was a tobacco fungus in Africa, he said, that was "similarly specific in its host." Was it not possible, asked Mister Wyatt, that the disease was in the pits, in the rootstock? Even I took note of that: the one thing I was certain of, the basis for everything we had done on the Retreat since 1866, was the purity of our rootstock. The professor offered a sarcastic snort. "No, Mr. Bayly, the fungus does not reside in the pits." I didn't understand most of what they were saying, but I can tell you this: you can watch two people arguing in a foreign language and you can get a pretty good idea of how things stand without understanding a word, and it was clear that day that Mister Wyatt didn't have the answers, but the professor didn't either. The difference was that Mister Wyatt was arguing for some cause that was new to science, and the professor wouldn't contemplate it. "What then is smallpox? What then is rabies?" That's what Mister Wyatt wanted to know. "*A plant does not get rabies,*" said the professor. "What you suggest is counter to all the experiences of botany. Absurd on its face. Wild superstition. If you don't mind my saying, the wild imaginings of the peasant."

What did it matter, in the end? Fine for Wyatt Bayly to treat everything we had done as a scientific study, but what was science going to do for us, for me? What was it going to do for this professor, whose life's work, even in his starched collar, remained out here among the trees. Oh, I got tired of being his handkerchief boy, but at least his heart was still in the fight. "Nature does not cure the yellows," the professor said, "so the farmer must. Simple as that. The farmer must continue the fight." And that was the way I saw it. Mister Wyatt had the luxury to back out of a fight he'd decided he was going to lose; he'd go through the motions because that's what a landowner does; he's got this vast plot of land and he's got to do something with it whether he wants to or not because people depend on him; but if he doesn't see the point, well then, you'd get someone who was sleepwalking like Mister

Wyatt was that day. What he didn't know was that most people, most of all colored people, spend their lives doing labor that has nothing to do with them, no enjoyment or product to be had that tastes of the sweat on our brows. So work was just the order of things, a way to live, to get food, to raise a family, to lie down with your wife from time to time. That was our lives; that was everything we had in Tuckertown. It was Mr. French's life; we were all in this as a business of living, and we saw the Retreat as a place to conduct this business, and now, for the man I admired the most of any person I ever met before or since, it was all about what could be seen with a better and better microscope, what could be filtered out with the finest mesh known to man, and what couldn't. That's where the science lesson ended in the lower orchard that day, amid the dying trees. Filters. Mesh. I didn't know what that meant, but I realized then that among all the people and livestock and crops and trees and products of Eden on the Retreat, it was the smallest of it all that was wiping us out. It was the snake in our Garden.

The next year, 1889, seemed like it was going to be a bad year. The trees began to blossom with an early spring in March, then the rains came, and a freeze, an ice storm, and we were back in winter for a few days and the cold sun made the orchards sparkle with crystals, and as beautiful as it was, it meant those pink blossoms were now hardened into the ice. The crop was lost, that's what we figured. We'd seen it before. But then a miracle happened. The cold passed and the ice melted, and the blossoms and buds just took up where they left off, as if they had been hibernating, and it was like this all over the county and everyone concluded that the ice had protected the trees from the deep freeze. There were jokes about growing peaches on the North Pole; people talked about dodging a bullet. I'm not sure it felt like that to me. By then we'd given up on the orchards by Queenstown Harbor, lost about five thousand trees to the yellows. Cut them down, dug them up, burned them. The smell of burning trees was constant all summer, all the next winter, the glow of fires along the river. Some of the children in Tuckertown coughed all the time.

By July of that year the evidence was plain to even our most unreliable pickers that the orchards on the Retreat were dying. Maybe half the trees were infected, the fruit all mushy, on the ground and rotting before we even set foot. You could smell it, this fermentation of rotten peach, and the hornets and yellow jackets were going crazy with all this abundance; we were all getting stung two or three times a day. When Mister Wyatt was in the orchards, he was on horseback, like a general getting reports that the right flank had failed. That year we tried to harvest only the healthy fruit, and it was possible to do it, teach the pickers how to tell the difference, dock them or fire them if they tried to fill up a basket with the diseased, but it didn't pay. The sorters couldn't keep up. Took the pickers too long, so we had to increase what we paid per basket. Mr. French told us it wouldn't pay before we even started; what was science for Mister Wyatt was dollars and cents for Mr. French, and at least dollars and cents was something we could see without a microscope, at least a day's wages would feed and clothe our families.

Everything was falling apart. Randall left for Howard and our daughters did what they could for their mama, but our house was a sad place, and my wife never recovered her hope. There was a darkness beginning to descend on Tuckertown; we could feel the tide turning against colored folk. In the Mansion House the troubles seemed to continue. Miss Mary still wasn't married, and Miss Ophelia was only there from time to time, and Mister Wyatt was starting to look old; every tree that died, every piece of misfortune, seemed to surprise him anew, as if ten or a hundred trees hadn't died the day before; he wore the look of a boxer who has just learned what a real punch, a foot-lifting jab, really feels like, has first learned that he doesn't belong in the ring with this opponent. The natural world had turned on him. He thought man led nature through science, when all we're really doing is following the twists and turns and gathering the leavings on the way. We were quite a pair out there in the orchards that winter—me fighting for my life and Mister Wyatt hobbled by this sense that God had betrayed him. We spent the winter marking trees with white paint for treatment with Paris green and potash, and with red for removal, and all winter you could hear the axes and saws at work and smell the fires smoldering, as if even flame was tired of all this. If it wasn't for

Mr. French—well, Mr. French and Miss Mary—we all would have given up, waited for the Retreat to wash away in the next hurricane.

So there we were one day, the three of us on the rivershore lands, not far from where the old dock had stood, just a few posts left, disappearing and reappearing with the tides. It was May, Miss Mary had come back, and we were all waiting to see what magic she could bring. The trees were budding—a sad sight, like an old dog still trying to run.

"Well, Abel?" Mister Wyatt had asked me how many trees I figured would give us good fruit.

I knew the answer but couldn't say it. So did he. Maybe none. If not none, then the few healthy trees would be so widely spread that it wouldn't pay to try to harvest them. It was over.

"Mr. French?"

"We've got eighty acres ready for corn," he said. "We could put two hundred acres in wheat in the fall."

"The peaches?"

"No." That was all Mr. French said. Not worth it, not wise, not a good bet. Not, in other words, the right crop for this land. The peaches, as it turned out, were just passing through. None of us had anything to say after that.

"They say Washington County will ship more peaches this year than any other county in Maryland." Mister Wyatt was almost talking to himself. "That's where the peaches are going, to the mountains, the Blue Ridge, the Cumberland Valley. Even to Georgia. Can you imagine that? Too hot in Georgia for peaches. They'll be wiped out in a decade."

"Yes, sir. I expect so."

"That professor was wrong, you know. It isn't a fungus. Stupidest thing I've ever heard."

We were all waiting for him to pronounce the end. To say that we would close down the peach operation and move the Retreat into some new line, small grains if Mr. French had his way. Dairy was what Miss Mary was thinking, but we didn't know that then. Yet we couldn't do any of it until Mister Wyatt said goodbye to his trees. That's why we had come out, to perform a funeral service. Mister Wyatt himself died two years later, but on this day we were burying our blood and sweat.

"There's nothing quite like a peach," said Mister Wyatt. "Just sweet enough. Good for the body. I had hopes for those Early Troths. How about you, Abel?"

I didn't know what all to say, so I answered that I found the Troths a little dry for my taste. Of the new early varieties we were planting, I preferred, I said, the St. Johns, better size, nice yellow flesh. But of all the earlies, I still liked the Hales.

"The Hales. Yes, a good fruit. But I'll tell you. All those earlies, the Hales and the Yorks, they are just marking time for the Crawfords. Now, that is a peach."

"Yes, sir," I said. "When you think of a peach, when you think of the peach you'd serve to the queen of England or the king of Spain, you're thinking of a Crawford." All this talk of peaches, my mouth was watering. This was getting a little crazy. I looked at Mr. French; it came to him, not me, to put the question.

"Mister Wyatt," he said. "Is this it?"

"Oh, surely," he answered, as if Mr. French was a little stupid for asking. "Surely you don't think we have a future here in peaches. Damnedest thing I ever saw. A plant that just up and quit."

So that was it. That summer we started to dig up the last twenty thousand trees. The piles kept burning for months. In the fall we planted winter wheat in and around the fires, and next spring the mounds were still hot and red with coals. I never want to smell that again; makes me heave to recall it. All that work, up in smoke.

Back then, we had our hands too full to think. What surprises me now about the whole thing is how short the success was and how sudden the end. A rise and fall of a whole industry, a way of life. Twenty-five years. That's nothing. People have been fishing and harvesting the Bay for thousands of years; imagine if it only took them twenty-five years to fish it clean of life. Even tobacco: it took a hundred years for tobacco to play out the soil. But this. I was a young man when the peaches began and still in the middle of life when it finished, and now another thirty years have passed and I am still here, telling this story. How could my life last longer than a tree?

I don't care what anyone says: it was the failure of the peaches that killed Mister Wyatt. And you know what? He was right about the yellows. Mr. French can tell you about this better than me. It wasn't a fungus, wasn't a bacteria. It was what you call a virus. A millionth of an inch across, they guess. No one's seen one, but they know they're there. Some Dutchman figured that out, but Mister Wyatt knew it all along. That's just one more sad thing: if he'd lived, if he'd kept at it, maybe he'd be the one the world over that gets the credit for discovering these viruses. And you want to know how they think the disease is transmitted from tree to tree? Leaf-cutters. I wonder if the professor is still alive. *The most harmless insect in God's kingdom.* Credit wouldn't have meant anything to Mister Wyatt, but I'm sorry he didn't live to see it all confirmed, because it would have pleased him to know that logic and observation had led him to the truth, even if we had no knowledge that could prove it. He would have admired that; it was science, after all, that he really cared about. So that's what we were up against.

(Now you keep out of the sun, you hear? Abel, these hot days I don't want to see you walking around in the sun with no hat on that shiny bald head.)

Well now. Miss Mary came back from France in July of '82, seventeen years old, went back to Baltimore to Miss Davis's, and the next year entered the Notre Dame of Maryland Collegiate Institute for Young Ladies in Baltimore, all part of her mother's plan, announced to Mister Wyatt one night without consultation. Notre Dame, she had heard, was now offering college-level studies for the daughters of elite Catholic families all over America, especially the Catholic daughters of Maryland. These daughters had brothers; Mary would study for two more years and then, certainly, would have attracted a suitable husband. This was the plan. The School Sisters of Notre Dame were from Bavaria, but quite acceptable nonetheless; Mary would acquire German. In 1876 President Ulysses S. Grant had presided over the first commencement; he was not a favorite, but his niece, Bessie Sharp, was a student there, a good Catholic girl. Notre Dame was in the process of seeking a charter to become the first degree-granting Catholic college for women in America.

Wyatt called it an attractive novelty and left it at that. They were sitting at dinner, a rare family gathering. Ophelia and Mary had returned to the Retreat for the summer. It was hot, with almost no air coming in the open French doors on two sides of the room; the candles didn't even flicker. Mary and Thomas were both silent, appraising each other back and forth across the table as their parents' awkward reunion unfolded. What Mary saw was a young male of the species, which was a promotion of sorts for him. What Thomas saw was a slightly less perverse version of the older sister who had bedeviled him for years. Neither Mary nor Thomas could know that from this time onward, few decisions she would make in the years to come would be unrelated to calculations about Thomas's well-being. He would never have imagined that Mary was his guardian angel, and at least for him, it turned out that the power of angels was almost unlimited. For Mary, it turned out that the source of angelic power was self-sacrifice.

Solomon brought in the dinner, a roast pheasant, which he deposited warily. He seemed to regard Mary with curiosity, Ophelia with fear. He backed into the darkness of the pantry without the usual banter about the weather or the occasional wry comment about Zoe's mood. Wyatt had forgotten how the staff mistrusted Ophelia, and as one more complication in these moments of conflicting emotions, it struck him as unfair that she should be forever shackled to her father—the Duke. No one was trying harder to escape what went on at the dock with the man from Virginia than Ophelia; she had sailed to Europe trying to outrun the schooner.

Wyatt looked at Mary, his daughter so long away that at times he simply forgot about her, thought of the two children in his life as Thomas and Randall. The light accentuated her profile; it was her blunt chin rather than her substantial nose that gave her a slightly manly look; still, a striking girl, perhaps not a beauty to anyone other than her parents, but no one would overlook her. Wyatt supposed that when her portrait joined the others on the walls of the Retreat, descendants would give it notice. Perhaps the portrait would not capture the dominion of her height, but neither would it reveal her gawkiness. Physically, thought Wyatt, Mary was as graceless as a heron. But determined. He wished Thomas had more of this, was sturdy like Mary. Well—that he was as sturdy and as quick and as clever as Randall.

"I'm delighted you will be returning to Mount Vernon Place," he said. Ophelia had just finalized the purchase of a house in the shadow of the monument, where she had been renting since the return from France and the rupture with her sister-in-law, who still blamed her for Cynthia's and Dolly's failures at the Hôtel Biron. The new house was just a few blocks from the Catholic Basilica. "Not much happening here, eh, Thomas?"

"Well," said Thomas, "I bet we're more fun than a pack of German nuns."

"Thomas. Show some respect," Ophelia snapped.

Mary glared at him and then appealed to her father for support. "Papa, there is still so much I want to learn. I hope to get a college degree."

"I gather that there are very fine colleges for women in New York and New England."

"Mary's place is not in New England among the Irish and the Unitarians. Baltimore is the seat of the church in America. Archbishop Gibbons is one of the country's foremost thinkers. Notre Dame of Maryland will become the Oxford and Cambridge of Catholic women in our country."

Wyatt did not argue this any further, though he considered adding that the archbishop, though born in Baltimore, was as Irish as Saint Patrick. Later that night Wyatt and Ophelia met in their bedroom, the bedcovers pulled back on both sides, her nightgown arrayed on her pillow, and amid the heat-soaked buzz of the tree frogs it could almost seem as if their marriage might continue for at least one night. But it was not to be. When Ophelia entered the room, she saw her nightgown on the bed and snatched it up, an involuntarily avid motion, full of pique at the servants who had not done as they were told. Wyatt observed this shirtless.

Ophelia looked at the garment in her hand as if unsure how it got there. "I'm sorry, Wyatt," she said. "I have decided to sleep in the linen prairie."

So, they would no longer sleep as man and wife. Wyatt could not say he was disappointed; nights with Ophelia were a rather distant memory. He could no longer in any way think of this woman and the person he married as the same; he admired her still—her determination to survive and outlast not just the Retreat, but history itself. Thus too went her faith: it was above history, as it was above the affairs of man. But now these instincts were turned against him. In truth, they had always been turned against him.

"I just think it is more proper," she said. "Perhaps . . ."

Perhaps what? wondered Wyatt. Perhaps she would visit for lovemaking from time to time. The linen prairie room was connected by an interior doorway. Perhaps she meant he should satisfy his male needs elsewhere. Well, he had been, from time to time. Had felt the touch of flesh, the firmness of another's body, had felt that no God, even Ophelia's, could deny him that.

Ophelia stood at the doorway, her hand on the knob, nightgown over her arm. "Thomas is a most unusual boy," she said. "If he isn't a scholar like Mary, he is a thinker. You should be proud. But I sense you have misgivings."

Wyatt, still shirtless, now bidding adieu to married life, did not want to enter into a discussion about Thomas, especially with the boy's erstwhile mother. "Thomas is an excellent student. I have no 'misgivings' about him whatsoever."

"And how is that other boy doing . . ." Ophelia seemed not to be finishing any of her sentences, trailing off into the void, her syntax floundering in the broad gulfs of their mutual experience.

"Randall. His name is Randall, and he is a remarkable young man. If you are right that this school you want Mary to go to will become our Oxford, then I predict that Randall Terrell will become the Abraham Lincoln of the colored. There is nothing between him and a distinguished career."

"I can see you mean that," she said. "And are things going well with our peaches?"

Our peaches. He noticed that she said "our." She might actually have been within her rights to say "my," but she didn't say "your." "Yes. Splendidly." He almost began a more detailed answer, the Waverly lands, Queenstown Heights, et cetera.

"That's marvelous. Good night, dear."

Ophelia closed the door to her new room, with its immense four-poster bed, as wide as it was long. She didn't know who had first called it the linen prairie. The room was in the corner of the house away from the water; next door to it was the room she had grown up in, had cowered in during the years of what she thought of as "her terror." The night view from there was across the graveyard, where the white marble stones seemed to swell in the moonlight as if being pushed from below, and then a cove and a scrubby point of land too small and wet for peaches, then the river, then the Bay. Betty Gale, who now always traveled with Ophelia despite having two children growing up with her parents in Tuckertown, had done what she was told—unpacked Ophelia's things into this armoire, put her brush and comb and nightcap on the washstand. Ophelia intended to ask Wyatt to install water closets in the Retreat; as she sat there combing out her hair, plumbers were engaged in modernizing the house on Mount Vernon Place in that fashion. Her nightgown; this was not an innocent mistake. This, Ophelia decided, was that terrible Tabitha's doing. Was there ever a house attended by a more ragtag corps of servants? The cook was crazy; the old—well, the *dear* old—Solomon was too frail to be trusted with a tray (that pheasant had almost taken a final flight to the floor); the girl Zula was a wordless simpleton; and Tabitha Hollyday was entirely too impertinent to be tolerated.

Ophelia dropped her undergarments to the floor and stood in the room naked for a moment, exposed to the moonlight, the ghosts, her memories. Her body's life journey. No one could have been more surprised than she that her body hair had grown in red, but then again, no one had warned her about body hair in the first place. The straw matting was cool on her feet. There was a small breeze coming across the orchards, and it was rich with the sweet fruit. For the rest of Ophelia's life, whenever she dreamed of the Retreat, the dream would bring with it the scent of peaches. One night years later, in a hotel in New York, she had a dream in which the perfume of peaches was so strong it woke her up, and the scent was still in the room the next morning; even the chambermaid remarked upon it. She had decided only today not to move back into Wyatt's bed, and only at the moment she saw the nightgown had she decided not to make love with him. She wasn't even sure, as she stood in the moonlight, proud of her nakedness, that she wouldn't now go in to be with him, but on balance, she had gotten used to celibacy. It was not the chastity of loneliness, not the abstinence of self-denial. Would the nuns be able to distinguish one sort of physical self-restraint from another? In this case it didn't matter; this was the purity of disinterest. There had been a man in Paris—a few daring conversations and then a note delivered, an inconceivable invitation late one night. Oh, but how silly to even think of that. She looked back at conjugal life with some fondness—she couldn't be certain she had ever experienced complete release, but she had felt physical pleasure—but no longer believed it would be decent with Wyatt. This thought motivated her to put on her nightgown. She wondered what Archbishop—perhaps soon to be Cardinal—Gibbons would say about her duties in her marriage; he was an intellectual, progressive in all things. She had not told Wyatt how much of her time in Baltimore was now taken up by being one of James Gibbons's "most trusted and reliable ladies." It was he who had insisted that Mary go to Notre Dame; as far as Ophelia was concerned, Mary's education had reached an appropriate level as it was. So much was swirling her head as she laid it on the pillow of the linen prairie. She would never get to sleep. Thomas—was she right to be so absent to him? Was it really Tabitha Hollyday who had put her nightgown on Wyatt's bed?

As Ophelia was attempting to calm the tumult in her head, her daughter was on her knees in front of the waterside window in her room, her elbows propped on the low windowsill. She had knelt to pray, but had been immediately distracted by the window and by the opportunity to resume a posture she had assumed countless times as a child, her small, bony elbows on the sill, her chin in her sticky palms. The fireflies were swarming over the terraces, leaving their short streaks upward, always upward, always as they rose. This supreme effort of light—it probably hurt to do it; the insects' bodies were probably sore and achy afterward. The brush, the water elms, and the cattails had grown considerably over the past few years, and Mary could no longer see the immediate waters of the creek, only the broader expanse of the river. In Paris she had missed the wide sheets of water, though the Seine, with all its traffic, offered the same kind of escape for the imagination. In Baltimore the harbor was a foul-smelling slough. She could not try to imagine what might be coming for her, but this would always be her home. Her mother's demons had not turned her against the Retreat; her mother's constant harping on the glittering opportunities of Baltimore had not completely convinced her. She made a note to say precisely this to her father in the morning. She was glad to be home, to see Thomas; she was almost old enough to appreciate what an evil sibling she had been to him—almost old enough, but not quite. He was so irritating sometimes. Especially tonight, when he made that comment about the Germans, though Mary herself wasn't entirely thrilled by the thought. There were several German nuns at the Hôtel, and she had liked them, but the French ladies were always making mean comments about them behind their backs. Mary was glad to see her father, but troubled by the coldness of her parents' greeting. She had overheard Tabitha and Zula talking about it: *Did you see that? The meeting of Robert E. Lee and Ulysses S. Grant.* And then, from Hattie's Mary, *You watch yourself, girl, or she's going to throw you out.*

Do I really want to be married? she asked herself.

She stood up and reached for her nightgown. A sprig of lavender fell out as she unfolded it—Hattie's Mary's doing, an old joke, really. Solomon tended the flower gardens and Hattie's Mary had gotten into this habit of folding a blossom into Mary's nightdress. She smiled at the thought. It seemed a very dear thing to do. She had no idea how old they were, but they were ancient, perhaps not long for this world. Suddenly, in the pit of her stomach, she felt a terrible longing for this home, a sudden fright that though it would always be home for her, it might not always exist. It was not permanent; that's one thing her mother had learned when they feared the mobs would come and burn them out. It could all be gone in an instant, washed away by rising waters, lost in a family feud, bankrupted by bad luck or bad decisions, cast off and abandoned like a sod hut in Kansas after a family moved on. Mary was still holding her nightgown, but swaying with this buffet of possible ends, this *eschatologie,* as she had learned to call it. Yes, she had been away for a long time. Hattie's Mary and Solomon were getting old, her father looked thin, tanned but thin, and Thomas was no longer a child. Over the years, she had just assumed that time stood still on the Retreat during her absences, but now she realized the opposite was the case: time accelerates during absence. The changes come quicker, the blink of an eye. Oh, she thought, what do I want? In front of her now: Mother de Lapeyrouse. *Ni une sainte ni une épouse.* Why had she said that to her? Neither a saint nor a wife. What was left for her to be?

Enough. She walked over to the door that connected with Thomas's room and listened for a while until she could make out his breathing. Still, she made sure the lock was turned before undressing and getting into her nightgown. She blew out the lamp. Her mother had told her that Mount Vernon Place was being wired for electricity, a marvel beyond imagining, light simply by pushing a button. As the curl of smoke rose above the lamp chimney, with its oily but reassuring odor, the scent of the close of another day in her life, Mary wasn't sure electricity was something she or anyone else would really need. She crawled into bed and lay on her back, staring at the ceiling. How many beds, she wondered, had she slept in during her life? She counted them: here on the Retreat, a crib, the baby bed, this one, Baltimore, Towson, bunks on the Atlantic crossings, hotels on the way to and from Paris, her cubicle at the Hôtel: fourteen, she decided. Fourteen pillows where she had trusted herself to God—and to her father or her mother or her host, or ship captains and hotel concierges, or the Sisters of the Sacré-Cœur—to keep her safe while she slept. *Should I die before I wake.* She wondered why safety was suddenly on her mind, why everything seemed so mutable. Sands shifting; Thomas says the duck pond inlet is widening, the whole river shoreline evolving. *Was it a vision, or a waking dream? / Fled is that music:—do I wake or sleep?* The Germans would never let her read poetry. Lord, preserve Mama and Papa and Thomas and Hattie's Mary and Solomon, and the Retreat.

With Ophelia at the Retreat, Mary's days were largely filled with calls to the Lloyds, the Wrights, the Peales, and the Cookes. Sooner or later these teatime conversations would end up with some cousin of someone being mentioned, and Mary quickly learned that "cousins" equaled "boys" or young men, or not-so-young men. She would have liked to meet young men, but she didn't get the feeling that what was being offered was the cream of the crop. "Would Mary like to meet our cousins from Talbot County?" The first step in the dance to snag a Mason—even if a Mason only on the maternal side, still a considerable catch. Ophelia was no more receptive to these suggestions than Mary: these "cousins" were from the Eastern Shore; they weren't Catholic;

they were not at all what Ophelia had in mind. Marrying some Cooke from Easton was not why Mary had been sent to Paris.

"It would be lovely," Ophelia would say, "but perhaps next summer. Mary has so much to do to prepare for college in the fall."

"College? I would have thought she was done with that" was how Mrs. Cooke replied, frosty, angry even, wondering why in the hell Ophelia Bayly had brought this awkward, too-tall and too-well-educated-for-her-own-good girl to call if she was going to snub what seemed, in the circumstances, a most generous offer. Typical Mason arrogance. This was an offer that would not be made again.

Once Ophelia had exhausted these potential avenues toward a marriage for Mary—she'd had no expectations that anyone suitable would be located on this side of the Bay; it was due diligence at best—she went back to Baltimore to supervise the modernizations, as she called them. Wyatt did not ask if she planned to live among the plumbers and electricians, or whether she had made other arrangements. The night before she left, she visited him in his bed, and it was pleasurable for her, but of all the faces to appear in front of her at the moment of Wyatt's climax, there was Archbishop Gibbons in Lenten purple.

Mary was now free to resume her father's side of the covenant, in the orchards, but if she had previously observed it all at her father's side, this year she dove into the labor. There was fellowship to be had. Harvest, the most pagan of feasts—even if the progression from early fruit to late fruit meant that picking continued throughout the summer, the moment of reaping what was sowed was special. Everyone felt it. Mary had seen many times before the way sweat-stained shirts and brows seemed to equalize—for a moment—the divisions, owner and hand, white and black. She had seen this but had not really understood it until her time at the Hôtel, when so much labor was apportioned and shared. At the Hôtel, Mary was never as happy as when working alongside one of the ladies, sewing, arranging the linens, sweeping the chapel, seeing to the vestments and altarpieces. The ladies said it all the time after a long day: *J'ai reçu bien plus que j'ai donné.* As far as Mary was concerned, what was received was a human gift, the pleasure of being able to do useful things with ones' hands alongside many other hands. Being selected by one of the sisters to do chores was a privilege, and everyone felt it; God was in the Hôtel always, within them all during worship and prayer, but never as present as in the fellowship of work.

Mary found the same thing in the orchards. She knew that what was pleasure for her was relentless labor for the families in the orchards, but amid all this toil there was joy. There was fellowship. Working from tree to tree, sometimes falling into partnership with another picker—usually with no idea who it was among dozens of families that spent the summer on the Retreat—for the morning, adopting a rhythm: *You get the high branches, I'll get the low.* Mary's height had never before seemed to her to be a virtue. *This tree's late, we'll get it in a few days.* Or not even having to say that, just a glance at the fruit and a nod and then moving on. Or sometimes working alone, slowing down to do a perfect job on a single tree, the diminished basket tokens not a problem for Mary as it would be for the pickers. She knew that in some way she was taking work from others who needed it very much, so performing less was a virtue. In any event, the job was a race against time; there was plenty for everyone before there would be nothing for anyone to do. It was the women who fascinated her. She admired these women, their strong, sinewy bodies, their lack of complaint. The women, the mothers and the older girls, they were not living the life they wanted. They had fallen, their husbands had lost the land they were working, they were migrants, they had been caught; or they were the "peach girls" hired right off the boat, not a word of English, but tough young women with none of the consolations of the hearth; or they were white girls from poor families in town who appeared out of the mists in the morning in twos and threes and were picked up at night by men in wagons—their fathers, presumably—who greeted them with palms out. Very soon Mary figured out that if anyone was ever out there slacking, anyone with a scheming eye who'd be all work and noise when her father or Mr. French came by and then slink back a row or two into the trees when he was gone, well, if there was anyone out there like that, it was a man, a husband, a father, a son.

Their women would defend them when they caught Mary's eye—*Don't you judge him, you don't know how we got here*—but they couldn't deny anything. Their husbands were worthless. They drank. They considered only the insults they had received, never the mercies. If these women had fallen low, it was because their men had dragged them down.

In the fall she rejoined her mother at the new house, in Baltimore, which was still very much invaded by odd people and devices—spools of wire, lengths of cast-iron pipe, a water closet cistern sitting in the back hall for weeks—and she commenced her studies with the German nuns of Notre Dame. She could not fault them for their scholarship, particularly in the sciences. It was a stern life, the girls all dressed in black cashmere or wool, with linen aprons—a school uniform that was varied only once, on graduation day, with white muslin and sash and gloves.

As usual, Mary excelled in her studies, and though the school could not yet grant college degrees, the nuns were determined to offer college-level courses, and they were hard, and at least once a month a girl would be sent back home for failing to keep up. Each time this happened, Mary recalled her own shame when her cousins Cynthia and Dolly had withdrawn from Sacré-Cœur. She never saw her cousins now, or her aunts or her grandparents; Mary was well aware of multiple reasons for rifts between the two families, but more and more it seemed to her that the main reason was religion. One might have thought this was one difference between families that would become less pronounced over time, but her mother had simply let go of anything that wasn't connected to her faith. Mary was getting bored with Catholics. They never saw anyone, Mary and her mother, who wasn't Catholic, and her mother seemed to be spending all her time at the archbishop's office and the Basilica. It made sense, really: faithfulness to the Calverts' scheme for an English Catholic colony in the face of resistance from the Anglicans of Virginia—well, that was Ophelia's family, the Masons at their most noble. Ophelia decried this constancy as something akin to martyrdom. But it seemed to Mary that her mother was being wooed and inducted into a special preserve, a sect of sorts.

Often, in the evening, she would return home flushed, bubbling like a schoolgirl, behavior Mary herself had long since outgrown. As far as Mary could tell, the appeal was political as much as religious: the plight of the working Catholic, the exploitation of Catholic immigrants, the general condition of laboring families in America, the stain of slavery. Mary thought these were fine things to be concerned about, but her mother's new allegiances seemed to require a revised family history. One day at tea with Mrs. Neale and her daughter Tessa in a rather shabby and dark town house on Maryland Avenue, Mary heard her mother say, "Of course, my father manumitted his slaves well before the war. You can imagine how popular *that* was on the Eastern Shore."

"Well, it was true," said Ophelia on the way home. "There were no slaves on the Retreat after 1857."

The school families held occasional tea dances, Saturdays from four to six; it seemed rather odd—and in the context perhaps even indecent—for the mothers to parade their girls in front of eligible males, but Mary didn't complain. They did their best to keep these affairs beyond respectable: pages of prohibitions about dress and behavior. At the tea dances there was to be none of this fashionable nonsense about demi-toilette, much less a hint of evening wear. What was so wrong with a nice visiting dress such as any respectable girl or housewife would wear making a call, something any young woman would feel complemented her looks without exposing herself to unvirtuous thoughts? A nice velvet was appropriate for all seasons.

The dances were held in the day girls' parlors, the furniture pulled to the walls for the nuns and mothers to sit and observe. The music was provided by Sister Ingrid, a large and very busty pianist; the girls made fun of her doing crossovers. The sequence of dances was waltz, quadrille, polka. Absolutely no lancers or gallops. But. Well, the girls noticed that Sister Ingrid gave a few extra pops to her polkas, that something resembling a smile came to her lips whenever she sneaked in a new tune, that she always closed the afternoon with a spirited rendition of "*Die alte Heimat*," as if they could now all complete the concluding niceties and fan out directly into the streets of Munich.

The boys were Loyola students or Johns Hopkins Catholics recommended by Father McVeigh, the chaplain. The Loyola boys were from local families: Irish, Italian—second generation. Mary liked them for their lack of airs, but her mother wrinkled her nose when Mary told her their names, visibly recoiled when she heard that the handsome blond boy Mary had danced with twice was named Stephen Paderewski. Where were the brothers of classmates from the best English Catholic families? Mary was aware of only one brother of a friend, and he went to Princeton. The Catholics at Hopkins seemed mostly from New England, which Mary found uninteresting, but they often brought friends to the dances, many from distant lands—California, Brazil. Mary always hoped to find a French boy with whom she could speak the language, but she never did. She was taller than some of the boys, but thank God, no longer taller than most of them.

In the winter of her second year, Mary danced with a boy named Gregory Belin, a somewhat lonely-looking Hopkins student. He was attractive enough, with warm hazel eyes, a high brow; he was a trifle skinny, and the fashionable high collar he was wearing made his scrawny neck look like a turtle's. He bowed stiffly in front of Mary, and when she put out her hand to him, he led her to the dance floor. As they were waiting for Sister Ingrid to begin the waltz, he told her he was from Worcester, Massachusetts, that his father was part owner of a new venture called the Norton Emery Wheel Company, and that his mother had died when he was six. "Have you heard of vitrified Pulson's wheels?" he asked.

Mary said she had not.

"Does your father's business require him to cut stone or metal or other dense materials?" From the way he intoned this question, it was clear that this was the way he opened all conversations with girls.

Mary was beginning to write off this dance, but it was a relief to talk with someone who was even more nervous than she was. She answered that her father was a farmer, but her grandfather and uncle had been in various industries, and in fact, her family's business had been quarrying stone.

The boy's face brightened. "There now. Limestone? Sandstone?"

"Granite, I think. I don't believe the company still exists." Sister Ingrid had returned from a brief break and was now arranging her habit, her limbs, and her bosom in preparation for the waltz.

Mary's answer had taken away the bit of enthusiasm. "I don't think we cut granite," he said.

Gregory Belin was an earnest dancer; Mary had no great gift for dancing either, and when they stumbled, he held her tight and bounced his head in time until they could pick up the downbeat again. Mary was pleased to have him return to sit with her. He told her that his father had sent him to Hopkins to study engineering, but in fact he was more interested in a medical career. "Our motto is 'Knowledge for the world.' The university is modeled after the German system. It's Johns Hopkins, not John Hopkins. Did you know that?"

"All of you seem very sensitive on that point," she said. "I wouldn't think a single *s* would matter all that much."

"Well, at home no one gets it right." She had knocked him off his game, stripped him of his next topic. They sat silently for a few moments, like virtually all the other couples. The whole thing was a little excruciating. Mary could see the mothers mouthing words to their daughters: *The theater—ask him if he likes the theater.* She couldn't tell what her own mother was trying to communicate—*Cross my ankles?*—but she had to say or do something.

"I'm a day girl," she said. "When I went to a convent school in Paris, I felt sorry for the day girls, but I like it here."

She had given him four or five excellent topics of conversation, and he did not disappoint. By the time boys were circulating the room looking for their next partners, Mary had told Gregory a good deal about her life, ending with the fact that she lived on Mount Vernon Place and with an invitation to pay a call for tea.

"He seems quite acceptable," said Ophelia on the way home. "Belin? An odd name, but certainly not Irish. Most Catholics from Massachusetts are Irish. Not that this would matter, of course."

"I don't know that he's Catholic. Not all the Hopkins boys who come to our dances are."

Ophelia waved off this possibility. "He seems to be a fine choice."

"Choice?"

"Well. We'll see how he does at tea."

"Choice?" Mary asked again. "I'm not going to marry him."

Gregory Belin behaved well enough at tea, and through the winter and spring he called now and again for Mary to take a walk with him. He was very intent on his studies; Mary learned a great deal about his professors. In May they walked across the new French gardens of the square to Mr. Walters's house for the annual public viewing of his art collection. Gregory announced that this was fine, but in Worcester they were laying down plans for an art museum to become the grandest in America; Worcester, he had been insisting, would soon surpass Boston as the major city in New England, and it was then, walking back across the square through the fountains and statues and other amenities of civic pride, that Mary realized she was mightily tired of hearing about Worcester, Massachusetts, and about abrasives and grinding wheels, and that despite Gregory's father's efforts to widen the boy's horizons by sending him to Hopkins, he was headed back home as soon as he could. Suddenly this entire winter of visits and tea seemed a complete waste of her time. She had been making inconsequential chatter with him for months, and even if she could recite whole lists of teachers and friends and activities in his life, he knew nothing of her beyond what she had told him the afternoon they met. What was the purpose of all this? What had been accomplished? As far as conversation went, she found her little brother, Thomas, far more insightful and provocative. When they reached her stoop, she turned and said, "I will be going to our farm on the Eastern Shore as soon as school is out. I have enjoyed our time together. Goodbye."

She spent the next few summers on the Retreat, less involved with the picking than before, but with an increased interest in the business as a whole. She had taken a course in home economics at school that had been taught on a fairly high level, and she found the concepts and the accounting techniques surprisingly applicable. She often spent afternoons in the office with Mr. French. He felt somewhat invaded, scrutinized at first, but Mary had a gift for figures. Odd, he thought. He was the father of three daughters and recognized that all he wished for them was to be happily married. Mary too, he hoped, for her sake, but he couldn't imagine it. He grew to enjoy her visits to the otherwise rather solitary place where he made his living. He cleared a table for her to use as a desk and found a lamp for her on dark days, and at times when she wasn't there, he would look fondly at that corner and picture her bent over her figures, her black hair shining, her delicate coral ear, her unblemished cheek. How pleasant it was to have a pretty girl in the room! Mr. French thought all young women were pretty. The office was in the back of the shop complex, behind his father-in-law's smithy, Raymond Gould's harness shop, the woodworking and repair bay, where a never-ending cast of unreliable carpenters, wheelwrights, and tinkers somehow kept the whole operation functioning.

"Mr. French," Mary said one afternoon as she was putting on her bonnet to return to the Mansion House, "do you think we will survive the blights the way Papa says?" This was 1887.

"I couldn't comment on that, Miss Mary. I truly couldn't. I don't know anything about the peaches."

"But just what you hear."

In fact, Mr. French heard very little. Whenever Abel and Mister Wyatt talked about these things, their conversation seemed subverbal. They spoke a sort of tree language: Abel holding out a leaf; Mister Wyatt glancing at it, then offering a piece of bark; Abel nodding, swaying a bit on his feet; Abel here in his office the next day, asking him to order more potash.

"I think we have to trust your father. This year we've had some losses, but it still seems fine, as you know as well as I do."

She came by to see him on the day before she was to return to Baltimore, to thank him for the time he had taken teaching her the mechanics of the business, for his kindness to her and to her family. The way she said it, "kindness to my family," gripped him. Mister Wyatt was at war with the yellows and Miss Ophelia was at war with her own history; Thomas, now into adolescence, was a reticent boy, especially alongside the glittering Randall. And what was going on between Thomas and Beal: no storm cloud rose darker over the Retreat than this, not even the blight in the peaches. It came to Mr. French in that moment that Mary was the strong one, that the troubles she saw or foresaw for her mother, father, and brother weighed on her; that she would now go back to Baltimore and satisfy her mother's most conspicuous impulses, but she was asking him to keep an eye on Mister Wyatt and Thomas. *Your kindness to my family.* Mr. French felt tears coming to his eyes for this resolute, serious girl. He had, in that moment, an unwelcome thought that returned to him from time to time in the years to come: she should run from them all, excuse herself from the Retreat. But of all of them, Mary was the one who would not afford herself the option of running. He wasn't sure why he thought that. She would be the last one standing. If he had a job and a place on the Retreat in the years to come, it would be because Mary had created it. Mr. French saw this plainly. But this was not yet the case, and that afternoon he wanted to take her in his arms and reassure her as he would one of his daughters, which might have been appropriate for that moment, but in years to come would likely be the thing he wished he had not done. So when Mary put out her large gloved hand, he shook it and told her all would be well.

Mary had taken Catholic education as far as it would go, had even taken a third year somewhat surreptitiously, and the nuns had now conspired with the archbishop to bring her back to Notre Dame as a French tutor and a proctor of the chemistry laboratory, both jobs that needed filling, but mostly a ploy to continue her reading in history and theology. "You have depth, but you must plumb it," said Mother Ildephonse, a typically brief but trenchant comment from her. Mary still missed the ladies at the Sacré-Cœur, but these women—Mother Ildephonse, Sister Erica—were intellectuals; they were certain of themselves, did not defer, did not waste time. Mother Ildephonse was curt because she had things to do; Saint Ildephonse, Mary had learned, was famous for beginning many treatises but finishing very few. The ladies at Sacré-Cœur had always been busy, but that didn't mean they were accomplishing all that much. Her mother's life in Baltimore, even with her philanthropies and good works, seemed more and more designed simply to expend hours. So much wasted time. This was crazy.

In October she met the brother of one of her French students, an astonishingly handsome man named Oswald Stafford. His sister was Oriane Stafford, a beauty herself. It was a Saturday, and Oswald was picking up Oriane from school. He had waited for her in the day girls' parlor and was walking toward the door with her on his arm when Mary encountered them in the foyer, and Oswald had to nudge his sister in the side to make her introduce them. "This is Miss Bayly, my French tutor," she said. "And this is my brother, Mr. Stafford."

He gave a slight bow, and so did Mary, exactly what she had read one was supposed to do in *Our Deportment* by John H. Young, a book on etiquette her mother had given her. She recalled that the person who was introduced was supposed to initiate the conversation, but it was unclear in this instance who had been introduced to whom. Mary was carrying a pile of books: Friedrich Schleiermacher, Ernst Troeltsch, a heavy load. Oswald asked if she wanted to join them. He would be delighted to drive her to her door. She lived on Mount Vernon Place, did she not?

"Mr. Stafford," she said. "How is it that we have just met and already you know where I live?"

He was unperturbed. "Miss Bayly, I am not the only man in Baltimore who knows where you live."

Mary took this as a compliment—she believed it was, even if it was slightly unnerving—but responded that her mother would have sent the carriage already.

"Then perhaps next week your mother might give her coachman the afternoon off and allow us to give you a ride home."

"*Donnez le coachman un congé pour l'après-midi,*" said Oriane.

"Quite good, Oriane," said Mary. "*Ce n'est pas mal.*"

"Yes. Give the coachman *un congé,*" said her brother.

Mary disliked the affectation of sprinkling French terms into English, just as she had come to loathe the obverse, which was practiced by certain French girls at the Hôtel Biron. If they wanted to prove they knew English, why not speak English? Still, she liked this man, a tall man with sharp features quite like her own; their children, she couldn't help imagining as the carriage made its way home, would have classic profiles, substantial noses, strong chins. They would look almost

French. Ophelia was ecstatic: a Stafford. Oh yes, fine family. The father a colleague of Mr. Mapp at the railroad, and the son had a fine junior position there as well. A fine Catholic family, long allied with the Jesuits. They worshipped at St. Ignatius. A fine choice.

Mary was surprised, and again a little unnerved, when the following Saturday she found that Oriane had gone home in her father's coach and Oswald was waiting for her alone in his runabout. "I asked your mother's permission," he said when she hesitated before taking an arm into the seat.

"I'm sure she granted it willingly." Mary had never taken a ride in a runabout with any man but her father.

"I hoped you would be willing to take a drive."

Mary said she was, and tried to arrange herself in the seat in a way that did not look altogether too intimate, too public, too attached.

"I thought you might like to visit the zoo."

"The zoo? Goodness."

"Not the zoo?"

"No, the zoo would be very nice," she said, and then reflected that it was actually a charming idea, to have one's first drive to the zoo. Along the way he mentioned that he had brought a picnic, and they could dine "*sur l'herbe*" at the lake or on the grounds by the Music Pavilion, and Mary finally figured out that he and her mother had planned a full excursion for her, and she wasn't entirely pleased. She said nothing more.

"I hope I haven't been too forward. *Arriviste.* Isn't that the word?"

"Well, sort of. But no. This is nice."

"I really don't know French. Oriane told me I should learn some words to use with you. She said you'd be impressed."

"I think English is up to the task," she said, a little more acidly than she intended. "Oriane's a funny girl. She's quite calculating, wouldn't you say?"

"I won't tell her you said that, but of course. My father says I should learn to think the way she does. It would help me in business."

This guilelessness won her, this lack of subterfuge; it was as if his handsome looks had a way of getting out in front of him and he had to reel them back with self-deprecation. She wondered how much of the day's plans—the drive, the zoo, the picnic at the pavilion—was her mother's idea; if she asked him, she was sure he would tell her the answer. They went to the bear pit, saw the famous boa constrictors in the reptile shed, felt both sorry for and repulsed by the lonely, mangy ostrich, whose turkeylike face seemed to ask just how it had ended up, the only one of its species, in Baltimore, Maryland. They must have brought two and the mate died, Mary supposed.

"I think we can miss the three-legged duck," said Oswald. By now they had exchanged first names. Growing up, his family had called him Scoot, he said, and he was never sure that Oswald would suit him.

"I think it's a fine name. At my family's farm on the Eastern Shore there is a portrait of some Mason called Oswald. He hangs in the dining room in his ruff collar. I was always afraid he was criticizing my table manners."

They strolled through a flock of sheep back to the stables on the lawn below the property's original mansion, reclaimed the picnic basket, and ate their sandwiches and cider sitting on a blanket at the lake. A family with four dark-haired young girls in white dresses went by in a rented skiff; Mary waved, but the bigger girls seemed embarrassed to be seen in this silly family adventure. Mary had never been on such an outing; there was no place on the Retreat or in her parents' marriage for such a thing. After they finished their picnic, a servant appeared to take away the basket, and they settled on the lawn below the Music Pavilion to hear a concert of marches and other patriotic numbers, Irish reels and German polkas, selections from Italian operas and even a Ukrainian folk song that Mary had often heard the peach girls sing. There was no French tune, at least not one she recognized as such. Mary still felt a little sorry that she had cut off Oswald's game so quickly. Why would anyone ever like her? But here they were, chatting away between numbers; she was far removed at this moment from her normal life. It was a gay and diverse audience, and it was thrilling to be there, to hear the surges of pride and applause from clusters of each nationality as the band worked through a survey of Baltimore's immigrant populations. She and Oswald never lacked for things to say, and she was glad as dusk fell that the servants had picked up the runabout and were ready to take them home in the family barouche. He took his place opposite and not beside her; John H. Young would have approved. It had become cool, but they kept the top down, and she was glad for the carriage blanket and would have liked to have a warm body at her side. She would have liked him at her side. Streetlights were twinkling in the dusk, and the glow from the houses, even the most modest row houses, was inviting. All seemed still and serene, almost as if the hustle and bustle had stopped just for her, to give her a second to appreciate the sudden stateliness of these Baltimore scenes. Mary hadn't felt this way about a cityscape since she looked across the Parisian rooftops toward the Right Bank during Christmas at the Hôtel. She'd never spent a day like this, never spent time with a man she liked more than Oswald, and refused to answer her mother's questions when she got home, but didn't mind the fuss she was making. She was twenty-three years old, and at last, she thought she might be in love.

Was there room in her life for love? That's what Mary asked herself in the days that followed. It seemed that love must occupy so much of one's time, and she had taken now as a motto of sorts *Waste no time.* It seemed that love pushed everything aside in her head; it was a big-shouldered thing, a big, heedless bear, masculine in every respect. Oswald left his card with her mother at midweek, and on Thursday she received a sweet note of thanks for accompanying him to the park, asking her to the theater the coming Saturday, and if she accepted—as she most certainly would—that meant he would be obliged to call upon her the following day after attending Mass with his family. So as she saw it, four days of this first week of their courtship would be taken over by him, by thoughts of him, by certain rituals and artifacts and evidences of his affection. And even on the other days, she found it difficult to concentrate on Friedrich Schleiermacher and higher criticism, not to mention the girls in the chemistry lab or the tutees in French, save one. There always seemed to be calculations going on in her head, which in each case promised one correct but unattainable sum, a sort of numerology of infatuation: three days ago, two days from now; four years older; seven-tenths of a mile; eighteen minutes late.

"I'm sorry," he said on that occasion, returning his watch to his watch pocket.

Mary said she hadn't noticed.

"We'll still have plenty of time to get seated for the first curtain."

It seemed a little unlikely. But Mary agreed. "Yes," she said. *Yes, dear,* she almost said. During the week, she had read and reread John H. Young's warnings and admonitions in his chapter on courtship several times: *proper conduct of suitor; falsely encouraging a suit; a gentleman should not press an unwelcome suit; a lady's refusal; a doubtful answer.* She didn't think she was making any mistakes. There was much about the parents' authority and vigilance; her mother needed no invitation to *watch her daughter with a jealous care;* if anyone was *rashly entering into premature declarations,* it was Ophelia.

That winter Wyatt and Thomas came over to Baltimore for the holidays, and Oswald joined the family for Mass at the Basilica the day after Christmas, and after that he came to dinner. Her father seemed uncomfortable the whole time, unwilling to tolerate the stresses of Baltimore, the war between his family and his wife, the pretensions of this society. In the evenings he dressed in a swallowtail coat he appeared to have found in some back closet at the Retreat, and in that getup, with his tanned and gnarled hands and weathered face, he looked exactly like what he was, a farmer lost in the city. Thomas was seventeen, and if, as a younger child, he had too much going on in his head to converse, he was now generally monosyllabic. The women in Baltimore, the men on the Eastern Shore—what sort of family was this? If her mother had not become, for all intents, a nun, the life she was leading would have been scandalous. Mary knew of no other family like this, where the divisions seemed to have little to do with affection or lack of it, but more with place and history and sensibility. Through Oswald the family could reunite; he was such an unaffected, honest person. Even Thomas, maybe especially Thomas, could see that; her father could do nothing but respect his work on the railroad. For dinner Oswald was seated alone on one side of the table, Mary and Thomas on the other; from there she could admire him, the firm answers he gave her father, the slightly risqué way he jollied her mother, the kindness of his glances at Thomas, and, above all, the impression he gave that he could manage all this, that if he was on a hot seat it didn't discomfit him, that this was his family as much as hers.

"I find them fascinating," he said on their walk that afternoon. It was cold, and Mary was fashionably dressed in her ermine-trimmed coat and muff. Below them, down the hill in the harbor, the decks of the schooners and steamers were white from a Christmas Day snowfall. Oswald offered his arm as they went down the stoop; there was some ice, but when they reached the sidewalk, she withdrew her hand. He had been calling on her for two months now, and it had become easy; she knew how to act with a suitor who was not yet a beau. She was glad for the muff, as it gave her something to do with her hands. In fact, she wondered if that's why muffs were invented: to take care of the vexing problem of hands and arms during the earliest stages of a courtship. But they seemed now to be awaiting a new phase; it was as if a *suit*—if that's what this was—were a series of clauses and the real meaning was found in their conjunctions, the punctuation. At the moment, as much as anything, Mary was a French teacher, and this is the way she thought. Any clause could be connected with "and"; any clause could be redefined with "but"; at any time, a period could end it all. She was also a young woman feeling as if her future was not really in her hands.

"Fascinating? What does that mean?"

"Well," said Oswald. "I mean, your father is an unusual man."

Yes, Papa was an unusual man; nowhere did he seem more unusual than in Baltimore. "He takes his work very seriously," she said.

"As all men should," said Oswald.

"But," said Mary, "you find his work a little—" She paused. He was already forming a look of surprise. "A little *simple*?" The surprise was hers as well; this charge seemed unjust even to her, even as she voiced it.

"No. Why would I do that? I don't think farming is simple."

"I thought you might inquire about his research. He's a pomologist of very high accomplishment."

They had stopped to cross the street, and before they engaged in the elaborate process of his offering his arm, her withdrawing her hand from her muff, et cetera, he turned to her. "Mary, it was not my place to question him about his work. How can you think otherwise? It would be bad manners."

"Yes. Of course it would be," she said, taking his arm.

But Mary could not quite get out of her head a feeling that this was not all there was to it, that good manners would inevitably not show Papa in a good light, that in this life she was leading, there would seem to be no forum for her heedlessly dressed father to propound on his researches into peaches, their varieties, the best conditions for their growth, or their resistance to blight and disease. Would she want Oswald to carry on about the railroad? Well, no; that was just his business, but the peaches were her father's distinction; he was an expert. Papa was a scientist, a man of letters. It was science itself that did not seem to have a place in the life she was leading, and if there wasn't a place for science in her life, then there was no place for literature, for ideas.

The winter of 1889 was brutal, with the winds slicing up Cathedral Street from the harbor, but then there was an early spring. A festival feeling took over the streets of Baltimore for a week or so: *early March and already over sixty degrees!* Vegetation blooming with the suddenness of a freight train. A lingering on the streets to pass the time, winter over, a feeling of relief that another trial has been confronted and survived. But not for Mary. The trial was not the cold winter past, but the warm break upon them. That was the trial, that was the curse, that was what was dangerous. The peaches. The peaches had suffused her thinking from the day she was born, from those days when she used to go out with her mother to see the men at work. For Mary, no matter where she was, she was always living two lives in two different climate zones: there was always another clock ticking, a thermometer rising or falling, a branch budding, blossoming, fruiting or not. The peaches were her border state mentality—always two sides to the issue. *Yes, but is it good for the peaches?* The answer was usually no. When one grows up in a family where success and livelihood are dependent on something as fragile, as flimsy, as a peach tree, there is always an apocalypse on the horizon. And that spring, the spring of 1889, she knew that apocalypse was drawing closer and closer. Mary would have been the last person on earth to look beyond her father's own prophecies about the battles to save the orchards from the yellows, and he was still mum on the subject, but it was hard to avoid the likely conclusions.

Then, after these days of early spring, the inevitable happened, which was a cold rain and then a spine-chilling, rock-hard freeze, and on the streets of Baltimore everyone resumed that back-bent, shoulder-hunched posture, shrugging their collars over their ears, hands in their pockets, and Mary knew what it meant this time: the crop was ruined. In a day or two those lovely white petals, millions and millions and millions of them, would be turning brown and dropping, the promised yellow fruit just a hard, desiccated pea, a stone with no flesh. She'd seen this before. At dinner that night she asked her mother if she didn't worry about the freeze.

"Oh. Those peaches!"

"I don't know how Papa will bear this."

"Your father is one of the most resilient individuals I have ever known. He has lost peach crops before. He'll lose them again."

Two weeks later, after the spring had resumed its more normal course, she got a letter from her father saying that a miracle of sorts had occurred, the kind of miracle science offers every second of every day, which was that when the thaw began again and the crystals fell off the trees and branches and blossoms and the sun came out, the petals, which had retained their color within the artificial carapace of ice, proved in fact to be alive, untouched, unmarred by the weather. "One can only conclude," wrote Wyatt, "that the ice put the blossoms into a suspended state and, in the meantime, protected them from the effects of killing frost. One would have to wonder whether that might offer some sort of strategy in similar seasons in the years to come."

He sounded like his old inquisitive and deductive self, but when Mary returned to the Retreat in June, from the moment she pulled up to the portico, the gaunt and unsure figure waiting for them on the landing was all but unrecognizable to her.

And Thomas. The schooling in the Children's Office was done; in the fall he would be going to Philadelphia to begin college. Ophelia was impressed; she had now firmly settled in Catholic Baltimore, but she had never gotten over her girlhood sense that safety from all she feared and despised was to be found in Quaker Philadelphia. But Mary knew with one glance that all was not well with Thomas. One afternoon she engineered a walk with him down the loblolly-lined lane that led along the edge of the orchards; the familiar sights and sounds of harvest were going on to their left. "You don't go out for picking anymore?" she asked.

Thomas had reached his full height now, a couple of inches taller than Mary, and they resembled each other to an eerie degree. In some dim or shrouded lighting, Mary thought, their shared looks worked better for a girl; in more direct sun, better for a man. When they were old, she thought, they might both become stout, but never fat.

He had not answered her question. "Does Randall still work in the orchards?"

"Sure. I guess. He has to."

"And his sister, that girl . . ." She trailed off, but she knew her name perfectly well.

"Beal. Her name is Beal. When people don't want to acknowledge her, they pretend they don't know her name."

"Beal. Okay. You know, people are talking about how much time you spend with her."

"I know they're talking, but there's nothing to say, so they should quit it. Beal's my friend. Look around you, Mary. Who else do I have to talk to?" He gestured toward the orchards, the deep woods.

They walked for a few paces; it had been a dry summer, and the clay of the roadbed was shedding yellow dust. They were both wearing broad-brimmed straw hats against the harsh heat and light. Mary might have wished that this scene—her brother, their straw hats—reminded her of their childhood together, but it didn't; they didn't have any kind of childhood together. "Are you pleased about Philadelphia?"

"Why should I be?"

"Going to college. I wish I could have gone to the University of Pennsylvania. I'm sure Randall—"

"Can we not talk about Randall? Papa's sending him to college too. Isn't that enough?"

They reached the end of the lane. If they turned right, they would head toward Tuckertown and Cookestown. Straight ahead were two miles of Retreat woodlands, then the bogs and cattails of Sawmill Cove, then the open water of the Chester. Mary recognized with dismay that Thomas would do whatever she wanted him to do; if she started walking into the woods, he would follow without question. She did not think his mind was completely empty as they remained on that spot, but she could not intuit even the tiniest crack in this blank facade. "Have you quarreled with Randall?"

"No. We're just not this Thomas-and-Randall thing anymore. In case you haven't noticed, we haven't been friends for years. I'm tired of people asking me about him."

"Is this about your friendship with Beal?"

"No, it's about me. I would like, for once, for someone to consider what it is like to be me."

"I'm sorry," she said. "I was asking about you, but you didn't answer. So I was trying another tack. Do you understand?"

He said he did, but he wanted to be asked a question, a certain question in a certain kind of way, and Mary was tired of trying to figure out what it was.

"Isn't the point that in Philadelphia you'll have to contend with neither the peaches nor Randall and you'll be around young men your own age? Isn't that everything you're asking for? Isn't that why Papa is doing this?"

"Sure," he said.

Mary left it at that. It was hot, but there was a nice breeze, clean sea air from the high west, perfumed by the treetops and not the wetlands; hard for anyone who had never lived here to imagine the many different varieties of winds, their textures, their odors, and their effects on mood. Mary forgot this in Baltimore, where all city winds were the same: gritty, confused in the lee of buildings, funneled like furies down the boulevards.

"So," he said. "Are you going to marry Oswald?"

"I don't know. He hasn't asked me."

"Funny his name is Oswald. All spring I've been picturing him with a ruff collar. In tights, with a codpiece."

Mary couldn't help laughing; she'd imagined the collar, the floppy velvet toque, the jeweled device in his hand—whatever it was—even the tights, but never, of course, that other thing.

"Did you know that codpieces were padded to make them bigger?"

"Thomas. Please."

"Queen Elizabeth discouraged them. I think they were banned in the sumptuary laws. She said men's privates were 'untidy' and attention should not be called to them."

"Thomas. Is this what you have been studying in the Children's Office?"

"Yes. As a matter of fact, it is."

In midsummer Ophelia brought Oswald over to visit for a week. Mary allowed her mother to show him off. If they had been engaged, Ophelia could have thrown a glittering tea. *Why is he taking so long?* she asked so many times that she began to sound like a simpleton on the subject. *It's clear you would have wonderful lives together.* Mary didn't know why he was taking so long, had no real opinion of whether or not they would have wonderful lives together, and wasn't all that unhappy with the situation as it stood. Without the engagement, without even the encouragement to call him Mary's beau, Ophelia was forced to bring him along on calls as . . . what? Mary's *friend*? How undignified. Mary's *companion*? Two maiden ladies who live together are companions. In the end, Ophelia was reduced to calling him "our guest." She had not made the sacrifices she had made in order that Mary should have a houseguest. Oswald endured this with good humor; he was always good-humored, a lovely man, everyone said, an attentive man. And so handsome! In this visit Mary was almost overcome by his kindness—overcome in the sense that she could see almost nothing but his kindness, an ecstasy of kindness. He expressed interest in everything and everybody. Perhaps chastened by Mary's complaint of last Christmas, he spent his first days on the Retreat pursuing her father from one end of the orchards to the other. "He certainly asks a lot of questions," said Wyatt after day two.

"Don't be harsh, Papa. He wants you to know he's interested in your work."

One evening she and Oswald were waiting under his namesake's portrait for her parents and Thomas to come down for dinner. He was filled with admiring comments about the whole operation. "Majestic," he called it. Mary kept trying not to look above him, and trying not to laugh.

"I met Randall," he said. "A most extraordinary colored boy."

Mary flinched, eyes darted up at the doorway to make sure Thomas wasn't entering. "Yes," she said. "He is, but please don't say that to Thomas. You can imagine how Thomas feels with everybody raving about him."

When they returned to Baltimore, they seemed to have made a further step into intimacy, and in September, Oswald proposed to her. She accepted with a joy that seemed magnified, if not heightened, by inevitability. She recognized the difference but did not probe it as a means of measuring her commitment. It had all been done according to Young: Papa consulted, Mama informed, blessings from his parents conferred. There could be no sweeter or kinder man in Baltimore who wanted to marry her; for Ophelia, no more eligible Catholic man on earth. As far as Mary was concerned, Ophelia had a right to her triumph. The engagement tea was flawless. All who were invited accepted and attended: the Cardinal, his bishops, selected families of Notre Dame girls, even some Anglican society, including Wyatt's parents and Cecile, Mary's engagement achieving the end of a rift that had begun when Cynthia and Dolly were expelled from the Hôtel Biron. Mother Ildephonse came in the Cardinal's carriage, and as soon as she arrived in the parlor, she darted for the sandwiches and lemonade and spent the rest of the tea in a corner, a little threadbare mouse.

"I wish you the greatest happiness," she said when Mary ventured into the corner, which other guests had ceded to her. "Two of our best families."

"Doesn't Oriane look pretty?" said Mary. "Pretty" didn't quite cover it; Mary had idly wondered what it might be like to have a sister-in-law who was certain of becoming a legendary beauty; one could hardly avoid having one's looks compared with hers. She knew that Mother Ildephonse did not like Oriane and was not surprised to hear her say that the girl ought to be more respectful of the body and more wary of the flesh.

"And me, Mother? What should I be wary of?"

"Goodness, Mary. I'm not here to play Cassandra."

"No one ever believed her anyway," said Mary. She missed this sparring with Mother Ildephonse; she was no longer volunteering at the school.

"You have nothing but achievement in your future. You can do anything."

"Mother Lapeyrouse once said that I would find happiness neither in a religious vocation nor in marriage."

"*Ach*. The French!"

"But really."

"I wouldn't expect anything conventional for you. I wouldn't resist unconventional choices." She glanced around the room: enormous wealth, highest society, ambient chitchat saturated in the tones and inflections of impeccable manners. Ildephonse was the first nun Mary had known who actively disapproved of wealth. "We hope to begin granting bachelor's degrees in a year or two. Nothing would give me more pleasure than to confer our first upon you."

"Come back to college as a married lady?"

"Why not? Your Mother Lapeyrouse didn't say you couldn't become a scholar."

Once the announcements were over, Mary and Oswald entered into the deferred life of the affianced. Certain behavior was now permitted: walking with her arm in his, accepting small gifts—a porcelain farm girl, a glass millefiori paperweight. As she looked forward, she knew they would have to begin making plans for their first home, but she also knew that the mothers would take care of it. She thought a good deal about her duties to Oswald in marriage: to do whatever was best calculated to please him; to encourage and facilitate him, by the example of her own frugality; to be economical, thrifty, enterprising, and prosperous in his business. She had read that should the need arise, she should "calm his perturbed spirits." She had never known Oswald to be the slightest bit perturbed, but she supposed that when they shared all, he might be from time to time. One thing that never seemed to force its way into her thoughts, even though she wished it would, was physical intimacy. It might come at the end of a long train of speculations; *Oh yes, that!* she'd exclaim. Her desires had awakened in her adolescence, but now they seemed, like everything else, deferred. Trying to anticipate the sex act with Oswald was hopeless. She couldn't imagine him in a state of passion. Ever. She had read her Jane Austen, her Flaubert; she had witnessed on these pages the shimmering of desire; she knew that true passion, of even the most proper and chaste sort, was a physical sensation. It was something read by the body. *A certain feeling.* A classmate at Notre Dame had described to her a scene from a new Zola novel in which mine crews ended each day of work by proceeding en masse to a nearby field and having relations like goats and bunnies. That's what this girl had said—*having relations like goats and bunnies.* Mary wondered how this girl had happened to get her hands on such a book, whether she had in fact merely heard of it, and whether it was true that such scenes could be in a novel and that such things could actually happen in real life. She wanted to ask her mother a very simple question: *If I don't desire him, if he doesn't give me that certain feeling, does that mean I don't love him?* But why ask a question, especially one as important as that, when you know what the answer will be, and whatever the answer is, you won't believe it. In fact, Mary could think of only one person whose answer she really would believe, whose opinion would really be useful, and that was Oswald himself.

In April she got a letter from her father in which he told her that he feared all was lost. "The life cycle of this disease is now well established, and on that basis, we are now at the end," he said with the dispassion of the scientist. "So much work. I fear for our employees," he added, with his enlightened regard for others. "I do not know how I will be able to bear the decisions in the months to come," he concluded, a scientist with a heart broken by the immutable logic and doleful progress of an incurable disease.

She and her mother were having tea as she read this letter. At reading that last line, she let it drop to her lap. "The peaches are dying," she said.

This news did not even make her mother slow the stream of tea into her cup.

"This time it may be for good." Her mother took a lump of sugar, held it in the tongs in front of her eyes, and flicked off a tiny bit of lint.

"I must go to the Retreat to be with him," Mary said.

At this, Ophelia did finally look up from her tea ceremony. She made an exasperated sound, a guttural hiss that sounded vaguely Polish. The Polish families in Fells Point, her current project. That's where she had found Dorota—lovely person, splendid cook, who made a hiss through the gap in her front teeth when something went awry.

"And Thomas."

This time the hiss couldn't work. Mary usually avoided saying his name, in order to avoid the outpouring of justifications, as indeed was occurring right now. *Made more sense . . . what he wanted . . . Wyatt's idea, that colored boy.* "By all reports," Ophelia concluded, "he is doing fine at the university. He is standing at the cusp."

"That's fine, Mama. I just feel that I am needed on the Retreat this summer. There's no reason for you to come."

"But what about your husband?" Her mother had been jumping the gun like this ever since the engagement. The wedding date had still not been set.

"I don't have a husband."

"At this rate you never will."

"Then whether I go to the Retreat or not won't matter to the husband I'll never have."

"You know perfectly well what I mean. Has Oswald given permission for this?"

Permission, Mary repeated to herself. When, she wondered, would there be a word or a concept or a custom associated with marriage that didn't seem designed to rob her of her dignity? "Oswald would never in a million years think I had to obtain his permission to spend the summer on the Retreat," she said, and it was true: none of this circumspection of her behavior ever came from him. *Oswald let you walk home alone? I must speak to him.*

"Oswald is too lax. I must speak to him," she answered.

"This is pointless, Mama," said Mary, standing up and reaching for her hat. "I must excuse myself."

"Please," said her mother, urging her back to her seat. "I'm very worried. I am worried that you are letting this wonderful marriage slip away." She raised her hand to stop Mary from interrupting, but in fact, Mary had not intended to say anything. "You both are too young to understand that even during these simple and glorious days of your engagement, you must be learning how to be together. The way you behave now will have great significance as you become established."

"Do you see any relaxation of Oswald's commitment?"

"Of course not. Not yet. But if you go off to the Retreat for the summer, what is he supposed to make of it?"

"I would think he would have respect for my devotion to my family."

"But that's exactly the point!" Ophelia exclaimed. "It couldn't have been any clearer if I had said it myself. Don't you see?"

Mary didn't see; she shrugged.

"It's devotion to *your* family. Your devotion is now due to *his* family. That is one way to demonstrate that you are completely ready to be his wife." She reached for her napkin; desperate tears were beginning to run down her cheeks. "Mary, what's to become of you if you don't marry Oswald? I can't bear to think of it."

"You are making all this up. I love Oswald and am going to marry him next summer. Why are we having this conversation?"

"Oh, the Retreat! That place!" Ophelia exclaimed. Mary had not seen her mother so exercised in years. "My marriage could have been so glorious: a fine and unusual man, a standing in society, but that place destroyed it. Now it is going to destroy yours."

"I wouldn't be going there just to be there. I would be going there for my father and my brother."

Ophelia ignored this distinction; it didn't exist for her—people, family, place: all the same. *Don't you see?* "Mary, the Retreat belongs to the Mason family. It came to me as a burden by accident, mistake, through senseless tragedy. But you're not a Mason. You don't have to be a Mason. You were born of the Baylys of Baltimore, and when you're married to Oswald, you will be a Stafford, a fine family. You will have returned to a family of the Faith. The Retreat, the peaches, the mules, the Negroes: they're Wyatt's problem. They're Thomas's problem, and he will take them on because that is his duty. But you are free of it. Tell me you understand that. You are free of the Retreat! For the last twenty years I have done everything I can do to free you of it. Promise me you will reconsider this plan to spend the summer there."

"I will," said Mary.

"You won't. You're going. I can see it in your eyes."

Mary blinked, but couldn't deny it.

"Then promise me this. Promise me you won't die there."

"Mama, whatever do you mean?"

"I mean what I say. Promise me one thing in all this, that you will not breathe your last breath on the Retreat. If I am assured of that, then I can hope for much more."

"All right."

"Don't you 'all right' me, Mary. Get down on your knees and make that promise to me properly."

Mary went the following week, even though a new letter from her father arrived a few days later. There was yet some hope, he said. Disaster might be averted. "I would not want you to feel that you must return, especially at this time of your engagement," he said, a line Mary knew he was transcribing from some frantic message dispatched to him from her mother after their conversation at tea. There wasn't even a tinge of irony to signal that he was saying this only because Ophelia made him; at first this disappointed Mary, but in the end it convinced her it was time to get home and see what was going on.

She was met at the peach dock not by her father, not by Mr. French, but by Tabitha and Robert Junior Turner. Even as the steamer nudged the pilings, she wasn't sure who the man was alongside Tabitha, and it was only a guess that this was he. She hadn't seen him in years. His father, Robert Senior, was often spoken of highly, maybe the next in line to Abel Terrell among the colored, but Robert Junior had never been liked. He was beckoned onto the steamer to unload Mary's trunks.

"That's Robert Turner?" she asked Tabitha.

"Robert Junior. Yes, ma'am."

"I guess I expected my father to be here."

"Yes, ma'am," said Tabitha again. "You surely must have."

"And?" said Mary.

"It's good you're back, Miss Mary. The heavens are bursting, is all I can say."

Robert Junior and the stewards loaded her luggage onto the carriage, and then came the earsplitting whistle blast from the steamer. Tabitha and Robert Junior waited for her as she watched the ship drift away from the pier in the current and begin to froth its way upriver. It seemed to be sailing off for good, as if she were being abandoned on an island. She understood the moment. She recognized her choices. She need not overstate her mission: the family was in disarray, clearly leaderless, but still, very plainly, this disembarking felt as if she had shifted her own flag and, for good or ill, was planting it on the Retreat.

They took off through what had once been the rivershore orchards, but there was no sound of labor, none of the fellowship she had once enjoyed in this place. Most of the trees were dead. Their bare, gnarled, and twisted branches made it seem that a battle had been fought on this terrain, that cannon-shot and minié balls had turned it overnight into a splintered wasteland. The fires were burning upwind, and as the carriage entered a cloud of smoke, Mary gripped her scarf to her nose and mouth. The smoke had some of the fragrance of Indian sandalwood in it, but it cloyed, was too sugary, like scorched chocolate.

Robert Junior and Tabitha were seated in front. There was something between them, Mary could tell that; they were a delegation, even if self-appointed. Their portfolio was not the farm, the business, or Mr. French would have met her himself. Theirs was the Mansion House. Mary wouldn't have chosen either one of them, but perhaps these were the people through whom she would have to work her will.

"How is Papa?" she asked through the folds of smoke.

Tabitha turned. "He's going about his business. He's still thinking he can win this."

"Really?" said Mary. "Do you believe he thinks that, or is he just saying it?"

Tabitha took a moment to answer. The smoke had thickened, and she waited with tight lips for the cloud to dissipate and then exhaled deeply. Mary could see peach smoke on her breath. "What he needs is for someone to tell him to let it go. That has to be you. No one else can do it."

No one else could. Mary could see it happening, night after night, slowly bringing her father to that understanding, interrupting the hopeless travails in his study, him hunched over his books and papers under the light of his kerosene student lamp, her saying, *Papa, come to bed*. Saying, *Papa, you're just one man; you can't stop the yellows all by yourself*. Saying, *Papa, it's cruel to prolong this; we must move forward.*

"And what about Thomas?" asked Mary.

Robert Junior turned his head to look at Tabitha. "We can't rightly say," she answered after a pause. "We haven't seen him since Christmas." Robert coughed once and then looked away. Mary had heard nothing about Thomas's Christmas recess at the Retreat. She'd seen him in Baltimore for a few days, and she'd been pleased to see that his face had matured, that girls at the theater kept stealing glances at him. Mary had been proud of him, but still, he did not steal any glances back. Mary got very little out of him about college; he spent most of his visit to Baltimore in his room.

They pulled up to the Mansion House and her father came to the landing as if he were surprised or delighted or flattered by this unnecessary gesture, but as soon as Mary looked into his lined face, she felt the troubles, the duties, the whole mess being passed along the sight lines from his eyes to hers and into her being. She knew she had done the right thing. But she had waited too long to do it. And when she was alone again with Tabitha, unpacking her things, she turned to her. "What did you mean about Thomas, that you 'can't rightly say'? What went on here at Christmas?"

It was clear that Tabitha had been waiting for this question, maybe hoping it would come, but she started with a disclaimer. "You got your daddy to think about, Miss Mary. You ain't mama to Thomas."

"But what?"

"He behaved himself as best he could, but we didn't gather any sort of change," she said.

"You mean about Beal?"

"Yes. That's what I mean."

"What about Randall?"

"Yes, Miss Mary. Thomas and Randall had a real set-to, so I gather. No one else was there."

"Will Randall give us time?"

"For what?"

"You know what I mean. No one likes what is going on any more than Randall does. But will he give us time to end it or is he going to try to do it himself? I don't have time to pretend I don't know what is going on. What do you think Randall is going to do about Thomas and Beal?"

This time, when Tabitha said she didn't know, she was telling the truth. "Maybe they'll get over it on their own. They's just children."

"Yes," said Mary, feeling reassured by this. Beal was probably the only young lady Thomas had ever spoken to. The first. The only. He seemed to have no interest in these matters, which struck her as alarming in itself, though she did have to concede that at his age, she herself had found the whole thing tiresome. "He doesn't know what love is. Not the honest kind that can last."

"Of course not."

"As you say. Still a boy."

A month later, after Mary had persuaded her father to accept the end, she found herself heading once more back across the Bay. Oswald met her at the steamship terminal on Light Street. Lean, as handsome as ever, but so white. What an odd reaction, thought Mary, but here it was. She'd never really noticed how pale his coloring was, how English his skin compared with her father or Mr. French, who were tanned and weathered, but here was her Oswald in a stiffer, taller, and whiter collar than she had ever seen him wear, and it attenuated his neck and made his head seem as if it would simply become invisible in the glare. Why, she wondered, in the tension of this greeting, this fixation on his skin tone and his collar, on this vision of evaporation? Because at the same time she saw his kindness, his regard for her, his forgiveness and complete understanding of what she had felt she had to do. It was at that instant, in those first few moments, taking his hand to enter the carriage, hearing his orders to the coachman, that she realized her mother had been right, completely right: he had given her too much freedom; at age twenty-five a woman must bind to a family, adopt its customs, assume its burdens, and she had chosen—or been chosen by—her own, not Oswald's. This was now irrevocable. It did not come with any particular dread or joy; it was not about east or west, father or mother. Oswald could have said a dozen noes along the way that would have brought her back onto the path toward their wedding, but he had not. Because he respected her, was just the sort of person you'd want to marry. Who wouldn't want a man so kind and thoughtful? He'd make a wonderful husband, a warm father, an upstanding citizen. If I am ever to marry, she thought, it will have to be someone like Oswald. When they reached Mount Vernon Place and settled into the parlor while the maids were bringing in her things and her mother was nowhere to be found, she realized that Oswald had already told Ophelia that he would be releasing her from their engagement, and he assumed she would accept.

"I'm sorry," she said. "You are too kind."

"Doing the right thing is not a matter of kindness. We have our duties; we have our hearts; we have our judgments."

"Yes," she said, feeling as if she were at a train station watching a departure, the last observation car now sliding past her, now beginning to recede, to pick up speed, to leave without her, soon to become a mere dot balancing above the shiny rails, like a memory. One never wants to be left behind; if there is leaving behind to do, one would rather be on the train than on the platform, but that doesn't mean it is the right place to be.

As it turned out, Oswald Stafford never married either. He rose in business with his family's money behind him, and he practiced all the philanthropies and good works on his side of the Bay that Mary was practicing on hers, and from time to time she thought how silly this was, the two of them living these parallel lives, walking similar paths, duplicating each other's efforts. How much simpler, how much more efficient it would have been had they married after all. She missed companionship. In fact, sometimes she felt she had made a mistake in not marrying him, but then again, there were those rumors, loud enough to have reached her across the Bay, about Oswald's bachelor life and his companion, Dickie Bennett, the two of them a most handsome pair.

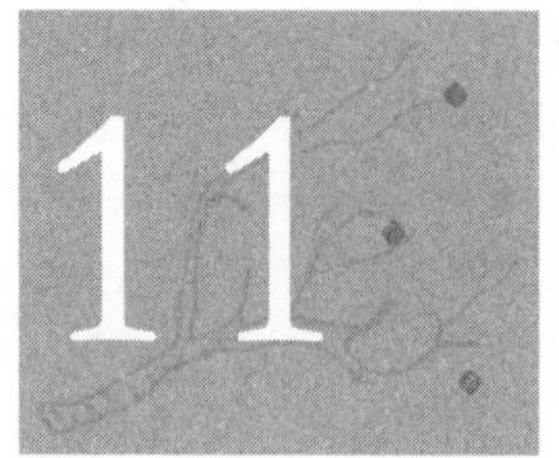

True love is forbidden love. That's what Thomas believed. That's what his short stint of university study had confirmed for him. A forbidden love creates the arguments against itself, but in so doing conserves its flame. Love is about overcoming. Love is not a state of mind or spirit, it is a reward. There is no place in literature for love that faces no barriers, not much drama if the man acquires blessings from the parents and offers his proposal and the woman accepts and children follow and certainly one or two of the children might die in infancy, and perhaps the woman lives out a slightly longer period of widowhood than she would have preferred, but all in all, a good life, a good marriage. None of that in the texts Thomas studied at the University of Pennsylvania. Nowhere to be found. Instead, infernal machines mauling doomed couples in the gearworks. Why would fate so devise it that simple desire was not enough? A joke, that's what it was. It was the gods on Parnassus amusing themselves by dreaming up the worst conceivable unions and then tossing the lovers into a rudderless boat on a stormy sea. Devising the most perverse trials: not only must Orpheus not look at Eurydice, he can't even tell her why. Fiendish! We turn to Pyramus and Thisbe, lovers for the ages reduced to whispering through a crack in the wall. Put a man and a woman together, raise them together, but then forbid their love? What did anyone expect would happen? Genius! Dido and Aeneas: Aeneas was a fool, thought Thomas; he made the wrong choice. He made that argument in class, which brought a stunned reproach: Aeneas chose duty, he chose honor, he chose sacrifice! was the reply. Oh well, *Si vis amari, ama.* Abelard and Héloïse: unquenchable love, secret marriage, ruination and mutilation. Why that cheerless story to survive all these years when there were countless Pierres and Moniques, Marcels and Amélies, husbands and wives buried side by side in a country chuchyard whom no one has ever heard of? Romeo: "I know not how to tell thee who I am. My name, dear saint, is hateful to myself, because it is an enemy to thee." Why is the greatest love story of all times a story of forbidden love, and why, indeed, a tragedy? Thomas put aside any elements of poetics and asked the question simply on the level of material: Why would forbidden love hold its ascendancy in the minds of poets were it not the truest form? This is what Thomas wanted to know. Because true love is the love that tests, that stymies, that persists, that enforces even unto death, that can finally only flower *with* death. "Yet they do wink and yield, as love is blind, and enforces." Oh yes, thought Thomas, I have been naked and blind, the "naked blind boy in her naked seeing self." Thomas did not need old Professor Rosencrantz—I mean, Rosenzweig—much less Shakespeare, to tell him that. *Credula res amor est.*

And, dear Papa, this is not just literature. It is science: opposites attract. Celestial mechanics, forces that cannot be resisted, equations that cannot be disproved. Planets will draw together until they are crushed by their love. The cardinal doctrines of motion, force, energy, and potential? Nothing but forbidden love. Said Professor Terwilliger on the first day of his *famous* natural philosophy seminar, "The entire body of physics is a coherent and harmonious system of mechanical truths. Are there any questions?" What sort of question can be asked about a statement like that? Thomas gazed out the window at the Philadelphia skyline, wondering what he was doing there. You ask me for a coherent mechanical truth? he thinks. Love is a coherent mechanical truth, Newtonian in the extreme. To Hell with the apple dropping on his head, was Sir Isaac ever in love? Love is binomial. $(X + Y)^2 = x^2 + 2xy + y^2$. Love is the sum total of its own contraries: male and female. Yes and no. Subject and object. Plus and minus. Odd and even. Right and left. My heart and your heart. Black and white. Yes, of all the forbidden binomials, let us not forget black and white.

So with all this impediment, what was the force that drew lovers together, the gravity? Thomas had only one answer for that: his own. His own life. He fell in love when he was twelve, thirteen, fourteen, and that never goes away. Never. That love is in your marrow; it grew taut in your body as your bones lengthened into adulthood; it's in the lenses of your eyes, and for the rest of your life you will see the world through it; it's in your breath, lodged in the parts of your lungs high in your chest that flutter every time you think of her, and for the rest of your life your air will be perfumed by it; it's the sound of her voice stored deep in your ears, a note that can come to you at any time like the sharp ping of a triangle from a crowded orchestra floor, as if every other instrument is suddenly hushed; it's that part of your cheek that was once kissed and now pulsates like a butterfly when she is near; it's those first astonishing words of a love returned, heard previously only in the wildest of dreams, but now, miraculously, coming from her lips. It's all that. It's a force you can't stop, a force you shouldn't try to get between, because no one knows what will happen then. Thomas had tried. All those years when she was just the little brat who was spying on them, then the girl who actually wasn't so bad to play with if there was no one else around, then the doe who was suddenly long-limbed and graceful and mysterious behind those pale eyes, then the beauty that no one, even his sister, Mary, could ignore or deny. Through all that, Thomas had resisted loving her. No! he said to himself at night in bed, before allowing himself to ease into the fantasy that he had just forbidden. He resisted loving her, felt it was wrong because she was all but his sister, too close; you're not allowed to marry your sister; you're really not supposed to marry your cousin, even though half the Masons in the graveyard had done just that. Randall had said, *But she's our sister!* Yes, in many ways she was, and Thomas resisted loving her because of it. He resisted loving her because she wasn't Catholic, which his mother wouldn't tolerate, and she wasn't from the landed class, which he figured his father and Mary would find unusual, and he wasn't of the community, which he figured would worry her parents. So through his teenage years he resisted Beal for all those reasons, but never once did he feel he had to resist his love because she was black and he was white. He knew others would, the Lloyds, Zoe, the dairyman Turville, people who saw the world through black and white, but he had been raised differently. His heart was shaped differently. When he looked at a colored person, he knew he or she was colored, just the same way anyone would look at his mother and know she had red hair. The question was, Did it matter?

In Thomas's room at Mrs. McPherson's, his friends gathered to debate whether Kant was right that the only moral act was one for which one would receive nothing in return; whether Plato was justified in his fear of the written word; whether time flows as Heraclitus argued, or was it a succession of instants, per the Eleatics. They met, Timkins from Chestnut Hill, Whitney from Pittsburgh, Anderson from Michigan—not the smart set, but not the sons of merchants either—in Thomas's room because it was the largest, a corner room, and as November began to chill the air, it was revealed as the warmest room, directly above the kitchen. From the bench by the window Thomas could see the Schuylkill winding a green, steaming path along its trampled banks, water shedding its essence, and he could only wonder what difference any of this made—Kant and Plato, this education, this sojourn in Philadelphia, a heartless city, an imperial husk. Randall should be in this room debating the nature of time, not he.

On into the fall, inspired by their readings and studies, Thomas's friends came to debate the great classical issues of moral and natural philosophy, but they said nothing of love. They had never felt love, the real kind, the forbidden kind—just a warm ease nurtured by familiarity and the approving nods of parents. Matches like his sister Mary's to Oswald, which seemed a matter of business more than love; he'd watched them this past summer and seen nothing of love. Out of their meager experience, when the time came, Thomas's friends were quite confident that there would occur an alignment of interests. They were content to leave the matter there, and Thomas judged that they were probably correct in their expectations. Nothing to discuss, really. Let's get back to Kant.

In Philadelphia he talked about her as much as he could possibly get away with. *Beal thinks this. She and I love to do that. That reminds me of the time we.* He described how beautiful she was, her eyes, her soft skin, that she was almost as tall as he was. Most of his friends preferred short women. He wanted somehow to reveal that there was something exotic about her, but the closest he could come was to say that she was "interesting," and his friends debated that quality in a girl and agreed they all preferred "nice." He mentioned that her brother was a brilliant young scholar who was excelling in his studies at—well, safely at a distance at Vanderbilt, but once it was at Harvard, a mistake that required some backtracking—and that her father was recognized as an orchardist and agronomist of note. As for his family's resistance, the reason his love was forbidden—because this aspect of his love had been featured in his tales from the beginning—he bundled all the complaints into a single all-encompassing metaphor, which was that she was not Catholic. He presented this as a barrier that all, especially his mother, regretted, but which, tragically, couldn't be ignored; they all loved Beal, but in life we must recognize . . . Having compartmentalized in this way to deceive his friends, he began to accept it as the truth, and it astonished him how easily all the other impediments melted away, passed into insignificance, became the kinds of problems that could be ironed out in a single frank conversation. Could be removed by the Pope. In his isolation in Philadelphia, even he began to believe his own gloss. He began to believe that his being exiled was a stroke of fortune. When his parents and hers, and Mary and Randall, saw that a mere year apart had done nothing to quell their passion, they would relent. They would have much to adjust to, and he imagined that when they sat down to discuss it, race would definitely come up as an issue, but it would not be the only issue; it would not become packaged as the single all-encompassing problem that, in his talking to his friends, religion had become.

"I believe natural law favors biology," said Timkins. Thomas had begun truly to loathe Timkins, his foolish, relentless philosophizing. "This is what I have been saying. Don't you agree, Thomas?"

Thomas had lost the thread. "Oh. Certainly."

"I'm sure your buddy Randall would agree with me," said Timkins.

"I'll ask him the next time I see him." Thomas could picture the way Randall's mouth tightened at the corners when he was truly excited by what he had to say, the way his eyes savored ideas, delectable new bits to ponder. From the Children's Office had emerged a *philosophe*, a polymath worthy of Benjamin Franklin; that's what everyone said, even if to every word of praise they attached the proviso "for his race." But Randall, genius that everyone supposed him to be, a genius colored boy, knew nothing of love. His mother and his sisters lavished him with love; he'd never drawn an unloved breath. Randall, who had been so admired, so favored in Tuckertown, so loved that he never had an inkling of what it meant to need love, to be forced to seek love, to find it, to discover that it is forbidden, and to surrender to it anyway. Randall believed that love should make sense, that one could reason with love, just as one should be able to reason with a bear that is planning to eat you alive. He didn't understand that without love, you might as well let the bear do what it wants.

That fall Thomas wrote to Beal constantly, two or three letters crammed in a single envelope, but he could never see the way clear to put any of them into the mail. He pictured one of his letters being handed from house to house down the line in Tuckertown until it reached the Terrells', smudged with thumbprints after being weighed, appraised, held up to the light at each stop. *What all is this? A letter to Beal? Now, just what all is this about?* As the pages mounted, it became more and more impossible. But still he wrote because during that time at his desk they were joined as one. *Miss Beal Terrell*, he wrote on the envelopes. *Her name is Beal*, he thought. *Miss Beal.* He could write for an hour and not even know where the time went. He had no similar experience with his coursework, which was the purest drudgery; there was no argument about duty or career or integrity that he could make to himself that might turn his focus to his studies. When he wrote to Beal, the words danced on the page, each syllable with its own radiance, like a star; when he wrote about the English Civil War, the words were so inert it exhausted him to finish a sentence. He wrote to Beal as if these letters might one day take their place beside Abelard's, and that they might end up as evidence to prove his love, should it come to that. He was assembling a brief. As a result of this potential third audience, his letters were all very proper, chaste, but full of love. A little of the tone of the conversations with Timkins et al. But also an occasional memory from childhood. *Remember the time we spied on Tabitha when she . . .* And: *Do you love me as I love you?*

So, yes. Forbidden though it must be, for reasons known only to the creator of this mortal mess, love must happen. *Who bids abstain. / But our destroyer, foe to God and Man?* Professor Chew said, "Let us not suppose Milton is espousing fornication." Oh, Professor Chew had encountered a generation of boys drawn tumescent by the imagery of Adam and Eve in their bower, *Iris all hues, roses and Jessamine,* but Thomas could only look down the lecture hall to this desiccated husk and wonder what exactly he was afraid of. Why did he feel that even the mention of connubial love required this dose of saltpeter? What bowers had this man ever occupied? In his youth he and Mrs. Chew—since there must be one—must have found in the parlors of Philadelphia and the dance floors of Rittenhouse Square a fondness, an attraction, a reason to plight their troth, but was it *adoration pure / Which God likes best*? Could that moment when young Mrs. Chew—let's call her Miss Shipley—glided up to him, the daring moment of ladies' choice, compare to the gentle brush of lace and flower he had watched Beal's ankles—for he had seen and loved those ankles—pass through so heedlessly? Had Professor Chew ever greeted his bride emerging at dusk from the spicy forest of the orchards like Pomona, goddess of fruit trees? Unlikely. *Sleep on Blest pair.* That's the line Thomas was waiting for. And would he and Beal not be so blessed by a God who had created them both human and innocent?

By the time Christmas recess was upon him, Thomas had become so expert at forbidden love, at denial, at absence, that he had no idea how to act back at the Retreat. He had no expectation that he would see her; one could expect only what was possible. It was too cold for meetings at the bench or the peach dock, and there it was: more truths. If forbidden love must sometimes snatch its caresses in the back halls, true love was of the air, of the natural world. The poet had this right: a dwelling for love, *inwoven shade / laurel and Mirtle, and what higher grew / Of firm and fragrant leaf.* Thomas did not want to steal moments in the dark back hall, and how was this supposed to happen anyway?

He understood as well as anybody on the Retreat that what might have passed as permissible last summer would no longer do; those last days of the summer, the last days of their youth and innocence, had been a clock ticking, with everyone just holding their collective breath until it reached midnight, until Randall left for Howard and Thomas for Philadelphia. The Retreat was where their love had begun, but it was not a place where their love could flourish. So the few times he happened to catch sight of her—at the head of the Tuckertown lane one day when he was driving past; when she came to the Mansion House to help Tabitha walk Zoe home—he looked away, or she from him, which was almost as sweet as a greeting, this private resolve to accept nothing but fullness.

Instead, he saw Randall, who came up to the Mansion House a few times to call on Wyatt, to make his reports to his benefactor. Thomas had made his own reports, and had wondered why he bothered. "I have finished my first term," he had said. He'd barely passed; the only reason he did was because he had entered so far ahead of the typical college freshman.

"Splendid. I'm proud of you. I never had any doubt that"—Wyatt hesitated, and then quite deliberately added the word he'd been unsure of—"both of you would achieve distinction." His skin looked papery, and there was a slight odor of bleach or chlorites or human urine in the office.

"I am studying what you recommended."

"Yes. A solid classical grounding in the literary and scientific. Rhetoric and poetics. The laws of the natural sciences. An appreciation for the arts. You are becoming a complete man." Wyatt coughed, as if he did not believe this last statement. Thomas had rarely felt so unloved.

"So now what?"

"What do you mean?"

"What will you have me do now? You have created me for something. What is it?"

His father seemed surprised and then baffled and then apologetic, as if acknowledging that yes indeed, there had been some purpose there, but it had slipped his mind. Even this did not surprise or hurt

Thomas anew: he had long ago figured out that the future, his future, had very little to do with his father's educational project. He was an experiment that had gone slightly awry; he was a train off its tracks, a boat aground on a sandbar, a mule backward in its traces.

"You are becoming ready to join the ranks of educated men," said his father at last, and Thomas was dismissed.

The last time Randall came to call, he and Thomas encountered each other warily outside Wyatt's office, but after a semester of Timkins, the mere sight of Randall gave Thomas a burst of joy. He no longer cared that his father certainly more eagerly and hungrily received Randall's news than his own; over the months, Thomas had successfully recalibrated his needs, and they no longer included either one of his parents. Randall was in a suit, a college boy. They shook hands, and Thomas gave him a questioning look and nodded toward his father's door. Randall returned a small shrug, but he drew his mouth and cheeks tight with concern. For so many years they had communicated in this wordless way—*How do you think he's doing? Not all that good*—and at the end of it they both laughed at this reunion in code. Thomas followed Randall to the kitchen, which for once was empty, and they sat down at the worktable. "So how is it in Washington?" Thomas asked. "Your school. Howard."

"Well, it wasn't founded by Benjamin Franklin or Thomas Jefferson."

"So what?"

"Yeh," said Randall. He gave Thomas the wag of the head that meant what he had just said should be disregarded. *Let's see if we can land a peach in the middle of that hornet's nest.* A wag of the head. *Tell Miss Henderson her dress is unbuttoned.* A wag of the head. "It's good. I'm grateful to be there."

"And you're already the genius of the school."

"No, I'm not. I never was. That was just what happened here," he said, waving toward the closed door of the Children's Office. "All that talk."

"It wasn't just talk. I used to be in awe of you. You were number one in the class."

They both laughed at that and then sat without speaking for a few moments at this table where they'd been grabbing snacks and lunches and stealing cookies and playing mean jokes on Zoe, moving things she'd placed carefully so she'd have to go hunting for them with her weak eyes. Beal had been there for a lot of this, which is where all the trouble between Thomas and Randall had started, and it was the topic that they both knew they weren't talking about.

"So how's Philadelphia?"

"Oh." Thomas shrugged. Washington and Howard were *part* of Randall now, Thomas could see that in his suit, in his face, in his defensive remark about Howard. He could see the broad avenues in his eyes, could hear the purposefulness and promise of the capital city in his voice. Randall was never coming back to the Eastern Shore, that much was certain. But Thomas and Philadelphia?

"Come on. It has to be meaning more than that for you. Thomas, this is your chance as much as mine."

"I don't see it. I'll just come back here being able to castrate hogs and quote Virgil at the same time."

Randall received this first with shock, then with resignation, and finally with a gathering understanding of the paralysis that had gripped Thomas's body and soul, the same plegia that had been assaulting him for years. As clearly as if he'd mouthed the words, Thomas had just told him that the only thing that gave meaning to his life was Beal—not labor, not ideas, but an impossible fantasy. "Why did you have to do it?" he said.

"Do what?"

"Start messing with my sister. What we had was enough, wasn't it? Your father's grand plan for us. Enough? Why did you have to go after my sister like some kind of massa?"

"It wasn't something I chose to do. Love doesn't work like that."

"Love doesn't have anything to do with it."

"Oh," said Thomas. "What exactly"—this was his topic, after all; Randall was ignorant in this arena—"does it have to do with?"

Randall got to his feet. The tiny moment of reconciliation, of cheer, was long over. "You think I'm going to let her end up like Tabitha? You think I'll step aside for that? You think I'll let you turn her into your little cuffee whore?"

Thomas took to his feet and threw his chair clattering back onto the brick floor. He was taller than Randall, not as heavy, but he didn't care if they fought and he ended up on the ground, as he had so many years ago in a fight begun in this same room over the same subject. "You call Beal a whore again and I'll kill you. I swear it."

They were both panting; neither of them wanted this to go any further, but neither wanted to back down. "Then what else," said Randall with a sneer; he was egging Thomas along to say something truly absurd. "What else can she be to you?"

"She can be to me whatever she likes."

"You're such a fool, Thomas. Just because you grew up with Negroes, you think you know how our world works."

"Then change the world. Isn't that what Dr. Washington is telling you to do?"

This cut. Thomas could see that; he'd scored a touch. And hated the feeling, scoring on Randall. Randall dropped his arms down straight, palms turned stiffly out. "I'm not going to argue this with you. What Dr. Washington says is none of your business." He flexed his arms again. "We're talking about my sister, and you're telling me she can be the next Mrs. Bayly? The lady of the Retreat? Zula and Zayne can say to her, 'Right smart of cream in your coffee, Miss Beal?' "

The idea of continuing his love for Beal as matron of the Retreat was so unspeakably horrific to Thomas that in genuine disbelief and amazement he yelled out, "You think that's what she wants? You think that's what I want?"

Their eyes were locked; Thomas saw Randall's anger dissipate somewhat.

"I know you think your love is pure," Randall said. "I know you believe you can find a way. But you're a fool if you think what she wants can ever make a lick of difference, or what you want can ever happen."

"I think we can outlast, we can endure."

"Endure? What does that mean? You think this is Shakespeare or something?"

Well, thought Thomas at that instant, the two of them inches from each other's face—and later, after they each backed away in mute defiance and parted—that *is* what I think. At swordpoint with his oldest and best friend. Shakespeare, precisely. But after the Christmas holiday was over and he went back to Philadelphia, he recognized that he had learned something from Randall, that his love could destroy the girl he loved. The infernal machine wasn't on Parnassus, it was on the Retreat: two centuries of slaveholding, the intimacy of plantation life, all of it shot through with desire. That was the real legacy of the place, that was the life that gets lived there, the life that imprints itself upon the ever-newer generations. And all these fruited couplings in the Garden, this heroic talk of myth and medieval fantasy, stone gates and oaken doors, whisperings from below the balcony, all these girded robes and kingly garb: none of it so hard to summon up, but wasn't this just a bit quaint? A sort of miscellany of whimsy? Randall had stood in front of him in the kitchen at the Retreat and had been anything but whimsical: *your cuffee whore.* What kind of depth of feeling would allow a brother to speak that way of a sister he loved? Because Randall wasn't talking about what Tuckertown would think, what they'd say in Cookestown; he was talking about what he would think. Turn his upper lip on Beal coming home in the evening as if she'd sold her workday not just to make the beds and clean the linen of the white master, but to lie in the sheets with him, let him jab his breath and will into her for a few pennies and an IOU of sorts that might be redeemed down the road if the going got tough. *You think this is Shakespeare?*

As usual, Milton had gotten there before him. Thomas had made it through only the first eight books before the recess, before *all Hell broke loose*, before the poet says *I now must change / Those notes to tragic.* Book Nine: Satan takes his revenge. *She eat; / Earth felt the wound.* And then Adam does. As knowledge flows into them, a gradual transformation; they repair behind a bush and copulate like dogs; he wants her body and despises her for it. They finish their deed and sit stunned into muteness, until Adam understands the disaster that has befallen them: *we find we know / Both good and evil; good lost, and evil got!*

Said Professor Chew in January, "See? The fruit she offered him was poison. Adam would have been destroyed either way, lose her and die of loneliness or eat the flesh and share her fate." With extra relish, it seemed to Thomas, the professor quoted Adam's concluding cry of despair: "'Thus it shall befall / Him who to worth in Women over-trusting / Lets her Will rule.'" He glanced up at this roomful of young men, boys, and released an imperial, urbane chuckle. "If I may speak from experience, gentlemen, heed that warning," he said, a line that always got a good laugh.

From forbidden love Thomas went back into the texts to find poisonous love. Not requited love that brings ruin, but love that destroys without even consummation after death. Not love that invites tragedy from the world outside, but love that is like a disease, like a blight. That curses without redress. Utterly pointless love. Where were the texts on that? But at that level, why would there need to be texts at all? And so what if there were? That fall he had been caught up in the perfumes of scholarship, like Timkins and his Kant. Did anyone in this wide world think for a moment that Augustus Timkins would read or care about Immanuel Kant ever again? At least Thomas had the advantage of knowing he had never been much of a student; he had tested himself against his father's Jeffersonian ideals and been found wanting; acknowledging that to himself had been the key moment of release from his father's power over him. All those hours in the Children's Office when he passed the time wondering what kind of sandwich he would have for lunch, whether he and Randall and Beal should spend the afternoon fishing off the peach dock, whether the gray would foal that evening and was it going to be breach as Pickle had predicted: the distractions of the immediate all seemed far more pressing than the abstractions of the theorem, treatise, or text. For many years he believed the problem lay in himself, and Beal had comforted him: *Who cares about all that stuff?*

Your cuffee whore. Oh, Randall knew how to drop the veil when he had to. That foul phrase reverberated, sliced through every possible pretension or delusion. For a time it seemed to Thomas that he had already done this to her that night on the peach dock, but no matter how he interrogated himself, he could recall nothing but purity in that moment. But yes, those were the stakes, the dangers along the road, and he began to feel that in his constant talk of her all fall, even though Timkins et al. had no idea what was really going on, he was dragging her into disrepute. She was defenseless against this chatter that so flippantly revealed her secrets, however doctored. There is a difference between forbidden love and impossible love, that's what Randall was saying: impossible love, to the degree that it goes forward at all, is incomplete; fractional love is impure, can never be anything better than that. That's what Adam and Eve woke to discover. *Our wonted ornaments, now soiled and stained, / And in our faces evident the signs / Of foul concupiscence.* Thomas wasn't much of a scholar, but he recognized the truth when he saw it.

To avoid Timkins, Thomas now took it upon himself to walk away the hours, especially as the winter season hardened. The inside spaces of Philadelphia seemed even more intolerable as the population retreated from the cold. The river was frozen, and after a late January rain turned the whole sheet to glass, there were skaters in twos and threes, happy family scenes, couples performing their own brand of ballet. Thomas had begun to notice what he had not been looking for earlier: young women, daughters and mothers making calls, young wives going to tea, couples in the half-light of the streetlamps bundling out of their carriages and into the theaters. Even if he wanted nothing to do with their society, he could not help but envy the ease, the lack of impediment, in these lives. Forbidden or impossible: What difference did it really make which, when either way he couldn't have what he wanted? At times like this he could ask himself whether he still had time to change his mind or his heart, whether—even going as far as he had—he had already stained Beal for life. Should he not take the conventional path, trusting in its uprightness? Release them both before anyone other than her brother dreamed to call her what Randall had called her?

But no. Because when he was with her, there was a force in the air between them; the molecules were charged with agitated delight. This was the best he could do at explaining the gravity between them—not Milton, perhaps, and not Newton, but it worked for him. And this had not gone away in the four months he had been in Philadelphia. He knew this because, in the end, he *had* stolen a moment, or a moment had been *given*, with her this past recess, though not a soul saw them and he told nobody. This was such a private moment that it infuriated him when Timkins said, with that sneer of his, "Did you see your girlfriend *Beal* when you were gone?" Well yes, he had. Ten minutes, if that. Solomon had fallen in his room and had been found senseless, and in the rush to call for the doctor, to help Tabitha comfort Hattie's Mary, to get Randall and Robert Junior to carry him downstairs, Thomas and Beal found themselves face-to-face outside the stable. It had snowed the day before, and all was white and clear, with a deep and boundless sky, sapphire blue, and Beal was wearing a wool hat and mittens that made her seem both childlike and inscrutable. Neither of them was expecting the other, or anyone, to be there as the commotion continued at the Mansion House—shouts, doors being crashed open or slammed shut, Mr. French clattering up in his carriage.

"Beal," he said, as if informing himself that this was she.

She also took a moment to compose herself. Both of them were gasping, as if the air around them had been replaced by some rarer, flightier substance. Finally, "How you doing, Thomas?"

"All right. I've missed you." The words, what he said to her, didn't need to be all that grand.

"Well, I guess I've missed you too."

"You guess?"

"I have wanted to be with you but didn't know whether it could ever happen again. Is that 'missing' you?"

This was a few days after his fight with Randall; everyone had heard the loud voices, the furniture being pushed aside, but Thomas did not know whether people heard what it was about. He could not tell if Randall had confronted her. "Yeh," he said. "That's what it feels like."

She smiled.

"I'm sorry I couldn't come to see you."

Her face showed her complete dismay at the thought, the mess of trouble a visit would have created if he had. When she recovered, she told him he didn't need to apologize for that. In fact, she was grateful to him for staying away.

"This summer," he said.

"I don't know, Thomas. I don't know what happens for us in the summer."

"I'm going to find a way for us to be."

"Really? You really think so?"

"If I can't, I'll go away and we'll never have to meet like this again. I'll leave you to live your life. I promise you that. If we can't be together in every way, we can't be apart just in some ways."

Despite the moment, she looked confused and said, "Huh?"

"I mean I can't bear it like this. I'm not living much of a life these days."

She moved closer to him, looked worriedly around, slid her eyes across the landscape for that little dart of motion that meant someone was watching. They had a moment. Thomas pulled her in to his body and hugged; her wool hat scratched his cheek; he reached for a hand and ended up with nothing but mitten. She slid her warm palm and fingers down his cheek. "I've got to go," she said.

"Me too. But I promise you, I meant what I said."

In the middle of May, Thomas received a letter from Mary in which she told him she had returned to the Retreat, the peaches were dead, she had broken off her engagement to Oswald, and their father had suffered a "collapse" and would probably need to be "minded to the end." Thomas was surprised by none of it; really, he had assumed all of it and was almost amused at the care and circumspection of language Mary demonstrated in her letter, as if, broached carelessly, any one of these jarring changes would devastate him. He could not help himself from theorizing that any or all of these events—events that threw the Retreat and everyone on it into disarray—could help him and Beal, could open a rip in the curtain of history, a little fissure to squeeze through. The world was cracking, and that was good.

He reflected on all this for a few days, continued his walks in the late-spring air. There had been no fragrance in the air with the early blossoms; the warmer air was bringing the scents of rot and decay. He daydreamed through a few classes and finally returned one early evening to Mrs. McPherson's to write the letter to Mary that he had imagined writing since Christmas. In it he proclaimed that he loved Beal; he wrote this as if it would be news to Mary, much as she had written thinking that what she said was news to him. "I know this may be painful for you, but I really must marry Beal." He argued that race meant nothing to him, but he understood the complications it created. He explained that the falling apart between him and Randall that had begun in adolescence resulted entirely from his feelings for Beal. He explained Randall's opposition and admitted he understood it, but he had been thinking he could overcome it, he could change his part of the Retreat just as it was falling on her to change the rest. But now? He could not be so sure. He could see now that he might have to lose her. That in almost every respect it would be better for them both, in the long run, if he did. He was in despair with that knowledge.

In the end, he repeated what he had said to Beal, that if he couldn't make her and their love honest, he would go away. To Mary, he went a step further: "I do not know exactly how to live without Beal and don't want to. Some of these days I have thought I should end it. You'll tell me I am speaking of unpardonable, mortal sin, and I will tell you that I am speaking of unbearable pain." He mailed this and then began the preparations to return to the Retreat and find out what awaited him.

Una had expected him in the afternoon. He had written that he would be leaving the city in the morning, should get to Baltimore by early afternoon, catch a steamer to Cookestown landing. He didn't know which one; he'd walk out to the Retreat. But when dusk was beginning to fall, he wasn't home, and Abel went out to find him. When Beal and Ruthie got home from work, crashing into the house yelling, *Randall, Randall*, Una made them some supper and then took up her place on the porch. "2 June," Randall had written—such an educated way of saying it—not the second of June or the first Monday in June, but "2 June." Everyone had started to say it. *When Randall gettin' back? Two June is what I hear.* For a month, *Two June*, and Una had decided that he spoke of it that way because there was so much on his mind: to be home again for the first time since December, to see his family. To see Beal. "I do hope you have been able to talk sense into her head." To get home before Thomas. Yes. "I shall plan to arrive on 2 June before Thomas returns from Philadelphia."

Una sat on the porch in "her" chair. They had two stiff ladder-backs, Daddy's and Mama's, for dining, and after supper was over and the dishes done and the little ones bathed and bedded, she and Abel used to carry their chairs out to the porch and sit in whatever breeze might pass by. There were always quarrels going on in Tuckertown, but Abel and Una were almost never part of them. Sometimes people would see them there and they'd make a beeline for them to make sure their side of the story got told first; or they'd wander up or down the lane as if otherwise engaged in business and lost in thought and then come to an abrupt stop opposite them, as if surprised to see them there, and give a little start and then a shake of the head as if *Why, there be Abel Terrell and Una! Why not go over and jaw a bit?* That was what Pickle Hardy did night after night, and Una could never resist saying, *Pickle, what brings you out this evening?* He would say, *Well, now,* as if there were a considerable story to tell, and he'd sit on the edge of the porch with his back against the post, but he'd never get to the reason he was out. Why not just say *It's a fine evening and my house is hot and I miss my Emma and I'm a lonely old man who spends all day talking to mules and at night I need a little human company so I can fall asleep without worrying that if I die before I wake, no one will find my body for a week.* Why not just say that? Una sometimes thought.

But no one came out this evening. It was 2 June, and Randall was supposed to be here by now, and he wasn't. As dusk fell, she heard the mules snorting for home at the top of the Tuckertown lane and she ran over to see them draw up, but it was just the one shape she saw in the dim cricket light. As he turned into the lane, Abel began yelling out to all who were there, whether in sight or not. "No cause for alarm," he cried out to Zoe on her porch. "The boy must have missed his train. Must have got detained leaving the city," he reasoned to the Gales, who were nowhere in sight. "Missed the last boat probably," as if in answer to a question shouted out from the house they still called the Everett house, even though the Everetts hadn't lived there for years. "Plenty of folks he can stay with in Baltimore."

Una stood as still as a post as he drew up. *Stop that,* she wanted to yell. *You hush up all those lies. Who in Baltimore's he going to stay with for the night?* She didn't need to say that; as soon as Abel saw her there, he closed his mouth and let the fear spread across his broad face. Ruthie and Beal had come out by now, and at the sight of these three members of his family Abel suddenly froze, and he got down from the wagon as if crippled. Beal brought out his chair, and Una walked him over while Ruthie saw to the mules.

"He's fine. Maybe he just got hung up leaving the city," said Abel when he sat down, and Una did not have to respond, did not have to say *White people "get hung up leaving the city"; white people "decide it is better to stay the night"; white people "are fine." Colored people are where they're supposed to be when they're supposed to be there, or they are "not fine."* At length she sent Abel and the girls to bed, but Una spent the night in her stiff chair on the porch. Some of the time she prayed, though she didn't place that much faith in prayer. Maybe her parents had known more than they thought when they gave her that name, a name her father had heard somewhere once, but not in church, not in Bible lessons: Una—one person—alone in the world. That was always the way Una saw herself, destined to be alone; her husband and family, they were gifts but could always be taken away, as her baby girl Michal had been.

Two June became 3 June, and the sky began to lighten. No one thought Randall would be coming home in the middle of the night, but no one questioned Una's vigil, her morning watch. Abel got himself up, ate breakfast, and left, and right after him Pickle went by in the red and ominous dawn without meeting her eye, but thirty minutes later he was back, and as he walked up this time, he was still not meeting her eye, had his head down and was rubbing his hands in front of him the way he did when he wanted something or when he was going to be yelled at.

Una stood up as straight as she could after a night in that chair. "Now, you say what's happening, Pickle. You say it right out."

Pickle stopped a few feet from the stoop. "Abel says to come up to the farm," he said.

"Pickle, you tell me. I don't want to run down that woods path trying to guess. It's Randall, ain't it."

"Yes, honey. It's Randall."

"What?"

"We found his body in the barn. He's dead, honey. Randall's dead."

From inside she heard Ruthie mumbling with Beal, and then Ruthie cried out. Una was still so determined to force Pickle to speak plainly that she didn't recognize he already had, spoken as plain as a newborn, used the plainest four-letter word in the English language. "How? How's he dead?"

"Stabbed dead," said Pickle. "Someone stabbed our Randall in the heart." With that out, Pickle couldn't help going on. "I found him lying in back of the mule barn, next to the corn grinder I use for feed. I couldn't at first make out what it was lying back there on a mound of corncobs. A deer? I wondered. A sack full of rags?" Pickle continued. He went up and looked at this thing . . . but by now Una had heard enough to prove what she already feared, and now she let out a scream that no one in Tuckertown could not have heard, and possibly as far as Blaketon people heard it, and it was a cry not of surprise or shock, but of confirmation that the worst, the worst possible, which had been so easy to imagine, had now come true exactly as she had imagined it. It was the cry one makes when history repeats itself. She kept screaming as she took off down the woods path, her gray hat brushed off by a bough, Beal and Esther now at her heels. Two June, Una kept saying to herself as her legs pumped and her lungs heaved. Two June, as if that day, the second of June, 1890, could simply be conjured to begin again, with Randall walking down the lane with his suitcase or arriving in the wagon. But no. The second of June was now and forever would be the day Randall died, the day she lost her only son.

By the time she got to the farm, everyone was there, ringed around the great midstrey doors as if there were to be an auction or a political speech, a word from the owner or overseer. The crowd parted for Una and the girls, and no one said a word to them except for Robert Senior, who said her name and reached out and seemed to be trying to grab her sleeve, to stop her from going inside or to make sure she knew he was there for her, but she kept marching.

She saw Abel first, on his knees, back on his heels, his arms slack and impotent. Randall was laid out on soft, dry hay, his hands crossed on his chest, his clothes straightened, his suit coat buttoned. Abel must have done that for her benefit, laid him out as if he were sleeping, but with his shoes on, his brown wool city hat positioned not on his head, but just above it, like a halo. Abel remained silent, looking at Randall. There was blackened blood on his white shirt and on his tie, but the way Abel had dressed him, Una could see no part of his flesh torn and gored. Ruthie began to moan and then to sob and then to howl, but Beal hadn't done that yet. She hadn't really said or done anything since Pickle came, besides coming along, tagging along to the barn. It seemed to Una that they were catching Randall still somewhere between life and death, that Abel's efforts to pull him down from his mound of corncobs and lay him out had restored a slight pulse through his sacred heart, that he would still be with them for a few more moments, so Una tried to see the living part, to stay quiet in case Randall wanted to speak. There were pigeons cooing overhead; the mules were clumping on the stall dividers and letting out an occasional light bray; there was a scuttering of rats; life all around them, and Ruthie had finished sobbing and was holding on to Beal. Randall's face was unmarred, the fine arc of his jaw still seemed assertive, his brow still analytic, his broad nose still waiting for the breath of God. None of these features had been altered by death, but his mouth, his lips—this was not what Randall looked like, this expression was not him talking or laughing or crying or being lost in thought. It was no expression at all, just an arrangement of dead flesh, and it would never, ever again be Randall's mouth, it would never again speak, and at that thought, Una began to cry.

Who could have done this to him? Why would anybody do this to anybody, but Una didn't care about anybody, she cared about her son. Oh, there were lots of people in town who didn't like what had been going on at the Retreat, Randall and his studying with Thomas. The whites didn't like it; the blacks didn't like it. From the night Mister Wyatt first proposed it, Una knew Randall had left the safety of his race. Lots of people, white and black, had gotten tired of hearing about Randall the genius. Black people aren't supposed to be smart, they aren't supposed to know they are smart. Randall going off to Howard—Howard *University*, named after one of those Yankee Freedmen's Bureau meddlers—and coming back wearing a tie and a wool hat; lots of people, white and colored, would hold a grudge about that. Una had worried about this for years, she knew it was a danger, but how many of those people would kill him? And Abel, during the years when the peaches were in full flower, had gotten uppity, with those fifty thousand trees he had created and tended. Lots of people were envious of Tuckertown and the colored on the Retreat, because where the Retreat had thirty years ago been a Babylon of enslavement and cruelty, it was now, if not a Promised Land, at least beginning to emerge from the darkness. Una knew that her family's upward arc was counterbalanced by a hundred Satans trying to pull them back to earth, but she could imagine no kind of hate strong enough to point a knife at her son and thrust it through his chest. So if not hate, what kind of love? Not the love of family, but some kind of twist in the road, a choice made between love and preserve and love and destroy. A mess of people get killed over love, Una knew that well enough—crimes of passion. But there had been no word from Randall about a woman. All he did at college was study, and there was no one here at home who was special for him; he didn't have time, at least not here at home, to get in that deep. That was sure. So what reason or what fate was it, yesterday, that put her beloved Randall in front of that man, or those men, the few who would kill him, and for what? A faded silk bow tie and a second-hand hat, or a glance and a few sweet words of love?

There was a knocking on the hay door, and it was Mr. French calling out that the sheriff had arrived and could he come in now. Abel took a poll of his family's eyes, all women now. Una nodded. What difference would it make if the sheriff came or not? Abel seemed to pause one last second, asking Randall if he was ready for the next episode of his death, and he nodded. They had to let him go. It was time. Time for the law to at least pretend it cared what had happened to an eighteen-year-old colored boy.

And then Una thought of Mister Wyatt. She couldn't remember if he had been out there in the crowd when she came in, not seeing the face of a single soul as she went by. And Thomas. Thomas was in Philadelphia, but Una thought he should be there, brother to Randall as no one else ever was or could be. The door parted behind them, let in one of its twenty-four-foot-high shafts of light, and it seemed to Una that this was perhaps Thomas, that the news had already traveled far enough for him to hear it and return on the wings of loss, but it was the sheriff, Sheriff Tubman, no friend of the colored even with that name, and Mr. French was with him. Una saw the tears spring to Mr. French's eyes when they rested on Randall. Una hadn't known that it was possible for a grown white man to cry over a colored boy, and with that, she melted when Mr. French put his arm on her shoulder.

"Una," he said, "let the sheriff make his investigations." Una could imagine little investigation except for a brief contemptuous look at her son, a curl of the lip that meant whatever had happened, *Boy, you asked for it.* But she took Mr. French's reassurance that there would be more to it. "You take the girls home to get ready for Randall, and I'll bring him by in the carriage," he said, and she tugged at Ruthie and Beal. They were gathering themselves to go when they all heard a commotion from outside, and it was a voice that often raised a ruckus, but never a ruckus quite like this.

It was Zoe, and she was screaming, screaming at Mister Wyatt, who was standing alone off to one side under the leathery, rattling leaves of a sycamore tree. Two hundred years of history recorded by the drops of her blood came pouring from her mouth. Zoe was past sixty, with deep creases in her face and arthritic hands and sore knees. She'd worked as a slave child in the fields and never met her father, who died before she was born. She didn't get to marry the man she loved; she might have been cast off because her eyesight was so poor, but Hattie's Mary had spotted her early as a bright girl and arranged to have her brought to the Mansion House, and that's why she stayed and was freed on the Retreat when her mother and all her aunts and uncles and cousins went off in the schooner of the man from Virginia.

"This is your fault!" she screamed, a bent finger pointing at the shape she'd figured out was Mister Wyatt. "You did this as surely as if you had pulled the trigger. You. You made him into something that had no place anywhere. You twisted his mind until he became nothing at all. He was dying when he left us, I seen it. I seen it with my own eyes that he was dying then, going to the city. He was dying when he come in December. He knew he shouldn't never come back, and still he tried. He tried to come home even though he knew it would kill him."

"Yes he did," said Stimson Rather, a peach picker who had been on the Retreat for the last ten summers, a troublemaker. "Yes he did," he called out, even though he and Randall had probably exchanged only an occasional hello.

"Why would anyone kill Randall? Because of you," Zoe said, finger pointing now over Uncle Pickle's shoulders, which were blocking her way should she want to advance. "This was whitepeople done this, in this place where they worked people of bondage. In this place where we lived our lives being worked to death. Randall wanted to be free of this place, and you brought him back here and nailed his hands and feet to a barn."

There were a few murmurs from the crowd, a few "That's right's," people beginning to see it as she did. Why kill Randall? There were perhaps twenty-five people there that day—all of Tuckertown; some of the pickers who felt they had a right or were simply taking this occasion to get out of the hot sun; a couple of whites; Jack Turville, who tended the livestock and dairy operation and lived in a small house next to the Frenches; and a white hand whom people remembered for calling Randall's death "a fuss." *Wha's alla fuss about? Tha's what I'm sayin. Wha's alla this fuss about?* If he hadn't been sent on his way that day, he might not have lived through the night, and the fuss, by God, the fuss then would have been considerable.

"What was Abel and my Una to do," Zoe asked, now glancing around the crowd, "with all this talk of schooling. They was wrong. I told them they was wrong, letting the lamb and the lion lie down together, but what was they to do? They let him go, should have said goodbye for good the first day he come up to the Mansion House, just a scared little colored boy. Just a slave boy you bought to keep your own child company," she said now, turning back to Mister Wyatt, who was still motionless under the sycamore tree. "That's all that was. Randall never lived a free day in his life."

"Never a free day," a voice in the crowd repeated.

Una had heard all this before. They all had. Whatever Mason or Mason spouse was in the Retreat, Zoe had been walking that woods path home day after day for fifty years, damning them to Hell, lamenting their hold over her. The lion and the lambs: who hadn't heard Zoe preach about that one? But today what Una heard was not Zoe's madness, but her hatred. An almost unimaginable thought forced its way into Una's head: Zoe hated white people enough, hated the Masons and the Baylys enough, to kill the one onto whom they had settled the most favor. Zoe's hatred was enough to kill Randall.

"Oh, why did the Lord bring whitemen to curse us so?" Mister Wyatt suddenly looked small and thin and stooped, almost a pathetic figure in the yellow light coming through the sycamore leaves; he was meeting Zoe's eyes. "Oh why in His creation, when He made us, people of the sun, did He make those people of the dark? How did they get ahold of us? How was we caught? He protected us against the Devil when we deserved protection, so why didn't He protect us against these devils, because we done nothing to them? Why did He let them come between Him and us? I tell you, I tell you now, we are all dead, and we will bury our dead, but there will be justice."

"That's right." It wasn't anyone from Tuckertown calling out from the crowd. But it wasn't just trash either, the men Abel told the children not to talk to, Jacob Beets and his sort, the reason Una didn't like Beal walking the woods path alone. These were farmworkers, decent people who generally kept their eyes open and their mouths shut.

"Why oh why couldn't things have stayed the way God made them? The Chinaman in China, the brown Indian in South America, the red Indian here, us colored in Africa, and the whiteman over there in England? Why wasn't that a good plan, a fine plan, for each of the colors to have theirs to do with what made sense to them? Where did the whiteman get the idea to rearrange Creation to his liking?" She addressed herself one last time to Wyatt, but she was tired now, and her grief had overtaken her rage, and it was as if she were appealing to Wyatt now, asking and not telling. "Why did you have to come here and bring us with you? Why did you have to do that?"

At times during all this, Wyatt's lips had moved in his gaunt face and his eyes had registered the wounds as Zoe pelted her words at him, but he hadn't said anything anyone could hear. Mr. French came to his side and gripped a steadying hand around his biceps. They were at the edge of the gulley, and beyond it was the stable, the coachman's cottage, the icehouse, the Mansion House, a backdrop of wealth and privilege, where all these troubles and wrongs seemed to have originated. It didn't matter that Wyatt had come from the western shore, that his family had never owned slaves; as soon as he set foot in the Mansion House as the new master, the history of it became his own.

"Why?" she repeated. It was a question she wanted answered; even in her rage and grief, the only person she could appeal to was the person she had accused of being the cause.

"I have tried to redress these wrongs," he said at last. He had spoken barely audibly, so when Mr. French looked at him questioningly, he repeated what he said at fuller voice. "I had hoped to change things. I tried to let the land redeem itself, but the soil is cursed. The dead child in there marks the end of my hopes. Don't ask for anything more of me. I have nothing more to give you, Aunt Zoe, or any of you." He waved his hand across the crowd, a congregation awaiting some sort of promise. "I have no way out of the world we live in. I thought once that I did, but events have undone everything I tried to build. We are cursed. This farm is punished."

There was a ripped silence, Zoe mute in the arms of her daughters Zula and Zayne. No, thought Una, this land isn't cursed; someone murdered my son. What other curses do any of us need?

"We can only pray that God forgives us our sins."

No, thought Una. I have committed no sins. I am innocent and someone has murdered my son.

"I'm sorry," he said finally, to no one. "I loved him like a son."

Una had never for one second doubted that Mister Wyatt loved Randall, loved him like a son, loved him not more, but better, Una believed, than he had his own son, who seemed to disappoint him so. Yes, Mister Wyatt loved Randall enough, too much. Randall made Mister Wyatt choose between himself and his own son. Was that enough of the madness of love to kill Randall?

Una knew she should do what Mr. French had said, go home and prepare to receive Randall's body. She could already hear Reggie Hollyday beginning to fashion his coffin in the woodshop. Zoe was being led back to Tuckertown by Zula and Zayne, and Una could still hear her cries from the other side of the farmyard. Jack Turville was urging the dairy hands to get back to work. But Una felt her place was exactly here, standing guard at the great doors of the barn. She could hear the sheriff and Mr. French reasoning that Randall wasn't robbed; no one had taken his hat and shoes; that Randall's body was untouched, so it hadn't been whites who had done it for revenge. Una supposed that if it was a white man who killed Randall, that'd be the last anyone heard of it; if it was a black man killed Randall, that wasn't a situation the law cared all that much about. Una knew that. What did it matter who had killed him? If it was a white man, then maybe it was Mister Wyatt's fault; if it was a black man, maybe it was Zoe's fault. What difference did it make?

Suddenly they were all gone. There was a steady breeze off the water that day, a soft white June day; she felt the air catch her skirt and flap the hem against her ankles, and she was suddenly back in the moment. Some minutes seemed to have passed, yet Una had no memory of them; the sheriff had gone, probably said something to her on the way out; Mr. French had brought the carriage around and was taking Randall's body to Tuckertown; all had dispersed, and it was as if people had left her there, as stiff and unmoving as a statue. She looked over at the sycamore tree and saw that she wasn't completely alone, that Mister Wyatt was still standing there. They looked at each other. What had they done? They had been partners, met as equals on the matter of Randall for a decade; they had shared him as their project, but all along, what they had been doing was driving him over a cliff. Una didn't have anything to say to Mister Wyatt, and it seemed he didn't have anything to say to her aside from the usual words of sympathy. She already knew she had his sympathy, and he seemed to know that he had hers, so they looked at each other for a few more seconds and probably nodded some sort of acknowledgment before they both turned and got on with the business of burying the dead.

When Una got home, Zemirah and Zoe had already bathed and dressed Randall's body, put him back in the suit he was killed in, because that was his best, got him a fresh shirt and tie, and Una sat with him until Reggie arrived with the coffin. When they had settled his body in, they moved the coffin to the parlor and rested either end of it on the seats of the two ladder-back chairs. No one but the dairy hands worked that day either at the Retreat or at Blaketon, and everyone from Tuckertown and people from Cookestown came by all afternoon. Some of them were people Una wouldn't ordinarily consider fit to make a call in her house, and some of them wouldn't normally think her house was a fit place to call, but it was all a comfort to her, who had always imagined that when tragedy struck, she would want to be alone. She never really thought of herself as one who had friends, but the faces that came through the door were darkened with her sorrow, and especially when visitors who came in had suffered the death of a husband or a child, she felt welcomed into a sisterhood of loss, and she didn't mind.

The face that came through the door at the end of the afternoon was the one she had both dreaded and yearned for. Thomas, alerted by telegram that morning, had been on a train from Philadelphia by noon. He had matured somewhat in his time away. He had been home over Christmas, but Una had not seen him, and in any event she had spent most of that two weeks ensuring that Beal did not see him. Una supposed that if Randall had arrived safe, he too would have the marks of another year of young adulthood, a firmer posture, a wiser and more knowledgeable laugh. Una gulped, thinking of the sound of Randall's laugh. Thomas stood for a long time at the edge of the coffin; Una heard him sniffle, then begin to cry, so she went up to him and put her arm around him. He said he was sorry, mumbled out a few of the words he was supposed to say, but they didn't sound like him, like anybody in the world, so she shushed him, said she was sorry for him, and thanked him for coming so soon.

And then there was Beal in the room.

"Hey, Beal," he said.

She said hey back.

Una was glad at least that they had this greeting to use, so much a part of their childhood with—and against—Randall. She was glad that this is what they could say, because even before Beal had begun to grieve properly for her brother, she must have tired of the looks, the promises of the River Jordan, the "chiles" and the "preciouses" she had been receiving all afternoon. Maybe later on she'd come to appreciate it all as Una had been doing, because their people were accustomed to absence and loss and probably knew how to do it as well as any people on earth. But not now. Beal and Thomas were looking at each other nervously, Thomas shuffling his feet, Beal fiddling with her shirt. Una didn't know why, but she believed Beal was thinking she was glad Thomas hadn't been killed too, because that's the way it had been for Randall and Thomas for so long, sharing everything, being where the other was—in a schoolroom or in front of a muzzle or at the point of a knife wouldn't be all that different. That's why Una loved Thomas, allowed herself to love him, because no matter what Zoe said, loving Thomas was just one more way for her to love Randall, and now that Randall was gone, it was the only way to love him.

Thomas said he was sorry to Beal, and she looked down at her apron and her maid's dress, the maid's shoes they made her wear that gave her blisters, and the Yes ma'ams they made her say, and still, for all that, she said back that she was sorry too.

Some of the Goulds from town arrived, and Una watched Thomas and Beal agree to slip out onto the porch. "Oh, Una. My child, my dear child," said Mrs. Gould, who was the mother of Raymond, Tabitha's husband.

From out on the porch Una heard Beal ask Thomas how he was, how he heard the news, when he got it.

"—and we know that he is walking with Jesus now," Mrs. Gould was saying.

"Did you hear about Aunt Zoe?" Beal said to Thomas.

Mr. Gould was a courtly man, a businessman who owned the Negro Market, as it was called, and he bowed to Una. "My condolences," he said.

"Yeh. Zula was at the Mansion House apologizing for her when I arrived. She didn't have to do that. We all know Aunt Zoe. We know she doesn't really mean it."

"We have lost our very best. We all mourn him. We will see him in the by-and-by, but that doesn't help now. I know that," Mrs. Gould said to Una. Una nodded; no, it doesn't help now, she thought. It may never.

"She does mean it," said Beal. "It's what that part of her means. But there are other parts."

Yeh, said Thomas, maybe that was a better way to put it. Beal started to cry. In the backlit silhouette through the window, Una could see her pull her apron up to her face and cry into it. Thomas stood with his arms at his side, the way the three of them had always done as children, waiting for the hurt to pass.

"We've brought a basket for you," said Mr. Gould. "Just some things to offer to company during the days ahead." The Goulds approached the coffin, and there was silence from the porch.

"What are we going to do now?" he asked when she was done crying.

"He was such a handsome boy," Mrs. Gould said.

Una mumbled a thanks to Mr. Gould and did not hear what Mrs. Gould said to her. But Mrs. Gould was talking, and she couldn't hear what Beal said either. What did they think their choices were? There was no flight for either of them, as there had been for Randall. Thomas was chained to the land, the dying land, and Beal's beauty could take her only so far. Zoe was right about that much: whether he came back for visits or not, Randall *had* left for good last September, and that's the way Una and Abel wanted it. "You go, Randall," said Abel on the dock. "You go as far as this boat can take you, and keep going." Una had forgotten that until this very moment, and yes, if he had truly heeded his father's advice, he'd be alive today.

The Goulds were now sitting opposite her, waiting for her to say something. "I'm sorry," said Una. "I'm done in."

"Of course. We won't stay a bit longer."

"I've got to go home," said Thomas.

"It's over, Thomas. It's got to be over now, with Randall gone. It's got to be done."

"You say it like we had something to do with Randall's murder," said Thomas, and for a moment Una's mind went completely blank, seized by an idea beyond her imagining, beyond it seemed Thomas's and probably Beal's, but an idea nonetheless. And even before she could fully emerge from this idea's grip, a relief came out of it, the relief that Beal was saying it must be over. Una could see the tiny ray of sun that shone through the pitch-darkness of Randall's death.

"The way for us to honor Randall's death is to prove him wrong," said Thomas.

Beal started to cry again. "No," she said. "No."

"We'll just be letting ourselves out, dear," said Mrs. Gould. Una did not apologize for forgetting that they were there. She heard Abel walking up to the porch. Una had let him go for a walk in the orchards when the visiting became too much for him. She strained to hear the tone of his greeting to Thomas: Wary? Accusatory? But no. "Your daddy and Miss Mary be needing you as much as us, Thomas. Don't you worry about us. We see you directly."

Wyatt asked if he could have a Mass said for Randall at Holy Redeemer, the Mason family church, and though no one in Tuckertown could see the need or the place for this within their own grief—Una did not want to hear Zoe on the subject—she could not deny him; she could not say he didn't have a right. Mary and Thomas and Mister Wyatt sat in their pew on the right, and Una and Abel and the girls sat in theirs on the left, and it was a strange admixture of whites and colored that came to this service. Tabitha came with her family, and Robert Senior and Robert Junior, their faces raw with a kind of anguish that surprised her. Una didn't know most of the people at this service. People paying their respects to the Masons, mostly; Una didn't know how she felt about that. She had started by then what would become an affliction for her in the years to come: every time she met or saw an unfamiliar man, white or black, a voice from within would ask, Was he the one? Because according to the law, the case was never solved. What Una did not know until years later was that Sheriff Tubman—he was there at the Mass—suffered from the same unhealed wound, spent the rest of his career and his life trying to solve this murder, even twenty years later walking down the street in Cookestown and thinking, *Was it him who did it, that murdered that colored boy?* Or, *Was it on account of her?* But he never figured it out. There were white crimes and Negro crimes, and white-upon-Negro crimes, and

Negro-upon-white crimes, and they all had their signatures, ghost marks of the passions or indifferences behind them, and this didn't have the mark of any of them. It was as if the boy had been murdered by a sort of person the sheriff knew nothing about, Barbary pirates come ashore for the night, or a band of Chinamen.

After Wyatt's service, the two families got into their separate funeral coaches—a carriage for one family and a wagon for the other—and went to the church in Tuckertown, where they sang, lamented, and wept. Una said little to the Masons, greeted Mary, and thanked her for coming, and Thomas spent most of the time at both gatherings standing alone, unconsoled by the words or songs of either service. He said nothing to Beal, and Beal seemed to have said nothing to him, and they were avoiding each other's eyes, but at the same time—Una saw this too—they couldn't stop their glances, drawn to each other like a compass needle. They were doing their best, these children; they pulled their eyes away as soon as they were able, but none of this was over yet.

June passed, and it was July now, an unusually sticky and humid summer: laundry didn't dry on the line, took a week for a dead fish to rot away, so little wind that the watermen didn't even bother to cast off from their landings. Mister Wyatt had once—long ago—said that slack air in the summer was good for peaches, but who cared about that now, what was good for the peaches? Nothing, as it turned out, was good for peaches. Una had lived her life marking the weather and the tides by that measure, as if it mattered the most of all, but now the peaches were dead, Randall was dead. At Blaketon they'd never followed Mister Wyatt into the peach business, mostly because the Lloyd brothers could never agree on anything, just kept at their grains, their berries, and a few lazy milk cows, and they had started growing hay for the horses of Baltimore, which meant that all summer and fall the haylands would be blooming with wildflowers. Una would often watch Beal as she walked to and from work through bedstraw, purple vetch and purpletop, chicory, and a wobbling of butterflies over the undulations of land, small gold coppers and blue hairstreaks; Beal had learned all these names from the gardener at Blaketon, an old white man who had taken a shine to her, and she told Una about it all at supper. Una was glad Beal had this peaceful walk on undamaged land, a kind of refuge from things on the Retreat.

At home there was no relief. Why would a seventeen-year-old want to leave the peace of Blaketon for this miasma? Una didn't blame Beal for feeling that her family's house, which used to be the prettiest, the grandest—with its turned posts on the porch and the funny little window that lit the stairwell—now gave off some kind of aura, evidence of a curse against her family. Una tried to shelter Beal and Ruthie and Abel, but none of them could walk up or down their lane without some Gale or Hardy or Hollyday or Turner asking was there word on Randall's killer, what was Mister Wyatt doing to solve this, did Randall have a wife he'd left behind in Washington, was it true that Una was trying to speak to Randall through that crazy Haitian woman in Cookestown or through Zoe herself? The rumor went both ways. Hard to imagine that a few decent people could be responsible for so much hurtful chatter. The only person in the family who wasn't being driven crazy by this was Esther, because she couldn't hear most of it. Una wanted Randall remembered, but what for? For a story about a wife he'd never had, never had the time to have? She wanted to grieve for him, but not like this.

And over at the Mansion House, who knew what-all? Mister Wyatt let Zoe come back, would even have let her cook supper the very day she damned him, without a single comment, but she had to have a "talk" with Miss Mary. Miss Mary was running the house now, even when Miss Ophelia graced it with her presence, which wasn't that often. Miss Mary. Twenty-five years old and no husband. All that schooling in France and college in Baltimore and no husband to show for it. Rumors of her failed engagement in Baltimore, with a touch of scandal if you listened to Zoe, or if you listened to Tabitha, a touch of heartbreak, or if you listened to Hattie's Mary, just the way of the world. *Most times, love don't work out the way we want it to. Remember that, child. Remember that love don't work out the way we want it to.* And Mister Wyatt. Keeping the investigation going, summoning the sheriff for reports, writing to Annapolis, spending hours in the orchards while Abel and his diminished crew proceeded to dismantle the dream.

From time to time Wyatt would ask that a certain tree be spared, allowed to stand alone while the fires burned around it, though no one could figure out exactly what he was up to. The research in his office was done. Maybe it was just visual; maybe they were just decorative, ornamental; maybe he thought of them as tombstones.

Miasma. Una had learned that word from Esther. Plague, clouds of death. Sounded about right.

The first clutch of grief had finally let go of her—giving way to the dull mourning that would be her companion for the rest of her life—when one day from her laundry tub she heard the murmuring and the scampering outside that always accompanied an unfamiliar person on the Tuckertown lane, and from the tone of the children's chirping Una knew the person was white. She dried her hands, went to her door half expecting to see Mister Wyatt, and was surprised, and then not surprised, to see it was Miss Mary. She was dressed in a purple day suit and was driving Mister Wyatt's runabout. This was business, not a social call, if indeed a social call could have been imagined. Una didn't think Miss Mary had ever set foot on the Tuckertown lane before, and from the way she was driving and peering around, it was clear she was trying to figure out which house was the Terrells'. Una walked through the door to her porch, and when Mary saw her, she pulled to a stop. *Lord have mercy,* thought Una; *will my children never be free of the Masons and the Baylys?*

They exchanged greetings and then said nothing as Mary stepped down, tied off the horse, gathered her bag, and walked up the oyster shell path. If Una blinked, she'd see Mister Wyatt standing in that precise place ten years earlier, so she did not blink. She asked Mary to come up onto the porch and went in to bring out the chairs. "No, thank you, Una," said Miss Mary after she had been offered a glass of water. Una wished she had said yes, but now she could do nothing but take her place in the other chair.

"Thank you for inviting me to sit," said Mary.

"You're welcome. Not so hot today, though, is it? Maybe we'll have a shower come evening."

"Yes," said Mary. "We could use some rain. It might cool things down."

"Oh, you know how it is, Miss Mary. A half hour of relief, then the wet air rolls back in like a fog." The conversation died, and they were silent until Una picked up again with the weather. "And for all that, the ground's so dry they're having to dig a new well over at Blaketon." Una didn't suppose Mary cared much about the water supply at Blaketon, but these words were calming her.

"Is that the truth? How's that well behind Aunt Zoe's? Always was the sweetest water on the whole neck, like some mountain spring."

Una didn't believe Mary had ever drunk a drop of it, but she was correct about the water. "Oh," she said, "water's right plentiful from Zoe's well."

"I hope you and Abel and the girls are getting on. I can't imagine your loss." Tears were in her eyes; her lower lip trembled.

"That's kind of you. We getting along okay. How is Mister Wyatt?"

"He's not well." Mary took a deep breath at the thought. "I don't think he'll ever really recover, to tell you the truth. Randall's death, and the failure of the peaches. He was maybe not as strong of spirit as we all thought, all those years."

Una had hardly expected such an honest answer. It was what they were all saying these days: *Mister Wyatt's done played out. He's used up. He ain't got the heart for the last quarter mile.* "I'm very sorry to hear that," Una said.

Mary smiled bravely, then nervously, and finally, warmly, at Una—the sisterhood of loss. "Well," she said.

"I expect we both know why you've come to call."

"Yes. I want to tell you that I'm proud of Beal, of her resolve. Thomas has told me that she won't see him."

"I'm proud of Thomas for respecting her wishes. They're both doing their best. Neither of them asked for any of this."

"They were wonderful friends, the three of them. Weren't they?"

"Randall never did like her worming her way in. He wanted Thomas all to himself."

They both laughed lightly at this, the way of blameless children. "Growing up, I was never in one place long enough to make friends like that." Mary almost continued to tell Una about the few girls she'd been able to love, Celeste at the Hôtel Biron, another Mary at Notre Dame, as if Una herself were on the list too, the confidante she'd never had. "But—" said Mary.

No need for Mary to finish the thought with Una. The truth was that neither of the children had forgotten about the other. They were neither of them free. Una tried to begin on a hopeful note, as if denying the truth would keep it away from her door. "They're both young. Beal's still a child. They will get on with their lives and forget about . . . this."

"This?"

And here Una began to talk, to share her private history with the one person, she suddenly realized, who would understand it. For years, she told Mary, she had worried about *this*, even when Beal was seven, eight, and following the boys and worshipping Thomas. In those days Ruth used to tease her about her "boyfriend." Then, when Thomas and Randall began to go their separate ways, there was a summer when Beal was twelve and she and Thomas played together in the farmyard—Miss Mary was at the Mansion House that summer, wasn't she?—even though they were both in the midst of puberty, and then these past few years. Una could not bring herself to describe these past few years. *This*. She could never in a million years share her fear with Miss Mary that Thomas and Beal might have been intimate. "For years I have tried to figure out what to do about them. What to do about Thomas and Beal? For a thousand nights I have gone to sleep asking myself that question. I have warned Beal over and over. I have tried to keep her attention on Blaketon. There are some nice boys who work over there."

Mary nodded from time to time. Yes, thought Una, they've been having the same worries in the Mansion House. The problem was plain enough.

"I think I'll have a glass of water after all, if you don't mind," said Mary.

Una fetched a glass for each of them and sat down again.

"I hope you don't mind, Una," said Mary, "but I have talked with Esther about this. I needed to know where Beal really stood."

Una was surprised to hear Mary use Esther's real name, surprised she even knew who she was, and couldn't quite imagine how or when they spoke. But she knew what Esther would have said: nothing was changing, nothing was happening except for this noble restraint of love, honor, and duty.

"Thomas believes that loving Beal is the only way to get over the loss. That he owes this to Randall's memory. He seems to think that by overcoming Randall's fears and objections, they'll win his blessing."

"Yes," said Una. "I heard him say something to that effect." That day on the porch: *The way for us to honor him is to prove him wrong.*

Mary's face registered some surprise: How and when had Thomas said this to her? But she pushed forward. "I believe the situation is this. Thomas is due to return to Philadelphia in the beginning of September. He's not a serious student, as I believe you know."

"Neither was Beal," said Una.

"He has to get more schooling. I don't know what he is going to do with his life, but whatever it is, I don't think it's here. On the Retreat." She waved her hand up the lane, through the timber stands, out to the rivershore, where the Retreat itself seemed to be claiming a whole new set of victims.

She's gonna take it on, Una said to herself. *It's happening in front of my eyes.*

"But I don't think he will go this fall if Beal is still here. I may be wrong, but I think he hopes she will see him again in good time."

"Oh, Lord," said Una. All summer she'd been saying to herself, *Just hold on until Thomas goes back to Philadelphia.* But that's how far it had come. Mary didn't need to spell anything further out to her. Beal had to be sent away. Last year she had sent Randall away to grab hold of his star, and this year she would have to send her baby away to save her life.

"Here's what I have been wondering," said Mary, and she went on to recall that when her father sent Esther to Hampton, she had stayed with a very respectable family in—Mary had been told—a fine neighborhood. She had been wondering . . .

"Yes," said Una. "The Whalleys. They took in Hampton students, from good families."

"I am sure," said Mary, "that they could help us get her an excellent position in a good house. She'd even have a chance to resume her education without distraction if she wanted. She's a very bright girl, we all know that."

"Yes. No sense, but a bright girl."

"It might only be a year or so. They'll both have a chance to meet more suitable young people. But Una," said Mary one last time, touching her fingertips to Una's sleeve, "we have to try this, don't we? They have made the first attempt. We have to help them succeed."

Una nodded.

"Will she go? I can't force Thomas back to Philadelphia."

"Oh," said Una. "Beal is sixteen, but she'll still do what she is told."

A week later Miss Mary confirmed that they had found a job for her in the house of an army colonel, and when Beal got home from work, Una sat her down and told her what was going to happen. "I ain't going to argue with you, baby. You're my last one, and nothing is going to happen to you but good, if I got any say in the matter. So here's how it's gonna be. Miss Mary and I have been talking—"

"Miss Mary? Mama, you been talking about me to Miss Mary? How could you do that? How could you do that to Thomas?"

Una paid no attention. "And we decided what was best is for you to go get your schooling in Hampton. The family Esther stayed with is all ready to watch over you. Mrs. French got family there too, and they'll keep an eye out for you. There's a colored school there, and maybe if you want to keep going, you could go to the Normal by and by."

Beal didn't speak. The whole Retreat in on this—Mrs. French, Miss Mary, Ruthie, everyone in on this. "This is because of Thomas," she said. "I haven't seen him since Randall's funeral. You know that."

"It's because of what's best for you."

"But look what happened to Randall," she said.

Una winced. "We don't know what happened to Randall. Whatever got him killed, it wasn't schooling. Besides"—and here Una could not keep tears out of her eyes—"this is for the good. We giving you a better life."

"But I don't want a better life!" Beal shouted. She jumped up from her seat on the steps, paced back and forth. "Not see you and Daddy and Ruth and Ruthie ever again? Not come back to Tuckertown? That's not a better life, that's being sent out all alone. I'd be scared, Mama. How am I supposed to know all the things they know down in Hampton?"

"You'll do fine." She got up. Supper to put on the table, life to go forward. Lose a first child, a little baby that weren't yet two, to fever; lose a son to a murderer; lose her baby daughter to the hope for a better life—not much choice in any of that, no alternatives. Beal could want a better life or she could not want one. Didn't matter. No staying on the Retreat, that's for sure. Nothing here but trouble. Trouble for Beal, trouble for Thomas, trouble for all of them. Run for your life, that's what Una thought. Mister Wyatt had only been the most recent person to say it: the Retreat was cursed, had been cursed ever since the day the slaves disappeared into that schooner. Run for your life. Throw your swaddled baby into the life raft; put her in a basket of reeds and send her down the Bay to Hampton. Praise the Lord.

"When?" asked Beal. "How soon?"

"Miss Mary is going to talk to the Lloyds about when they can let you go."

That turned out to be sooner than Una thought. If left to the Lloyds, it would have been never; they still wanted to own people, one way or the other. But it wasn't left to the Lloyds, because the Baylys wanted her gone, wanted her away from Thomas—what they all wanted, except for Thomas.

The last evening, they had supper, their depleting family. It was not a happy event. In the morning Zula would ride with Beal on the train down to the tip of Cape Charles, and that night they'd stay at the colored house where everyone stayed when they were catching the ferry in the morning. Zula would put her on board, and that would be that; the Whalleys would be waiting for her in Newport News, and if they weren't, she was to catch the two o'clock ferry back, and Zula would bring her home. If Beal wasn't on that ferry, all would be well.

Beal told them that Thomas was going to come up in a carriage to say goodbye, a sort of proper thing, after all this, that he would pay an evening call to take her for a ride or sit with her on the porch and say goodbye. After the summer, no one could object; it was such a seemly request that Una took heart from it. They didn't ask how this message had been relayed to her; they knew it was Tabitha who brought it. But if Thomas came to take her for a drive, what would he be in? This all started with Mister Wyatt showing up at their house in a depot wagon, with Thomas in the back, and that was right, that was the old way, before they lost Randall. Then Mary had come by in a runabout. And now, a carriage? Not a carriage. Beal and Thomas, together, were too much master for a dray, too much servant for a carriage; they meant too little for horses, too much for mules. What world were they in? That had always been the problem. Thomas could depart from neither the barn and Uncle Pickle nor the stable and Phineas, the coachman. When Randall was alive, they could, the three of them, have ridden together on something, but not Beal alone with him, beside him on the seat. That's the way Una saw it; that was why they were doing all this. And in all this, Una proved to be correct. When Thomas showed up that evening to say goodbye, he came the old way, by the woods path, on foot. He was a good boy. A fine young man. But whatever Una felt about Thomas, friend of her son, in love with her daughter, whatever she felt about him, she hoped that when she heard his knocking on the doorframe and looked through to see his handsome young face, this would be the last time she would lay eyes on him on this earth.

13

At least now he could write to her. After she had been sent off, he demanded her address and said that if Mary did not give it to him, he would go down there and find her. That fall he wrote her often. They were plain letters, but ardent. Occasionally he would glance back at the sheaf of unmailed letters from the year before, and the language in them—all this idiocy about forbidden love, all this literary reference—made him ill. As if Randall's death were part of a costume drama. Beal responded now and again, asking him to stop. He had expected this, but he couldn't. He was lonely. She was the only person in the world he cared about and, with the exception of his sister, who cared about him. The real problem with her letters was that they were written on stationery from the Freedmen's Bureau. There must have been vast quantities left over after the office in Hampton closed, and perhaps the Whalleys, not about to let paper go to waste, had acquired reams of it. He couldn't think of a way to explain this to Mrs. McPherson or, should they spot one of these letters in his room, to his friends. The latter weren't that much of a problem. Timkins and Whitney had joined clubs; Anderson spent all his time these days in the library.

By the end of his second year at the University of Pennsylvania, Thomas's ardor for correspondence had waned a little, and his resolve was truly tested when she wrote him the longest of her responses, in which she told him how much she enjoyed her life in Hampton. She wrote, "The azaleas have bloomed, and all of us have picked flowers for our rooms. I don't know when I've ever seen anything so pretty." She had not picked up again with her schoolwork, as Thomas had hoped, but "Colonel and Mrs. Murphy lend me books to read from time to time." She wrote, "Last night a band played in the park at the end of our street and we was all dressed up and looking right fine." Her English grammar was beginning to suffer. And then, the reason that she had written any of this: "My Mama and Daddy believe it is best for me if I stay in Hampton for another year, as it's plainly good for me."

Now it starts in earnest, Thomas thought. Now we are being tested not just from the outside, but between us. As dark as our prospects may appear, the light at the end will be so much the more brilliant.

Thomas returned to the Retreat that summer with the flame he was nurturing and little else in hand, and almost nothing to look forward to. When he left for college the first time, it had seemed there could still be miracles to save them: no matter what his father said, many of the trees were heavy with fruit; Randall was departing, and there might now be time and space for him to see the light. He and Beal had plighted their troth on the dock at the peach landing, Mary was announcing her engagement, the souls and ghosts of the Retreat were fat, too content to do anything more than occasionally terrify Hattie's Mary or stop in for a pleasant chitchat with Zoe. When Thomas returned this time, Randall had been dead a year, the orchards were burning, most of the rivershore fields were once again bramble and scrub waiting for someone to devise a use for them, and his father's eyes were vacant of plan or interest. Everyone at the Retreat and in Tuckertown was waiting for Wyatt to die before a single thought of the future could reenter for any of them. Even his father was waiting for this event and, if anything, doing what he could to hasten it, eating less and less, often doing nothing for an entire day but sitting in his chair in his office and staring at the dusty laboratory equipment, the dried piles of peach twigs, desiccated fruit, hundreds of samples of bark all labeled as to year and variety. Toward the end, he'd felt the answer lay in the bark, which was one of the few areas where he was wrong in his theorizing on the yellows: the answer lay in the roots, a sickness of the soil.

His first day back, Thomas paid his usual call to his father in this place of business.

"What shall I do?" Thomas asked, allowing his voice to rise. "What's the plan? Why did you have me believe I was following a path when there wasn't one?"

"You must follow your heart."

"I don't think you'd really want me to do that."

His father hesitated, then waved his hand in a gesture of helplessness. He glanced toward the door, as if Mary might come in and relieve him of this misery. Vacant, irresolute, even recalcitrant, and why might it be otherwise? Wyatt's dreams were now uncouth. Such, thought Thomas, is the power of the Retreat. Every space and cavity of the farm seemed blackened by the stench of burning peachwood. The very air of the place, once the breath of life for Thomas, was now sour, brackish with salt, yellowed with the ash of blight.

"What should we do with the Retreat?" he asked.

"Oh, the Retreat belongs to your mother. Why don't you ask her."

Well, he wasn't going to ask his mother, so he did the next best thing. Mary claimed she had no real idea what should happen to the Retreat, that one day the place would be his anyway, that they were all simply trying to keep everyone fed and their father comfortable. *Comfortable to the end,* she implied. Mary's return to the Retreat had a permanent air about it; she had taken over her mother's old slant-top desk in the back library and had begun a project to improve the lawns and gardens around the Mansion House. She had mentioned to Thomas that she was reflecting on a mix of varieties of grass: crested dogstail, yellow oat grass, hard fescue, white- and redtop, and—for fragrance after mowing—a handful of sweet-scented vernal grass. Thomas couldn't imagine where, and why, she had learned so much about grasses, but for some time he had noticed that she was filling a selection of Mark Twain Patented Scrapbooks with clips from *The American* and other Baltimore newspapers. One afternoon when she was out, he guiltily took one of the scrapbooks down from her shelf and was astonished by what he found. From the first entry, "Raising Large Cows," he found that his sister, educated in France and the pride of Baltimore's Catholic elite, had assembled a textbook on husbandry, on cattle and poultry, expert opinions on the diseases of livestock and their treatments, the business of farming, the marketing of meat and produce, the implements and practices of agriculture, the chemistry of food—for example, that the fat globules in milk diminish in size as the cow approaches the end of her milking period, though to compensate, they are much greater in number. Useful to get that learnt, thought Thomas. There was one rather chatty piece on the six reasons for planting an orchard, in which the first was to leave an inheritance to one's children. Through what savage impulse of irony had Mary cut out and mounted *that*? What dismayed Thomas most was that the whole approach seemed so much like his father's, so methodical, so scientific, so prideful. The sequelae of that approach were right in front of her in the barren stubble of the cursed riverlands and the sad wreck of a man who rarely left his chair. Thomas wished he did not feel that pure doggedness, blind loyalty, was driving much of this—loyalty to their father, loyalty to the Retreat, loyalty to all those dead Masons buried just feet away from the Mansion House, as if it all could be redeemed. All these choices, dutifully considered and researched, seemed in the example of the Retreat to lead to the same place: being thorough seemed no match for pure fate. *Spes alit agricolam.* What also saddened him was that Mary had kept all this secret; his interest in these scrapbooks had been aroused initially when she slammed one shut upon his entrance to the room. He could imagine lots of reasons for this, including the fact that the Retreat theoretically would be going to him, and he was especially intrigued to see, among the many clippings devoted to model farms and particularly successful agricultural businesses, a clipping headlined "A Woman's Big Farm." In it, Miss Sara Pollard of Polk County, Minnesota, was introduced as "a prosperous farmer and does not wear male attire." She was quoted as saying, "One mistake I feel it my duty to correct, and that is, I do not wear male attire. When working on my farm I don a bloomer suit, which consists of a short skirt that falls just below my knees, with pants to match."

Thomas put the book down, dropped it, wishing he could undo having read this last bit. He felt sad, thinking of his sister in a bloomer suit, thinking of her having to defend her choices in such a way. *I do not wear male attire. I want you to make that clear. I do not wear male attire.* It was 1891, for heaven's sake. Haven't we gotten to the point where people can be who they want to be without being shackled to the roles, to expectations, to the land? Can we not love whom we love?

Well, no.

Not once all summer did Thomas mention her name. It was the only way for them. He went to Randall's grave and promised him that he would honor her; he felt that Randall's soul would not rest until he had proved his intentions. There was a relatively recent handful of flowers on the grave, and Thomas knew they were from Blaketon's gardens, and for a moment he imagined that Beal had put them there on her way home from work. But Beal was in Hampton, not an exile, but an emigrant, left home for a better life. One night he felt Randall visiting him in his room, sitting on the chair by the window, as if prepared to wait until eternity. At the time, what struck Thomas most about this was the realization that Randall had never before set foot in his bedroom, just as Thomas had never set foot in his. But when Thomas awoke, he was filled with joy because it meant that Randall was watching him and, in due time, would see the truth.

He did not write to her and she did not write to him. Everything was a test. Silence was honor. His surrender to duty that summer was so complete that it obliterated the conflict, made it moot, made it deniable. *I can't imagine what you are talking about.* Thomas knew he was prevailing, but he could not help taking solace from the fact that his restraint was eating away at Mary. Anytime Beal might have been mentioned, even as part of the most innocent childhood memory, his silence became purple. He could hear Mary drawing in breath to argue against her or letting out breath to signal that there would be no further discussion. In times like this, Thomas almost hummed a little tune to himself.

Finally, he knew he had triumphed when she said to him, without any prelude, "Don't you see? It's against the laws of our society, the mingling of the races." They were sitting in the back parlor; they both had books in their hands. She must have read something that started all this off, and he had sensed it from her, a rising agitation; the outburst came to him as seamlessly as if they had been debating miscegenation for the past quarter hour.

"The races have been mingling on these farms for two hundred years," he said.

"Like Papa and Tabitha? Is that what you mean? That's not anything but sin. That's an argument for nothing but sin!" she shouted. "That is between Papa and God. He's living in sin."

He slammed down the book he was holding. "What Tabitha and Papa might have done has nothing to do with me. Beal is not Tabitha. We haven't committed any sins. I promised Randall the last time I saw him that my heart was pure, and it is."

She waved her hand, as if this little fact could be ignored. She wasn't going to debate; this wasn't a college seminar. "Hasn't enough happened to Abel and Una?" she said. "They've lost their son, and now their daughter is gone from them. They want her back, Thomas, but we can't let that happen until you both give this up."

"Both?" He jumped on it. "Both?"

She'd made a mistake and had to acknowledge it. Yes, she said. Una had suggested that perhaps, despite her refusal to see him, Beal too was unrepentant. It was like a message in a bottle, words reverently passed along through intermediaries, as good as a letter. His heart stole the air in his chest.

"You know who will pay for this, don't you?" Mary said. "The mob won't come to our door, will it? It'll come to the Terrells'. And I don't mean just whites. Their own people don't like this either. Is that what you want?"

"No. How can you say that?" The mob, the torches lit; it was sick for her even to say that. "I don't want that to happen, which is why I'm asking you to help us."

"Help you? How?"

"Shelter us. Shelter us all."

She took his hands in hers. "I wish I could," she said.

And that was it for the summer of 1891. Thomas returned to Philadelphia for his third miserable year at the university, and his correspondence with Beal resumed. She was happy in Hampton; she was becoming a city girl. She was casting off the Retreat; he could be jettisoned along with the other burdens of history. Why not? So he had to adjust his strategies, back off a bit, write her less—a good thing, since he was beginning to fail his courses—cool his rhetoric, simplify. All according to some sort of plan, but still, these were the worst days of his life, the darkest winter, the least redemptive spring. He broke off finally with Timkins et al.; he hurt their feelings, but it was Anderson who came closest to the truth when he said, "I don't think this girl, this girl Beal, exists at all. Nothing adds up here. This Randall genius who died of tuberculosis. I think you're just making the whole thing up." Thomas knew he was skirting some kind of madness, recognized that through his studies of forbidden love had flowed a current of lunacy and obsession. By the spring he was rarely leaving Mrs. McPherson's; she did not like Thomas, but she worried about him, and he didn't know exactly how to feel about that. To receive concern and care from someone who dislikes you. *Jesus, Mary, and Joseph,* as Mrs. French used to say. The letters came from Mary at the Retreat: their father's decline was now irrevocable; there had been no revival with the first of the spring breezes. But she always closed with encouragement about Thomas's studies, about the comfort they brought to Wyatt. "Papa is more proud of you than you suspect. I wish you understood that." He'd stopped going to his courses; graduating from the University of Pennsylvania was now the last thing on his mind. "I'm real sorry you are feeling poorly," wrote Beal. "You must take a Purposeful Walk for at least forty-five minutes a day. That is what the Colonel says. We all do that together, and the winds from the ocean restore us. This summer the Colonel will be in the Philippines, and we are expecting many fine hours in the sun."

In midsummer, Papa's health began to fail. No one had told him that Thomas had been counseled not to enroll in courses at the University of Pennsylvania in the fall; the letter to Wyatt to that effect had been intercepted by Mary. The heat had come on, the humidity rolling in sheets up the Bay from the swamps and marshes of Virginia and North Carolina, and the haze fell from the clouds and settled on the landscape. This was the time in dead summer when the peaches had seemed to suck the gold out of the sunlight; the peaches had loved this time of year, the syrupy indolence of it; when the breezes bent their branches, they bobbed up and down like children on a seesaw. It was also the time of year that marked the men and women who could thrive under these conditions and those who could not. Papa had been one of those who could, a relatively rare white man who went out into the mouth of it in heavy canvas pants tucked into his boots and long-sleeved shirts buttoned at the neck and a broad straw hat pulled down over his ears, but this year, the summer heat did him in. There was talk of his demise. Ophelia came over to try to buck him up, and they spent many hours together in his office, because whatever else had happened, there was much affection between them. They had always understood and respected each other too well for the sake of a conventional marriage. Thomas stopped by to eavesdrop a few times, the low voices muffled through the thick oak doors, and one time he heard his name, but it seemed to be a memory of a sort, not a discussion of present circumstances. Another time, she was reading to him, and to his shock Thomas realized that she was reading aloud a letter Wyatt had written to her long ago, and Thomas tiptoed away because there was much about his parents and their courtship, their marriage, he did not want to know.

The night before Wyatt died, Thomas and Tabitha helped him upstairs to his room. It was the last week in August and the heat had broken. "Oh, that breeze is nice," he said when they paused on the stair landing for him to take a look out the window, down the lawns and to the water. The fireflies were swarming in the moonlight, a last, desperate attempt to attract females before the cold air wiped them all out. "They're still at it," said Wyatt. "Late this year." Thomas remembered him teaching them about the life cycle of the firefly, or "lightning beetle," as he insisted they call it; he remembered going out in the early evening with Randall, armed with paddles made of cedar shingles, and swatting them into their last illuminated death arc. They helped him up the last flight and into the dark hall. "Good night, Papa," said Thomas at the door to his room, and Wyatt put out a hand to pat him before Tabitha took him into his room. In the morning he couldn't speak; he didn't appear to be entirely all there, so Thomas took that pat, the comments about the fireflies, and the appreciation of an evening breeze as his father's parting gestures. Thomas had been raised by him in this unique bachelor arrangement, the two of them in this huge house attended by a full staff of servants, and even if the bulk of the schooling was handled by the succession of tutors, his father had been his one and only teacher; even if his mind never wandered from his work, there was always room and time for him to answer Thomas's questions; but still, Thomas could not say he had known his father all that well, and he had long ago figured out that the way children get to know their parents, the way they form an intimate portrait of the person they call Mama or Papa, is by watching them interact, which hadn't happened much for Thomas. He grieved with all his heart for the disappointments his father suffered in his last years, and he missed his companionship and love, but he realized that he was going to be one of those sons who does not cry at his father's funeral.

Which wouldn't have happened in this case anyway. Because one finally has to move forward. Because a whole community like the Retreat and Tuckertown that has conspired to change the course of history finally has to test its work, see if the great river, given the choice between its old course and the man-made one, will do what it is told, see if love—if that's really what it was—can be brought to its senses. And finally, there are devotions that must be practiced, gratitudes that must be acknowledged, honors that must be paid, and for all those reasons—hoping it was now safe, inferring this from Thomas's apparent disinterest and Beal's demonstrated dispassion—Beal was summoned home for Mister Wyatt's funeral. When Mary took Thomas aside the morning of the service and told him Beal would be there, he said nothing. There was a long, unreactive silence. "Did you hear what I said? Thomas?"

"Yes. I heard you."

"Did you know about this already?" she asked sharply. Was there communication already, all along? Had all these efforts in the past years been completely pointless?

"No. I didn't know this."

She eyed him skeptically, but then took it as the truth, or as much of the truth as she was going to get. "She got home last night. This is about Papa."

"I know it."

"Please," she said. She was sitting under the portrait of Oswald at the dining-room table, and for the first time, she looked not older, because she'd always been older, but old; her face was thinning, her nose sharper. Her beauty was fading in this place. *I do not wear male attire.*

"Don't worry," he said. "It's going to be all right." What, exactly, did he mean? he wondered. All right? Well, this: that at this moment, the moment when his sister used Beal's name, it landed inside with a strange leaden thump. Beal. *Her name is Beal.* The truth was, he could hardly picture her. If it was the Beal from three summers ago—the love they had felt that last summer together, the promises they had exchanged—that Beal was no longer there. She was gone. Imagining this reunion in a mere matter of hours, he understood for the first time that in these months and months of solitary passion he had created a person who might not really exist. He hadn't guessed for a second that this was so; he hadn't had reason or opportunity to test his ideals against reality. But now she was returning, and honestly, he could summon up little more than her name. Maybe, he thought, we can just drop the whole thing; it was a little complicated, after all. He'd just been through a hellish year and had no desire to sink that low again in his life. As many, many times as he had imagined the scene of their reunion, whether it was a joyful all-is-well sprint across the fields into each other's arms or a tragic wrenching apart, like Abelard's farewell at the gates of Argenteuil, it was always accompanied by rapture. Never, God in heaven, accompanied by ambivalence. A lot—*a lot*—had transpired to have it end in indifference. But for the moment, for today, this was how it was going to be: he would be sitting in the front pew in Holy Redeemer with his mother and Mary, and with Cecile and the two girls, whom he hadn't seen in years, and there might be over his shoulder a rustle and a groundswell of complaint, because at that moment the black community—the Terrells and the Hardys and the Hollydays—will have entered en masse to assume the very back rows, and Thomas would know that Beal was there, and if he turned, if he allowed himself to look back, would he love her? Would he love the Beal he saw? He didn't know. He could trust the hours as long as they were endlessly unfolding, but now that the end was here, who knew what to trust? As he was dressing for the service, it had suddenly come to him that for as long as he had been assuming that she would have to fall in love all over again for them to go forward, the same was true of him. Their love was so unlikely as to be an impossibility, a miracle. Could one expect two miracles in one life?

He did not look back. Just as he had imagined, the colored came in with a rustle of disapproval, which only added to the chitchat of discomfort from all these Episcopalian worthies, Methodist tradespeople, Calvinist eccentrics finding themselves at a Catholic funeral Mass said in Latin in the shadow of the Pope. Thomas hardly heard any of the service. When it was over, he and the other pallbearers recessed with the casket down the aisle, and that's when he saw her, when he glanced first at the row of black faces at the back of strips of white, like stripes on a flag, and he glanced down the line of those various hues of skin, and there she was between her parents. She did not smile or even acknowledge him as he passed by, but one look into her amber eyes told him that all was not lost. She'd had the advantage perhaps of watching him through the long service, the back of his head as he listened, his shoulders as he kneeled, a glimpse of his profile as he looked from side to side, his young back as he stood, and maybe all during this she was asking herself, *Do I still love him? Is this right? Is this worth it?* She'd had time, and she'd also had the one thing that seemed in such brutally short supply, the privacy to reflect.

Outside, all the carriages and wagons and the hearse were pulled up, and before any of the colored stirred, even ruffled a fan or stood to stretch, they would have to wait for every white man, woman, and child to vacate the sanctuary. Thomas was heading to the Retreat before she appeared. Oh, he had felt something in that one glance, a yearning, perhaps just a memory of yearning, but he knew why, in that one glance, he had once loved her. When they got to the Retreat graveyard—being buried there was Wyatt's choice, just as not being buried there would be Ophelia's—they waited for the colored to arrive in their buggies, but again, they stood at the back of the plot, back where slaves had been buried for years in unmarked graves and now servants were beginning to find resting places under a wooden cross or a pool of concrete, names scratched in while it dried. At the end of the burial service the guests were invited into the Mansion House for refreshment, but that was it for the colored, the ones who weren't working in the kitchen. Thomas ran up to his room with its window looking over the drive, and he watched her walk back to their wagon. She was between Ruth and Ruthie this time, as if the family had agreed to surround her at all times lest she bolt. Just as he had earlier predicted to himself that it must, selected instants in the years of their life together had to replay in his mind, beginning with the image of the frightened child with smudged, tearstained cheeks backing herself into the covering embrace of her brother for protection. *Her name is Beal.* Standing away from the window so he could not be seen, Thomas said her name aloud a few times. This is the person I love; her name is Beal. She'd taken off her hat and was carrying it at her side; her hair was severely pulled back and bowed, and the top of her head shone. She was in a blue cotton church dress; her ankles and wrists were slender; he'd never really noticed before how broad her shoulders were, but how delicate they seemed, how beloved her back. The years were streaming by in his mind; he was reinsinuating the mysteries of the times they spent on the beach, in the orchards, in the haylofts and barns; he felt that kissing this girl's cheeks, he should be kissing the whole Retreat rivershore. There's no accounting for the person one loves, but this person was his. She was laughing with Ruthie even if everyone else was solemn; how glad she must be to get home and to be with her family. He didn't blame himself for her exile; on the contrary, it seemed unfair to him that on her first day back, her family had her all to themselves, that he had to attend to this function of state, the burial of the king, and she could go home and take off her shoes and fancy things and come out to the porch barefoot in a pair of overalls and sip lemonade with her parents and sisters. Thomas shifted from foot to foot. From downstairs he heard Philomen Lloyd's "Boy, I'll have some of that bourbon," the murmur of condolences, the rhythm of Ophelia saying all the right things, the sound of someone mounting the stairs, probably sent to retrieve him. Beal jumped into the front of the wagon and turned around to say something to her mother. She was still laughing, and finally, this vision of her in the seat, in the mercy seat, in the gold of the sun that made her skin radiate youth and beauty, with an expression both impish and coy, this legendary child beauty who seemed to love him was there in front of him, and as the knocking on the door came to him, he had fallen in love all over again, this time for good and forever.

"Come in," he said. He did not try to pretend he was doing something like finding a cuff link, combing his hair. It was Tabitha.

"Miss Mary is wanting you downstairs," she said. He could tell that she knew what he had been up to, yet of all people, she did not regard him fearfully, she did not make him feel that he was bringing ruin upon their world by loving the girl he loved.

"She's still beautiful, isn't she?" he said. He pulled the curtain all the way back to catch the last sights of her departure.

"Oh yes, Thomas. That she plainly is."

He watched the wagon reach the end of the Mansion House lane and swing left through the gate. Tabitha had stopped in front of the mirror on the dresser to inspect her hair and to stretch the skin on her cheeks with her fingertips.

"What's going to happen to us?" he said, somewhat absently, as if all this drama was about actors onstage. This was the last thing he planned to say, but he'd been asking Tabitha the biggest questions in his life since he learned how to talk, so it didn't seem out of place.

When he said this, her fingers stopped in mid-cheek, and she turned to look him in the eye with disbelief, a horror at the question. He had expected her to react with the kind of soothing reassurances she had always given him, that's what he was seeking. But this time she was, of all things, angry. "Well, I guess you're going to have to step forward and take her. I declare. 'What's going to happen to us?' If you don't know the answer to that, how is anybody s'posed to know. You hear me? Time for you to act like a man."

Thomas dropped his hand from the curtain. "I am a man," he said, aware how lame it sounded. He meant: *I have been truer to her than you can possibly imagine.* "I'll follow Beal to the gates of Hell."

"No," said Tabitha. Her face had become hardened; the look around the room now showed contempt. *What you doing hiding up here, looking out a window like some peeper-man?* "You don't follow the girl. The girl follows you. You take her out of this place. There's no life for anybody here until you do that. We've all just been waiting for it, like we were waiting for your papa to die. How long has this been going on? How much longer are we going to have to wait for you to take her?"

"Is that what everyone wants?"

"Who cares what people want? No one anywhere in the county who knows anything doubts that you two love each other. More people done more to protect you than you know. Time for you to show that you're man enough for it. Time to show that it was all worth it."

He said nothing, but she wasn't waiting for a reply. She turned, repeating that Miss Mary wanted him to join the funeral party. He followed her back downstairs and did his duty, and after the last guests had left, Mary found him sitting on the porch and thanked him. Thanked him for stepping to with the guests, thanked him for creating no scene, for doing absolutely nothing that she had observed to invite comment. She questioned him wordlessly, a quick furrow of her brow, a tipping forward of her head inviting reassurances. *That's right, isn't it? You did nothing to invite comment?* "It's all right," he said. "Everything's fine." As far as he was concerned, it was.

The next afternoon around two o'clock he was knocking on the Terrells' door in Tuckertown. He'd come by the path, through the heat of airless woods, and he was sweating and panting. Una came to the door. "Oh, Lord," she said.

"Hello, Una. Can I see her?"

"Thomas, please." She leaned her head out to see who was watching him; she couldn't see anyone, but by evening, everyone would know he had walked up to their door. Zoe was the one she was most afraid of. She pulled him aside on the porch. "There's no way forward for this. We can't live with this."

"I need to see her. If she'll see me," he said.

She shook her head and arched her eyebrows. *Oh, she'll be willing to see you all right.*

"Can she meet me by the rock?"—the white boulder in the path on the way to the Retreat—"Would you tell her that for me?"

She nodded, to get rid of him as much as anything. He jumped down from the side of the porch and made his way to the path in the woods by a route that the children had learned many years ago exposed them to the least scrutiny from Zoe and, to a lesser extent, from her sister Zemirah Hardy: make your way to the chicken coop between the Terrells' and the Hardys', run along the back wall, dart to the big chestnut where the shed of the Everett brothers' house shielded the view, then jump into the safety of the woods. In those old days, this final sprint had left them giggling with guilty relief, like stealing tomatoes from the house garden at the Mansion House, like whitewashing a cow, like sneaking away from peach picking. They—Thomas, Randall, and, later, Beal—always got caught for these things in the end, and here, Thomas knew there was no keeping things quiet.

He reached the rock and clambered up to the top of it. He held his breath to listen for her footfall, but there was no sound. It was a sort of magical, great living thing, this boulder, an otherworldly object to children who grew up with pebbles and stones, to farmers who had never received the spine-compressing jolt of driving a plow point into something unmovable, to a community built on sand and clay. Beal always moved quietly but, of course, never as silently as she believed; they always knew she was there. *Beal is a big fat pig and I know she can hear me!* A community built on slavery learned to move quietly, to keep its secrets, but now that was all done, wasn't it? All people free to do what they wanted? And just then a rustle, a rattling of holly leaves, the snap of a brittle pine twig. Thomas's heart was pounding so hard he was surprised he could hear these sounds over the din from his chest; this was love, and her name was Beal. The stone beneath him was hot with the sun. He moved a little to surrender a tiny bit more of the flatness, a place once big enough for three children, now barely big enough for two adults.

She came to the edge of the clearing and stopped. She was in town clothes, in the slimmer skirt and fuller shirt of the city, but she had her hair in the two spiky pigtails of her youth; her fine-grained skin was still unscarred, maybe untouched. She wasn't smiling, and neither was he. This was a grim business, this reunion; no margin for error here, nothing, no thought, no issue, no doubt to be put off until tomorrow; if intimacy was sharing thoughts and deeds that redounded to no one but the lovers, they enjoyed little intimacy. What they decided today would be writ large by evening. They knew that. Una had been only the most recent person to tell Thomas that there was no way forward in this, at least no way forward without turning the Retreat on its head, and she had no doubt said the same thing to Beal as she left: *This can't work out, child. There is nothing but danger and sadness here.* No smiles when that is what your mother gives you as a blessing on your way to meet your lover. But if there was no way forward, what Thomas now understood was that there was no way back, and that where they were now was intolerable.

"Hey, Beal."

"Hey, Thomas."

"You can come on up," he announced. A slight softening of her jaw, a small wash of cheer in her amber eyes. That was one of the rules of the rock: if it was occupied, climbing aboard required an invitation. This had been a rule solemnly devised and sworn to years ago; since the only people who ever occupied the rock were Thomas and Randall, it was a rule designed entirely to exclude Beal. If they found Beal sitting there, they'd just keep walking because they knew she was only there to deny an invitation in return. Oh, thought Thomas, how simple and sweet that was. How much he'd loved her even then, how the image of being mean to her hurt him now, even if it was years ago.

She came over to the base of the rock and pitched herself up; she was in shoes, not the bare feet recommended for climbing on rocks, and he reached out and grabbed her hand. She landed beside him, her hips tight against his, but dropped his hand. She arranged her skirt.

"I have missed you," he said, not that differently than he might have if she were Randall or just a friend. Except that his pounding heart seemed to suck the air out of his windpipe.

She said she missed him too, was sorry that sometimes she didn't answer all his letters. Sitting so close side by side, it was difficult not to speak these words straight ahead, out into the woods.

There was nothing more to say for a minute, and then it was a few minutes, but Thomas wasn't dismayed by wordlessness. He felt as if his whole body were readjusting to her presence after these many months of absence, recalibrating, getting everything set and in order before his brain could concentrate on what to say next. "Well," he answered finally, defiantly. "We didn't need letters."

"No. I guess we didn't."

"So how is Newport News?"

"Hampton," she said with a touch of civic loyalty.

"I don't know why I said Newport News. I wrote Hampton enough on envelopes." He offered a slight furrow of self-mockery, which she did not return. Instead, she said she liked it, that they lived like proper free people there; she said this almost as if she had forgotten that she had written such things to him over the years.

"You are free in Hampton. Not like here?" he said, a pointless question mark on the end of an absurdly obvious statement.

"I don't know, Thomas. What difference does that make, for us?"

He didn't think it made any difference at all for them, but then he wondered why she had made the point in the first place. He dropped it. Her body was warm; he could feel her hipbone against his. How strange it was to love another person, to love even that person's bones, as if they were any different from anybody else's bones.

"I'm sorry about Mister Wyatt," she said. "It didn't sound happy for him, these years I've been gone."

"Has there been anything but misery here since you and I left? Misery was waiting for Randall the night he came home."

She stiffened, and Thomas took her hand. They both looked down at this combined thing, the white fingers interlaced with the black ones; they both knew that if anything was to happen for them, they would have to keep these dissimilarities joined by force of continuing will. Relaxing their grip would lead only to slipping through each other's fingertips. Her hands were surprisingly small, and he'd always loved that about her; the only other female hands he knew anything about were Mary's, and hers were large and heavy, like her feet. Beal was as strong as Mary, but she moved like a nymph. He squeezed her hand, and she squeezed back.

"That night on the peach dock . . ." she said.

He blushed, and he could feel the blood run in her; for all this time he had lived with the knowledge that he had made her do something she didn't want to do. "Yes," he said, nodding, which meant, *It was a mistake. I wish we could forget about it.*

She reflected on his response. In the creek, just through the trees, something upset the swans—which wasn't all that hard to do—and there was a loud squawking. "Well," she said. "I've been chaste. I've lived without sin."

"So have I," he said quickly, and he squeezed her hand again to attempt to hurry to an end of this topic, but she was not yet ready to return the sign. She dropped his hand. To live without sin: he didn't know what she meant by that. She was saying she had not been with anyone since him, which filled his heart with joy, but it was odd, her saying "lived without sin"—so Catholic. The church in Tuckertown followed Daniel Payne Coker as much as anyone; he'd preached on the Eastern Shore often. Thomas didn't know what the AME thought about sin. Didn't know what Tabitha meant earlier that day about God judging her sins. Sin was not an issue in his life. To acquire the freedom he needed, he had to throw it all out the door: sin, law, commandment, protocol. "I don't think it was sin," he said. "I don't care what my mother's church, what Mary's church, says about it. I don't think I'm a Catholic. I think I love you, that's all. That's enough for me."

She drew in a breath, sucked it in sharply, and held it. She tipped her head slightly and tickled his neck with her pigtail. She let out her breath in order to ask him, "Why? Why do you love me, Thomas? What are we doing?"

He answered that he loved her because she was all he ever thought about, and in that case, he'd go mad if he didn't love her. She laughed a little at this; he hadn't intended to make a joke, but it was sort of funny. He said that he spoke her name all the time, that this was how he got through the years without her, and just saying her name made him happy, and since she was the only person named Beal he had ever heard of, this joy must have something to do with her. He said he felt they had proved their love because here they were together on the rock, where no one else on the planet wanted them to be; their love was forbidden, and strangers the world over who knew nothing about them would hate them for it. "But that's okay," he said. "I don't care about anything else but being with you."

"Your family? The Retreat?"

"Let it all sink into the Bay. Let the waves lap over the floors of the Mansion House. Let the stones in the graveyard submerge. I don't care." There was nothing on the Retreat for him, he said. If the peaches hadn't died, he'd probably be chained to the place, but now they had been wiped out, and he was sorry for the disappointments endured by both their fathers, but he was glad at the way things had worked out. The Retreat was what it had always been, just a big plot of land that no one knew what to do with. He—they—were free of it.

The sounds closed in; soon enough they would hear the return of the workers at the Retreat—Tabitha; the new cook, Loretta. Thomas wasn't quite sure who all worked at the Retreat these days. Zoe seemed to have retired, or been fired, or quit. Beal shifted her position; on that side there was a small ridge in the rock, a vein of quartz that was comfortable only if you positioned it right between your buttocks, between what the boys called their "ass crack."

"I still miss Randall," he said. "I miss him every day."

"Me too." She added that she couldn't really talk about him.

"But he was wrong about us. He was wrong about me. He should have known better, that I would never be mean to you, or use you."

She used his arm for leverage as she shifted her position again, and the touch of her fingertips seemed to have opened five points of entry for her to flow into him and he into her. She left her hand there. He had planned to ask her if she loved him, because now that she had renounced the night on the peach dock, she also may have been withdrawing the love she had proclaimed she felt for him, but the hand made it unnecessary.

"So what are we going to do?" she asked. She leaned her head on his shoulder.

"When are you supposed to go back?"

"The day after tomorrow," she said; she'd been given four days off.

"They sound like generous people."

"They're quality. The colonel is. The lady not so much."

"I don't care who they are. You shouldn't be a maid for anyone."

She let out a bitter laugh. "What else am I supposed to do? Would you rather I picked crabs or shucked oysters? Or do you think I can get a job in a nice shop selling lacy things to white ladies?"

"Beal," he said. "I'm going to change all that." He turned and kissed her cheek, the hollow of it.

"You think loving me changes all that?"

No, he didn't. But the one thing he did know is that if they got away from here, wherever they might devise to go, it would be better. A year ago he'd figured out that they had to leave the Retreat—a middle-of-the-night revelation in his bed at Mrs. McPherson's, the realization that *going somewhere* was among the options. A why-didn't-I-think-of-that followed by a now-what? Where? Massachusetts, maybe. As he recalled, it was a Massachusetts regiment that had arrested his grandfather during the war, Massachusetts regiments that refused to return runaway slaves to their owners despite the fact that Lincoln had ordered them to do so. Or was it New Jersey? It didn't matter; he could promise that anywhere else would be better. But it was the second time she had expressed this bitterness, and he wasn't sure he knew what to make of it. No, he didn't think loving her changed all that, but why did she seem angry? Her parents weren't angry. The peaches ripped the heart of Abel and his father in equal measure. It seemed to Thomas that things were getting better for the colored all the time, not that he thought of her as colored, as Negro, as black-skinned, any more than he went around reminding himself that he was white. It wasn't that he didn't see it, it was that he didn't bother to name it, any more than when he saw his mother, he named her red hair, or when he saw Mr. French, named the spectacles he always wore, or when he saw his sister, Mary, named her height. Actually, now that he reflected, he did often think of the word "tall" around Mary, because during their times apart he tended to forget that she was almost his height, and when they were reunited, it shocked him. But Beal was Beal, that was the only feature he needed for her, and when he was with her, he loved her skin because it was perfect and fine-grained and deep.

But now, sitting on the rock, two lovers with very little going for them, she was resisting him. *No, I don't think loving you changes anything for anybody but us.* But maybe that wasn't enough for her. Maybe he had to change the world before she would go with him. Forget Hercules and his twelve arduous labors. Maybe this was all slipping through his hands; maybe he was going to lose her after all. In a few short minutes he had used up his store of reassurances, and without them he was looking into the abyss. He had been battling the insurmountable barriers to forbidden love for years, but he had always made the assumption—without it, what was left?—that she would be by his side, that she would both love and do battle, and suddenly, at this moment, he felt his gut drop: this was hopeless. Whether she loved him or didn't, what difference would that make? The forces that forbade it were too much. What would he do now? Where would he go? he asked himself, with a groan.

"What's wrong?" she said. She nudged into him when he said nothing, a silent intimacy: *This is me. You have to answer.*

"What do you mean?"

She mimicked the sound he had made. Suddenly companionable, suddenly gay and girlish.

"There's no way for us. Nowhere for us. Is that what you think?"

She put her arm around his back and dropped her head onto his shoulder again. They sat like that, in the comfort of hopelessness, which allows one not to think beyond the moment, and in the unspoken trust in magic, which sometimes makes things happen.

"Is that what you think?" he repeated.

"No. I think you will find a way."

"Okay," said Thomas. He said it brusquely; he was being petulant at this of all times, but she'd hurt his feelings, and the human passions have no sense of scale or scope.

She gave him a few more minutes of silence and then said she'd have to go back to Hampton.

"I know," he said. Yes, this was step one: Beal goes back to Hampton. "Of course. You have to go back. They won't let us alone here anyway. You have to go back and I'll make a plan. Do you trust me?"

She was getting ready to answer; he could feel it; she was placing her all with him, giving him what he asked for—time. But just then they heard swishing and footfalls from the path in the direction of Tuckertown, a slight pained grunt, a growl from a large female chest, and they both knew exactly who this was before Zoe broke into view. She stopped at the edge of the clearing, glared up at them while they attempted to pull apart on their small seat. There was horror on her face; her madness came from horror and not rage. She would live only a few more years, and her sense of her approaching death had only loosened her tongue and quickened her spleen. She'd come after them, no question about that—seen Thomas's hat bobbing through the trees as they ran, or caught a flap of Beal's skirt as it disappeared into the woods. But maybe not. If she'd seen them, she'd have put down her rolling pin, wiped her hands on her dishrag, and given chase. So maybe, thought Thomas, Una had told her, sent her out—the enforcer—to break this up, not that Una ever asked other people to attend to her business. Or maybe everyone in Tuckertown was aware that Thomas and Beal were meeting on the rock, and they'd all conspired to keep it from Zoe, which they should have known was the sure way to alert her to some agitation in their midst.

"You!" she said, pointing a finger on an outstretched arm that bobbed as she caught her breath. "You!" she said again, and Thomas didn't know which of them was in for the full force, but it turned out it was Beal. He was not addressed; he was beyond reason. "What are you doing with him? What are you doing with that devil? You come down from there." Beal had her arms behind her, her hands on the rock, as if she would push herself up, but she made no movement. "Isn't it enough that he cut down Randall? It was him that did it. Not his daddy, not his mama, not his sister. It was him that did it. You can't wash black blood off white skin; the Lord will see it on his Judgment Day, will see that black stain on his hands and send him straight to Hell." She had advanced into the center of the clearing, and at this, Beal hiked herself to the very top of the rock, pulled her feet up so they couldn't get clasped in those arthritic hands. Zoe came to the base of the rock; she was nearly bald, just a few gray wisps. "You lie down with your brother's murderer," she said. "You sleep with the Devil and your female parts will burn. You'll make a Monkey child with this devil, and on the day you are delivered, it will come out of your chest with your heart in its claws." She was out of breath from this, and while she gasped, she kept jabbing her finger toward Beal: *you, you, you.* "You think he's going to take you away from us? You think he's going to lift you out of our bondage? You're a fool if you think that. We deserve what happens to us if you think that. Hold up your legs for his irons! Offer your wrists! Lean your neck forward for his iron collar! Do it now."

Beal stood up, wavered a bit, and steadied herself on Thomas's shoulder. She looked down at Thomas and shrugged slightly. Because, after all, it was Zoe saying this, not Una, not one of the Hollydays, not even Zemirah, but Zoe. She dusted off her backside. "I've got to go," she said to Thomas, as if she had chores to do, as if she were being called home for supper. "I'll see you directly." She jumped down from the rock, landed a little closer to Zoe than she had intended, and Zoe took a step back. "Come on now, Aunt Zoe. You take my arm and I'll walk you home."

Zoe eyed Beal with surprise, as if she had lost the thread, as indeed she had, and she took Beal's arm gratefully and leaned hard upon it.

Thomas got back to the Mansion House around four o'clock. Mary was waiting for him at the stoop. "Are you insane?" she shouted as he approached. "Have you completely lost your mind?"

"What did I do?" he said. He meant: *What was it that I did that was so bad, or why was it that what I did was so bad?* "We just talked. I love her, and we just talked at the rock."

By evening, it seemed, everyone knew that Beal and Thomas had met "at the rock," even people in town who had no idea what "the rock" was, as if this place were a public monument, as if they had desecrated hallowed ground. Thomas stood by in dumb amazement while Mary conferred with Abel and Una Terrell, Mr. French. The world, Thomas thought, was going mad. A boy and a girl passed what was supposed to be a sweet hour and the world went mad. Everyone knew about his father and Tabitha, and twenty-four hours ago he was being eulogized as the "finest man on the Shore in this century." Emancipation was almost thirty years ago! Thomas wasn't stupid. He wasn't a child. What was happening around him that he couldn't see? He sat in the kitchen. The stove was cold. He wished Hattie's Mary were there, but the funeral had tired her out; Solomon had died a year ago, and now she was slipping away. "What did we do?" he asked Abel and Una, and neither answered, just looked at him with fear in their eyes, and sadness, maybe even sympathy, but no anger. Mostly fear.

"Things are changing around us," said Abel.

"Where is Beal? Is she safe?" he asked, not even knowing safe from what. Yes, so okay, so there might be people in town, broken and bitter white men, evil trash that might make it their business and concern that a white boy loved a black girl, but they had always been there, in town, with their belts cinched tight and their hungry brown eyes, drawn to any passing carriage like dogs hoping for scraps, approaching with their hands on the brims of their hats and limping back to the pack with a snarl when nothing was forthcoming. They had always been there; one of them, everyone assumed, had killed Randall. No one had any doubt about that, a Caldwell, a Todman, one of the Bayards. But since when did Thomas, the Baylys, or the Masons have to pay them any mind? Since when were men like that anything to be concerned about? If anyone's safety was an issue, why didn't they all just come up to the Mansion House, as they had done in the war, and wait it out?

And then Mr. French was driving up in his victoria, with Turville the dairyman beside him, and the side curtains were down, and Thomas knew—how, he couldn't be sure—that Beal was in back. "What's happening?" he asked Mary. They were still in the kitchen.

"They're taking her to Easton. She'll be safe there."

"Do we really have to do this?" asked Thomas. "Why would Beal be in danger?"

"Don't be a fool," said Mary. "You're the one they hate, but they can't touch you. No one would dare try anything with you. You know that. You've never known anything different. We can't protect Beal. You've taken away the one thing that could protect her."

"What's that?"

"Her honor. Her virtue."

Your cuffee whore.

"No," said Thomas. "We have risen above that now. Even Randall knows we have risen above it."

She looked at him with dismay, wondering if he was the one who had lost his mind, but she did not question him. "We'll talk about all that tomorrow. For the moment we'll get her out of harm's way."

He ran out through the summer kitchen, yelling for Beal. It had begun to get dark, and there was a chill on the air; the stifling heat of the summer had broken the way it always does on the Chesapeake, with a wind from the northeast. She was standing on the far side of the carriage with her parents and Ruthie, and at this point there was no more secrecy, nothing more to be lost or gained. She lurched for him and he to her, and they held on to each other. He ran his hands down her back and up to her precious shoulders kept warm under a shawl, and he leaned his cheek against the top of her head. She was hugging back hard and their hipbones were touching, and the fronts of their thighs, and they stayed like that for a minute or so, rocking a bit as they resisted losing their bipartite balance and tumbling over, but it seemed to Thomas that if he wanted to protect her, this was the very best way, to make them as one, to extend his body over hers. He looked up at Abel, Una, and Ruthie, and there was little emotion on their faces, but how could they resist someone who loved their daughter, sister, with all his heart. He'd been more than right, earlier, on the rock, when he realized that there was no more time for uncertainty between them; they were lucky to have had that hour of decision as it was. They'd grown up side by side, and there were very few things about each other that they did not know, and the only question had been whether they truly loved all those things. They did. They had thought so on the rock, and now they knew so. They pulled apart; he held on to one of her hands and turned. Mary had come out at some point, so there they all were, her family, what there was of his family, Mr. French, Turville, maybe even Hattie's Mary from her third-floor window directly above them. No one said anything; the horses pawed the ground and the wagon wheels rocked.

"We better go," said Mr. French at last.

"Then I'm going," he said, pulling Beal closer.

Mary and the Terrells glanced at one another. Thomas was not surprised; they'd been scheming for an hour.

"No," said Mary. "The first thing to do is take this precaution, to make sure Beal is safe, and then we'll try to decide what to do."

What to do! We've won, thought Thomas. He could let her go. *I should not have let them take you from me, else I believed that we would soon be reunited in this world.* Abelard was wrong, but he was tricked by those who wished him ill. No one wished Thomas and Beal ill; they were, thought Thomas, perhaps arrogantly, the flower of the Retreat, a joining of all the families. Beal understood just as plainly what had been said. She left his side and went to her mother, like a bride taking leave; Una was sniffling into her handkerchief—her youngest, her baby. Abel stood off helplessly to one side, the befuddled father, not knowing what to do with his hands. But what an odd ceremony, a wordless, brutal betrothal. A getaway carriage with its curtains lowered, horses' hooves pounding in the night. This is the love that has come to me, thought Thomas. Love happens in the midst of war, of plague and famine; it happens when and where it should not and is forbidden, but it wins out. Love is ordinary even in extraordinary circumstances, and why therefore would one not embrace the ordinary and the extraordinary, the carriage with its armed guard, this gathering in the dark and the chill, the danger. He felt blessed; he felt unworthy.

They drove off. Much the same group, or the same sort of group, had stood in this spot watching the carriages bearing Thomas and Randall to college, and just as Randall had never come back, so it seemed that Beal would never come back. Thomas knew what he had done to Abel and Una, to Ruthie and to Ruth, and at that moment he wanted to say that, to acknowledge and apologize for the fact that his love had torn their youngest daughter from them forever. He would say he had never wanted to hurt their family so much. They deserved nothing of what had happened to them, but neither had his mother deserved her nightmares and her wanderings, nor had his father deserved the peach yellows. The Retreat was always claiming its tariff. But this was all in the past now, and he could not blubber like some child, *Oh, I'm so sorry, I'm so so sorry for what I have done.* Beal had left the Retreat, and soon—he did not imagine quite how or into what arrangement—soon he would follow her, for good. He was giving up as much as she was, less of family love but more of material wealth. But soon he would follow her.

Later that evening Thomas and Mary sat at the kitchen table; the new cook, Loretta, had left a chicken, roasted for the funeral just the day before, and some tomatoes ready to be fried, some spoon bread. They ate side by side at the long worktable in the middle of the room, and at one point Mary reached over and lay her arm on Thomas's shoulder. He returned the gesture, until he needed his hand to rip off a drumstick. Neither of them could speak, and Thomas assumed that Mary's silence was the result of too much in her head, as was his. Of all things, what Thomas was thinking of, in these hours of spiritual union for him, was Mary's solitude. She was sitting with him in this darkened kitchen, and he saw ahead with deep sorrow and the certainty of revelation the many days and nights to come when she would be here, for all appearances the only living soul in this heavy ark of a house. He saw that he was abandoning his sister to this place, that she had seemed to come back from Baltimore happily to run the household in their father's last years, but this had been temporary until Thomas was ready to take up his duties and responsibilities, to accept the Retreat as his gift or his burden, as if it mattered to anyone which it was. But that wasn't the way it was going to turn out for him, and, more important, for her. She wasn't unwilling; it was plain to everyone that she wanted the place, wanted to run it, to fashion it in her image. She had ideas, she had her scrapbooks of farm clippings, but not everyone thought it was a good idea; not everyone saw much joy in it. *I do not wear male attire. I don a bloomer suit.* So much had been decided in the previous several hours, and almost none of it had been articulated. Around eleven Mr. French poked his head in the door and said all was well. Thomas helped Mary clean up and waited while she blew out the lamps, and in the light of their two candles as they parted in the upstairs hall, they exchanged the final wordless agreement, that tomorrow they'd have to figure out exactly what to do.

That time three years ago on the peach dock—that time they both now regretted, which might have ended everything—Thomas had first mentioned the word "France." If he was to be honest, he wanted her so badly then that he would have said almost anything to make her believe they had a future. They let white and colored marry in France, he had said, but he didn't know whether it was true; he had simply assumed that if any people anywhere were willing to let lovers be joined despite barriers, it would be the French. So what if Abelard and Héloïse were torn asunder; that was in the twelfth century. (So what if Abelard had been emasculated; he wrote later that it hadn't hurt.) The French were people of love. Back when Mary had spent her year there, he had always been reluctant to tell people that's where she was because it seemed vaguely sinful. Even the convent wasn't quite enough to remove this tincture of loose morals from the word. So it didn't surprise him, but it did bring this old association to mind when the next day Mary said they could go to France. "That's all I can think of," she said. "If you are willing to marry—"

"Willing?" he interrupted, trying not to raise his voice. "That's what we want. That's all we want. To be married and left to live our lives."

She paused long enough to express displeasure at his outburst and to restore suitable emphasis on the condition she was laying out. "Willing, as I was saying, to be married in the Catholic Church."

"The Catholic Church? What difference does that make? I wouldn't have thought the Catholics would be any more keen to marry us than the Episcopalians."

"You underestimate us, just the way Papa did."

Thomas had no interest in a debate about this. "Beal isn't Catholic," he said.

"That can be changed, if she's willing."

Sin, he thought. Sin and confession. She'd have to confess the fact that they had sinned on the peach dock, but in that instant it occurred to him that this was just what she might want to do. *I have lived without sin.* She seemed already to be adopting the worst of it, of Catholicism, so why not the best? Why not accept absolution and awake the next day in a different world? "I think she would be."

"Good," said Mary. Neither of them spoke for a minute. They were sitting in their father's old office, the implements of research, of chemistry and horticulture, all around them: a sad place, the locus of yellowed dreams, a symbol of the failure of science. Like all Masons, including his sister, Thomas had abilities as a scientist, as a man of numbers, but no interest. "I didn't think you'd object," she said, continuing her own presentation. "Mama is coming back."

He groaned. She'd been there for the funeral and had left on the first steamer she could catch within the bounds of any sort of propriety. Thomas imagined that had been her final visit to the Retreat. He had no idea if she knew anything at all about Beal, if she even knew Beal existed.

"And the Cardinal."

"What? Why him? Are we going to get all this done today? Is he going to celebrate Mass for us in the parlor? Confessions all around?"

She stared at him for a moment, a hardened, unflinching face. "Don't be sarcastic," she said finally, with the effort of someone who really has no time for the present moment. "He's a great man, and he'll help us. You ought to be more than grateful. But gratitude, acknowledgment of what you're putting everyone through, awareness of the dangers, simple recognition of the issues you are throwing into other peoples' laps like a ten-year-old . . . Well, Thomas, none of that seems part of it for you. As brother and sister, we've never had a chance to be close, have we? No, I agree, Mother's choices didn't help. But no matter what, I'd think that as Masons we'd share some sense of duty. Don't interrupt. Some sense of the appropriateness of our deeds. Yes, this is something a Mason would do; no, this is not something a Mason would do. But I have no idea how you think. To my mind you have no morals at all except those driven by your own interest. Well, fine. We'll get this done. But there is one thing in all this you have to understand, Thomas. You and Beal are up against bigotries and hatreds and ways of life and cultures that are bigger and more powerful than you and I can imagine. There's only one force on earth that can contend with hatred of this magnitude, and that's the Catholic Church. We can send you to France, and the Sisters of the Sacred Heart will get you settled and watch out for you, but only if you're Catholic and only if you are married. There is no priest in this country who would marry you without the Cardinal's approval, and even he can never admit he gave it. Does that spell it out for you? Or do you have a better idea?"

Thomas did not have a better idea. When his mother entered later that afternoon with Cardinal Gibbons, breathtaking in his garb, Thomas had to acknowledge that if this august and assured presence was on his side, maybe everything was going to be all right. He was, after all, the de facto Pope of America, a plenipotentiary who had taken over in Baltimore, the Vatican of America, and his job was to pronounce the future. He had a narrow face and sharp eyes; "shrewd" was the word that came to Thomas's mind. A calculator. A born Marylander. He had a laugh that seemed both comforting and patronizing, and when Abel and Una entered, he stood up and greeted them with a bow. They sat in the waterside parlor and did indeed conclude their meeting with a prayer, but before that it was all business. Beal, who was now back in Hampton, would begin her instruction immediately with a Josephite priest who was preparing to open a parish for colored in Norfolk and celebrated Mass once a month in a colored school building in Hampton. None of this was easy or ideal, said the Cardinal. There were . . . political issues for him in Virginia, once his diocese, but no longer. But when she had finished her conversion, the Josephites would marry them in that rough sanctuary and they would get on a ship to France and be put into the hands of the Sacred Heart. There had of course not been time to arrange any of this, much less to see if any one of these individuals or institutions would object, but Thomas realized no real impediment was likely to arise as long as the Cardinal had given his blessing.

The Cardinal turned to Una and Abel. "I know how difficult this is for you. But you have nothing to fear."

Una said she appreciated that, but they were still losing their daughter—to France, a place she knew nothing about, even if she was inclined to trust Mary's assurances.

The Cardinal could have given a more vigorous defense of the French—not that in his heart he would have believed much of it—but he moved forward into the business of the day. "Do you approve of this marriage? Have you given your consent?"

Una said their consent hadn't been asked for.

The Cardinal turned his sharp visage to Thomas and gave out a vexed stutter of breath. The Cardinal was displeased; usually when pastoral matters of this sort came to him, all the preliminaries had been attended to. No matter; it was the Masons, after all; he'd take care of the boy. Thomas felt that he was being unfairly whipped; the nature of forbidden love was that consent wasn't part of the conversation. He had never once imagined asking consent from anybody, especially because he knew that if articulated in that way—if the word "consent" was in the sentence—the answer would have to be no. As far as he was concerned, assent for their love, if not consent to marry, had been given the night before, at the carriage. In the presence of everyone gathered, he and Beal had proclaimed their love. But no, when all this abstraction was done, he had not asked Abel and Una the most fundamental question. The Cardinal kept him in his gaze and tipped his head toward them.

Thomas felt like a fool, and he addressed himself to Abel, who he thought was the easier target, and he used the words required. He asked for permission to marry Beal, acknowledged that he was not the perfect match, not the match they might have wished for, but that no one would love her more faithfully than he would, and if they had to go to France for now, they would come back just as soon as the foolishness, the "current confusions" about race, had passed.

The Cardinal smiled and leaned back; all was in order. A word from Abel remained, and then there would be tea. Eliciting obedience, finally, was what his job was about; it didn't seem to matter much what was done in the church's name, as long as it was done obediently. He turned to Ophelia, and it seemed they would now engage in Baltimore small talk.

But Thomas could tell that Mary had something on her mind. "Mary?" he said.

"You have to understand—and Beal and Abel and Una, all have to understand—that you will almost certainly never be able to come back. As a couple, anyway. Papa raised you to see no difference between yourself and Randall and between yourself and the colored on the Retreat, but that's not the way it is, and it's getting worse. Some places might have seen the best, if that can be said, of slavery, but it seems now that we're going to see the worst of Emancipation. And Maryland will just follow along the way she always has. Laws against marriage between whites and colored are just the beginning. Despite," she added, "the leadership of the church."

The Cardinal coughed into his palm, but he wasn't going to argue that Mary was wrong. Cardinal Gibbons had devoted his ministry to progressive causes, and he had felt the forces of repression moving north as much as anyone.

"We understand," said Abel. "We give our consent. We can't change anything, least of all our daughter's choice for a husband. We tried, but it's what she wants, what she's always wanted. We've known it for years, only we could never imagine it happening. So we should be glad, shouldn't we? Shouldn't we give thanks?" he asked, not of himself, not of Una, but of the entire group. "Shouldn't we give thanks that it is going to come to pass?"

"Well now," said the Cardinal, quite overcome with this last speech from this surprisingly articulate colored man, with the perfect transition to a prayer, the way cleared for tea, so pleasant to get out of the heat of the city for a day. And the Retreat: an English Catholic monument was now even more firmly in Catholic hands; in years past it had worried him to hear Ophelia describe Thomas's faith as less than firm, but whatever other rearrangements, legal and spiritual, would be required now, the Retreat was going to be in Mary's hands. A splendid day!

Two months later, Thomas and Mary boarded the new *Alabama* in Baltimore for the trip down to Old Point Comfort, the first leg of what Thomas—adopting the family history in reverse—had come to think of as his retreat from the New World. Their mother was on the dock to see them off, and the previous evening they had enjoyed a surprisingly gay, almost festive dinner. It was to be the last time Thomas saw Ophelia, and he treasured her cheer even if he didn't quite understand it, even if he didn't quite trust it. She might have been trying to demonstrate the pleasures of the life he was leaving, but he knew little of his mother's life on Mount Vernon Place anyway; he had to be shown to the bedroom he would stay in, and he assumed it would be one in the back, so no one would know he had come and gone. But when he came down to the parlor for an aperitif, he discovered that she had invited guests, a single woman—not a nun, as it turned out—and a couple not much older than Mary, for a sort of bon voyage dinner. He did not know what any of them had been told about his trip to France, and no one volunteered the fact that in three days he was to be married. But it was terrapin soup, rockfish, pheasant, apple fritters, and wine, and the woman turned out to be a professor of French and eager to talk of Provence, and the couple were transplants from Massachusetts, all Catholics, of course, but jolly. Mary had been the quiet one, and halfway through the dinner it occurred to Thomas that their mother had invited the couple in order to present a positive side of marriage, even a marriage as late as Mary's would be, if she ever did it. No wonder Mary said little.

The mighty *Alabama*: steel-hulled, all electric lighting and call bells and steam heat. Of the four vessels required to effect this retreat from the New World, it was an irony that this leg down the Chesapeake, the night boat on the humble Old Bay Line, not even the French Line's finest, would turn out to be more comfortable, better-appointed, more impeccably crewed—a high-water mark, as it turned out, for Chesapeake steam packets, not that Thomas and Mary were thinking of such things. They cast off at 4:00 p.m. from Light Street with an exquisite yellow October sun at their backs, and once out in the Bay, they sat on deck chairs on the port side and made out the lands and waters of the Retreat as they passed by on the opposite shore: Eastern Neck, the mouth of the Chester, the Love Point Lighthouse, Kent Island. As far as Thomas was concerned, it was all Mary's now, though she had refused, for the moment, to allow him to sign it over to her.

He asked Mary what she intended to do with the place, and she answered that she had a vision for the Eastern Shore, for the Retreat, and that vision—well, it could seem a little silly when said like this—was something soft and sweet. Jerseys. Sad-eyed Jersey cattle. The finest herd of Jerseys in America, and the most modern sanitary dairy on the Eastern Shore.

"Not exactly needlepoint and altar flowers."

"No," she said. She held up her hands—big, broad male palms and fingers of a practical shape. "These weren't made for needlepoint."

"Will you be happy? Will you find a husband?"

"I don't think I have to find a husband to be happy. I'm not like you. I don't have the capacity to give my heart no matter what it costs. The truth is, I admire the nature of your love, but I don't envy you. You've seemed ensnared for all these years."

"But whether you admire it or envy it, you have made it possible."

"Whether or not you recognize this tonight, it has cost us all much."

Yes, it had cost them much. Mary had no idea how long he had held on in order to outweigh the madness it had created. "When I think of Beal, I feel I am the luckiest man on earth."

They were seated for dinner on the port side as Tilghman Island slid by, and they enjoyed oyster stew, crab cakes, and pork loin. Their fellow diners were a rough sort for this kind of luxe: merchants, traders, men sloppily groomed; there perhaps lay the flaw in the business plan of the Old Bay Line. By the time Mary and Thomas were enjoying the stew, Una, Abel, and Ruthie had arrived in Hampton after taking the train down the cape and the ferry across the mouth of the Bay. It was the first time Una had ever been off the peninsula, first time ever to such a city as Hampton, where the colored lived in houses with wraparound porches and had their own public library, their own college. She cried when she saw Beal because she was so beautiful and happy, and because Una couldn't understand this love; she couldn't believe it would not fail and then how in the world would they ever find her and bring her home from France?

Mary and Thomas resumed their seats on the port rail in time to see the Hooper Strait Light twinkle faintly from the choppy and dangerous waters where the Nanticoke became Tangier Sound. On the bridge, Captain McDaniels remarked as he always did that it was time for someone to build a proper light off Hooper Island in the Bay, to replace the lightships in that location that never seemed to be there on the dark nights they were needed: sunk by Confederates, burned to the waterline by a careless cook, dragged off moorings by winter storms. It was cold now, and the steward was surprised to find this young gentleman and lady still on deck, took them for a young couple, and brought them blankets and pewter cups of hot milk. Thomas talked into the night; this was not a deathbed confession, but it seemed the time to empty whatever he had to his sister, whom he really didn't know that well. What he thought of things, the Retreat, the peaches, their father, Beal, Randall. Things he regretted, both here and in Philadelphia; things he hoped to make right. "I am interested in grapes," he said. They both paused on this, and then Mary started to laugh. "Grapes? Why not throw in some peaches?" she said. Thomas was done with his reflections by the time the *Alabama* slipped over the fluid demarcation into Virginia waters. And they were in their staterooms but not much asleep as the ship wound past the slendering finger of the cape to the east. To the west were the mouths of the Rappahannock and the York, and they sailed into Hampton Roads as they ate breakfast and by 9:00 a.m. were on the dock at Old Point Comfort, where a carriage waited to transport them and their luggage the two hundred yards to the Hygeia Hotel.

The priest paid a call on Mary and Thomas at eleven. He was a threadbare young man with a thin face and monstrous eyebrows, and he was nervous, if about nothing else, about being around all the moneyed milieu of the Hygeia, rubbing shoulders with all the army officers from Fort Monroe next door. But tea in the fabled dining room offered considerable pleasures. "Of course," he said as soon as the introductions had been completed and they had been seated, "this has all been very rushed." He helped himself to a wide selection of cakes and sandwiches.

"I would suppose," said Mary, "that this is not the first time in the Josephite mission to the Negroes that certain accommodations had to be made in service to a much greater goal."

Father Langlois was reaching for the butter, but bristled somewhat at Mary's suggestion. With his hand in midair, he said, "Those who oppose us in the church and outside the church argue that our converts have not undergone all the inquiries and scrutinies. I assure you, they are well prepared for a life faithful to the gospel." Only after Mary apologized did his hand continue to the butter dish.

"We presented her as a catechumen," he said.

"And why was that necessary? She is a baptized Christian."

"Ahh," said Father Langlois, his pique forgotten. He seemed delighted to encounter a layperson who understood these matters and relieved to be able to sidetrack into ancient Catholic principles. "But as far as we can tell, as much as she herself could describe the practices of her own local sanctuary, she was not baptized in the trinitarian formula. This is typical of our converts."

Mary nodded, but did not enter into debate about this. "But she has been received into the full communion? That is correct?"

"Of course. The Cardinal," he answered. The Cardinal had made it quite clear—"a personal favor to me," he had written—that Beal be received as quickly as possible. Father Langlois would later feel that the Cardinal had overstepped his bounds in this matter, which he had, but never until the day Father Langlois died did he deny that coming into contact with, having business with, the great man was an apex of his ministry. "I regret that she will not be with us for mystagogy."

For a moment, hearing that word, Mary slid back to the Hôtel Biron, to the Holy Mysteries of the Catholic calendar, but now was not the time. "That can't be helped," she said.

"No. But she is . . ." His mind seemed to wander off.

Thomas had been inattentive to these liturgical discussions, but he sensed instantly where the priest was going.

"She is the most lovely young woman. I have enjoyed my conversations with her, as brief as they have been. I daresay she is the loveliest of her race that I have ever encountered. Her eyes—"

"Yes, yes," said Mary. She moved him on to plans for the wedding the next day, and as he was leaving, with a small picnic basket of tasties assembled by the kitchen, she gave him an envelope with an offering check that was sufficiently large to complete the fund-raising for the St. Joseph's church he hoped to build in Norfolk and to pay for a bell for the steeple and a massive parlor stove that, when cranked up, could keep the baptismal font well above freezing. As for himself, personally, Father Langlois was completely satisfied by the tea cakes.

Thomas spent the afternoon and evening composing the last of his various gratitudes and confessions to all, to his mother, to Mary. To Abel and Una he confessed that toward the end of his and Randall's unusually intimate common upbringing, into those last few years of study in the Children's Office, they had grown apart, but Thomas had continued to foster their friendship because it was the way to see Beal, not only to meet as farm children in the barns, but to be greeted as her brother's best friend. He thought they should know how strongly Randall had been resisting their love in the past few years, know that he had resisted for all the right reasons, a matter of principle, a fear for what would happen to every one of them. He would prove Randall wrong, he said, and in so doing would validate Randall's principles. He wrote Oswald, Mary's former fiancé, to tell him that he was moving to France and that he was worried about Mary falling too deep into the Retreat, and he hoped Oswald would invite her over to Baltimore from time to time out of old loyalties. He took tea with Mary just after finishing that letter, and he felt both disloyal and sad; perhaps neither one of them was going to live a conventional life. Something about their parents' marriage, or about the Retreat itself, had seemed to turn them both away. They both took dinner in their rooms, by now needing a break from chitchat, and thus it was that Thomas spent the last night of his life in America in Phoebus, Virginia—room 309, the Hygeia Hotel—eating fried oysters and having a glass of cider, thinking about his love, his future wife, the little Negro girl, prettiest-thing-you-ever-did-see, Beal Terrell. He laid out the clothes he would wear for his wedding day and reassembled his steamer trunk, which was full of what he would need for the voyage, the first months in France. He'd brought very little of this life he was now departing: a few of his father's texts on viniculture, his copy of *Paradise Lost,* a drawing of Mary by one of her friends in the convent, a string of peach pits he and Tabitha had carved into miniature baskets, and a driftwood carving of two boys that Randall had given him for his birthday so many years ago.

He wrote one final letter to his lawyer, and when he was done, he went to the window and looked east. The waters of Hampton Roads were pebbled in the moonlight; retreating Masons from England in 1657 had passed by here, perhaps even stopped for water on their way up the Chesapeake. The Emigrant, the man whose name was almost never spoken: Catholic gentleman, by family lore the surgeon to Queen Henrietta Maria before she fled to France—yes, thought Thomas, we all flee to France—running for his life with two ships full of livestock, indentured workers, and chattels such as the portrait of his grandfather Oswald, a family genealogy recorded not in a Bible but in an account book, and his most treasured possession, a letter to his father from Robert Catesby written in the hours before Catesby's execution, a hero, a martyred patriot, a great man now forgotten.

In the past three years Thomas and Beal had spent about ten hours in each other's presence; before that, they had spent their lives together. For such lovers, three years was not a long time. This is what Thomas was thinking as he and Mary boarded the carriage for the short jaunt over to Hampton, and he was still reflecting on this as they stepped down from the carriage in front of the simple wooden structure. This was what colored schools looked like, a structure set up on brick piers, a small door into a single barely lit room, but it was still a sanctuary when a priest was in attendance, and a sanctuary was needed, as what Thomas and Beal, not to mention Father Langlois, were doing was illegal. There was a well-dressed colored family to the side of the door, two women in white hats and three or four children, and all of them were staring at Thomas and Mary; a face appeared in the smudged window, then quickly disappeared.

"You leave us when you enter that door," said Mary. "You and Beal go to a world of your own devising."

"We didn't devise it," answered Thomas. "I wouldn't have invented such a thing. This world was already there, always had been. It's just that you never had reason to look at it."

"All right," she said. "All right, Thomas. I just want you to be happy."

"I am happy. And I want you to be happy."

And there was Beal at the door. She was wearing a blue traveling suit; her hat was a little toque, blue lace, a tiny glint of gold braid, lilac flowers. She stood stiffly in these unfamiliar clothes, and she gave him a bashful smile, as if she were more unsure of the hat than of marrying him. "Lord," said Thomas. How far they had come! What a mystery is life! Thomas would have liked to stand there a few moments, Beal in her suit, her long arms now reaching out to him, a moment of joy frozen, something in a dream.

Father Langlois came to the door beside her and beckoned to them. *Come quickly,* he was saying. *Let's get this done before someone reports us to the police.* When Thomas reached her, she took his arm and squeezed, brought her warm body to his side, and they processed to the altar like that, and there were Una and Abel and Ruthie but not Ruth, along with the family Beal had been living with. On the other side of the aisle there was a single distinguished-looking white man, sitting on the groom's side, but only because he was white and not because Thomas had any idea who he was. Father Langlois sped through the liturgy; Una and Ruthie cried and Abel was stoic. The Father blessed them at the end, and he said it finally, as if he meant it. Then they were married, and on the way out they met Colonel Murphy, the man whom Beal had worked for, and he handed her an envelope in which was a letter from his commanding officer, a General Something, asking that all courtesies and services be rendered to Mr. Thomas Bayly and Miss Beal Terrell as they set sail. "Use this if you need it," the colonel said, adding yet another global power, the U.S. Army, to the list of their protectors. He was to die of malaria in the Philippines in a few short years. Thomas's and Beal's luggage had been loaded into the colonel's carriage, and after so many goodbyes of such different varieties in the past few months, this one was brief. They clattered back to Old Point Comfort and boarded the packet to New York as two unrelated individuals, a gentleman and, in the parlance of this particular maritime enterprise, a nigger girl. When they reached New York the following morning, they boarded the CGT liner *La Touraine* as gentleman and maidservant—an unusual ménage, but just barely acceptable as cover—and in the course of that splendid passage, despite the fact that this steamer was considered the handsomest *paquebot* afloat, despite the cuisine and entertainments of the most fashionable sort played out in the decks above, this gentleman barely left his state-room suite, being served his meals by his maid, and when they arrived in Le Havre seven days later, they walked down the gangplank to France arm in arm, as man and wife.

The carpenters arrived before first light, before Mr. French had finished his coffee, laced his boots, fed his chickens, and gathered their eggs. There were three of them—the Irishman, Mr. O'Donnell; the Italian, Mr. Bigotti; and the Ukrainian, Mr. Prodan. Mr. French had always liked and admired the Ukrainian families they had hired as pickers, and in the years to come, he grew to like Mr. Prodan by far the most and to trust Mr. Bigotti by far the least. Mr. Bigotti didn't really steal things; he was a pilferer, a scavenger, a collector of things fallen out of favor and forgotten. The same was true of his wife; they were both strident and dark, like crows. Mr. O'Donnell was a dour, nasty man, but he kept his most noxious ethers to himself outside of his home; when their home was still a tent, it was obvious to all that he did not keep them to himself inside. They arrived in carts with their families, wives, children, and parents, and by the time Mr. French walked to the farmyard, the men had laid out the foundation lines of the first dwelling; the women and children had erected the tents they would live in while their houses were under construction; and the stovepipe out of the cook tent was already smoking. It looked as if the Massachusetts Eighth had impounded the place yet again, though Mr. French had not witnessed that episode firsthand. From the tents came the cries of children, the sharp scolds of the mothers, in three languages. How long, wondered Mr. French, would this arrangement hold together?

Sawyers had been at work for two months at the sawmill they had set up in the woods, and the orderly piles of lumber in the farmyard had reached prodigious heights. Enough lumber to build an ark. One of the surviving slave quarters had been filled with nails, hundreds of pounds of them, along with all the hardware, the hinges, hasps, locks, door sets required for a dozen houses, barns, coops, and dairies. There must be a hundred new doors in the old granary, thought Mr. French, lined up like soldiers; how could there not be waste in all this copiousness? Sash makers and glaziers in town had been delivering windows constantly all winter. Enough shingles to roof over the Roman Forum.

In the shafts of first sun Mr. French could see the three carpenters surveying the storehouse of two-by-eights, two-by-tens. As the lumber accumulated, he had asked the sawyers where were the posts, the sills. Where were the stout members out of which a solid frame was to be constructed? He had been told, not without some sarcasm, that such things were in the past, that all the new structures on the Retreat were to be balloon-framed, box-silled, all held together by nails. "These things is engineered, Pops," said one of the sawyers. "I see," said Mr. French. Engineered. Balloon-framed. Ah.

"Got everything you need?" Mr. French called out to Mr. O'Donnell, in theory the foreman. Mr. French thought of this question as a small joke, not that he allowed himself too many episodes of humor during his workday.

"Brick?" said Mr. O'Donnell.

Oh yes, Mr. French said, there was brick aplenty, and mortar, for the piers and for the chimneys; arriving in the predawn darkness as they had, they must have missed the stockpile of brick under the gray tarps.

Mr. O'Donnell did not thank him for this information. The Ukrainian, Mr. Prodan, gave him a small bow, a friendly and respectful acknowledgment. The Italian smirked, as if he were wondering what use he might have for four tons of brick. There was to be no chatter. It was now only forty minutes into the dawn of the new Retreat—the way forward, the answer to the age-old question, What are we to do with this place? The same question the Emigrant himself must have asked on his first morning—*I left all that I possessed in England for this low-lying swamp?*—and Mr. French was starting to feel extraneous. He'd located these men and the sawyers, and he'd ordered the sawmill from Worcester, Massachusetts, and the nails and the doors, and haggled over the best price or arrangement in each of these transactions, but his opinions and judgment had not been solicited. He'd been on the Retreat for almost thirty years, and the last four or five had tested them all to the core: Randall's murder, the failure of the peaches, the death of Mr. Wyatt, the flight of Thomas and Beal. Tested them all, and he could only welcome what Miss Mary was doing, which was to be done with all that, to move on. To create a sanitary dairy that would serve as a model for the entire peninsula. Pure milk. Certified by a committee of doctors. The new idea. To save the children who drank it. To put an end to the white plague. Mr. French could not argue with any of that, couldn't imagine, given the vast sums being invested, that it would ever really pay, but that didn't seem to be Miss Mary's first order of concern.

Still. Mrs. French, née Yeardley, daughter of a blacksmith, born on the Retreat, hardly a day or night of her life spent away from the place, was troubled by all these innovations. "Well," she said when he took the time to lay out the full extent of the plans to her only a few weeks earlier, "it seems unseemly. Not proper."

"Not proper in what way, Mrs. French?" He called her "Mrs. French" when she was being bossy or propounding on decorum and protocol, which she loved to do. "It's not as if we are still in mourning. Mister Wyatt died the day we burned the last of the peach stumps."

"Well, Mister Thomas had hardly packed his bags before she started all this."

Mr. French recalled the letter Thomas had sent him last fall, on the night before his departure. *Of this there must be no doubt or hesitation: the Retreat is Mary's to do with what she feels is best. Upon my mother's death I will renounce my claim, if I ever really had one. Mary won't let me complete my instructions yet, but with you, Mr. French, as a witness, I renounce my claim. I renounce it.* "She'd been planning this for years. She was ready to go."

"Wouldn't have done any of it if Mister Thomas hadn't left."

"Then we're lucky he left and she stayed. Honestly, Alice"—the conversation was turning more pointed—"if England can be ruled by a queen, I think the Retreat can be run by a lady."

Mrs. French stiffened, gathered her posture in an indignant shake of her shoulders. "I declare," she said.

He wasn't sure what she was declaring. "Just let the Masons and the Baylys be, my dear. Let Miss Mary do what she wants to do and let Thomas and that dear child find happiness wherever they can find it."

" 'Dear child,' " she repeated. "Mr. French, I wish you worried and fretted about your own daughters as much as you do about that Negro girl."

Her familiar complaint. He'd very much wanted to go to the wedding, but it would not have been permitted. "None of our daughters has moved to France."

"Jesus, Mary, and Joseph."

Sometimes Mr. French, a Quaker from Pennsylvania, wondered how it was that he had fallen in among all these Catholics.

But no, he didn't entirely disagree that this all felt too sudden, wholesale, and improvident. These carpenters: they had been invited onto the Retreat with the understanding that whatever they saw that they needed or wanted, they could take. He'd need to keep an eye on that Italian, that was sure. The sawyers had laid waste to the woods like a plague of insects. None of these people showed the least respect for the past; none of them had any knowledge of history, and how could they? Mr. French knew what his wife was complaining about: the only way to read this complete transformation was as a repudiation, Miss Mary's repudiation of everything that had gone on at the Retreat in their lifetimes and before. As if this were the way to escape its curses, to run from its past, Randall's death. With her carpenters and cows, Miss Mary was renouncing the Retreat as definitively as Thomas had in his letter. If the mule barn was the one structure on the place besides the Mansion House and his own home that seemed not to be slated to be replaced, well, what did these tradesmen know or care that it was where they had found Randall's body? If they gazed over the fields that would soon become pastures for the dairy herd, they did not, as Mr. French did every single day, every single minute, see the thousands of peach trees that had so recently stood there. Barbarians!

Mr. French was brought back to the moment. As the carpenters pawed through the piles of lumber, contemptuously rejecting a piece now and again with a sarcastic multilingual snarl, Mr. French could hardly keep from shouting out, *Who are you to pass judgment on our trees?*

He saw movement over at the livestock barns, a lantern, a shadow in the doorway. These barns would be razed soon enough. Laid out for an earlier time: pigs, chickens, cows together, milk here, eggs there; the leopard lies down with the kid. Oh, Mr. French remembered Zoe's outburst the day they found Randall's body. *Wolves and lambs,* he had wanted to shout out; *wolves and lambs, not lions and lambs,* as if getting the passage right would restore Randall to life. *Rest in peace, Aunt Zoe.* She had died during the winter; the church was full of wails and laments, but all of Tuckertown, all of the Retreat were relieved to see her pass. But what was to become of the men who worked here? Jack Turville, the toothless old dairyman, hardly the person to create a model of purity and sanitation. Jack Turville bathed once a season; his wife sewed up the rips and tears in his clothes only after she grew tired of looking at his undersuit. As long as a pail of milk was still warm from the teat, Jack Turville had once explained, it stayed sanitary no matter what foreign matter caked to the flanks of the cows might fall into it. "That's nature's way," he said. Jack Turville was out, but one of his hands, Robert Junior Turner, for reasons Mr. French couldn't quite gather, was in. A decent enough worker, it seemed, if not at all the man his father was. Miss Mary often requested him for help on special projects. Robert Junior—and his young pregnant wife, whatever her name was—would find a place in the new Retreat, that seemed certain enough. But Abel? Mr. French could hardly bring himself to think about what was happening to Abel. Mr. French would have thought that the first person Miss Mary might settle in at some dignified and useful work would be Abel. Abel and Una were *parents-in-law* of her brother; Mary was *sister-in-law* to Beal. But she seemed not to care about that, seemed content to continue his salary at the very decent level it had reached with Mister Wyatt, but not to accord him the respect of meaningful work, a title. Mr. French had for some time decided what it should be: chief of the grounds. That's right, all those gardeners that were beginning to come in, let them all report to him; those plantings, the grounds, let that all be Abel's duty. Mr. French wanted an office put into one of those new buildings with a plaque saying CHIEF OF THE GROUNDS on the door. But she wouldn't hear of it. Mr. French had proposed this to her twice, and the first time she listened without comment, and the second time she cut him off. *The gardens are for flowers, not crops.* More to it than that, surely. What sort of wrong had Abel done to her, or what sort of memory or association would he inspire that she would want to avoid? Mr. French could not imagine that she blamed Abel for Thomas and Beal. If there was blame in that, they all shared it; they all saw what was happening to those children long before the children even knew it themselves. The hardness in Mary did not surprise Mr. French; they'd all had plenty of opportunity to observe this willfulness, and he didn't fault her for it. When she came back before Mister Wyatt died, they'd dumped the whole mess in her lap, leaned right hard on her, and she'd taken the strain. She'd opened her arms like Jesus and the little children, said "Suffer them to come to me." She'd leaned over like Atlas, ready to take the weight of the world. He admired her strength, her self-confidence. But these burdens had not been without cost: the studious girl, the winsome young woman, the cheerful apprentice, even the loyal daughter had all gotten lost somewhere in the back halls of the Mansion House. And on this matter of Abel he could make no accommodation. What was that all about?

Later that day Mr. French paid his customary thrice-weekly business call on Miss Mary, and they sat in Mister Wyatt's office in front of a pile of architectural plans about two inches deep. Houses for the carpenters, a house for the dairyman, and houses for his staff, a new hundred-stanchion tiled dairy barn, a milk chiller room, bottling room. New granaries, corncribs, equipment sheds. A building for the live steam and power plant she anticipated installing. A farm office and a hospital barn. In the hospital barn, a small space labeled CHEMISTRY OFFICE. Mr. French had thus far not been charged with locating a qualified chemist, which was a relief, as he didn't know what a chemist would be hired to do. A new stable, half of it designed for horses and carriages, the other half for motorcars! A new cottage for the coachman to live in. A house for the groundskeeper. (Abel's job!) Doors to this and access to that; efficiencies built in as if the architects were engineering people's lives, the comings and goings of hot-blooded creatures, all reducible to these blue lines on the page, and what for? *I'm getting into a state,* said Mr. French to himself. He tried to break free of his gloom by asking Mary about the children.

This was not, of course, an ideal topic for small talk, but Mary answered him. "I've just had a letter. They're in Montpellier, a city on the Mediterranean. The sisters think that is an excellent place for them."

"Why do they think so, if I may ask."

"Because there are many Arabs and Africans who live there. Some are wives and children of French officers who served in Africa." She paused, as if deciding whether she should continue. "They sound very happy. They have suffered little prejudice against them. I pray for them every night. I pray for Beal's safety and for Thomas's soul."

Mr. French found this distinction a little hard to understand—Beal's body but Thomas's soul. If one feared for them, why not also for Beal's soul and Thomas's body? Perhaps this was something Catholic, but those had indeed seemed the stakes during the last years at the Retreat, the night of Beal's final departure. He cared for them both equally, however they were parceled up. They moved on to business. He said that the carpenters had arrived.

"Yes. I heard them coming in this morning."

Well, Mr. French had not, even though his house was closer to the road they traveled than the Mansion House. In any event, he reported that they seemed to be settling in and, as planned, were at work on the three-family row they would move into. It was to be right next to the creek, which made the plumbing for water closets convenient. He reflected silently that there were no water closets in his house, and he couldn't imagine the need for them, but all was to be modern here, the last word in sanitation. He wondered if the cows were to be taught to back themselves up to the creek bank whenever they had to let fly.

"Mr. French. You seem—" she paused. This was the way she spoke, always looking for the right word. "You seem troubled by all this."

He admitted that all these changes, the arrival of the carpenters—it was a lot to take in.

"For me also," she answered. "But it seems that the Retreat is now my problem, and we have to find a way forward. You do agree, don't you? You'll give me all your best efforts? I'm alone without you."

Of course he would. He was not too old—fifty-five—to be starting anew. The last time, thirty years ago, the sap of his youth and Mister Wyatt's and Abel's ran along with the peach trees; this time, not so much sap, but maybe the wisdom to use what he had more productively. He preferred trees to cows: quieter, they gave off sweeter odors. But if circumstances offered this second chance, he would not flag. He'd help Miss Mary get it going, and after he died, she'd find someone to replace him, and his soul—if he had one—would seep back to where it seemed to have settled in life, the earth of the Retreat, and if in decades to come his house was still referred to as "the French House," maybe one or two people would know why. Yes, he thought. My heart this morning goes to death.

It took the carpenters five weeks to build their housing. Balloon framing, whatever that was, did seem to facilitate matters, and he had to applaud the habits of the crew, pounding their hammers away from first light to deep dusk. However they communicated, they got the job done. Perhaps the men were driven by the international discord among the families in the cooking tent. It was the Irish and the Italians mostly, chasing each other with iron skillets; Mr. French had observed that there was a quite pretty—"comely," said Mrs. French—Irish girl and a dark and smooth Italian boy of about the same age, which couldn't be helpful. In the new house this young pair would be living side by side, talking to each other through a crack like Pyramus and Thisbe. The structure was plain, the sort of row-house tenement they might have moved from, but here along Mason's Creek, under two large honey locusts, it seemed more gracious, and the repetition of the three front facades struck him as elegant and economical.

The carpenters turned next to the dwelling for the dairy manager. This was to be a proper house, something suitable for a professional family, with a separate entrance to a corner office, which would allow easy access to the new dairy complex. For now, it seemed a door to nowhere, but at least they had decided on the man, a McCready, an old Eastern Shore name. He was younger than Mr. French wanted, but as the second son of a successful family in Caroline County, he'd come highly recommended. Mr. French liked him immediately—his wide face and lustrous black eyes, bovine eyes, you might call them. A kind person, it seemed; you don't want a cruel man tending livestock. Mr. French took him to the Mansion House, waited for him while he was interviewed by Miss Mary, and brought him back to his house when the interview was done. He seemed a little overwhelmed, especially by the stack of books and pamphlets Miss Mary had given him to read. "Lewis F. Allen, *American Cattle: Their History, Breeding, and Management*," he read off the spine of a particularly fat tome. "William Hoard, *The Dairy Temperament of Cows*," he read off the cover of a stained pamphlet. "Nathan Straus. Henry Coit. Who are these people?" he asked in a slightly desperate tone. "I mean, we're talking about cows, right? This one's"—he peered at it—"in French, I guess. Does she expect me to read that? Someone named Goffart. Get it? Go fart."

Mr. French forgave McCready's outburst. "Miss Mary's made quite a study of these things. It's the way her father went about planting peaches. You won't have to worry about the breeding or the herd, the Jerseys. That's all Miss Mary."

"That's a relief," Mr. McCready said, not sounding relieved.

"I wouldn't worry about the French one. That must have been a mistake."

They were in Mr. French's carriage, and they passed by the construction site of Mr. McCready's new house, the tall, spindly studs of the "balloon frame" sticking two stories in the air. It looked as if they were building a cage for some very large beast, a giraffe or a pack of gorillas.

"Miss Bayly says there's going to be a county milk commission that's going to be inspecting the operation regularly. What's that all about?"

It was true. This milk commission was being created at Miss Mary's insistence. "Look," he said to McCready. "There's lots of ideas around these days about milk, and Miss Mary has chosen to sell what's called certified milk. That's what the commission does. It certifies. They've got their ways about them, but it shouldn't matter that much to you. It's all to the good."

"It's just about keeping clean," said Mr. McCready in mild defense of himself, his family's operation in Caroline County, of smaller fry everywhere. "I don't know about all this science. It's just about keeping the operation clean and the milk cool. It's about the children who will drink it. Isn't that all there is to it?"

"Yes. I believe so. I believe science just tells us why simple good habits work best."

McCready continued. "I don't mean any disrespect, but a good farmer can produce sanitary milk without all this expense." He waved back at the construction site receding behind them.

"Well then, let's say you take a good farmer like yourself and then go to all this expense, you're going to make *really* sanitary milk. You're going to make milk as pure as the drops from your mother's breast."

They both laughed; McCready would do just fine.

"I hear she almost got married but called it off."

They were pulling up to the Frenches' house. "Don't you worry about that, Mr. McCready. I'd advise you to keep your mind and attention on this side of the gulley."

When the carpenters finished the McCreadys' house, it was time for masons to come in and lay up the cinder-block walls of the dairy complex and—while the carpenters built the lofts and roofs above—to lay the gleaming tile on every surface. It was winter now, the winter of 1894, and Mr. French could feel the incipient twentieth century being thrust upon them with its agricultural sciences, its germ theories, and its campaigns for the poor, for social justice. The scientists, the reformers, bespectacled men and dour, plump ladies, were coming and going at the Mansion House, and Mr. French sat in on most of the meetings and presentations and learned that pasteurization destroyed the nutritional qualities of milk, that winter feeding with silage could increase annual yield by thirty percent, that certified milk in jars—bottles!—could save the babies *and* fetch prices double that of typical urban milk ladled from a can. Save the babies of the rich, he thought, but did not say. Still. He felt this was all to the good, but it was leaving him behind. Himself and Abel. He often saw Abel in the mule barn, now that Uncle Pickle Hardy had died and it had fallen to Abel to care for the mules in the building where his son's body had been found. One day in spring Mr. French and Abel sat in the open door of the equipment floor and watched as the dairy complex seemed to be rising out of the mud. The masons had moved on to what were called "silos," an innovation that had the whole county, the whole shore, clucking. "We should be glad, Abel. We should be proud to be part of this."

"Oh. I know that all right. Miss Mary. She's right fixed on this."

Mr. French took out his pipe; tapped it on the doorframe; filled it; riffled through his clothes for a match, but couldn't find one. "You want me to hunt up a match for you?" asked Abel.

"No. Smoking's probably bad for you, like everything else. What we're learning is that living is bad for you."

"I don't think it was ever any other way. Much as you gain, you lose more. Like all this," he said, waving his hand. "Miss Mary's got all the money in the world, so why not. But it's hard to think this really amounts to so much."

"Listen to us," said Mr. French.

"Yup," said Abel.

They watched the work in front of them, the masons raising a pallet of blocks with a pulley, the carpenters throwing up rafters into space. "I'm sorry, Abel. I'm so sorry you had to lose so much."

Abel didn't need to reply; he knew Mr. French was sorry, Mrs. French. They all missed Randall. They all missed Beal.

"Have you heard from Beal?"

"Oh, she gets word to us from time to time," he answered, but Mr. French knew that Beal did not write often, that she was not keeping her parents informed of the changes in her life. Mr. French could understand it—so many oceans between Beal and her parents now; she could be excused for thinking a letter simply couldn't travel that far. "In some city in the south of the country," Mr. French said. "No one bothers them. They blend right in with all those different people on the Mediterranean.

That what you hear? Thomas is thinking about buying a vineyard, growing some grapes, if you can imagine that. That Beal's pregnant, expecting anytime. That she's happy? I'm sure that's what you and Una have been hearing."

"Right. That's about what we have been hearing."

Once the dairy complex was finished, the carpenters moved to the hospital barn with its vast herd office, and then they kept going to the other side of the gulley and built the stable, the coachman's cottage, the groundskeeper's cottage—oh, Mr. French found him too, a prissy little bachelor from New England, a white man to do the job that should have been Abel's—and anytime the carpenters didn't know what to do, they'd build a shed, a chicken coop, a kerosene shack. In the nearly seven years that they lived on the Retreat, they built, Mr. French reckoned, thirty-three structures. And then one morning in the spring of 1900 they packed up and left. The Italian boy and the Irish girl had long since sneaked off, and the girl had come back with a babe in arms, and that babe was now walking and talking, and the Prodan children had distinguished themselves as uncommonly bright. The middle one was a prodigy, they said in town, couldn't even speak English when he started and had now skipped ahead two grades. The Prodans moved to Cookestown, where they would no doubt prosper, and who knew or cared what happened to the others. The last thing the carpenters did on the way out, on Miss Mary's orders, was to strike a match and burn their row house to the ground. A shame, thought Mr. French; perfectly good housing for one thing, and he'd grown to like the way the building sat right on the creek under the two honey locust trees, as if it were floating.

That Fourth of July, Miss Mary held the first of her teas for the workers and the families of the Retreat. "I should like all to attend," she said to Mr. French, which he understood she meant as a generous gesture, but it made him wonder exactly how to communicate this word to the guests—as an invitation or a summons? He needn't have worried. They all would have come either way, and by nightfall it was known throughout the town that Miss Mary Bayly was opening the doors of the Mansion House to every damn shitkicker and nigger she could find. That was the way they spoke of her, of the Baylys. *Her brother run off with that nigger. You hear about Mary Bayly and her Jersey bull?* They might have felt such hatred, no reason that they shouldn't, really, when Mister Wyatt was alive, but they'd been quieter about it, a cur's snarl rather than this open contempt. But now, with Mister Wyatt dead, no reason to hold back. It was that she was a woman, pure and simple; that's what Mr. French believed. She'd become a tough woman, with more than a bit of her grandfather's mathematicism: a cow lived and died on the Retreat by her Babcock tests, a pound and a half of butterfat a day—that's twenty-four ounces, not twenty-three—or she was gone, even if she was a pretty light brown with big, blameless Jersey eyes. Miss Mary was a hardened person, but still a lady; no one who worked directly with Mr. French was allowed even the most veiled ironies about her, much less smirks, haawws, or hand gestures, but he couldn't do much about the chitchat at the hardware store, the barbershop, the park bench.

The invitation was for 5:00 p.m., late by the etiquette of tea parties, but milking had to be done, every cow, with precisely twelve hours between morning and evening milking. And so it was that Mr. McCready and Robert Junior and young Hollyday and the new white milk hand Clem—or was it Clay? Mr. McCready hired and fired his own crew and Mr. French had trouble keeping them straight—had finished milking and the preliminaries of cleanup and had gone home to bathe and dress. Mr. French too. No one could deny that this unusual gathering had been imparting a festive air all week. The Fourth of July! A national holiday in the bright, thick cream of summer. The first Fourth of the new century! I'll be. Miss Mary's motorcar was due to be delivered any day. Imagine that. Nineteen hundred! Mr. French was not too far past sixty, but he could not resist a few moments of pleasure. All that construction done and the herd assembled animal by animal, a fine business in certified milk, the only dairy on the Shore that could meet the standards, truly a model. Not as pretty as the peaches, but it wasn't supposed to be; this was the age of mechanization, of science. The Retreat had risen, and it was a second chance for all of them, and if Mr. French harked back to the youthful satisfactions of those first days and years of the orchards, he did not dwell on the precedent set by the failures. Better now to look forward.

Mrs. French had been dressed for an hour before he got home, and therefore she put her full energies into his preparations.

"Mrs. French. Please. A little privacy," he said.

"You will need help with your collar."

"If I need help with my collar, I will ask for it."

She took a step back from him, then another, placed her fingers on her sweet round cheek, a sign that he had wounded her.

"Dear," he said.

"Yes?"

"You look very lovely," he said, and she did, a fine green dress with a quite snappy jacket thing, lace, bows; if her waist was not quite as trim as it once had been, she had broad shoulders and made a fine figure. He reached out to pat her arm and then ran some of the ornament of her sleeve between his thumb and forefinger.

"Cheviot," she said.

Mr. French wasn't sure what she meant, but he was caught up in the pleasures of the moment, and he would have liked to delay this dressing a bit and lie down with her, but it was out of the question. Through his window, down his lane to the county road, he could see a line of wagons bravely up from Tuckertown, seven of them, Abel and Una and Ruthie almost surely at the lead—yes, that did seem to be Abel's shiny bald head, uncovered as usual, in the first wagon—followed by Gales and Hollydays and Hardys and Turners and Tabitha and her husband, Raymond Gould. Mr. French could see a pretty froth of pink and yellow ribbons in the girls' hair, and the dots of white collars on the men who had suits, and on all the women, such wonderful hats, feathers, flowers; in the slight distance the hats became their heads, and this modest hallucination was funny, joyful. He relented on the collar, and his wife came back full force, rasping the starch into his skin, battering his poor Adam's apple. It reminded him of the way she used to brush their daughters' hair, so grimly, viciously, as if this were their penance for being female.

The wagons had run out of steam at the top of the Mansion House lane, curled into a circle as if expecting attack. Mr. French knew what they were feeling; he was feeling it himself. It was not as if he had ever been all that comfortable in the Mansion House, even with Mister Wyatt, with its ghosts and whispers of sorrow. In the French House there were just the two of them now, but the sounds of their daughters were in every room, happy sounds for the most part, the noises of dressing for a future anticipated with pleasure, not with this constant pulling back, this worried continuing, this fear that for all this effort, nothing but reverses awaited them. Well, Mr. French hoped such premonitions could at last be lifted from the Retreat, and if it happened, he would have Miss Mary to thank, they all would, but this party—what was it going to be like? Except for the servants, Mary had little directly to do with the workers, and they all kept their distance. As to what went on in the Mansion House, Mr. French had no inkling, had no way to imagine Miss Mary sitting down to dinner alone. *Thank you, Wylla, dear. You tell Loretta that her rockfish was perfect as always.* No, Mr. French could not quite figure that sort of affectionate comity. So what was supposed to happen at this party? Were people supposed to talk, or was Miss Mary going to give a speech? Were they really all going to be in the same room? Really? Or were there to be two parties, separate but equal? Were the men supposed to stand and the ladies sit, or was it the other way around? Was the food going to be enough of a dinner or would they have to go to bed a little hungry? Would the children behave, the girls say *Yes, Miss Mary* or *No thank you, Miss Mary,* as they had been told; would the boys sit still and keep their hands out of their pockets; would the babies please not cry?

Mr. French could drive the direct route through the farmyard, past the new silos, the new dairy, or out their lane and back in the Mansion House lane. "We'd better go rescue them," he said as they climbed into their carriage.

"Poor things," said Mrs. French. "This isn't fair to them."

"This is Miss Mary's idea of paying back, showing her gratitude."

"Seems to me a side of bacon and a turkey to every house would do that better."

"There isn't a person in the county who wouldn't come to this party if they had a chance, no matter what they say."

Mrs. French humphed, but there she was in her cheviot—a garment? a style? a kind of fabric?—she'd spent the last three weeks sewing.

They drew up to the wagons, passed down the line of nervous faces. It was Robert Senior driving the wagon with Eleanor, Robert Junior's wife, and his baby—they called him Robert Baby—but no sign of Robert Junior. Where was he? Mr. French wondered; always just one step out of trouble. Abel and Una were in the lead. "Ready for it, Abel?" asked Mr. French.

"You can't say she doesn't mean well," answered Abel. "There'd be no reason to say that."

"No. There wouldn't," said Mr. French, and he gave a little tsk to his mare and the line of mules and wagons fell in behind him. When they reached the Mansion House, he drove right up to the front portico and wheeled around in his seat to beckon the wagons, which had stopped at the summer kitchen entrance, to follow. Ralph Peters, the new butler hired over from Baltimore after old Solomon had died, was standing at the top of the portico steps, and he seemed not to know what to make of this crowd, these rough country Negroes, all these children. He was a formal city man, no more to Mr. French's liking than the new gardener, Mr. de la Tour. De la Tour! Murphy, more like it. But there at his side, to Mr. French's slight surprise, was Robert Junior, in his suit, acting like a host.

"What's Robert Junior up to?" asked Mrs. French.

"Damned if I know," he answered.

"She just needs a real man at the door," said Mrs. French, and she was right. There was hardly a male of any description in this house of women: Miss Mary; Loretta; the girl Delia in the kitchen; Tabitha's daughter, Ajax Gould, moved in to take care of laundry; the front maid Wylla; and Tabitha doing whatever she did. Hardly a male on this side of the gulley, unless you counted the coachman, whom Mr. French was planning on firing any day now, a drunk, a thief. They'd only just gotten rid of Mr. Bigotti. The Retreat had always seemed starved for men; it ate them up, it drowned them, it demanded offerings of a few men of every generation: Miss Ophelia's brothers, Mister Wyatt, Randall, casualties of the Retreat, fallen heroes.

"Robert," said Mr. French when he reached the top of the stoop, "what are you doing here?"

He expected remorse, shame, but what he got instead was truculence. "I'm doing what Miss Mary asked me to do."

"Which is what, exactly?" His wife gave a tug on his arm; he was needed to lead the group inside.

"Helping her with this picnic."

"Oral, leave him be."

"You just be careful, you hear me? Don't try and take anything you aren't owed."

"You can trust that, Mr. French," he said. "I'm not taking anything I ain't owed. You can trust that."

Robert Junior. Why are some people never really trusted? Even as children, three little boys at the door, two of them are trying to fib or whine or charm their way inside and the third seems to be taking a different route; what he's got isn't any more subtle, but it's more reckoned, it's contrary, it's unholy. You feel as if you can give a simple no to the first two, but the third needs to be engaged for a second longer. That was always Robert Junior.

"Oral!"

Miss Mary was waiting inside the door in the hallway that ran from land to water, from the portico of the entrance to the tall glass doors onto the porch. Mr. French was glad that the few moments it took for his party to squeeze through the door gave him time to clear his mind. Robert Junior was just not the person to whom Miss Mary should be entrusting any portion of her life. Why not Abel, for God's sake? Not that Abel would stand at the top of the stoop in a suit. Not that Miss Mary's relationship with Abel was uncomplicated. Well, he'd ponder this later, but for the moment, he had to move on. His wife was standing beside Miss Mary, and Mr. French was struck with the fact that what she was wearing was not at all unlike what his wife was wearing; they met clothed as equals. He knew Alice would be pleased and relieved. Was that cheviot? Miss Mary knew the names of more of the help than Mr. French would have expected, and once she got straight which family was which, she addressed each one of the children by name, which terrified them but couldn't help but flatter their mothers. Miss Mary was trying very hard with this, not all that natural to her makeup to give a party no matter who the guests were. She was much more comfortable in the herd office, out inspecting the milking, or meeting with her band of milk activists in Mister Wyatt's office. "What a lovely baby. It's Sarah, isn't it?" Miss Mary would never have babies of her own, never marry, and Mr. French thought that was too bad for her, even if he assumed she wouldn't agree. "Mr. Gould. Thank you for the basket of peas Ajax brought round." Mr. French had never heard her try to charm the hands like this. "Please make your way to the porch. These two lads look positively parched. It's James and Peter, if I'm not mistaken." Most of the colored had attached themselves to Mrs. French, and she understood their need and showed them the way out onto the porch. *Thank you, Alice,* thought Mr. French, because he stayed in that end of the hall with Miss Mary as she greeted the white families who were now arriving in a similar desperate little clump: the McCreadys were performing the same role for them that the Frenches had performed for the colored. Behind them were Clem and his cousin Clay—so that was it! there had been two of them all along, Clem and Clay!—the milk driver Staley and his loose, sloe-eyed wife and all those kids, the worst-dressed and worst-behaved on the Retreat; the mechanic and smith Olian, a genius, but sort of a nut who mumbled to himself as he worked; Olian's wife and her children of a widowed marriage. Mr. French didn't know why he felt his place was here, lurking protectively at Miss Mary's side, except that she seemed so alone greeting people, this once-great family now reduced to its last daughter. It seemed, at this moment, a lot to bear. Mr. French pictured a pyramid inverted, the point resting on top of this poor woman's skull, something out of the Inquisition. He had not expected this rush of solicitude, had not expected of this day the realization that the image he had of Miss Mary, a child back from Paris, sparkling at her father's side in the orchards, was now many years in the past. Yes, he was a man with many daughters, and it was natural to pull other young women under his wing, especially those who were struggling. Mr. French had a sixth sense for young women in need; he could see it past the makeup and manners; he had been seeing it all his adult life.

The grandfather clock on the stairs pinged the quarter hour. The portraits of the Emigrant and his wife glowered down from the stairwell.

"I believe that is everyone," he said to Miss Mary. "I wouldn't expect to see the coachman."

"Indeed," she said. "I fired him this morning. He was drunk."

"Ah," said Mr. French. "I had been intending to do the same after church on Sunday. I'm sorry I was too late."

"No need to apologize," she said. "I do hope this is a pleasant event for our people." From the porch came a slight murmur, though Mr. French could picture the scene well enough: everyone standing; black on the end of the porch closest to the kitchen, the one place in this house where they might feel comfortable; white far at the other end, at the corner where the breezes now building off the Bay flowed freely.

"I guess I need to go out and entertain. I don't know what to say. I spend very little time socializing."

"You don't have to entertain, Miss Mary. But I guess you do have to go out."

"Thank you for standing with me," she said.

"Your father would be very proud of you," he said. He could barely remember the good old days, the days of Mister Wyatt's prime, his quicksilver manners, his light, common touch. Miss Mary had none of these gifts, these advantages; she had tried to school herself, but the lessons always showed, as if she had written cues on her palm. "He'd be proud of what you have done with the Retreat."

"It had to be done. Didn't it? It couldn't go on the way it was. I couldn't have borne it."

"Of course," said Mr. French, and then, quite without intending it, he offered his arm to her, and she took it.

The scene they entered was more relaxed and genial than he had imagined, though it was true that each group had established a home base where he expected them, and no one thus far had the courage to brave food or beverage. Two heavy mahogany tables had been placed in the center of the porch, and one was covered with platters and boards of tea cakes and seedcakes, bread and pots of marmalade and honey, sandwiches of potted meats, and, on the other table, two enormous crystal bowls of iced tea and lemonade, with about a hundred small punch cups fanned out to either side. There was food and crockery enough for twice, maybe three times the number of guests. Mr. French knew that all the food not eaten would go home to Tuckertown and to the help houses on the Retreat in baskets, wrapped up in napkins, parceled in waxed paper, and that this was Miss Mary's idea of lavishing the people who worked for her, for overcoming their resistance with generosity, but of course, the opposite was happening. This abundance made no sense. *What is all this here for? Must be laid out for another party later, when we go home.* Even Wylla, stationed at the food table, and cheery, fat, well-loved Delia at the beverages could not seem to overcome the fears, white and black. "Please," said Miss Mary in a quiet and slightly desperate voice. "Please do help yourself to some refreshment."

No one took a step forward. The children looked up at their mothers but held their ground, and just when it seemed to Mr. French that it had fallen to him to overcome this impasse, he heard a familiar voice say, "Well, now. Don't those seedcakes look darling." It was Mrs. French, and she had already been doing her bit, standing with the colored at their end with Robert Baby in her arms. "I think Robert Baby would like a little munch of that seedcake." She proceeded to the table, broke off a small corner of a slice, and nursed it between his firm, demanding, infant lips. "Mmmm," she said. "Is Robert Baby the only little boy or girl who wants some of these cakes?" she asked, and with that, finally, the two sides began to inch toward the middle and, at last, to take plates. And from these groaning tables there seemed no reason beyond unnecessary custom for the children not to take two or three snacks, and for the men, almost weak now with hunger after this long day and the stomach-churning minutes of anticipation, not to take a good slab of bread and a few sandwiches, and for the women not to take small bits of everything because they knew the whole display was young Loretta's magic, who despite her age had already been the cook at the Retreat for nine years, the nine years since Zoe had finally become too unstable, too angry, too full of grief to bear it.

"Well then," said Mr. French to Miss Mary. She had dropped her arm, but not left his side.

"Yes," said Miss Mary, "this is a house for the people."

Mr. French wasn't quite sure about that one, but he let it go, and just as he was beginning to worry about what to do with her, Mrs. French came up to Miss Mary and asked if she wouldn't like to come visit with some of the families. Mr. French would never have expected such a thing from Mrs. French, but as he watched her, he could easily reflect on the way she organized their family holidays with their daughters and families, children redirected and given tasks before they got into trouble, sons-in-law seated in the front parlor, sisterly rivalries blunted. She'd been caviling and complaining about this party for weeks, but when it came about, who else could take over like this? She was born on the place. She knew all the stories; the history of the place, as it now survived, was probably as much her invention as anyone else's. Who'd been there longer, now that a whole generation had died, her own parents among them, and among the dead all the colored who had stayed with the place since Emancipation, kept it going for good or ill: Hattie's Mary and Solomon and Zoe and Zemirah; Uncle Pickle Hardy and Reggie Hollyday? Robert Senior had a few years on her, and she had a few years on Abel and Una, but no matter what, she was the only person who could take over the party and make something happen that all could feel good about.

By now the boys had been sent down the steps to run on the lawns and terraces, and a few of the fathers had followed in order to police the games and keep them out of the flower beds. There were giggles and shouts from behind the box bushes, and then one by one the girls followed, slid off the porch onto the ground, pumping their skinny black and white legs, pigtails flying. "Oh well," said Mrs. McCready. "They done good so far." Mr. French surveyed this scene, Miss Mary now on the lawns, showing a small group of ladies the flower beds, and he couldn't help marking how little this sort of thing had ever—as far as he could tell—been part of life in the Mansion House. What could it have been like for Thomas to grow up here, with just his father as family? No wonder he attached himself to Tabitha and Hattie's Mary and Randall. No wonder he fell in love with Beal, with the *idea* of her family, with Ruth and Ruthie, the older sisters he'd never had until, in those last years and months, he found a sister in Mary.

Mr. French was standing not far from where he had originally landed with Miss Mary, his back up against a long shutter on one of the sets of French doors, the tables in front of him, the columns of the porch, and then the lawns, terraces, the water of Mason Creek, and in the distance, the loblolly pines of Hail Point. He was enjoying these reflections on kith and kin when the butler, Ralph Peters, came up to his side. Mr. French had had nothing to do with selecting and hiring Ralph Peters, and he disliked him from the first moment: language and diction too precise, too white, manner too subservient and punctilious for a self-respecting black man. Mr. French could divine nothing about him that seemed genuine.

"Mr. French, I should like to show something to you."

Mr. French's sugary smile was still there on his face, he supposed, but he could feel it begin to drain. Back to work. "Is this something here in the Mansion House?"

"Yes, sir. It surely is."

"What is it?"

"Well. It's something I'd like to show you."

This was not going to get anywhere, so he raised his hands in a manifestation of surrender and told Peters to lead the way. They proceeded through the hall, past all those brooding portraits that had always seemed so sinister to Mr. French. Why would anyone choose to live in a place where eyes from every wall seemed to stare with such disapproval? They went through the swinging door into the butler's pantry, past the glass-fronted cabinets of china and crystal, into the kitchen, where Loretta was sitting smoking her pipe, surprised by this intrusion and clearly not pleased that it turned out to be Peters, and then up the narrow back stairs into the servants' wing. This was a part of the house that had been built in the 1750s, it was said, the wing that had survived the fire of 1839, and the ceilings were low and the corridors not wide enough for two to pass, and too many people had lived in too small quarters for so many years that the air was fetid and greasy. Mr. French had never been up here; it seemed none of his business, not his place, and he felt doubly that he was invading someone's private space because he was being led here by Peters. He could imagine Peters searching the belongings of everyone who lived there on a regular basis, and he had begun to assume that this was what he was being shown, something stolen found in Delia's wardrobe, evidence of men in Wylla's cubicle. But Mr. Peters took him to a window in the hallway, a small window that looked over the Mason graveyard, and he pointed. Mr. French didn't understand. He looked through the window and wondered why, whatever it was out there that was worth this episode, it had to be seen from just this place, through just this window. But then his eyes settled on the glass and he saw that on one pane something was scratched. He leaned down to bring the scratching into a slant of sunlight. MISS MARY BAYLY, someone had written. 2 FACED.

"You see?" said Ralph Peters.

Well, Mr. French did. Two-faced. He had to think what it meant, scratched here in the servants' wing, and the answer was not so difficult. Who isn't two-faced—one face for the home, the family, and one face for the world. Mr. French's mind went, for some reason, to the image of himself at Christmas, playing Santa for his grandchildren. Now, that was a face he wouldn't want the people he supervised to see. But there was Ralph Peters, smoldering not about disloyalty to Miss Mary, but about an affront to order. An affront to himself! Oh, shoot me now, thought Mr. French.

"Someone on the staff did this," said Peters.

Mr. French nodded. Two-faced. Could there be another story unwinding alongside the one he knew, an unnoticed stream running along the train tracks? Mr. French couldn't imagine it. He supposed, in the shrouded darkness and solitude of the days and nights at the Mansion House, there must certainly be secrets that he knew nothing about, and yes, in the past few years the Mansion House had begun to feel like a force pulling in upon itself, from which nothing could escape: no light, no sounds, no air. Through the centuries the Mansion House and its predecessors had occupied their place as the locus of law and the repository of wealth, the keep of this castle, and even if there was nothing remotely fair or equitable about this, it was to the Mansion House that people turned in times of trouble. But these days, occasionally Mr. French would glance across the gulley and almost expect the Mansion House to be gone, as if it had so little do with its surroundings that it had floated off, looking for a happier situation down the Bay.

But what of all that? He snapped himself back up to full height. This message was just a slur, a weak moment etched into permanence, and he thought it was sad that someone would write such a thing about Mary, a person at this very moment trying so hard to keep life and limb together for all, an awkward young woman—this was the first time Mr. French had ever thought to use that word about her: "awkward"—playing the hostess, taking these working women for a tour of her flower gardens, promising a cutting of this, a bulb of that. Her performance today had shown a face of Miss Mary that Mr. French had not seen before, but it was so plainly a mask, a social convenience, that it was hardly a revelation that needed to be scratched on a pane of glass. It was only human.

"Well?"

"I guess I'm sorry to read this," he said. "I'm sorry that someone would say something like this about her."

"This here is Ajax's hand."

"Ajax?" he asked. He knew who Ajax was, but what he was really asking was how Peters could be so sure it was her handwriting; a slogan scratched angrily into a pane of glass with a point of quartz or something would hardly be a fair sample.

"Ajax Gould. Tabitha Gould's daughter."

Sure, Mr. French thought. Now it gets interesting, but I'm not heading into this swamp. The one thing that had truly surprised him was that Tabitha had not been swept out of the Mansion House on the morning Mister Wyatt died. Tabitha was Mister Wyatt's companion, Thomas's protector; the women distrusted and hated her. But the opposite had happened; Tabitha had assumed some sort of housekeeper role and had hired her daughter. It seemed to Mr. French, in fact, that of all the people in their community Miss Mary could have chosen for her helpers, her circle, she had chosen the least trustworthy: Tabitha, her daughter, Robert Junior; a person with so many human needs apparently unmet, Miss Mary had surrounded herself with people who could not be counted on to speak the truth, but rather might whisper into her ear, reach into the darker organs of her fancy. In fact, the "staff" had been thinning out for years; more and more it was just the cook, Loretta, and Tabitha and her daughter and Robert Junior who had anything much to do with the Mansion House, except for big occasions like this. Mr. French knew that Ralph Peters would be gone soon. With all that in mind, he could only conclude that he knew nothing about what was really going on in the Mansion House, that he would do his best to protect Mary, but he had little leverage if she didn't want to be protected.

"What are you suggesting?" asked Mr. French.

"Why, sir, to let her go."

"Nonsense." Imagine the row that would cause.

"Might I know why?"

"No reason," said Mr. French. "Except that it seems hardly necessary. And you can't prove who it was anyway."

"Then I would like permission to have this glass removed before it inspires others to deface other pieces of property."

Mr. French looked again at the inscription. He could imagine the bruised moment when whoever it was—Ajax was as likely as anyone—was smarting from some criticism and felt there was something that had to be said, a righting of the balance even if nothing about the situation would be changed. He could imagine Delia and Wylla, and Loretta maybe, and who-all else passing by this window and reading this statement and saying, *Yes, yes, yes. Tha's the way it is. You speaking the truth now.* In fact, Mr. French had the brief notion that it might have been written for him, as the person who might indeed be able to take Mary aside. Truth, it seemed to Mr. French, was better spoken than unspoken. *It's done now, writ into glass for the ages.* No way that it was going to be taken away. If Mary had one face for her servants and one face for the rest of the world, better to have this learned all at once than a little bit, drop, drop, drop, at a time.

"No," said Mr. French again. "We'll let it be."

Peters protested again, but Mr. French had had enough, made it clear that by "letting it be" he meant it was not to be touched, that if the house survived for another hundred years, he expected that the inscription would still be there and people could come by and wonder what it meant, about Miss Mary Bayly, about the Retreat, about the way they had all lived in this first year of the new century. The black Americans of the new century would have their chance, and it would begin by proclaiming the truth. Yes, and if anyone was going to keep them down, it was people like Peters. Mr. French knew he shouldn't, but he snapped one last time, "Don't touch it." He left Peters there, retraced his steps down the narrow, winding stairway; he hoped, as he walked back toward the party, that he had indeed said *Don't touch it*, rather than the more pointed *Don't you touch it*. A certain resonance in recent memory suggested the latter. When he returned to the porch, he found that the party, now officially a success, was coming to an end. Well, thought Mr. French, if Miss Mary was considered two-faced, let the public one be seen as sufficiently generous and kind to offset the crueler private one. Mrs. French had established herself as the unofficial hostess of this event, and for as long as it continued, twice a year, Christmas Day and Fourth of July, she would fill that role; she became, indeed, the real face of the party as Miss Mary slowly withdrew and, in the end, didn't attend at all. But this time Miss Mary had taken up her place again at the door as her guests filed out, loosened and sated with food, satisfied that they had accounted themselves well, and relieved to be set free; many of them chanced a warmer phrase or two than mere thanks, something about the seedcakes, the flower gardens, the fine evening, the Fourth of July, a fond memory of her daddy. All the little boys were smudged and shirttailed from their games, and the ribbons in the girls' hair were flopping to one side or in their mother's baskets, and they all said *Thank you, Miss Mary*, or *Much obliged, Miss Mary*. And when they had all paid their respects and Mrs. French had gone ahead to their carriage, Mr. French and Miss Mary had a moment to reflect.

"Did it go well?" she asked. "Was it a success?"

He told her it was, a big success. That it would elevate morale on the Retreat—not that morale was bad. That the Mansion House was indeed a house for the people. That she had shown her generosity and her eagerness to demonstrate that the Retreat was a family, that even if there were squabbles, naturally, from time to time . . . Mr. French went way overboard on all this, talking back to those scratches in a pane of glass that had so wounded him, and Miss Mary was looking at him somewhat guardedly, and he was able to reel it back in and wrap it with his own "Thank you, Miss Mary," and then he was out the door and heading back home with his wife.

The Retreat was now a model dairy, finest on the Eastern Shore, its daily scorecard of equipment and method, condition and cleanliness, judged never less than perfect, one hundred percent. They were producing and shipping certified milk, the highest possible grade, and fetching a dandy price in Baltimore. Mr. French was back in the business of shipping perishables, but in this case, the difference between fresh and spoiled was not a matter of days, but minutes, the morning and preceding evening's production bottled and chilled and out the door on the way to the steamer or the refrigerated Railway Express cars at 10:00 a.m. On the dock on Light Street or the station in Philadelphia at 12:00, in the select stores by 1:00, ready to be purchased by the maids, cooks, nannies, housekeepers, of the families wealthy enough to afford this superquality item, and down the blameless, innocent, sterile gullets of the babes at suppertime. These babies, at least, would be drinking the real thing, even if, across the rest of the city, less advantaged children were drinking a product from God knows where, days old, adulterated with formaldehyde to retard bad odors and colors, ladled from open wooden casks, in some cases, with bacteria counts approaching that of raw sewage. "Behind its veil of opaque whiteness," said a prominent Philadelphia official, "every quart of milk hides a potential peril to public health."

Mr. French was quite aware that behind the discrepancies in the beverage drunk by the two different babes lay a considerable debate. He had heard parts of these debates as a somewhat unwilling observer in Miss Mary's office over the years. Pediatricians from Baltimore. Sanitarians from New Jersey. Rich activists from New York City. Fellow dairymen from New England. But when you came down to it, it seemed to Mr. French just what Mr. McCready had said—just about keeping clean. As the years went by, Mr. French did not warm to cows, even if from time to time, in the evening, they made a pretty sight filing out into the pasture beneath a fiery sky, a vision out of the prints of rural England that his wife so loved. *The Lowing Herd Winds Slowly o'er the Lea. Morning in the Highlands. The Lost Calf.* Things like that. He could look out his window and see those red-brown hides, white cowbirds perched on their withers, and think it all looked rather peaceful, but then they'd start switching their tails and his attention would be turned to the back end, with their explosions of steaming piss and corn-studded spume, and he'd reflect that he didn't much like them, that it was a funny business, this harvesting of their bodily fluids. He wondered at Mr. McCready's patience; even as he might be beating a wayward or recalcitrant animal over the head with a cane, he was doing it without rancor.

In those years Miss Mary was in her office in the hospital barn from eight to eleven in the morning, and about once weekly in the late afternoon when she would randomly take over the task of filling out the daily scorecard. The data poured in: Babcock results, Kock assays, Sedgwick tests, tuberculin screening. After a while the responsibility for accumulating these figures and, in simpler cases, for conducting the tests fell to Robert Junior, which was fine with Mr. McCready, as when he wasn't milking the cows he was busy growing their feed. Mr. French would enter in the morning to find Miss Mary, always dressed like a lady about to pay a call, seated at her desk, and Robert Junior standing in front of her, delivering his reports. Robert Junior deserved his chance, Mr. French could admit that, but how had he obtained it? And why didn't Mr. French approve? Maybe it was the way one or the other of them would glance up when he entered in the middle of these meetings, as if he were interrupting something; maybe it was the fact that Robert Junior often seemed to be assigned jobs that Mr. French knew nothing about. But it was crazy to object to that. Why wasn't it appropriate for Miss Mary to have a right-hand man to take care of the sorts of petty tasks that she herself would perform if she were a man? Why, to get right down to it, was it not understandable that she might enjoy male company? But then, thought Mr. French, to make it proper and to guard against rumor, Robert Junior should be given a title on an office door: ASSISTANT TO THE OWNER or RECORDSMAN FOR THE ESTATE. He liked that last one quite a bit—"recordsman" was his own coinage—but whatever, without this title Miss Mary and Robert Junior were heading slightly off the rails.

He consulted Abel on this, one mild evening in early spring. It was 1904 or perhaps '05. They were sitting on a newly toppled tree trunk on the banks of the creek, in theory discussing whether to remove it or just let it rot or float away in the decades to come. The water was slightly greenish, the unhealthy pallor it took on during the snowmelt and spring rains. "So," Mr. French said after they had exchanged pleasantries, after they had pieced together Thomas and Beal's news as best they could from their various sources, after Abel had protested that he was right content with taking care of the mules. "What do you hear of Robert Junior's mind?"

Abel did not seem to be surprised to be asked this question, but still, he began by deflecting it. "Fine job he's doing. Like his daddy, a good man."

"Oh. That's certain," said Mr. French. Neither of them believed this for a second; they both knew that Abel meant quite the opposite of what he had said, but without rancor: not Robert Junior's fault. They watched a pair of winter swans paddle by, the male showing every willingness to steer closer and beat them with its wings. "But what's his mind? That's what I'm wondering."

"About Miss Mary? That's what you're asking?"

"Yes."

"Well, Mr. French, I'd say Robert Junior is looking out for himself, but no more than I would expect of a man with a family to raise. He had a wild side as a boy, but he seems to have wised up. Far better than

I would have predicted, to tell you the truth. Yes indeed. If he can do a favor from time to time for Miss Mary, he'll do it. We all would, if we were asked."

This was true enough, thought Mr. French.

"He never went out of his way to be chosen," continued Abel. "No one would say he was trying to make something from nothing. But when she was looking for help, he didn't hide, the way some folks would."

Oh, yes. If they saw Miss Mary's eye sweeping toward them, they would duck behind a haystack just as fast as they could, become real busy, too busy to look up. Mr. French remembered that feeling from grade school.

Abel continued. "We all know that even back to Miss Ophelia, everybody felt real bad for Robert Senior that day at the dock. Losing Emily like that. Emily was the kind of girl who gave her heart, and she gave it away in North Carolina the second time, when she thought all was lost, and it tore her up. I think everybody believes there's a little extra kindness to his family to be made up. To Robert Junior and Robert Baby."

"If that's what we're trying to do, we can quit now. No way to make one bit of that up."

Abel nodded.

"But that was almost fifty years ago," Mr. French said.

"I'll be," said Abel. "Fifty years."

That was all Mr. French could do for the moment, and over time Robert Junior's pay was duly increased and the butler Ralph Peters was sent sniveling back to Baltimore, and when Miss Mary announced that she did not need a manservant, it was generally understood that anytime male brawn was needed in the Mansion House, Robert Junior would provide it. Maybe Mr. French just worried too much. That was what his wife said about most things, that he "fretted" too much, except for those times when he was "positively blind, deaf, and dumb" to dangers swirling all around them. Oh, Alice, we have spent too much, or not enough, of our lives together. Besides, by then Miss Mary was more and involved in her associations, the Dairymen of America, the

Jersey Breeders Association, the Milk Board. On this latter, over the past several years Mr. French had begun to hear a more partisan slant than he had noticed earlier. The meetings he attended now seemed less like discussions of various alternatives than mapping out strategies to prevail over rivals. As much as Mr. French didn't want to be there, he realized that he was at risk of being branded disloyal.

"Dr. Knox is coming over tomorrow," Miss Mary announced one day.

"Ah," said Mr. French.

"Dr. J. H. *Mason* Knox," she said. "Probably some cousin." And she added contemptuously, "The Baltimore Babies' *Milk* Association."

"I'm sure we have discussed him."

"We certainly have. He says we are devoting too much of our efforts on the 'tiny heirs of comfort and luxury.' He's a regular Louis Pasteur."

Where oh where, Mr. French wondered, did this edge come from, this sarcasm? He had failed; he was supposed to protect her from the worst, even if it came from within, and he had failed.

Mr. French understood from all this that he was to attend the meeting the next day, that it was to be a confrontation rather than a consultation, that the evil forces of pasteurization were sending Dr. Knox because he might serve as a go-between, a man of the middle ground, and a Mason to boot. For this last reason Mr. French was not surprised that the greetings on the landing of the Mansion House the following day were cordial and full of flatteries.

Dr. Knox began it all as soon as he stepped out of the motorcar. "Miss Bayly, as you well know, Mr. French, has done more to promote milk safety than any farmer in America. We in the cities owe her the greatest gratitude."

In response, as if Mr. French's opinion of these matters could not be left uncorrected, Mary said, "Dr. Knox's work at the Wilson Sanitarium and the Babies' Milk Association has no equal. Tens of thousands of children have survived infancy in Baltimore because of him."

"Not at all," the doctor said, and then allowed himself and his companions to be shown into the front hall. "Ah. The Retreat. It's been many years." He was a big man, full white whiskers and a solid belly; he filled the space as if he could own it. A man with this sort of presence was an unusual sight in the Mansion House these days.

Mary asked which side were the Masons in his family, and he replied that it was his father's mother's mother. "Just a drop of the blood at this point," he added.

Mary showed them into the dining room, where tea had been laid out, and she beckoned them into seats she had roughly assigned—Dr. Knox and his two rather charmless assistants, a shifty man and an unusually large woman, on one side, and Mary on the other, and to his shock and dismay, Mr. French at the head. As referee? They sat, took their tea. The house was silent.

"Now then," said Miss Mary.

"You know why we're here," said Dr. Knox.

From here on, Mr. French was simply trying to stay afloat. "The Good Ship French," as his wife called him, being buffeted in the winds blasting between the forces of pure milk on one side—Miss Mary's—and the masses in favor of pasteurization, Dr. Knox's side, on the other. Mr. French tried to keep his composure by keeping score.

"We do not need to compare pure milk to any ideal standards," said Dr. Knox. "What we must do is compare the splendid product of the Retreat"—he was still trying flattery—"to that which the ordinary child is being served this very day. That discrepancy is our challenge."

Mr. French thought this was a pretty good point: instead of looking at the matter from the height of perfection, one ought to try gazing up from the depths of misery. Dr. Knox seemed to be saying that if one could not, in the end, ensure that all milk entering the city was fresh and in a sanitary condition, then the main effort must be on intervention, on the middleman, the processor. Science permitting, raise what came in the door, buzzing with flies, fizzing with swarms of bacteria, to at least tolerable standards.

Miss Mary heard this all with apparent disinterest. When Dr. Knox was done laying out his points, she waited a moment, took a drink of tea. "Then you have no response to Dr. Flugge's findings? You believe that it is acceptable if the ferments are simply boiled away? You at the

Wilson Sanitarium are prepared for an epidemic of scurvy and rickets? We might as well let the flash pasteurizers have their way."

"Miss Bayly," Dr. Knox said, clearly furious, though Mr. French could not figure out exactly what was Miss Mary's most inflammatory charge. All these names, these competing claims; perhaps he should have been more attentive over the past few years. Dr. Knox added a few more names to the mix. Conn and Rosenau. A few more technical parameters—at 60 degrees centigrade for twenty minutes. "You have always been a person of science," he concluded. "Why can't you accept that these new discoveries have solved the problems we all admitted were real?"

This went on. Dr. Knox struck Mr. French as a reasonable person, a man in the middle with children's health his only portfolio. Later, when Mr. French reflected on this afternoon, he realized that out there in the realms of science and public policy, the tide had turned. Miss Mary, it was suddenly clear, had made a choice early on for all the right reasons, had taken the fundamental position that purity lay in nature, that it was technology's purpose to preserve as much of that purity as could be done by fallible, fallen human beings. This was perhaps Mister Wyatt's view, as it was Mr. French's; possibly, it was to be all their undoing. Science had now offered a new way of thinking in this golden age—that through human intervention, through science, man could achieve higher levels of perfection than the Creator Himself. This was a radically different kind of science from any Mr. French had previously imagined. He did not spend much time thinking about the Creator, but Miss Mary certainly did, and over the months to come, as he pondered the changes around him, he realized that Miss Mary's view was most Catholic: that participating in nature was to join fully in the Divine Plan. The rituals of the dairy barn were perhaps not so different from those of the sanctuary. The new technology was an arrogant sacrilege.

There was a silence. Mr. French wished Delia or Wylla would come bursting in with fresh tea. At last Miss Mary turned directly to Mr. French. "Do you see? This is what they have been saying to me for years. They have never had the science on their side, they have never proved that pure milk wasn't better, just that it is too difficult to provide in bulk. Therefore, I should not provide it at all. This is not a world I understand." She waved toward the guests but kept her eyes on Mr. French. "Please tell our guests that I am grateful that they have dropped in. Would you be so kind as to show them out?"

She remained seated while she shook their hands, and Mr. French showed them to the door and down the steps. As the very large and silent lady was hefting herself into the cab, Dr. Knox turned to Mr. French. "She has changed," he said. At first Mr. French thought he was referring to the woman in front of him, that she had gained about three stone, but the sorrow in Dr. Knox's voice made it clear he was talking about Miss Mary. "She has the soul of a reformer, but her positions have hardened."

Mr. French said he'd noticed this, but he couldn't really comment on the positions themselves.

"Oh, that's not the point. Her contributions to this cause are unquestioned, whatever the opposing views. I'm worried about her. She's here too much. She's alone too much. You know she maintains a home on Park Avenue."

Mr. French said he understood that. In fact, he was the one who located it, not far from Ophelia's house on Mount Vernon, arranged for its purchase, maintained it, paid a housekeeper year after year to live in this otherwise empty house. All at Miss Ophelia's direction. *Just in case Mary ever comes to her senses.*

Dr. Knox reached into his waistcoat and pulled out a card. "I know she respects you, as her father did. Perhaps you could encourage her to leave the operation to you for a few months and come to the city for the winter." He handed the card to Mr. French.

"That's really not the sort of opinion I am expected to provide," he said, eyeing the card.

"Damn it," said Dr. Knox. "What difference does that make?" Something like that, something that stung Mr. French as they drove off, because he didn't deserve to be scolded, but Dr. Knox was right: Mr. French had known, cared for, and worked for Miss Mary almost since the day she was born. And he had more reason and more cause to be worried about her than this man ever could or did—the hours and hours into the evenings he spent pondering the direction things seemed to be going, the gaps in the story. Mrs. French told him to "pay attention to the farm and leave all this storytelling to Mr. Dickens." Still, over the months to come, he tried from time to time to suggest that Mary might enjoy a break, mentioned that he had ordered the front parlor on Park Avenue repainted and wouldn't she like to see it, commented that February on the Shore could be right mournful, with the winds across the fields and the honking of the waterfowl, but she sniffed it all out, seemed to know that Dr. Knox's card was burning in his pocket.

The good doctor did not let it go. Two months later Mr. French received a letter from Thomas—he wrote from time to time, seemed to understand that whatever personal information he told Mr. French would be passed along to Abel and Una—asking him to intervene, if he could, with Mary. He'd had a letter from a cousin in Baltimore. Thomas said that he had invited, asked, begged her to come over to visit them for the winter at their vineyard, to see her nieces and nephews, to keep on going to Rome, for heaven's sake, a place she had never been. The Pope would no doubt give her an audience. "She respects you," Thomas had written. "You may not know this, but your opinion is the only one besides her own that she values." Mr. French was getting tired of being respected, given the fact that he seemed to have less and less influence over the situation. He didn't know what to do with this letter, decided in the end that no one could make the case more eloquently, more lovingly than Thomas had, and he simply gave the letter to Miss Mary. She made no comment about it, but afterward he felt he had violated not one but two confidences. And then, a few months after that—summer again—who should sail over on a sloop from Baltimore to pay a call but Oswald Stafford, her old beau and former fiancé. He landed at the new pier below the terraces of the Mansion House, and Mr. French walked with Mary down the alley of box bush to the dock to greet him. She was very pleased, dressed in a white summer costume of light, airy fabric in place of the darker and darker and heavier and heavier dresses she wore these days, no matter the heat. Mr. French almost let his jaw drop when she appeared so lightly draped at the stoop, as if he had forgotten that she had legs and a figure, that she was a fine-looking woman who still knew how to dress for a gay occasion. Mr. French remembered Oswald as the young man who had visited the Retreat almost twenty years ago now. He was still extremely handsome, and it would have been lovely, would have cheered Mr. French, would have come as a rapture to Miss Ophelia as she headed to her grave, if Mary had simply boarded the sloop and they had sailed off to renew their engagement and ultimately to marry, and Mr. French and Mr. McCready would be left to evolve the Retreat dairy toward the newer model of milk production, and Mary would return from time to time looking younger and happier with each visit, thinking, perhaps, that in those years at the Retreat she had lost her way a little, the tragedy of Randall and the peaches, grief over her father's death, grief over Thomas's departure, and had transferred everything to the cows and the dairy—*Whew, I was lucky to get out at the last minute, lucky that Oswald came to rescue me. Dear Oswald, always knew what I was thinking, knew when I broke off our engagement that this was what I was going to do, heard me calling in my darkest hour and hired a ship and crew to save me.*

But of course it didn't happen. A cordial greeting, a fine lunch under the portrait of the earlier Oswald, a stroll through the gardens, and with the tide beginning to make navigation out of the creek a challenge, he was gone before the afternoon began to wane. And the next morning Miss Mary was back in her drab outfits, receiving reports from Robert Junior.

When Miss Ophelia was dying, in 1908, Mary did return to Baltimore to nurse her through her last days, though there seemed at least a dozen nuns and doctors on hand, and when she died, the church took over all matters, and her funeral was in some ways a swan song for the mighty Catholic Church in Baltimore, the death of one of its few surviving English aristocrats. The church in Baltimore was to be all Irish and Poles from there on out. The way was prepared for Mary to take over her mother's place as Catholic philanthropist, and she did take up some of that mantle and was seen in Baltimore during the cold months from time to time, but she never really left the Retreat again.

Out there, the milk trade had taken its decisive turn, and though there was still a market for milk from the Retreat, it no longer commanded the premium that could make it pay. Miss Mary's Jerseys had once been a bloodline everybody wanted a part of, but new breeds were attracting attention, like those monsters from Holland and Switzerland. Mrs. French had begun to speak of retirement, which Mr. French found preposterous; he'd be dead in six months if he allowed himself to become idle. That's what he said, and he meant it for the most part, but what he really meant was that he couldn't give up on Miss Mary, couldn't let her become the crazy recluse of the Retreat, just she and her servants, Tabitha and Robert Junior. Mr. French must have had a hundred conversations with Robert Junior about this, slyly offering to get him out of it, find him a good job in town, Robert Junior arguing that it was fine, that this was his home, that Robert Baby was now pretty grown up and was fixing to join the army as a mule skinner if the United States came in on this thing in France, and he wanted Robert Baby to have a place and a job to come back to.

And then one day little Valerie—Darby's daughter and Zoe's granddaughter—came running to Mr. French just as milking was getting under way and said there had been an accident at the Mansion House and he should come quick. Who was hurt? he asked, and she said it was Robert Junior. Robert Junior had scalded himself somehow, his face, and it was already puffing and blistering red. By the time Mr. French made it up to the Mansion House, Robert Junior had staggered off and Loretta and Ajax were in near hysterics—that he was blinded, that it was coffee, hot coffee thick with sugar, Miss Mary's coffee that had ended up on Robert Junior's face. And Mr. French said to himself, I knew it; I knew something like this was going to happen. He had done what he could to stop it. He'd never have guessed that she'd hurt him, hurt him so badly, but there was now something loose inside her, and he believed what he heard without a moment's argument: she'd thrown a pot of coffee in his face.

There was no time for confronting Miss Mary. He had Loretta call in town for Dr. Ashley, but as it turned out, the doctor wouldn't come treat a colored man, so it was Dr. Rawn, a drunk and a pederast, who showed up later that evening at Robert Junior's door. Thank God Robert Senior was dead by then: that's one thing Mr. French was thinking. Thank God Robert Baby was still in France. Mr. French was running by then, following Robert Junior across the barnyard past the barns and the dairy. Everyone had seen him go by, clutching his face, staggering, howling in pain, and Mr. French finally caught up with him at the rock where the children used to play. He made him take his hands away from his face. Robert Junior was rubbing dirt and sweat into the wound. Mr. French could see the outline of the splash on the side of his head. It had scalded his ear and burned some of his hair off, but he hoped it had missed his eyes. The skin on his cheek was so hot it must have still been doing damage, and he was in pain and frightened, asking if it was bad. "Am I blinded? Is my ear still there?"

Mr. French held his hands on Robert's shoulders to keep him from touching the wound, looked him in the eyes, and told him he was going to be fine, the doctor was on the way, and then he couldn't help it: he took him in his arms and held him for a few seconds, thinking, *Lord God Almighty, this is just one of us, a man trying to live a life, this is a brother to me, and look what we have done to him.*

Valerie had gotten to his house, and just as Mr. French was turning to lead him down the path, his wife, Eleanor, came running out of the woods. Eleanor screamed when she saw him, and Mr. French could hear it all over again as if it were coming straight from dead Aunt Zoe, that Robert Junior had been lying like a lamb with a lion. Mr. French just shook his head; he didn't know what else to do. He followed them as they helped Robert Junior down the path and to their house, waited on the porch for the doctor while they tended to him. It sounded as if something they did caused him so much pain he passed out for a time. There didn't seem to be much treatment available at this point, just clean it off and cool it down and pat it with lard. Una came over and asked him how bad it was, and he told her he didn't know, but Dr. Rawn was on his way.

She looked at him with wild rage. "Him. He'll kill poor Robert Junior if he's sober enough to do it," she said, cranking it out as if no one would ever care for what happened to them. Oh, dear God, he thought;

this is Una, my friend, saying this to me. At this horrific moment all he could think was to try to defend himself; all that he had done, the justice he tried to preserve, the friendship he felt in his heart, was lost to him.

Una went in, and others came and went; people were milling around in the Tuckertown lane, and Mr. French wanted to go out and be with them, to hear what they were saying, to show his horror, but he knew that on the porch he had found the one place where he could be tolerated. Robert Junior had come to by then and was just moaning, still asking about his eye, his ear, his hair. It was getting dark when Phillip Rawn arrived, stinking of bourbon, and Mr. French told him if he didn't snap to and do every damned thing for Robert Junior that a white doctor would do for Woodrow Wilson, he'd cane him in Courthouse Square. But there wasn't much to be done. On his way out, the doctor said the ear would heal. Maybe the hair would grow back; maybe it wouldn't. There'd be scars, but Negro—he'd started to say the other word but thought better of it—Negro scars weren't as visible. The question was the eye. He didn't know about the eye.

Mr. French made it back to the Mansion House at about nine o'clock. Miss Mary's supper was cold on the table, so he knocked on the office door, and when she didn't answer, he let himself in. For seventy years the rich smell of coffee had always been a pleasure to him, had always reminded him of his father, whom he had lost many years before, but the stale, charred fetor in that room cured him of coffee forever. From that day on, he couldn't have a single bean of it in his house. The silver coffeepot lay dented on the floor, a pool of coffee in front of it that looked like dried blood. Miss Mary was sitting at her father's old rolltop desk. She must have hardly moved since the incident. Mr. French could not help it—her ravaged face, blackened eye sockets, wild hair—she looked possessed. She was holding a handkerchief, perhaps the one she had immediately withdrawn from her sleeve to wipe the searing liquid off Robert's face. She hadn't meant to do it, of course she hadn't. She hadn't meant to do it at all, so that's what he said to her first, that she hadn't meant to do it, he knew that, that the last person she would want to harm would be Robert Junior, a man who had done her such service and kindness these past few years. She asked how Robert was, and he told her everything the doctor had said to him, but he didn't tell her it was Rawn and not Ashley, because he wanted her to believe they were doing everything that could be done. He told her he didn't know about the eye.

"Oh Lord," she said. Then she said what sounded like a prayer, in French.

He took a seat. The room was almost dark, just a yellow line of light under the door. He remembered wondering what the point was of all this electricity, why she had bothered to install it if she was going to sit in the dark.

"What happened?" he asked.

"I don't know," she said.

"Well," he said, "what were you doing when it happened?"

"We were talking about the milk reports. I'd been writing a letter to the *American Dairyman*."

"And?" he said.

"I lost my temper. I wanted to throw something, and the pot was in my hand. Valerie had just brought it in hot from the stove. I threw it over there." She pointed to it on the floor, across the room. "But all the coffee came out and hit Robert Junior. I was just trying to throw the pot. I didn't think about the coffee, where it would go."

He asked her if Valerie was still in the room when it happened, and she answered that Tabitha was. He wondered why Tabitha would be in the room when they discussed the milk reports. "That's odd," he said out loud, though it was really directed at his own thought process. That old threesome again, drawn into this inner sanctum. And then his heart simply heaved in his chest, as if a hand had reached past his ribs and given it a shake. Through Miss Mary's fevered eyes he could see that long, dark cave she had been dropping into these past few years, these past twenty-five years, dropping into no matter how hard he had tried to keep her out of it, to pull her back to the surface of the earth in the life-giving sun. In this cave, she was heading for the bottom.

And what he saw, at the bottom of the cave, was Randall. That young, beautiful man gazing upward as if bemused, perhaps intrigued by yet another challenge to his considerable reasoning abilities: What am I doing here? How do I get out?

Mr. French gasped, and despite what slender effort he could interject into such a sudden jolt, he tried to look away from her. Tried not to see what he had seen, to look instead at his boots: *Hmmm, that lace is about to break*; at the floor: *See how the desk chair has worn a groove into the bricks.* But it didn't work. And she knew it, met his horrified expression with a kind of gratefulness that he would have imagined only at the final breath of a long and painful death. No words formed on her lips, but if any had, he could imagine her saying, *What took you so long? Who else?* Mr. French did not want to be subsumed by knowledge; he did not want to be inducted into this unholy trinity, Miss Mary, Robert Junior, Tabitha. He took a slight step backward; in fact, given the bruise that blossomed later on his thigh where he came in contact with a small table, he must have jumped back violently, as if afraid of falling into the abyss in front of him. The abyss out of which Mary gazed at him, still wordless. He could not imagine what role any of them might have played in Randall's death—no role was imaginable, really—only that they all three had a role. He could imagine no scenario for any one of the three of them, holding a knife while Randall cowered, or charged, or froze in disbelief. Even that brief flash of theater sent a skull-cleaving stab of pain through his brain. He tried to make his mind go blank so that it would not invent more of these moving pictures, but the next one that popped up in front of his eyes was Thomas and Beal embracing before the departure the night of their meeting at the rock. He'd suspected it—he was hardly the only one—that Randall's murder had something to do with Thomas and Beal; but with Wyatt, certainly, and Thomas and Mary above suspicion, he could never connect them. It still didn't make any sense to him—what for good God's sake would harming Randall have accomplished—but with the Mary he now beheld in front of him in the picture, he could see with a terrible, almost mathematical symmetry that it could have happened.

He had failed them all; he had not found a way to be the friend and protector he had promised to be. The Mansion House, with Miss Mary in it, had years ago fallen into the deep, or risen into the sky, sailed away with secrets, stories he would never know, could never have known. He was a farm manager, a man good with figures, a clerk; he would have saved them all if he could, and died with the assurance that what he had in the end was what he had given away, but this simply wasn't a path he had been fated, or equipped, to walk.

"They should call the sheriff," she said.

For which crime? he wondered, but looking at her, it seemed likely that she meant both, or either—that it didn't matter which. And did that mean he was supposed to bring this news back to Una and Abel, who were at this moment trying to minister to a man who had something to do with their son's death? No. If he could take his pick of which crime, he'd choose today's assault. "I doubt they'll bother."

"Will you make them do it?"

"No," he said. He wouldn't make them call the sheriff if they didn't want to, wouldn't make them invite the law into their lives when it so often meant nothing but trouble for them. It was all up to Robert Junior and his family, but he would make sure they understood that she wanted them to.

"You're very . . . kind."

He said he didn't think he was. He was just trying to see it from every point of view. That's all he had ever done. Calling someone kind; it's what people say as a way of forgiving the fact that they can't measure up, even to that simplest of human obligations. He stood up. He was tired; he was hungry. His right knee hurt from running all over the place. There was a stain of rose-colored sweat on his shirt from where he had held Robert Junior, though she couldn't see that in the dark.

"What now?" she said.

"I don't know that there is any 'now,' Miss Mary. Same as before, I guess."

Loretta and young Valerie were still in the kitchen when he came out. What now? they wanted to know. *What now?* Wasn't it the deepest irony that here on this place, Mason property for over a hundred years before the founding of the nation, people were always wondering, What now? What's going to happen to us? That's what the slaves were saying the morning they were herded out onto the rivershore to wait for the schooner. What might have created a sense of permanence seemed only to instill uncertainty; you try to grab the Retreat and the sand just flows through your fingers. What now? they were wondering in Tuckertown as they tended Robert Junior in his pain. What now? wondered Mr. McCready: We going to keep shipping milk, or is there something new on the horizon?

Mr. French walked home in the dark—limped home—to tell the truth. He hoped Mrs. French wouldn't ask him a thousand questions, and she didn't. She had a nice juicy pork chop and a pot of beans waiting for him. She pulled up a seat next to him as he ate, put a hand on his shoulder, and in all their years together, he thought, he never felt luckier, never loved her more than at that moment.

Six months later Mary Bayly announced that she had been diagnosed with cancer, that it was going to kill her, that she would be concluding her affairs at the Retreat, and when she had, she would move to Park Avenue and await her demise.

"Well, Mr. Mason," says Mrs. French, dabbing her eyes with a dish towel. "I do declare that Mr. French has told you some things about us that even I do not *recollect hearing him say to me.*" The glance at her husband strikes Edward as somewhere between horror and boundless love.

Edward feels wrung out. It is nearly five, the hour when he has to return to complete affairs with Miss Mary. This will have to be quite a performance. Mrs. French gets up, gathers the lemonade glasses. Edward reflects that after this day of lemonade, he could sail around the world five times in a row without a touch of scurvy. He and Mr. French sit, watching the slight currents of air rasping the surface of the creek. A north wind, says Mr. French. Edward can't think of any response to that, and what finally comes out of his mouth, despite the moment, makes them both laugh. "What now?" he says.

When they have finished enjoying his joke, Mr. French moves on to the point. "With what, sir?"

"Well. The dairy, I suppose."

"We'll keep running it as we are as long as Miss Mary lives, but there's no real return in bottling our own. We'll just ship it to the plant. Let someone else be a model of something and give the Retreat a rest. Sell off the bottling equipment. A much simpler operation, McCready and a couple of hands. We've been planning this for a year or two now."

"The Mansion House?"

"That's going to be your problem, I guess."

"You know my wife and I are moving to England in November?"

"Yes. I know about that. We'll keep an eye on the Mansion House. No one's going to bother it. Too many ghosts."

Edward reaches into his waistcoat for his watch. Is he going to admit to Miss Mary that he has heard all this history or play dumb? Probably wouldn't get away with that. He feels he has been painted with story, pieces of narrative hanging off his body in strips; he'll never be able to clean up enough to fool her.

"Mrs. French," calls out Mr. French. "Pull me up, will you?"

Apparently she didn't hear, so Edward helps Mr. French clamber out of his chair. They stand for a minute, Mr. French holding on to Edward while he gets his balance. "Don't let anyone mislead you," says Mr. French. "Getting old is Hell on earth."

There is nothing else to say.

"And what now for you?" asks Edward.

"I'm eighty-two. There can't be too much 'now' for me left to fill."

"I wish you and Mrs. French every comfort. Retirement may be 'preposterous' "—Mr. French smiles, hearing his own word—"but I would imagine taking time with your family would not be unwarranted."

"No. I suppose it wouldn't be."

Edward takes his fond leave of Mrs. French and again of Mr. French when he drops him off at the Mansion House. Even if Mr. French might soon be working for him, neither of them suggests that he will ever see the other again. Edward assumes that Mr. French would have relayed only a fraction of this tale if he had suspected otherwise. Edward mounts the six steps to the portico. It seems fifty or sixty years ago that he had done this and not a mere nine hours ago—though his day has been by any measure a long one. What was her name—craziest names they used around here—oh yes, Ophelia peering out at the burning dock from the window just above where he is standing, Mary departing for the convent, Thomas leaving so unwillingly for Philadelphia, Beal entering the church for Wyatt's funeral, the Retreat teas. All through this door. After he has announced his presence with the massive bronze door knocker, Edward reflects that humans should probably not construct things that last so very long; over the years even the most modest spaces get crowded by souls, all jostling for their bit parts in the tales. *I sat on that bench for six straight hours that day. You did not;*

you'd gone to town with the corn. No, I remember distinctly, she was wearing that blue bonnet . . . Edward is deep in this spectral argument when the door is opened by the elderly butler. The last Edward knew, based on the stories, there was no butler; Ralph Peters had been sent packing. This man, despite his age, was clearly a late addition, someone brought in to relieve Robert Junior of the obligation of ever coming to this door again.

"Miss Mary is waiting for you in the parlor."

No coffeepot in her hand, I trust, Edward wants to say. A nervous jollity, thankfully unspoken.

She is sitting in a large wingback, a hairy-clawed Chippendale, reading a book. She has a blanket over her lap and one foot propped on a small footstool. She wears the look of someone who has been installed there by nurses, with a cup of tea next to her, and she asks him to help himself from the teapot under the cozy on the butler's table. The thought of ingesting another drop of liquid in his entire life makes Edward gasp for breath. He thanks her, but declines.

"You've had the full tour?"

Yes, he says, he most certainly has. Mr. French has been extraordinarily generous with his time; he has shown him the Retreat in the most complete detail. "Really, every corner of the operation," Edward says, hoping he can account for the entire morning and afternoon with this exhaustive tour. It is remarkable, what she has done. He really had never reflected on what was involved in producing clean and healthful milk. He himself, he says, had grown up drinking bottled milk in Boston from a local dairy called H. P. Hood & Sons.

"Yes, the Hood boys," she says. "I know them quite well."

Mr. French has introduced him to a number of the staff, he says, hoping she will not ask, *Did you meet Abel Terrell? Did you meet Robert Junior Turner?* She does not. He says he found the technology quite remarkable, the layout of the operation. Much to consider as he embarks on modernizing his operation in England.

"That's fine, but the dairy business, as perhaps you have learned, went in a different direction. I am a dinosaur."

Hardly. A visionary. A person determined to introduce Christian values into the business of milk.

She scowls.

But, he continues, of all that he has seen, what perhaps most impressed him is the beauty of this—he searches and can do no better at the moment, so infused with the sad tales he's been hearing all afternoon, even though he hardly wants to allude to any of it with Miss Mary—pitiless landscape.

"Pitiless?"

"In New England one grows up with hills and valleys. Almost all views are intimate, just a little piece can be seen at a time. It seems to me that events and memories keep their place in New England. But here, in this flat and almost seamless meeting of water and land, it seems"—well, in for a penny, in for a pound—"that nothing can be hidden."

Mary hears this with a start. She would have expected no such depth, no such uncalculated candor from this man. Yes, she thinks, Mr. French has shown him around, through the acres and through the years. Just as well; in fact, it was what she hoped would happen, for him to hear some of the stories from Mr. French, from whom much of it might be conjecture based on scant evidence, but none of it would be untrue.

"Then you have heard our story?" she asks.

"Yes, ma'am. Your father. The peaches. Your brother and his wife. It seemed part of the tour. I trusted Mr. French not to say anything indiscreet, or else I would have cut it off."

That is right; Mason has correctly judged the man. She is less certain about his rather empty-headed but well-meaning wife—for Miss Mary, all women are empty-headed, but not all of them are well-meaning—but she has as much right to these stories as anyone. That is one part of the Retreat everyone can own. It is the one part of the Retreat that one can put one's trust in. Something that can survive slave auctions and peach yellows and the forces of pasteurization. Lay not up for yourselves treasures upon earth, Mary reminds herself, where moth and rust doth corrupt.

She feels a tinge from her abdomen. From her female parts. "I should tell you that my brother has retained no claim of ownership. If it comes to you, it will come entire and unencumbered."

"I had assumed so. But have you offered him a final time to reconsider, given the fact that it would go to someone with very little connection to the place?"

"Yes," says Mary, and adds no more assurances. Thomas had never wavered from the moment on the deck of the *Alabama* when he told her that he and Beal would never be coming back, that he had signed every possible document ceding the Retreat to her upon their mother's death, and all she had to do, now or in the future, was to sign it to make it law. And now, his life, his vineyards, his five children, each one, if photographs were to be trusted, more beautiful than the last—why come back here? His success with grapes that had so outstripped his father's sad experience with peaches. Rootstock. Scions. Harvest. All those words in his letters, once mouthed on the Retreat, echoing back from France. Faced in the phylloxera plague with the same sort of ruin their father faced in the yellows, but Thomas survived. Oh, no time to go into the ironies in that! And Beal. Sometimes at night, when Mary can't sleep, she plays a game she calls "Being Beal." Born into little more than a shack with three older siblings, a flighty girl, too silly as a child to understand that her future was all but writ in stone. And now, as Mary understands it from the letters, she is partner in one of the most important new wineries in France, a hostess speaking French with an accent no one can ever spot as American. Some kind of African princess, the daughter of an Arabian potentate, a priestess of a long-lost sub-Saharan people. Beal will live forever in history and in legend, the way people do in Europe; here in the United States, what survives is at best gossip, at worst pure fiction hardened into myth.

"You have more connection to the place than you suppose," she says, but she is not surprised, given the pause, the extended silence, that he has lost the thread.

"I'm sorry?"

"You're a Mason. You're the direct line from the Emigrant, even if you are from a branch of the family that did the politically wise and expeditious thing, which was to become Anglican, but you are a Mason and a Catholic. Some of your blood escaped." Escaped the persecution in England, she means, but does not explain. "I'm quite ill," she says to Edward.

"Yes. This is what I understand. I was sorry to hear it. I hope the pain is manageable."

She thanks him for that. Manageable with stiffer and stiffer doses of morphine, but that is science, isn't it? One must trust in it even when it seems the result is not going to be happy. Modern medicine cannot quite cure her of the disease, but it can make it manageable, give her time to get these last details attended to. All of them now attended to but one. Just one more burden to be placed on the shoulders of this complex man. She feels she had misread him somewhat in the morning. She misread him, or he has come back from a day on the Retreat transformed.

"You heard, I am sure, the story of Randall. His death?" When this day broke, she'd had no intention, no thought of discussing this with Edward Mason, but as the hours wore on and she imagined him hearing the stories of the lives on the Retreat, it had seemed to her that she must. When it comes to gossip, truth is always better than speculation. But there is more to it: if she cannot tell the truth to Edward Mason, there is no reason to suppose she will be able, on her deathbed, to confess all her sins and to earn at least the slight hope that she would be forgiven.

Edward Mason admits that he had, but only that. "The murder of that remarkable boy," he says. But no more. This is one piece of information he got from Mr. French that even thumbscrews would not force Edward to divulge. "Unsolved, I gather. Back then, I'm sure the murder of a Negro did not get the serious attention that it should have." He waits for her to turn her penetrating gaze upon him, to force him to say more, but at this point she is not scrutinizing him; it's almost as if she's forgotten that he's in the room. In any event, she clearly doesn't care what he has heard or not heard.

"You're wrong. My father spent many months thinking about almost nothing but solving his murder. Nothing but trying to figure out why it happened."

"But he never did."

"No. I think he did, and couldn't bear the answer. In some respects, he chose an early death rather than follow his research to its obvious conclusion." She looks at Mason. Yes, broad, needy, as she had described his face to herself earlier in the day, but not unintelligent. Maybe even shrewd. He is holding his head quite stiff, looking her right in the eye.

"Randall was very proud, a very proud man. He believed in his race. His year at Howard had done nothing but strengthen his resolve. He believed the Negro would only prosper when he cast off the whites completely. Randall was a visionary, and everything about Thomas and Beal's love was wrong to him."

"And also his fear that his sister would be ill-used, or seen to be so?"

She does not manifest the slight shock this—"correction" is the right word—causes her. "Yes. You are correct about that too."

The question—Who did it?—is hanging over the conversation like a gargoyle. Edward tries a misdirection. "Did people speculate that it was Thomas?" Edward has met none of these people; he can suggest Thomas as the murderer as easily as one could accuse a character in a book.

"Some people thought that. Some people still do. But no. He was in Philadelphia that evening with a boy named Timkins. An odd name. Maybe that's why I remember it." Another twinge from the abdomen; out of the gray of discomfort is coming the blue, the sharpness of sting; soon this one will be purple and will need to be attended to.

Edward does not think this moment has devolved into a guessing game. He says nothing.

"It was an accident, but it was my fault," she says. "My arrogance killed him. My belief that I could influence the future, bend God's will."

"Ma'am?" It's the maid, Valerie, knocking on the door. She pokes her head in. "You getting ready for your medicine?"

Mary sends her away. "Three of us have borne this truth for thirty years."

"The woman, what was her name, and Robert Junior," says Edward.

Yes, the Frenches have told all, but from the tone of this deduction, it seems clear to her that they did not lead Mason to believe it was Tabitha and Robert Junior who confronted Randall that afternoon. "Tabitha," she says.

"Ah."

"They were going to speak to him. I wanted to find out whether he would work with me. Whether we might send Beal away, or keep Thomas away. I didn't know what. I just needed Randall to be patient with Thomas and Beal. Thomas needed Randall to show the way. Thomas wasn't a very strong person, as maybe you have gathered. Perhaps a late bloomer would be the way to describe him. I worried about his health. I mean, I worried about his mental health. I wasn't sure he wouldn't take a hand to himself, as he had once threatened to do."

"But Randall wouldn't."

"No. I don't need to describe to you what happened. Robert had brought another man in, I don't know why. To scare Randall, I suppose. A man named Jacob Beets, a man who had once been a slave here. He killed Randall. It was his way of taking revenge. By killing Randall he found a way to take revenge on every family, every soul, on this farm."

Edward remembers that Mrs. French described her husband as "the good ship French." He's trying to stay afloat here, hoping he can make it out the door in one piece, beginning to wonder whether owning this farm is really worth entanglement in all these tales. Too much . . . humanity, he thinks; too many humans, all their desires and cross-purposes shoehorned into this little postage stamp. These revelations cling to him like flypaper; Mr. French had figured out more or less what happened, had suffered the knowledge in silence, and now, poor, dumb Edward had appeared as a likely confessor. God in heaven! He hadn't signed on for this. Sooner or later he'd have to confess in turn, pass it on down the line, this hot potato.

"So there it is," he says miserably, lamely: mystery solved!

Miss Mary is not listening to him. "Robert is not a bad man, and he has paid dearly for this mistake. So have I."

"And the woman?"

"Tabitha is dead now. I don't think anyone ever figured her out, but one thing became clear to me over those years, before and after. That she wanted Thomas and Beal to happen every bit as much as Randall didn't want it to happen. That her loyalties above all else went to them as a couple."

"As I gather it," says Edward, reflecting on the fact that this day of stories has given him the right to say any damn incautious or scandalous thing that comes to his head, "she must have had some loyalty to your father as well."

She fixes her eye on him and then allows a sort of smile that acknowledges the absolute insanity of human behavior. "She hated him. She did what she had to do with him. What happened with Randall may have changed my life and Robert Junior's, but not Tabitha's. Not one bit."

They're sitting now in the reddening sky of a September evening. Geese are honking overhead and a single cow is raising a ruckus over at the farm. Edward finally says what seems to him the honest truth—that Mary could hardly feel that she had caused this tragedy.

She brushes him off. Oh, he realizes that there is not a single word or idea about this that he could conjure from now to eternity that she has not already considered.

"Did Thomas know?"

She looks at him with pure horror. He has no words to describe the look on her face, maybe more physical pain—her "medicine" being delayed—but more probably the pain of the one thing that would have made this all for naught. "No. That was the reason behind everything I did, almost everything I have done for the past thirty years. When I thought I would die of guilt if I did not admit my role, all I had to remember was that if Thomas knew what had happened, he could not have lived with it. If there was a mortal sin to be committed in all this, I would commit it gladly to ensure that Thomas would not. I had already destroyed Randall. I could not destroy Thomas and Beal too."

"And you have told no one this. No one but me," he says with an accent of incredulity.

"I have told no one else," she says, but he can tell she's being—is "coy" the right word in such dramatic circumstances? She doesn't know what Mr. French may have said; Edward has successfully kept that from her.

"You have not—what do you call it—confessed this?"

"I have not confessed and sought absolution for my sins since the morning Randall's body was discovered in the barn."

"Surely your church . . ." He trails off.

"I did not ask anything further of my church on this. It was the part I was given to play. In the end, Thomas and Beal were our redemption. Thomas was right about that. Our shining moment. If you'll forgive the thought, they were given to us as children to do this for us. Theirs is the story that will be remembered about us."

This thought calms her, but it has also worn her out. The silence is quite long—long enough for Edward to worry that she has lost consciousness.

"I must leave," he says. McCready will take him to Love Point.

The pain is starting to inflame, to blaze from that little knot of horror attached to her cervix. But quite honestly, she has enjoyed this meeting. She feels she has given away, relieved herself of, a good bit more than a farm on the Eastern Shore of Maryland. "I have enjoyed meeting you," she says.

Edward tries to take this without looking dumbstruck. Nonetheless, it offers space for a final gesture. "Could I make an impertinent request?" he asks.

"Certainly," says Mary, a woman who has lived an impertinent life. She seems momentarily energized by the idea that she will have to contend.

"Do you have a photograph of Thomas and Beal? Might I see it, if you have one?"

At first she seems disappointed, as if she had been relishing a final round of debate about pure milk versus pasteurization, but then a small glimmer of sorrow softens the hardened brow, which is followed by the barest smile. She starts to get herself up, and Edward rises to give her a hand. When she is on her feet, he realizes that this is the first time he's seen her standing, and that yes, she is as tall as he is, or would be if she weren't stooped over to favor her abdomen. She leaves the room, and he hears her slowly, painfully mounting the stairs; the photograph she is seeking must be one that sits on her bureau, or on the mantel in her bedroom, on the wall of her dressing room. One she wakes to, or bathes to. Her favorite. She returns with a small frame, a photograph of Thomas and Beal and three or four children, and if Edward makes it out right, vineyards in the background. In the high contrast of a not very clear photograph, Beal looks darker than he expected, but so does Thomas. The photograph seems to have captured no real elements of her beauty or of Thomas's fine, sharp features or of the children's exotic mixed parentage. Edward supposes that there are far better likenesses of them in the house, yet he believes he understands why Mary has shown him this one. He gives it back, thanks her, shows himself out, goes back to Baltimore and thence to Boston, becomes a father, moves to England, assumes the helm of his company, becomes a father for a second time, and strays from his marriage, looking for something he cannot identify, and at each stage of his life, at moments of accomplishment and of defeat, he thinks of that blurry photograph of Thomas and Beal and asks himself, Will I ever know such happiness? Will I ever be visited by so much grace?

After he has gone, Miss Mary remains in her chair. Valerie comes in with a hypodermic and injects her with morphine. Not long now, but much accomplished. There is talk of a tropical storm on the way up from Florida, and if she is to make her last crossing of the Bay, from the right-hand shore to the left, she'd better do it tomorrow morning. She is not dismayed at the thought; it will be lovely to behold the Bay one last time, this drowned river valley, this geologic feature that seems so timeless and permanent but which, it appears, is probably not a whole lot older than the Pyramids at Giza. The land is sinking; this is what they say; another thousand years and the whole peninsula will be a vast sandbar. Not an uncomforting idea. The houses, the graveyard, the dairy buildings, all submerged as if gelled in amber. Horseshoe crabs and rays and rockfish swimming in and out of the windows; oysters and barnacles crusting the tombstones; a few seagulls bobbing happily and heedlessly on the surface with no idea that only a few feet below them rests what used to be Mason's Retreat.

Not her problem. In any event, time to close up shop. She'd made a number of promises to her poor mother and broken every one of them, but fulfilling this final promise seems to offer a special kind of peace. It was only fair, she had long ago concluded, harking back to the covenant that had helped her make sense of her own east and west, of this geographical distress that had ruled her life since the day she was born. So this is fine. *Yes, Mama, I will not die in the Retreat.* She can hear Loretta and Valerie outside the door, packing some of the mementos she has decided to take to Baltimore. Loretta is singing a hymn, a recessional: "Jerusalem, My Happy Home." A favorite on the shore. How nice, thinks Mary, but she'd always taken issue with the line "My soul still pants for thee." She had not lived her life, come this far, in order to be likened, at the end, to a dog.

Acknowledgments

I am deeply grateful to my agent, Geri Thoma, and my editor, Jonathan Galassi, and all the talented and dedicated people at Farrar, Straus and Giroux for bringing this book to life.

I am grateful also to the Virginia Center for the Creative Arts, where I completed large portions of this novel during several residencies.

Almost all of the historical research I conducted was in contemporary materials available online or in the magnificent collections of Alderman Library at the University of Virginia. Three superb modern texts were invaluable to me: Barbara Jeanne Fields's *Slavery and Freedom on the Middle Ground: Maryland During the Nineteenth Century*; Richard A. Meckel's *Save the Babies: American Public Health Reform and the Prevention of Infant Mortality, 1850–1929*; and *Commonwealth Catholicism: A History of the Catholic Church in Virginia*, by Gerald P. Fogarty, S.J. I apologize to them for everything I got wrong despite their best efforts.

The story of the rise and fall of the peach industry in Maryland first came to my attention in Jane Scott's introduction to Shirley Hampton Hunt's *The Vanishing Landscape: Documenting a Changing Way of Life*. On the futile battle to preserve orchards from the yellows, my primary source was a long treatise by W. K. Higley in *The American Naturalist* of November 1881. Most of the lines of dialogue attributed to "Professor Quigley" are quotations from this article.

The Compagnie Générale Transatlantique, known as the French Line, appears here and elsewhere in my fiction, and I am guided by the photographs and captions in William H. Miller, Jr.'s *Picture History of the French Line*. Certain details in my brief account of Mary and Ophelia's transatlantic crossing are borrowed from Harriet Beecher Stowe's very funny letter to her children describing a stormy crossing in 1853, included in Mary Suzanne Schriber's *Telling Travels: Selected Writings by Nineteenth-Century American Women Abroad.*

Some historical figures appear in this book, but I have no basis in fact for most of the actions and utterances I attribute to them. Most notable in this regard is Cardinal James Gibbons, archbishop of Baltimore from 1877 to 1921. Cardinal Gibbons was a remarkable man, a true progressive, but there is not a shred of fact behind the role his character plays on behalf of Thomas and Beal. Another historical figure who makes a cameo appearance is the extraordinary Mary Aloysia Hardey (1809–1886), the Maryland-born dynamo of the Society of the Sacred Heart.

WITHDRAWN